Queen of Thieves

Queen of Thieves

A Novel

Beezy Marsh

wm

WILLIAM MORROW
An Imprint of HarperCollins*Publishers*

P.S.™ is a trademark of HarperCollins Publishers.

QUEEN OF THIEVES. Copyright © 2021 by Beezy Marsh. All rights reserved. Printed in the United States of America. No part of this book may be used or reproduced in any manner whatsoever without written permission except in the case of brief quotations embodied in critical articles and reviews. For information, address HarperCollins Publishers, 195 Broadway, New York, NY 10007.

HarperCollins books may be purchased for educational, business, or sales promotional use. For information, please email the Special Markets Department at SPsales@harpercollins.com.

Originally published as *Queen of Thieves* in Great Britain in 2021 by Orion Dash, an imprint of The Orion Publishing Group Ltd.

FIRST U.S. EDITION

Library of Congress Cataloging-in-Publication Data has been applied for.

ISBN 978-0-06-323484-0

23 24 25 26 27 LBC 5 4 3 2 1

For my friends

Queen of Thieves

Prologue

The sleek sable wrap feels so sumptuous between my fingers, I simply can't resist it.

The fur is heavenly and soft; it's exactly what I'm looking for. The whole street is going to be dolled up to the nines for the Coronation Party and I don't want to disappoint because I'm royalty too; Queen of my manor, that is.

The minute the shop assistant's back is turned, I snatch it from the rail and begin to roll it, quickly, into a tight, furry bundle.

I yank open the baggy waistband of my skirt and shove the wrap down the leg of my knickers. They are voluminous, real passion killers, with elastic at each knee, designed with one purpose in mind: going shopping.

Clouting, we call it, and I'm the best in the West End of London, stepping away from that clothes rail as if I haven't a care in the world.

It hasn't always been this easy; I've had my fair share of close shaves, especially in the early days when I was learning my craft. Even now, the thrill of stealing mingles with a fear of being tumbled by the shop staff, which makes my hands clammy.

Being a thief wasn't the career I had in mind when I was growing up but if there's one thing I've learned, it's that you never know the way your life is going to turn out.

I

By the time I left school, I'd never even pinched so much as a sherbet lemon from the pick 'n' mix at Woolworths.

All that changed after we won the war.

Victory tasted sweet but as I soon found out, it couldn't stop the hunger pangs. Beating Hitler was one thing, but Britain was broke.

Rationing got worse and before you knew it, most folks were taking a bit of crooked, just to make life more bearable. It was all well and good for politicians to tell us not to grumble, but they never went short, did they?

Wherever you looked there were bomb craters and piles of rubble. Weeds and wildflowers sprung up among the ruins, and excited kids claimed bomb sites as their playgrounds, no matter how many times their mums told them not to. Life went on but there was little or no money to rebuild.

In London, battered by war but bursting with people hungry for some fun and what little luxuries they could afford, the black-marketeers and their bosses saw a golden opportunity.

After all, gangland was a man's world.

That's what they thought.

But us women, well, we knew different.

This is our story.

Chapter One
ALICE

Waterloo, London, June 1946

When we won the war, I didn't know whether to laugh or cry.

I was sad to see the back of the blackout because, to be honest, losing it was bad for business.

Night in the city was paradise for me and my girls. We made good use of the cloak of darkness to shift the stuff we'd brought home from the shops during the day. Now the gas lamps were shedding light on things I wanted to keep hidden and that made life more difficult.

We'd got used to running the gauntlet of an air-raid warden or two in the Blitz and when the siren went, you'd get some funny looks scurrying off to the Underground with bags stuffed full of finery, with a mink stole slung about your shoulders. But I'd be damned if I was going to let a German bomb deprive me of the spoils of a hard day's work.

But with the blackout gone, there was more risk of being tumbled.

Round our way, most folks have always known better than to ask too many questions, no matter what they saw coming and going from my flat. They're happy enough to pay for a bit of stuff on the side when they need it, especially if it means they don't have to keep slapping gravy browning on their legs, because I've got them some nice new nylons.

And if anyone feels compelled to talk to the law about me, well, let's just say they'll soon realize that my jewels aren't just for show. Diamonds are hard, and they can come in handy as a knuckle-duster when you have enough of them. I wear one on every finger. Alice Diamond by name and diamond by nature, as I like to say.

You can call me a thief, but I prefer to say I'm a hoister. I liberate clothes from shop rails and coat hangers and find them good homes. Perhaps I'll give a working-class girl a chance to shine in a dress that she could never dream of affording, never in a month of Sundays. However, after a particularly busy Monday spent in the West End of London, I can make all her dreams come true, for a fair price, given the risks I'm taking.

Shoplifting with my gang, The Forty Thieves, is a proper career, with skills honed over years; a tradition that's passed down by word of mouth, from one generation to the next. I get teary-eyed when I think of it really, because we can trace our heritage all the way back to the days of good old Queen Victoria herself.

I bet she could have stashed quite a few furs in her bloomers, given the size of Her Majesty. I could have made good use of those when I was out shopping.

No offense, Ma'am.

It's a year to the day since the war ended and everyone's having another knees-up for the Victory Parade but I ain't exactly in the mood for a party.

Everything but the air we breathe is still on coupons. Make do and mend, Mrs. Sew-and-Sew, clothing on the ration; forgive me for saying, but those things are for mugs who want to wear moth-eaten jumpers and go around with holes in their stockings. And don't get me started on the utility dresses they've still got in the shops. I wouldn't be seen dead in them. What kind of victory is that?

It's a matter of pride that no matter how hard up I am—and believe me, there have been times I've been down to my last brass farthing—I've still kept up appearances, just like the quality over the water in Mayfair. The posh folk might say we are all in it together, but they're not going without like we are. They ain't fooling me, not for a minute.

I can honestly say, everything about me, every stitch I've got on, is crooked. But I've worked hard for it, just the same; harder than quite a few blokes I could mention, who spend their wages down at the pub and leave the missus short for the housekeeping. Talk about doing an honest day's work! And what with the prices of things in the shops these days, it's hard to say who's robbing who when you pay for things at the till. Not that I've done that very often, but at least I'm truthful about it.

And don't go thinking I've lost touch with my roots, even if I am dolled up in my finery. Some of my best contacts are people you wouldn't bat an eyelid over if you met them in the street.

The flower seller at Waterloo Station looks like nothing more than an old drunk, but she's sharp as a tack. She's called Lumps and Bumps because she's always falling down and hurting herself when she's been on the sauce, but she's my eyes and ears in that neck of the woods. Old Lumps has the alarming habit of warming the cheeks of her arse by the fire in the local boozer and she doesn't wear knickers either, so that sight is not for the fainthearted. Her skirts haven't been washed since the General Strike, I'd wager. Her teeth are like moss-covered tombstones and her breath reeks, but I always listen closely because her tip-offs are pure gold.

Last week, she heard that a couple of girls from Waterloo had got a little ruse going where they were knocking off some rolls of silk from the cloth factory by winding it around themselves and waddling out of work like a pair of Egyptian mummies. They made a pretty penny, but they forgot to pay me my dues, so I'm in the neighborhood to see what I can find out about them, before I plan my surprise visit. Anything crooked on this side of the water, on my manor, goes through me and that's that.

I just need to remind them who's the Queen of Thieves round these parts and then we can all be friends. I've brought my silver-topped cane to make that point, and Molly, my second-in-command, has her hatpin, just in case. She's quite handy with it when she needs to be.

Meanwhile, there's time for a quick drink at their local, the Feathers, just in case they happen to be there. I've a packet of stockings to drop off for the landlord's daughter, and he owes me for those.

It ain't my usual neck of the woods; I'm from round the Elephant and Castle, but I like to keep an eye on things, just to let people know I survived the Blitz, in case they were wondering where I'd got to.

I'm sure they'll all be pleased as Punch to see me.

The row of two-up, two-downs that nestle by the River Thames behind Waterloo Station has quite a reputation but it don't scare me or my girls. The same can't be said of the local policemen—cozzers, we call them—who will only walk down the streets round there in pairs.

Some tatty bits of Union Jack bunting have been strung between the lampposts, and kids are out having fun watching a dog and a rat having a scrap on the cobbles. Some of the older ones are running a book on it. Makes a change from the bare-knuckle fights they have on a Sunday at the top of the street, and that's including the women, who like to settle scores with fists.

There's quite a gang of us as we walk into the pub, and heads turn. A banner declaring "GOD SAVE THE KING!," last pressed into service a year ago, on VE Day, has once again been proudly displayed above the bar.

An accordion player in the corner squeezes out a few notes of "Roll Out the Barrel" to liven things up a little. A few old blokes, nursing their pints and picking their teeth for want of anything better to do, struggle gamely to sing along, and some wisecrack jokes that it sounds as if a cat is being strangled down the back alley, which raises a laugh.

My girls are dressed like film stars, with hair like spun silk gleaming beneath hats of the finest felt, in colors and styles you'd only seen in magazines; not even in shop windows, not since before the war. There's a dainty blue pillbox with a veil, a derby hat in lime green, a bright beret in zesty orange, and the finest of all, my red fedora with enough plumage to make a peacock proud.

Our clothes are nothing like the drab, worn, shapeless utility wear that stalk the streets of Waterloo, on the ration.

Our jackets have nipped-in waists and there's material, *extra* material, for frills and tucks on the dresses. My girls' legs aren't stained with gravy browning either. They wear stockings, silk stockings, and they're all laughing and joking with each other because the world they come from doesn't involve making do and mending.

A hush falls over the room, right into the darkest corners, stained yellow by years of tobacco smoke. I could swear the peeling wallpaper wilts a little more at the sight of us.

Men stare at the floor and shuffle their feet, suddenly taking great interest in their bootlaces or the sawdust and cigarette butts under the tables.

"It's quiet as the grave in 'ere," I joke to the barman

with a throaty laugh. "Someone died, have they? Where's the party?"

Right on cue, the accordion player starts up again and half the pub starts singing for dear life, as if to please me. Men tighten their ties and flick imaginary dust from their trousers as they make their way over to buy my girls a drink or ask them to dance, or both.

I turn my back on the party and murmur something to the barman, handing over a small package. He nods and pulls a wodge of cash out from under the counter and hands it over. I flick through it briefly before stuffing it into my carpet bag.

Things are livening up a bit now and I tap my silver-topped cane in time to the music, my row of diamond rings twinkling on my right hand.

The barman pours a whisky and pushes it toward me: "It's on the house."

As I raise it to my lips, that's when I spot her, sitting at the end of the bar, looking lost . . .

Chapter Two

NELL

Waterloo, London, June 1946

I didn't mean to stare, but I'd never seen anything like it in all my born days.

They were glorious, like exotic animals in the zoo or mouth-watering cakes in the baker's shop.

Leading from the front, like a ship in full sail in a red fedora hat, was a woman standing as tall as any man. Her face was broad and her piercing green eyes glinted as she scanned the pub, almost willing someone to meet her gaze.

Her black hair was rolled up and set at the front and the sides, to accentuate her rounded features.

This woman caught me gawping at her and gave a little wink: "Cheers, love!"

Well, that made me turn scarlet. She must have thought I was a proper nosy mare.

Just then, the barman chipped in: "Cheer up, love, it might never happen," and pushed a drink my way.

I pulled my old woollen cardigan closer around my middle. As far as I was concerned, it already had. Even at just four months gone, I was showing.

My blouse was straining to contain the new life growing inside me. It wouldn't be long before people started to notice that I was in the family way. A blush started to creep up my neck at the very thought of it. Our street was a tight-knit place, where the walls were thin as paper and people looked out for each other, or poked their noses in, depending on which way you looked at it.

The whole of my childhood had been overshadowed by two terrors: my dad's temper and German bombs raining down from the sky.

And now, just as things were supposed to be getting better for everyone, I'd gone and done something stupid and ruined it all.

My stomach lurched at the thought of what Dad would say. The stares and knowing looks from the neighbors were nothing compared to what he'd do to me for getting myself into trouble. He was handy with his belt at the best of times and once he'd hit me so hard with the buckle, he cracked one of my ribs. Mum kept me off school and told the neighbors I had scarlet fever. It was our little secret, and I didn't breathe a word about it because my parents loved me, and it was all my fault for being so bleeding cheeky in the first place. Dad said so.

But that wasn't even the worst of it. He had a way of brooding, ignoring me for days when I'd upset him, which was worse than the beatings. It made our two-up, two-down in Tenison Street, just a stone's throw from the River Thames, feel like a tinderbox. Just opening my mouth to speak could be the spark that set it all ablaze.

The war had sucked every last bit of good humor out of him and there wasn't much of it to spare in the first place, if truth be told. I'd rarely seen Dad smile, except with his mates down the pub. He was forty when the war broke out, too old to fight, and nights spent sheltering on the cold floors of the Underground had played havoc with his lumbago, so he'd volunteered as an air-raid warden, which only made him more irritable, mainly about the stupidity of people who failed to observe the blackout. His days were spent loading packing cases full of jam onto lorries at the Hartley's factory down in Southwark, and his nights were spent grumbling at Mum, finding fault with everything, from the way she boiled the potatoes to the lumps in her custard.

Mum spoke in whispers and lived on her nerves, but she was an absolute rock to other women in the street during the long years of the Blitz. She was always there with a cup of tea and listening ear, calmly doing what she could to help. The uncertainty of war was nothing to her because she'd lived under fire from him indoors for so long anyway. He'd never raised his fists to Mum, not that I knew of, but his anger was so volcanic that the aftershocks would continue for days.

The end of hostilities with Germany had brought hopes of a truce with Dad, thanks to the return of his one true passion, greyhound racing. The evenings when he went to have a flutter on the dogs were among the happiest in the house, simply because he wasn't there.

And then, along came Jimmy.

Jimmy just strolled into my life one summer's day not long after the war ended, sauntering around the corner, whistling low between his teeth. It was as if the sun that ripened the peaches piled high on his barrow had seeped into him, from the roots of his sandy blond hair to the twinkle in his sky-blue eyes.

His jacket was loose about his shoulders and thrown back slightly, his tie tightly knotted at the collar of a crisp white shirt and shoes polished to a shine.

He was a fixer, someone who could get hold of things if you needed them, no questions asked. Half the neighborhood had been in hock to Jimmy at some point but there was no shame in that, it was just the way things were. He was reasonable about repayments and if anyone was daft enough to try to diddle him, it wouldn't be Jimmy who got heavy, but some fellas sent from the bosses over in Soho. No one could blame Jimmy for that, he was the monkey, not the organ grinder.

I'd watched him selling overripe fruit to hatchet-faced housewives in headscarves with such charm, I couldn't help but giggle. He'd even put an extra apple in their paper bags for them, by way of apology, giving me a wink as he did so.

So, I started to look forward to seeing him when I was running errands or escaping Dad's black moods, or sometimes both, by going down to the shops in The Cut. There were always queues and that was an excuse to linger, to bat my eyelashes at him and pretend not to notice when he treated me to the broadest grin. When he smiled, it was like the clouds melted away.

Soon we were stepping out together, meeting at the cinema on Friday nights.

It wasn't long before word reached Dad.

He sat brooding in his chair and when he heard the latch go on the front door, he went off like a clap of thunder, leaping up and grabbing me by the collar of my dress as I stepped over the threshold.

"I know what you've been doing, my girl, and I'm telling you now, it's over!"

His eyes bulged out of their sockets and I could see the spittle in the corner of his mouth. Lying about seeing Jimmy was pointless because the curtains had been twitching as we walked up the street.

I stared at the floor, knowing that protesting would only make matters worse. "Yes, Dad."

Mum came dashing in, wringing her hands together, almost in prayer, whispering, "Please, Paddy, please don't be too hard on her . . ."

But all that fell on deaf ears.

"And if you so much as go near him again, you will feel the back of my hand!" Dad shouted. "Now, get to bed."

Jimmy was still hanging around by the lamppost outside and to my horror, Dad saw him off by yelling: "Stay away from my daughter, you spiv!" out of the window.

So, if anyone in Tenison Street had missed the row, they certainly heard that.

It didn't matter that Dad was wrong about Jimmy because by then it was too late.

The way we were together, the way he made me feel, was something new and shiny and special, like finding a lovely sixpence in your purse that you never want to let go.

Dad would never understand that, never in a month of Sundays, so what was the point wasting my breath trying to explain it?

There were no shouts, no banging of fists, no disapproving glares from my Jimmy. He wasn't that kind of fella. He knew how to treat a lady, to be kind to her, with flowers and even a box of chocolates, which must have cost a fortune in coupons. That meant so much to me, seeing how Dad had Mum at her wits' end the whole time and he'd never so much as pulled up a daisy to give her, despite everything she'd done for him her whole, miserable life.

Now, don't get me wrong; when I was walking out with Jimmy, I wasn't just some silly little schoolgirl hanging around with a good-looking barrow boy. We were making plans for the future, our future. Maybe not tomorrow, but one day soon. He said so. Being with him was easy and fun.

So, it was only natural that he wanted to take things further. When we went for a night out to the Trocadero down at the Elephant and Castle, he wasn't eyeing up other women who were all dolled up in the foyer. Jimmy only had eyes for me, like I was his goddess, and after the film, in the freezing night air of a London winter, he pulled me into the alleyway and stole a kiss.

"Nell, my Nell, my forever girl," he whispered, his eyes half closing. "You're so beautiful tonight, how can I resist you?"

My heart fluttered, like a thousand butterflies in my chest.

I felt his fingers at the hem of my skirt, pushing it upwards. I clasped his hand for a second and he looked deep into my eyes, and I relaxed and kissed him. If this is what it took to be his forever girl, then I was prepared to let him shrug my knickers down my legs, which were blotchy with cold, and let him explore further.

I draped my arms around his neck, as I'd seen the actresses do on-screen, and let him explore my mouth with this tongue.

His fingers wandered higher up my thighs and when he touched me, I winced at first at the shock of it, so he nibbled my ear and held me tightly, his sweet nothings making us both giggle. His soft laughter was infectious and before long, I was giddy with it.

He put my hand to his fly, which was bulging and firm, and I tensed at that. How on earth would that fit?

"It won't hurt much, I promise, and you'll like it," he said. "Then you'll be a woman, *my* woman."

"Alright, Jimmy," I whispered, nervously. "You can."

I felt him, insistent, pushing at the top of my thighs and suddenly he was inside me. As I gasped at the sting of it, he stroked my hair and covered my face with kisses.

"It's you and me, Nell, forever," he breathed. "Just us."

As we moved together, we weren't hard up against the bins in a grimy alleyway at the cinema; we were in paradise.

Now I understood what those actors in the films were on about, not to mention the noises that came from Mum and Dad's bedroom after they'd rowed. I didn't want it to stop.

Then a couple of months passed with no bleeding. Mum

was too bound up coping with her job up at the waste-paper factory and with Dad's temper to notice that I hadn't thrown anything on the fire lately. Living on rations meant everyone felt hungry from time to time but I could lick the plate clean and still have room for more. The horrible truth dawned. I was pregnant.

That was a couple of weeks ago and now the waistband of my skirt was getting uncomfortably tight.

I scanned the smoky pub for any sign of Jimmy, but he was nowhere to be seen.

The woman in the red fedora hat was watching me closely, a row of diamond rings sparkling on her right hand. They were spellbinding.

Just then, the pub door swung open again and another crowd tumbled in, shaking off the rain, which was coming down like stair rods. "Flaming June, flaming nuisance, more like. It's a washout!" said a woman with a mane of red hair, which hung about her shoulders like a damp fox's brush.

Trailing in her wake like a little tugboat, with a stupid grin on his face, was Jimmy.

"Let's have another one, ladies," he slurred, barging his way to the bar, slinging his arm around his companion, who had a beautiful black suede handbag to match her shoes, which had been ruined in the downpour.

She turned, planting a wet kiss on his cheek, so that he was branded by her lipstick, which was red like the post-box at the end of the road.

That set me off. I felt vomit rising in my gullet. I hadn't suffered any morning sickness and now was not a good time to start. My hands turned clammy. He hadn't even noticed me, the feckless sod! There I was, like a bleeding gooseberry, perched on the barstool. I pulled my cardi tighter around my middle, poking a finger through one of the holes left by the moths. I wished the ground could have swallowed me up, there and then.

The redhead, she was all eyes, wasn't she? She spotted me staring at them and gave Jimmy a sharp nudge in the ribs. He looked over and blanched.

"Nell, I wasn't expecting you," he stammered, straightening his collar and wiping the lipstick from his cheek, leaving a horrid smear.

"I can see that," I said, wondering if I could get away with picking up her handbag and clobbering him round the head with it.

"Come and meet the girls," he said, throwing his arms open to me by way of apology.

In an instant, I was swept along the bar in Jimmy's beery embrace: "You look gorgeous as ever, petal. Come and join the party!"

The barman took pity and threw Jimmy a lifeline, asking him for his order. That left me and her, and an awkward silence.

The redhead looked me up and down for a moment and then lit up a cigarette. She blew a few smoke rings in my direction.

"Funny," she said, with eyes as cold as a dead fish, "Jimmy's never mentioned you."

I opened my mouth, but no words came out.

The redhead pressed on, moving closer, so that I could see the smudges of red lipstick on her teeth. "Are you one of the many, love? I can see what he sees in you. Pretty little thing, ain't you? What's your name?"

There was a silence.

"Cat got your tongue, has it?"

"It's Nell," I replied, staring at the floor. Mum always said I was a good-looking girl, with big brown eyes and fine features, but my hair was a different story. It was mousey and never did what I wanted it to. What with the war and rationing, there was barely a picking on me, so I looked younger than my years. Next to this woman, I was just a foolish schoolgirl, and for some reason, I was behaving like one.

"Does your ma know you're in here, Nell?"

"That's enough, Molly," said the woman in the fedora hat, leaning across and extending her hand to me. "Can't you see the poor girl's shy? Leave her be."

Molly turned to leave.

"I'm Alice," said the woman, giving me the full benefit of her startling green eyes. "Alice Diamond and it's a pleasure to meet you."

The unmistakable drone of airplanes could be heard outside. A few years ago, during the war, that would have sent everyone running for cover, but now customers stampeded out to see the fly-past. Jimmy vanished with them, and I made my excuses to Alice Diamond and went after him.

Rain sploshed down, running in filthy rivulets into the gutter, as everyone craned their necks skywards to watch the planes fly over in formation, toward Buckingham Palace.

My hair was soaking wet, plastered to my head, and my blouse was soaked through, as I stuttered, "I'm in trouble, Jim."

"Whassmarra, darlin'?" he said, with such a glazed look in his eye, I felt like crying.

"I'm going to have a baby."

I clung to him as a look of shock swept across his face, but then Jimmy, God love him, pulled me into a big bear hug, swaying slightly on his feet.

"I think you're smashing, Nell," he said, giving my tummy a little pat. "It's a bit unexpected, ain't it? But I will sort this out, you'll see. You're my forever girl, ain't you? Shall we have another one to celebrate?"

"But . . . we've gone and put the cart before the horse," I mumbled. "Me dad'll kill me!"

There were ways of doing things. Women who didn't were whispered about or worse. The GIs had plenty of fun in the war but all anyone remembered now was who'd dropped their drawers for a packet of nylons or who'd cheated on their husbands while they were serving overseas.

Love didn't come into it. Marriage was about respectability and, from what I'd seen, sacrifice.

Iris, my mate from the factory, who lived a few doors down, had made herself sick with worrying during the war, waiting for news of her fella, Tommy, who'd been captured in Burma. When he returned, he was nothing like the six-foot docker who used to swing me up in the air to make me squeal with laughter when I was a kid.

Poor Tommy was more like a living skeleton. Iris had done everything she could to make him feel safe at home; she'd cooked him all his favorite meals, which he'd insisted on eating alone in the bedroom. He couldn't bear any noise from the kids in the street and he'd been so short with Iris's mum, who had gone a bit doolally after she was bombed out, that the poor old dear sat crying on the doorstep one afternoon and wouldn't go back indoors until it got dark. But Iris stuck with him because that is what women round our way did.

Now I was in the family way without a ring on my finger, but Jimmy thought he could sort anything, easy as pie, because things just seemed to fall off the backs of lorries and into his lap whenever he needed them.

"Just leave it with me, sweet," he said, kissing me on the cheek. "Now, I've got a bit of business to sort but I'll catch you later. Why don't you get to know the girls a bit? They're lovely."

And with that, he was gone, like a rat up a drainpipe.

★

Alice Diamond strolled over as I was standing there and put her arm around me.

"Got yourself in a spot of trouble, have you?" she said, pointing her cane toward my belly.

"No, no, I haven't." I lowered my voice to a whisper. The last thing I wanted was the whole pub finding out I had a bun in the oven.

"Calm down, sweetness," said Alice, giving me a little pat. "You just looked like you had a little secret to tell Jimmy, that's all, and it wouldn't be the first time where he's concerned."

"What do you mean?" I said, panic rising in my voice.

"Why don't you come back inside, and we'll have a little chat?" said Alice, steering me back through the door of the Feathers. It was more like an order than a question.

Inside the pub, more people got up to dance and someone was hammering on the piano now, "When the Red, Red Robin Comes Bob, Bob, Bobbin' Along." That song always made me smile when I heard it on the radiogram at the factory. It's fair to say I could more than carry a tune, but right now my voice had deserted me.

Fellas grasped whatever their dance partners were prepared to offer—a hand, a waist—clinging to each other as they jostled their way around the floor, which was sticky with spilled beer. They'd all survived the war. They'd all won but they'd all lost too, and when someone started to sing "We'll Meet Again," there were a few tears.

Alice settled herself on a bar stool and motioned for me to join her.

"We'll have two whisky macs," she barked at the barman, who jumped to it.

Alice swirled the amber liquid around her glass for a minute and I copied her. I'd never drunk whisky, that was a fella's drink, but when I sipped, it warmed me from the inside and it felt lovely and reassuring.

"Now, you're in a spot of trouble ain't you?" said Alice, looking deep into my eyes.

"I don't think I want to . . ."

"You can tell me, duck. It's my business to know things about people," she continued, like a steamroller, ignoring my reply. "I notice a lot, how their clothes hang, for one thing, and yours are looking a bit tight around the middle. Been eating a lot of pies, have we?"

"No, 'course I haven't."

The very idea of it, on rations!

Alice pointed to the girls she'd come in with, who were attracting men like bees to honey. "These girls here work for me. In fact, I could find a job for you, if you like . . ."

"That's very kind," I said. "I've got a job, though . . ."

A few other customers who'd had enough of the rain traipsed back indoors, like drowned rats, but Jimmy wasn't among them. My heart sank.

"Think about it," said Alice, relaxing her grip. "You can find me down at Queen's Buildings on Scovell Road at the Elephant and Castle. We can have a chat about it. Everyone round there knows me."

"But I've got a job at the fur factory . . ." I began again.

"Not for long, in your condition, love," said Alice, matter-of-factly, buttoning up her jacket. I felt like I'd been slapped, but it was true, pregnant girls got their marching orders, especially ones who were unmarried. The boss, Miss Pritchard, was a proper witch. All that was missing was the broomstick.

"I'm not sure Jimmy'll want me to work when I'm

married, and I'll have the baby to think about too . . ." was all I could manage. My whole life seemed to be spinning out of control and this woman had seen right through me. Jimmy had buggered off and left me in the lurch.

"I'll let you into a little secret," she said, murmuring softly in my ear. "I've known Jimmy a long, long time and with the best will in the world, he makes a lot of promises he can't keep. He means well, honest he does, but if I had a quid for every engagement ring he's palmed off on innocent young girls like yourself, I'd be a millionaire by now."

"That's not true," I gasped, "I don't believe you!"

I freed myself from Alice's grasp and ran out of the pub, blinded by tears.

"Suit yourself," said Alice, shrugging her shoulders.

I could still hear her laughter ringing in my ears over the music, as the pub door swung shut.

I stood alone in a crowd on Waterloo Bridge, as darkness fell.

People milled about, a mass of dampened spirits, wet flags and sodden shoes. Searchlights crisscrossed the sky and then the first of the fireworks exploded overhead through drifting clouds, to a chorus of "oohs" and "ahhs" from the people below, who were desperate for a spectacle.

Jimmy was nowhere to be seen. I'd searched the boozers down The Cut and all his usual haunts, but he'd vanished into thin air.

What if Alice Diamond was right?

The thought of him making out with the redhead made me feel queasy again.

No one could say what the future held. The war had taught me that much, with houses there one day and gone the next, and all the poor souls in them too.

Then there was Mum, spending every day dancing to Dad's tune, and Iris, her nails bitten to the quick dealing with a stranger in her own home. And now Jimmy, flirting with floozies. He'd played me for a fool, that's what Alice said.

There was something about those women in the pub, how happy and carefree they looked. It couldn't hurt to find out more, could it?

God knows, I hadn't made it easy on myself. What the hell was I going to do? I was only just turning twenty and I had a horrible feeling my life was headed one way—downhill.

Chapter Three

ALICE

Elephant and Castle, London, June 1946

Call it instinct if you like, or the devil's luck, but I'm rarely wrong about who has the makings of a good hoister. I have always had the knack of picking them off the streets of South London to work for me.

Take this girl, Nell from Waterloo; she's fresh as a daisy and a bit wet behind the ears but that's perfect for us right now, with stores employing more walkers, who want to make our lives difficult by watching our every move. There's something quite appealing about a girl next door, with a wide-eyed innocent look about her, because she won't draw too much attention to herself.

She could go far, as long as she doesn't lose her bottle. Being a good hoister takes guts and daring. I suspect she's got something sparky in her, even if she don't really know it yet. I'm not a betting woman, unless I know which way the odds are stacked, but I'd lay money she'll be knocking on my door soon. It's amazing how being down on your luck can focus your mind. With a bun in the oven, she'll be keen to please and open to a new opportunity. I've seen that many times over the years and I've got a feeling young Nell's going to come in very handy, if she plays her cards right.

My girls need to be fast learners and have nimble fingers and being a fur factory girl will stand her in good stead.

The first trip up West is always an easy one, just me and the new girl and my trusted second-in-command, Molly, to keep an eye on things. You could trust your grandmother to Molly; although she'd probably bring her home one over the eight, she'd show her a good time while she was out.

The way we operate is that if we are going for a proper spree, which happens three or four times a week, we have teams of us out there, with drivers at the ready. The Forty Thieves don't work for men, ever. They work for us. That's how it's always been and that will never change, not as long as there's breath in my body.

Money talks and I make sure I pay the drivers well, so they're loyal to me. A few of them are brothers of the girls, which helps keep things in the family. Molly's brother, Jack, is my top wheelman. He has a straight job too, as a porter up Covent Garden, but he knocks off early, which means there's plenty of time to take us shopping.

Petrol is on the ration these days, so that makes it a bit more tricky to run a nice big car with a roomy trunk, but I've got a Chrysler I keep down in a lockup off the Borough market. I had to work bloody hard to buy that car and it's my pride and joy. Everyone round the Elephant knows when the Queen of the Forty Thieves is in town when they see me gliding by in it, with my best mink wrap on. And nobody dares lay a finger on the paintwork or I'll give them what for.

Jack drives us up to town in it and parks up outside the stores, while me and the girls go inside. If a cozzer asks him why he's there, he'll just say his missus is running an errand. Meanwhile, I will come downstairs and meet one of my gang in the stairwell or just outside the shop and give her a bagful of goods, and she will swap me back the exact same bag as mine; this one will be empty for me to refill it. Works a treat, that one, hoisting stuff into a bag and swapping it. If we have to make a quick getaway, Jack is there waiting.

I've got lots of tricks up my sleeve.

Jewelry—tomfoolery—is a particular favorite because everyone likes a sparkler, don't they? Diamonds are best; they're small and expensive. Stones are easy to move on and gold can be melted down, just ask my friends up in Hatton Garden, who'll be happy to oblige. But getting hold of them takes skill, especially these days. Fellas like the smash and grab but that usually ends up with the cozzers chasing them down a dark alley and all that drama and headlines in the papers the next day, which makes it harder for anyone to do an honest day's thieving.

Some might get off on the thrill of the chase, but I enjoy bringing a woman's touch to the fiddle, to keep things more discreet. It's less brazen and you can get more done, making a real day of it down Bond Street if you can do more than one shop. It's brains not brawn that The Forty Thieves are all about.

Me and my girls might pretend we're interested in a ring, but we will already have a worthless paste one that matches it tucked away in a pocket. Indecision is the hoister's friend, along with the desire to "see things in the light," by walking over to a window, where you can perfect the switch. You've got to keep the patter up while you do it. I have had a few good fiddles where I've slipped an entire tray of rings into my carpet bag by keeping some old fool of a jeweler talking and back in the old days, there were friends of mine who made a habit of haring out of the shop with fistfuls of whatever they could lay their hands on. But being behind bars gave them a long time to consider why that was a mistake.

Now, I've never been one to fall for a handsome GI but some of my girls have, and as well as getting silk stockings without having to nick them, they discovered American gum. It always looked a bit unsightly to have a girl chewing the cud like some blooming cow in my opinion but having a bit of gum to stick a ring or two into under a little ledge at the edge of the counter works a treat to park a ring for a while, until I send an accomplice along to pick it up later.

The golden rule for The Forty Thieves is you never wear what you have hoisted, ever. Anything you nick belongs to me, first and foremost, and I will pay you handsomely and take a cut for fencing it. That means you have a ready supply of cash to go out and buy yourself something nice, without having to nick it.

My girls know the joy of stepping into Selfridges or Marshall and Snellgrove and going up to the snooty shop assistants waving a wad of pound notes to make them dance to their tune. They can get their hair done, go out to dinners and dances up West, all on their own pay packets. There's no other job round our way can provide all that; at least not one where you can keep your knickers on. I ain't got time for my girls being brasses, that just lowers the tone, but if they want to have a boyfriend that's fine, as long as they remember where their loyalties lie.

But I won't have two girls fighting over the same fella and if it comes to it, I will bang their heads together and they'll be banned from seeing him for good.

I won't stand for all-night parties and I dock their pay and give them what for if they turn up to work looking like they've pulled an all-nighter. It's a bit like being a mother to these girls and raising them right, especially the younger ones. I like to give them a good work ethic. Going shopping is going to work and it's early to bed and early to rise. That's always been the way, ever since I was a nipper, because if you are too hungover, you get sloppy and it puts everyone at risk.

The number one rule is never grass or help a cozzer. To grass is to bring shame on you and your family and we won't ever forget it. In a close-knit community, that can make life very uncomfortable, but anyone who snitches has got it coming, in my opinion.

The only other hitch is getting caught. But we can cross that bridge when we come to it . . .

Chapter Four

NELL

Waterloo, London, June 1946

"Is that it?"

Dad sat hunched over a tiny slice of bread, thinly spread with jam, as Mum wrung her hands in despair.

"I'm sorry, Paddy, it's the new rations. They cut the bread we get because the people in Berlin are starving."

"I don't give a shit about Berlin!" he shouted, banging his fist on the table, which looked as if it might be about to give way. "Seems like only five minutes since they were dropping bombs on us and now we're bothering about what they have for breakfast! How's a man supposed to do a day's work on an empty stomach?"

He took a bite and chewed thoughtfully for a moment.

"And I saw some German POWs cleaning up the mess from the Victory Parade the other day up in Hyde Park and I can tell you, they didn't look like they were starving," he said.

I stirred the pan of watery porridge on the range. I was famished, but given that the button on my waistband was threatening to pop off, I kept quiet, in case my parents looked too closely at my expanding figure. My back had started aching last night, a niggling pain that I couldn't shift. Oh, I'd give anything to go for a good old soak in the tubs down at the Manor Place Baths, but that was a luxury we could rarely afford at sixpence a turn. The word was that the attendant was getting parky about putting more than a quarter of an inch of hot water in, with requests for "a bit extra, please" being greeted with icy blasts from the pipes, which made it feel more like Siberia than a lovely, steamy bath. Still, it was better than cramming myself into the tin tub in the scullery where Mum might catch sight of my protruding stomach.

Dad ran his hands through his slicked-back hair.

"I'm sorry, Mary," he said, glancing over to Mum, who was scouring the cupboard in the scullery for something else to feed him, "I know it ain't your fault but if the government keeps this up, there'll be a revolution, I'm telling you. The common man will not stand for it."

He swallowed the rest of the bread in one gulp, threw his jacket over his shoulder and stalked out of the door.

I had some sympathy for the Germans. I'd seen some terrible things on the newsreel at the cinema, of their cities in ruins and listless kids lying on hospital beds, their bellies bloated with hunger. I honestly didn't mind going without some bread to help. They were ordinary folk like us, who just happened to live in Germany and be on the losing side, that's all.

Mum sighed and took our ration books down from the mantelpiece. She handed them to me. They were a mass of complicated instructions.

"Tear this portion off" and "Write in this margin—official use only" and boxes filled with capital letters for the shopkeeper to tick off; the newest one was B for bread.

"See if you can get us some sausages for his tea on the way home, will you?"

I nodded as she spooned the porridge into my bowl.

I'd been planning to go down to the Elephant in search

of the mysterious Alice Diamond after work but standing in the queue to get meat would take over an hour. The butcher wasn't fooling anyone with the slimy gray lumps he was palming off on the neighborhood; they tasted like wet crumbs with a bit of sage added, mostly because that was what they were. Complaining was pointless because everyone wanted the best cut they could get with their coupons, but there were stony glares in his direction when his back was turned. People had barely forgiven him for providing turkeys which looked more like sparrows for the first peacetime Christmas.

Mind you, at least he had some birds to sell. A fella down in Southwark had all his stock half-inched on the day before Christmas Eve and there was nearly a riot. Our butcher up The Cut wasn't taking any chances and he slept under the counter after that, with an old army revolver as a companion, to deter looters.

Mum searched my face: "Are you alright, love? You're looking a bit peaky. Not sickening for something, are you?"

"No," I replied, "I'm fine, honest, just trying to get this down me. It's like swallowing glue!"

Mum started to heat some water on the range for the washing up and set about blacking the grate. She was on second shifts at the factory, so she usually got some of the housework done before she left. We didn't have much: some blue and white china, a few ornaments, a clock in a walnut case, threadbare tablecloth, a picture of Brighton, where they went on their honeymoon before the war, hanging off a nail and piece of string, but Mum kept everything neat and tidy. There were no carpets, just bare boards and a rag rug by the range, which she used to sling over the washing line in the backyard to beat once a week.

As I pulled on my coat, I'd decided there was only one thing for it: I'd have to nip down to the Elephant in my lunch break and pray Miss Pritchard wouldn't notice if I was a bit late back.

Stepping out into the street, the women who worked up in the wastepaper factory with Mum, round on Belvedere Road, were traipsing out of their houses, with shouts of: "Morning!"

They had sacking tied around their legs, to keep the rats away. That thought made me shudder; the longtails crawling over their feet as they sorted through bales of old news-papers.

The Alaska Fur Factory, where I worked, was a step up from that. There was always the stench of the dyes and resins to contend with, but at least the animals weren't crawling all over our feet.

I'd started there two years ago, helping the war effort. We'd made thousands of sheepskin linings for RAF flying jackets, as well as some for the US Air Force. My section made yellow hoods for the RAF, which were used to help the Air Sea Rescue find airmen in the water when they bailed out.

The boss, Miss Pritchard, spotted I had a very steady hand and an eye for detail and so after the war, I was put on the beaver lamb section. She had a way of peering at me over her horn-rimmed spectacles, which put the fear of God into me. It turned out she was watching me like a hawk because she had a bit of a promotion in mind. She was a hard woman, stiff as a board with a mouth like a thin red line, which only ever turned one direction: downwards. She had no friends at the factory and she never joined in any of the socials or the once-a-year beano to Margate. How could she? She was the boss and I'd seen her make grown men cry for screwing up dye jobs on the furs, giving them their marching orders, with a glint in her eye. I think she enjoyed it, actually.

I was a given a job as a groover, someone who painted the stripes on conditioned, trimmed lambskins after they had been dyed brown. That meant I had to paint resin in long, black stripes to make the sheepskin look like a row of beaver pelts. Miss Pritchard said we'd make a really beautiful fur which could pass for beaver, for a quarter of the price, as long as we didn't muck it up, in which case we'd get our cards. I could lose myself in that fur, the details of every hair I painted, but the responsibility of it meant the first time I did it, my hands were trembling. The lines had to be straight, dead straight. Even with the fear of being fired, it was better than the jobs most of the others had to put up with.

My pal Iris came running down the road toward me, fixing her hair into place as she went, and coughing her guts up, as usual.

She worked in the fur-beating room at the Alaska factory; it was the worst job in the world, feeding rabbit pelts into a machine with flailing bamboo rods, which whacked the living daylights out of them, sending rabbit fluff up your nose and down your throat. Iris, bless her, was a bit cack-handed and there was no way Miss Pritchard was going to let her loose with a paintbrush near a pelt, so her days were spent in bunny-fluff hell.

"Tommy's going to look for work down the docks today," she said brightly, after she'd stopped spluttering.

We both knew this was a lie. Tommy would spend the morning staring at the wall or swearing at Iris's mother, before traipsing off to the pub for a lunchtime pint, as usual.

"Maybe I could ask my dad to have a word with the foreman at the jam factory, see if there's any casuals needed?" I said tentatively.

"No, no need," said Iris. "He's got plans, big plans; he

kept me awake half the night talking about it, which is why I slept in. Things are looking up for us, I can feel it."

Iris clung to hope like a kid grasping a melting ice cream.

The tallyman was waiting with his cart at the top of the street, with his old nag quietly chomping on a nosebag of oats. He was tall and almost boyishly good-looking, despite his thick mop of silvery gray hair, which was tucked under a cloth cap. The tallyman was a real charmer, handsome, with the gift of the gab, and the housewives up Tenison Street and Howley Terrace loved to have a natter with him because he knew all the gossip and had a way of making them feel special. Buying a teatowel or two usually involved swapping secrets about people from the neighboring streets. He soaked it all up, like a sponge, safe in the knowledge that he could squeeze it all back out a few streets away, and no one would ever find out it was him.

I'd always thought there was something shifty about him, the way his blue eyes darted about and he'd sidle up to people, like a nasty little crab. He walked a bit wonky too, knock-kneed, which is how he'd got out of doing the army.

"I'll catch you later," he murmured to Iris out of the corner of his mouth, as we hurried past. I caught the look on Iris's face. It didn't sound like a question, more of a statement, and Iris had gone a bit pale.

Everyone needed the tallyman, for everything from candles to cutlery, but no one welcomed his visits because it always involved paying him for the stuff they'd had on tick the month before. Dad called him "that blasted, lanky con man" and was always fuming about the interest on repayments, which seemed to go up weekly, but that didn't stop Mum from being a name in his little red book of customers, which he kept in the top pocket of his waistcoat.

Iris thrust her hands deeper into her pockets as we scurried along Belvedere Road and up the steps toward Waterloo Road, to catch the tram down to the Elephant; from there we'd always get the bus down through Bermondsey to the factory gates.

"It can't be easy managing on just your wages," I said, gently. "Is everything alright, Iris?"

"'Course, it's fine," said Iris, without looking me in the eye. "We're getting by."

That's the best that any of us could say, I suppose.

We squeezed into a seat side by side on the tram, which was full to bursting with other girls, all headed down to the factories, which were known as the Larder of London. The only problem was, these days, the larder was looking quite bare, and everyone was heartily sick of paying through the nose for what went on the table.

When Miss Pritchard wasn't on the prowl that morning, the other girls snatched a moment to gossip about what they'd got up to at the Victory Parade. I didn't have much to talk about, for obvious reasons. "Yeah, me fella went off with a tart with red hair and left me up the duff." So, the less said, the better.

In any case, I was too busy watching the clock 'til lunchtime. When the bell went, the others shuffled off over the road to the works canteen and I quietly slipped out of my green overalls. Our factory wasn't as bad as some, but that canteen, good Lord, what they did to the food was verging on criminal. The stench of boiled cabbage and spam fritters was enough to make me retch, so I didn't mind missing out.

I hopped on a bus back up to the Elephant and made my way to the tenements in Scovell Road. Now, where I lived wasn't what you'd call a white-curtain street, by any stretch of the imagination; the kind of place where office workers rubbed shoulders with dockers, and everyone's nets were starched to perfection. But to find anything positive to say about Scovell Road in them days, was like saying there was a tasty end to a lump of shit. And by the time you'd thought about that as you made your way down Scovell Road, you'd probably have stepped in it anyway.

Rubbish was blowing about outside the grimy windows of the local pub, which squatted opposite huge, redbrick tenements looming so high that they blotted out the sun. A bomb had done for the houses next to the pub, making somewhere for the kiddies to dice with death when their mums became sick to the back teeth of them. I glanced up to see washing strung between the flats, graying vests and holey sheets, fluttering high up above me. Down below, the shouts of little ones running amok echoed in the courtyard.

In a heartbeat, two of the little sods were on me. They were bomb site kids alright, snotty noses, matted hair like straw, covered in filth and God knows what else.

"Gi'z a penny, Missus!"

"Shouldn't you be in school?"

"Mind yer flaming business, you nosy cow."

I went to take a swipe at her, for cheeking me, but then I realized her face was all scarred and her little friend was holding her hand tightly, because she couldn't see, the poor little mite. She must have been caught near a window during the Blitz.

"Alright," I sighed, reaching into my purse. "There's a penny but you've got to tell me where I can find Alice Diamond."

"If it's the cozzers, she don't live here no more," said the blind girl, as her mate kicked her in the shins.

"Ow!" she yelped.

"Not supposed to say nuffink, stupid," said her mate, scowling at me.

"I'm not the police, for Gawd's sake, I just need to talk to her," I said, glancing at my watch.

The shin-kicker snatched the penny, so I held on to her collar, to stop her legging it.

"Flat 32 on the third floor in that block over there," she said, pointing to a doorway in the corner of the courtyard before breaking free and scarpering, pulling her chum along behind her, like a little rag doll.

There was an eerie silence as I climbed the stairwells, which stank of carbolic soap, but even that couldn't cover the stench of urine in the corners. My nerves almost got the better of me but I'd come this far, so I ignored the butterflies in my stomach and rapped gently on the green front door of number 32.

It swung open and Molly, the ginger tart, was standing there.

"Well, look what the cat dragged in," she drawled, puffing away on a roll-up. She glanced over my shoulder for an instant. "You alone?"

I nodded.

"Better come in, then."

She led me down the hallway, past a room which was like an Aladdin's cave, with a clothes rail stuffed to the gunnels with expensive-looking coats and dresses. Perhaps Alice was a seamstress of some sort and took in piecework for wealthy ladies? They probably had more call for posh outfits now the war was done. I spied a Singer sewing machine in the corner too, a really fancy one. I loved sewing. I was a dab hand with the needle and thread, which came in very handy during the war, but I'd never been able to afford an actual sewing machine, so I was craning my neck to get a look at that. Molly tired of me dawdling and shoved me, quite hard, down the corridor toward a tiny kitchen.

Alice Diamond was sitting at the kitchen table, surrounded by more bags brimming with clothes, grinning from ear to ear.

She had an enormous teapot in front of her, covered by a Union Jack cozy, and she poured me a brew. It was the brownest, most delicious-looking cuppa I had seen since rationing began. Our tea was like dishwater, from reused tea leaves, but hers looked like paradise.

"Thought I'd be seeing you again." She smirked. "Had a little think about my offer, did you?"

She motioned at me to sit down and I pulled out a wooden chair, which screeched on the tiled floor.

"Yes," I said, sipping the scalding liquid. I was so keen to taste it, I almost burned my tongue.

There was no point being standoffish. "I'm in trouble, and like you said, there's not many opportunities for a girl in my situation. I don't want Jimmy to find out I've been here, but I want to know more, that's all."

"Not still harping on about him, are you?" said Molly, serving herself two boiled eggs from a pan on the gas stove—two, if you please! We only got one a week, at the best of times. She saw me eyeing them, sliced the tops off, took pity and pushed one toward me, along with a slice of thickly buttered toast. I ain't ashamed to say I accepted it and started gobbling it up before she could change her mind.

Alice smiled, warmly: "What you do with Jimmy is your business, love, but in our line of work, it helps not to have too many strings attached. And like I told you, he ain't all that reliable. You seen him since the other night?"

"No," I said, tracing a few crumbs around the tabletop with my fingers, avoiding her gaze.

Alice went on: "Speaks volumes, don't it, Molly, not to check on his girl?"

Molly nodded, smugly. For some reason, I was dying to give her a clump, egg or no egg.

"What is it, the work you are offering me?" I asked, between mouthfuls of delicious yolk.

"Well, we go shopping to earn a living," said Alice. "But there's skill involved because we think the prices in the big shops like Selfridges and Gamages are too high for the likes of us."

She jabbed the air in front of her with a bejeweled finger as she spoke, to underline her point: "And it just. Ain't. Fair."

"You nick stuff," I said, the penny dropping. "It's all stolen. I ain't a thief!"

"Pickpockets, dippers, burglars," said Alice. "They're the lowest of the low, stealing from old ladies' coats, people's houses and women's handbags, the filth.

"The way I see it," Alice continued, taking a slurp of tea as a fat, tabby tomcat strutted in and jumped onto her lap, "we are skilled workers. The posh folk are pinching from us every day of our lives. They treat us like mugs. We work our fingers to the bone."

I had to admit she had a point, but Molly's cigarette-stained fingers, with red nails like talons, didn't look like they'd done a hard day's graft in their life.

Alice continued, as the cat rubbed its head against her hand, purring: "And all we get is coupons we can't live on, rent we can't pay, even after the sacrifices we've all made in the war.

"Not the quality, oh no, they're over the water in their posh houses, Mr. and Mrs. Lah-Di-Dah, dressed up nice, going out to dinner, bending the rules or breaking 'em because when you're rich, Nell, the rules don't count.

"And in any case, the shops have got insurance, so they get the money back. We're just nicking a few things here and there to help give people, our kind of people, stuff they want, at a fair price. We ain't really robbing from anyone if you look at it that way. We're helping ourselves because no one will help us."

Molly grinned at me, and I noticed her teeth were yellowing: "We're hoisters, Nell. It's a trade you have to train for, but it will set you up for life."

Just then, the kitchen door swung open and another couple of girls, the ones from the pub at the Victory Parade, stepped in and started pulling things out of their pockets to lay them on the table before Alice.

One of them lifted her dress and produced—no word of a lie—an entire fur coat from the most enormous pair of bloomers I have ever seen in my life. They had elastic at each knee and were proper apple-catchers, reaching all the way up beyond her belly button. As she unrolled the fur, still on the hanger, she laughed: "Ta-da!" and Molly gave her a little round of applause. It was sable, the softest and most beautiful pelt, and I knew it would cost a bleeding fortune.

"Well done, Em," said Alice. "Turn out your pockets, Patsy," she said to her companion, who was fishing around inside her coat. She was blonde, with freckles, and looked like butter wouldn't melt in her mouth. With expert fingers, she produced several pairs of leather gloves, some stockings, and a watch, as Alice looked on, approvingly: "Nice work. Any problems up West?"

"Gamages are getting wise to us," said Em. "I had a few near misses."

"These are some of my girls," said Alice. "We look after each other. It's a bit like a family." She produced a fistful of pound notes from the pocket of her apron and gave some to each of them, just like that, as if money grew on trees.

My dad was killing himself at Hartley's Jam Factory for four quid and six shillings a week and I was grafting all week for two.

"We stick together, and we don't tell no tales ever," said Alice. "It's a proud tradition, hoisting, goes all the way back to the times of Queen Victoria herself. The cozzers call us The Forty Thieves."

I was listening, open-mouthed. It sounded like something out of the talkies, Ali Baba and The Forty Thieves, only this was Alice Diamond and The Forty Thieves. It was thrilling, to be honest.

"The bosses up in the shops in the West End are getting too clever for their own good, the sneaky bastards. We have our methods but they're getting walkers on the shop floor, to follow us around, spot anyone acting suspicious, which is where you come in, love.

"Who would ever suspect your innocent little face? And let me tell you, that bump of yours is only going to get bigger, which means you can shove more down your drawers and get away with it!" she said triumphantly.

"What if I get caught?"

"You won't get caught because I will teach you everything I know. And I know plenty. And in any case, you're pregnant, which means they will be more sympathetic. You could have just been having a funny turn, couldn't you?"

She turned to Molly, who was admiring the watch, which had a beautiful mother-of-pearl clockface: "Moll, when was the last time anyone went up before the beak?"

Molly shrugged her shoulders: "Maybe three years ago. Eva got time but that was during the war when they were clamping down on us and even then, it was only six months in Holloway. The prison cocoa was nice from what I hear."

"And did I look after her?"

"Yes, paid her wages weekly and she had it all when she came out, with interest," said Molly.

I had no intention of going to prison, ever, but stealing a few clothes and earning easy money did sound like an attractive prospect. Besides, the way Alice was talking and given my situation, I didn't really have a choice.

"I want to be able to get some money together to help raise my baby," I said, the words tumbling out before I even knew what I was really saying. Jimmy had made promises about the future, *our* future, but right now he was nowhere to be seen and I needed to do something to make things better for myself and this baby. Supposing it had all been a load of hot air and he'd done a runner, given I was in the family way? It wouldn't be the first time a bloke had left his girl in the lurch at the first sign of trouble.

I'd heard of a few women who'd had babies with GIs who were going it alone, and they were on the waiting list for council prefabs. The clever ones put their kids with an aunty and they went out to work during the day. You never saw them out and about because they were always working or at home, and frankly most people didn't want to talk to them, but at least they were living life on their own terms. I knew my dad would never let Mum help me out, but at least if I had money, I could pay a babysitter . . .

"That's a lovely idea, ain't it, Molly?" said Alice. "D'you think we'll be able to help Nell stand on her own two feet with her little one?"

"Can't see why not," said Molly. "The best girls easily earn a fiver a week, Nell, and I should know."

A fiver a week! I'd be living like a lord on that.

"But that's more than fellas earn!" I gasped. Jimmy or no Jimmy, earning that kind of cash was like a dream and I wanted to know more.

"It is," said Alice. "I have a few blokes working for me, to help us get shopping away from the stores in a hurry, and I pay them fairly, but my girls are my priority. There's no other job in London that'll pay you more than me. Well, none that will let you keep your knickers on.

"Now I've let you in to some of our secrets, I'll need you to prove yourself, but first why don't you come and pick something nice, just as a welcome present, for joining our little gang?"

She was so persuasive, almost homely looking, in a pinny and fluffy carpet slippers. This Alice wasn't a bit like the fierce woman in a fedora who'd commanded such respect in the pub. She was softer, motherly almost, and she was a million miles nicer than my boss, Miss Pritchard. I didn't care that the bell would have sounded for the end of lunch break by now and everyone would be hurrying back to their places in the factory. I simply did not give a fiddler's damn about it anymore.

Alice was offering me a different life: money, big money, more than I'd ever earned, standing on my own two feet with no man being the boss of me.

She put her arm around me as she swept me down the hall and into the front room, where the clothes rail stood.

"Help yourself." She smiled.

My fingers ran the full length of that rail, feeling the softness of printed cotton, silks, and taffeta. Those were other people's lives on that rail, rich people's, but I was allowed more than a glimpse, I was allowed to touch, for once.

There was no way I needed a fancy frock in my condition and I'd never be able to explain that to my parents. In a bag on the floor, I spied some underwear.

My bust was barely contained in my liberty bodice these days. My boobs were looking more like two barrage balloons.

Bending down for a closer look, I pulled out a brassiere and a silk camisole. I'd seen a picture of one in the adverts in the *Evening News* but never dreamed I'd feel one, let alone own it.

"Don't be shy, try them on," said Alice.

I slipped out of my blouse and undid my bodice, heaving

a sigh of relief as I eased into that bra, feeling the softness of silk camisole next to my skin.

Alice picked up my tatty old liberty bodice and twirled it around before chucking it in the corner.

"You won't be needing that anymore, love."

Then she rummaged in an old wooden chest and pulled out something else, holding it aloft.

It was a pair of those ridiculous hoister's bloomers, with thick elastic at each leg.

"But you will be needing these.

"Welcome to The Forty Thieves."

Chapter Five

NELL

Waterloo, London, June 1946

It felt like I was hopping the wag from school.

"You're doing what?" whispered Iris in astonishment, as we sat together on the tram the next day.

"Old Pritchard nearly blew a gasket when she realized you were missing all afternoon," she went on. "Shouldn't you go and face the music? At least tell her you're leaving?"

"No flipping way," I said. "I'm not going back, and that's that. Just tell her I've gone to look after me sick nan down in Kent, will you? I've got bigger fish to fry now."

As far as Mum and Dad were concerned, I was going to work down at the Alaska factory every day, just as I always had.

In reality, I was holed up in Scovell Road, learning how to be a hoister, taught by Alice Diamond, the Queen of The Forty Thieves, who was the best pilferer in the business. Molly Hall, her light-fingered second-in-command, was planning to take me out on my first shopping expedition up in the West End, but first I had to learn the tricks of the trade. Molly dispensed advice in between slugs of gin from one of Alice's best china teacups.

"Alice has three other teams working for her, but they leave their shopping with local fences, for safety, in case of police raids, so they don't come round to Scovell Road," she said, topping up her cup. It was not yet lunchtime, but she could drink like a man, for sure. "And if the cozzers did show up, things would disappear into other flats, as if by magic, wouldn't they, Alice?"

"They can't search the whole of Queen's Buildings," said Alice, strolling into the kitchen. "They know I'm crooked, I am right down to my smalls, but they've never been able to prove it."

"Now, let's get on with it. Have you got your hoister's drawers on, Nell?"

Pulling on those stupid knickers, Gawd, I looked a sight. I was doubled over laughing.

"Passion killers," said Molly drily. "They'd work better than a chastity belt."

"Wish I'd had them on round the back of the Trocadero a few months back," I replied.

That broke the ice between us.

I can't say I liked Molly, given how she'd been all over my Jimmy, but she was a good teacher and she did her best to make amends: "If I'd known he was walking out with you, doll, I wouldn't have touched him with a barge pole, honest." She smiled but her eyes didn't. I was prepared to let that slide.

When I say "my Jimmy," well, he wasn't really my Jimmy anymore because he'd done a bunk. No one down The Cut had seen him since the night I'd caught him boozing with The Forty Thieves. His barrow was still parked in its usual place, up an alley, but he'd upped and gone, like the Scarlet Pimpernel. I tried not to dwell on it, but the thought of being without him made me feel properly queasy in the pit of my stomach.

"You look a bit pale, love," said Alice, coming to my side. "Expect it's a bit of morning sickness. It'll pass. Come on, let's take your mind off it. This will be fun."

We used Alice's kitchen table as a counter, and I practiced sweeping things off and into my bag. The bag swap took place between me and Molly, across the threshold of the front room to the hallway. She'd had a few by then but was still steady as a rock on her feet.

"Speed it up," said Alice. "You've got to be quicker, Nell."

God knows, I was trying my best, but she was like greased lightning when she did it.

"You're doing fine," she said. "It takes years to get fast at it, but you've got real potential, ain't she, Molly?"

"Oh, she's a natural!" she cried. I think it was the drink talking.

We practiced distraction, where Alice would knock something off the table, and I would swipe scarves and gloves and stuff them in my pockets.

"In the changing room, keep asking for clothes in more than one size, throw it all off the hangers, into a heap, so you can filch a few things and if you have time, put them on under what you are wearing."

"On the shop floor it's about speed and distraction. We will always work in a team," said Molly.

"Clouting," said Alice, "is the art of rolling a fur up, nice and tight, and shoving it down your knickers. I can get one in each leg, but you should just aim for one smaller item, for now. Here, start with a mink stole."

She threw the soft fur wrap over to me and I rolled it, as best as I could with one hand, while I flicked through the clothes rail with the other. I lifted my skirt and quickly shoved the fur down my drawers, but the end of the mink trailed out down my leg as I walked away.

"No," said Alice. "No good, go back and try it again."

Just then, there was a knock at the door. It wasn't just one knock, it was three in quick succession.

"It's alright," said Molly, as a look of panic swept across my face. "It's one of the fellas, that's their signal."

She sauntered off down the hall and called after me: "You've got a visitor."

I yanked the fur out of my knicker leg—that was no mean feat—straightened my skirt and made my way to see who it was.

Jimmy was leaning on the doorframe, scuffing his shoes on the mat.

Well, you could have knocked me down with a feather. I wanted to slap his stupid face and kiss him all at the same time. Instead, I stood there glaring at him, pursing my mouth.

"Heard I'd find you here," he said, glancing up at me with that little-boy-lost look of his.

He was sporting some new threads. The shoulders and lapels were wider than before, and he'd started to grow a little pencil moustache. It didn't suit him.

"There's something stuck on your top lip," I joked.

He didn't find it amusing. "Give over, Nell. That's the style for all us Chaps up in Soho."

"What's a Chap?"

"Someone who's on the pavement, looking for work, ready to help out."

"But you're a barrow boy."

He looked hurt. "You have no idea what I've been doing but I tell you this, Nell, I've been doing it for you, to show you I'm serious."

"What do you mean, serious?" I said. I wasn't going to make this easy for him, not after what he'd put me through these past few days. "Seriously sticking your tongue down Molly's throat like you were the other week?"

He shook his head. "Nah, you got it all wrong. I want to get married, to put a roof over our heads, so I can provide for you and the baby."

He talked as if it was going to be the easiest thing in the world, like one of his little errands he had to run.

"Well, you've got a funny way of showing it. You just upped and disappeared!" I spat. I was fighting the urge to grab hold of him and feel his arms around me. It must have been the pregnancy doing funny things to me. I'd heard about that. Women throwing pots and pans at their blokes in screaming rows one minute and then their knickers to the wind the next. What the hell was happening to me?

"Oh, Nell, don't be too hard on me, girl . . ." His blue eyes twinkled, and I felt my stomach do one of those silly flips. "Life is meant to be about having a bit of fun, ain't it? It was a party, and I'd had a few, but there was nothing in it with me and old Molly, she's just a family friend, honest to God."

I folded my arms. My bump really showed when I did that.

"I know you're brassed off with me, I get it, but I had to go and do a bit of work for someone, call in a few favors, because I'm trying to pull in all the cash I can. I'm serious about us, Nell. I want to provide for you and the baby. I want us to have a proper wedding and everything."

"With me looking like the back end of a bus!" I scoffed. "And my mother dying of shame in the front pew of the church."

He pulled me to him and nuzzled into my neck: "Are you forgetting who you are, my forever girl? I'm made up about our little family."

"But you've got a girl in every port, Alice said so," I protested. It was more like a half-protest. I could feel the smile starting to curl at the corners of my mouth. Jimmy had this way of soothing my anger, of making me think of strawberries and sunshine. It just oozed out of him, and I craved his touch.

"Don't believe everything she tells you, Nell! We can

do this together, but you have got to believe in me. Trust me. I may not be around very much while I sort things out, that's all."

"I'm scared, Jimmy," I whispered. "Scared about the future for me and the baby. People will talk. My dad will kill me when he finds out what we've done."

"Why don't you let me take you home? I can face him, man-to-man," he said.

"Oh, Jimmy," I choked. "He'll never let us get married. He'll have your guts for garters for what's happened, and I'm finished when he finds out . . ."

A voice came from over my shoulder.

"You alright, love?" It was Alice.

Jimmy's face hardened. "What have you got her into, Alice?"

"Nell don't need you to be the boss of her, Jimmy," said Alice, her mouth twisting into a sneer. "She's on a promise for me and she can think for herself from what I've seen."

Jimmy reeled back, like he'd been shot, and then he made a grab for me, with a wild look in his eye: "You don't know what you are getting tangled up in here, Nell, for God's sake! Let me take you home, we can iron this out with Alice later . . ."

Alice gave a snort of laughter. "Typical fella! Thinks he can waltz up to my door and dictate how things are going to work on my manor."

Molly swayed into view down the hallway, clutching her bottle of gin. "What's all the racket? Are things getting interesting?" She stopped, put her hand on her hip and pouted at him: "Oh, hello, Jim."

I pulled away from him. "It's alright, Jimmy, I want to do this, I'm happy here. I reckon I can earn good money and we can make good use of it, you'll see, it's for the baby." I owed Alice for what she'd taught me so far, I knew that, so

I couldn't just leave, but I'd also seen how her girls lived, the independence they had, the things they could afford, and I wanted some of it. It was different from the way I longed to be with Jimmy, but I was chasing the chance of a better life, which would help us in the long run. If only he'd see it that way.

He looked crestfallen, and I felt tears prick my eyes at that and they started running down my cheeks before I could stop them.

"But I'm going to provide for us, just give me a chance," he mumbled, shrinking in Alice's shadow as she loomed toward him.

"She's making her own decisions, Jimmy," she said curtly. "Now, I respect you, we go back a long way, but you're on my turf and I won't have you upsetting my girls because that would be a flaming liberty. So, you'd better sling your hook, chum, before I run out of patience."

She shut the door firmly in his face and as I turned, I found myself weeping on her shoulder.

"There, don't upset yourself. Just a lovers' tiff. He ain't worth it. No fella is worth it."

She gave me a little squeeze and as she gazed into my eyes, I noticed, for the first time, that hers were flecked with gold.

"Come on," she said. "Let's go shopping."

Selfridges on Oxford Street stood like a monument to wealth and luxury, with huge columns all the way along its frontage and tempting window displays drawing crowds, even on a boiling hot day. I knew it from my childhood, the times I'd spent with my nose pressed longingly to the glass, admiring the toys at Christmas. Sometimes Mum and me might wander through to look at things, with her words "Look, don't touch!" ringing in my ears.

Today was different. We were very much in the business of

touching things and taking them home—without paying—and I felt almost giddy with nerves. We'd hopped on the bus to cross the river because Alice wanted to save a bit on petrol and her Chrysler had been in the garage for repairs, so the plan was for her driver, Molly's brother Jack, to park up nearby in an hour or so, when we were finished. Alice had given me a summer frock to wear, a beautiful cotton dress printed with sprigs of flowers, and belt in the same material. I had a petticoat under and my hoister drawers over my knickers. Molly and me had matching carpet bags slung over our arms, and Alice had the most enormous leather handbag.

Alice had spent some time doing my hair up nicely, rolling it at the sides to give it a bit of lift, fastening it with some grips. "Makes you look pretty, shows your cheekbones off a bit," she said.

She was wearing a light overcoat, of gaberdine, which I knew had secret pockets sewn into the lining, and a smart straw hat with flowers on the brim. Even in the heat, she was cool as a cucumber.

"Now," she said, as we hopped off the bus and she pushed open the heavy double doors to the shop, "I need to see if you're game enough for us, Nell."

"Of course, I am," I said. "I ain't bottling out now."

She gave a little "hmm" of approval.

"I'm not expecting you to hoist much," said Alice. "Just some easy stuff: hankies, stockings, scarves. Sweep them into the bag, using the technique we showed you."

I nodded.

"I'll keep the assistant busy," said Molly, "then we'll do a bag swap out in the stairwell, and I'll get the bag out to the others on the pavement outside. You stick close by me."

The thieves worked in teams, inside and outside the shop, so that they could get their loot away and come back for more. It was a simple plan, but very effective.

It made me feel special, important even, walking through that store knowing I was working. I felt sorry for my pal, Iris, spending all day every day stuck in that bloody factory, bashing the life out of rabbit pelts. That was soul-destroying. This felt like freedom.

We had to push our way through, past the crowds of women on the cosmetics counters, squirting perfume on their wrists, to get to the stairs up to the women's clothing department.

A well-dressed woman with so much face powder on she looked like she'd rolled in flour was pulling out her purse to pay for some Eau de Cologne and a lipstick.

"Mug," muttered Molly, under her breath. "Makeup is easy pickings, I'll show you that another time."

When we got upstairs on the shop floor, I started to feel my heartbeat quicken. Alice peeled off left and we went right, over to a table with scarves on it, all neatly folded.

Molly picked one up and pretended to admire the pattern for a moment. "It's rayon, not silk, won't be worth as much but we'll have a few of them."

She strolled around the counter with the scarf still in hand, as a little birdlike shop assistant made her way over to us. I stuck to the side of that table like glue, waiting for my signal.

"Anything Madam would like in particular today?"

Right on cue, Molly dropped the scarf. "Oh clumsy me!"

As the assistant bent down to pick it up, I held the bag open just under the edge of the table and swept a few scarves in. I glanced up and saw Alice, in the corner, trying on a hat. She flashed me a grin, like the Cheshire cat.

I closed my bag, turned and walked off toward a display of stockings, which I knew were valuable to The Forty Thieves. Every self-respecting woman needed them, and they cost three coupons a pair. More were coming onto the market because of a new factory making British nylons, but they were still in short supply.

The assistant was busy advising two matronly women on their underpinnings. They looked like they still wore whalebone corsets, the poor old dears. The stockings were arranged on a carousel, so I sneaked around the side nearest to the wall and grabbed a few packets from the bottom, stuffing them in my bag. Molly appeared at my side and filched a packet too, which I assume she must have put in her bag, but I swear I never saw it happen; she was so fast.

The little sparrow of an assistant from the scarves' counter started to walk toward us, with a quizzical look on her face.

"Can I help you ladies? Any size in particular?"

"No thanks," said Molly, wiping a bead of sweat from her brow. "Terribly warm in here, think we need some air."

Now, Molly normally spoke like all the people round our way did. We were Cockneys. But when she was working, she sounded like she had a plum in her mouth. I stifled a giggle and she dug me in the ribs, hard, which winded me, so that I coughed.

"Oh, my daughter's feeling faint too," she said. "Perhaps you should open a window in here?"

Molly put her arm around me, and we walked together to the door, where she took my bag, and I took hers. She didn't hesitate and was already hightailing down the stairs as I walked back into the department to find Alice.

She was nowhere to be seen.

I made a show of looking at the scarves again and went and tried on a few hats. Maybe it was fear that made me do it, or daring, but before I knew what was happening, I was sauntering toward tempting rails of lingerie. I gave the flannelette nighties a wide berth; I could hear Alice guffawing with laughter at the thought of selling those matronly threads.

Instead, a lovely display of negligees caught my eye. I picked one up, marveling at the softness of the fabric. Was it silk or rayon?

"Silk, Miss," said another shop assistant, who had appeared out of nowhere and was built like a brick shithouse, pardon my language. "Very expensive."

I imagined what Alice Diamond would do.

I fixed her with a steely look. "I'd like to try it, please."

My fingers developed a life of their own, messing up her neat display. "And a few of those ones too." She started trying to tidy up, and in the confusion, I plonked my bag on the table and pushed a nightie to the edge and onto the floor.

"Do mind the stock, Miss," she said acidly. "Your bag may damage the delicate fabric."

"Silly me," I said, moving the bag and bending down to scoop the silk and shove it inside while she fussed over the neatness of her display. I'd done it! It only took a few moments and I stood there, coloring up. There was no turning back now.

A thin smile formed on her lips as she looked me up and down. "I would like to try them on," I said, adding thoughtfully, "Please."

"I see," she said, clasping the garments to her bosom, as if they were her most prized possessions. She moved at quite a lick for a well-built latrine and what with the nerves, I was almost out of breath trying to keep up.

"Well, do try and let me know if there is anything in particular you like," she said.

"I'm here with my aunty, shopping," I said, by way of explanation, as we headed toward the changing room. "She wants to treat me for my birthday."

"Lovely," she replied.

My heart was pounding as she yanked open the curtain and then pulled it closed behind me. I surveyed the nighties, in pale blue silk, shell pink, cream and, of course, the one I'd shoved in my bag, in purest white. They were all beautiful and cost more than two weeks' wages for any woman.

I stared at my reflection in the changing room mirror. I looked terrified, with two high-colored patches of scarlet on my cheeks where I'd got so flustered. But I'd gone and done it now. It was easy to stand in a changing room, but I had to get the goods out of the store and to safety before the assistant did a stock check.

I started to undress, to make a show of trying them on. I swear my boobs had grown an inch since the morning and when I pulled the scrap of silk over my head, it got stuck. Panicking and fearing I'd rip it, I pulled it off again, sharpish, and counted to ten, breathing deeply.

"Well, Miss," she boomed from the other side of the curtain, "how does it look?"

"Lovely," I lied. "I'd like my aunt to see it before I buy it, could you possibly hold it for me for an hour?" I wriggled myself back into my summer dress.

"Of course," she said. "Just one hour, though."

I pulled back the curtain and greeted her with a cheery smile, handing over the heap of nighties. How hard could this be? All I had to do now was make for the oak-paneled door in the corner but for some reason, my legs were shaking, and my knees had gone a bit wobbly.

"Are you feeling alright, Miss?"

"Yes, just a little hot today, isn't it? I think I need a little fresh air. I'll be back shortly." I set off across the shop floor.

The bag on my arm suddenly weighed a ton and every mannequin seemed to be staring at me accusingly. The door loomed in the distance and my feet were wading through treacle, but I kept going and I didn't look back, not even when the assistant said: "I'll look forward to seeing you later."

"Not if I see you first," I muttered under my breath.

Suddenly, the door was right in front of me. Pushing it open, I was greeted by a gust of cool air in the stairwell, and I leaned against the tiled walls to steady myself. As I was making my way down the flight of stairs, Alice was standing there at the bottom, with a face like thunder: "Where the bloody hell have you been?"

She grabbed hold of me, and her grip was like being caught in a vise. She dragged me, bodily, through the doors, clamping me to her side. Alice was talking, out of the corner of her mouth, in a low whisper, with words that stung like hell, her green eyes blazing: "You little bleeding idiot! What the hell d'you think you're playing at going off and getting lost like that? Just you wait 'til I get you home."

"Let me explain," I squeaked. "Give me a chance to—"

"Shut it!" she spat. "Just let me get us out of here."

Suddenly we were moving, very fast, across the ground floor. The makeup counters passed in a blur. We whizzed through the revolving doors at lightning speed and out into the car, where her driver was waiting with the engine running.

Molly was in the front seat, grinning from ear to ear. She'd gone and dumped me, and she knew it, but I wasn't going to grass her up to Alice over it.

"Now," said Alice, as the engine revved and we pulled away up Holborn, "explain yourself."

Molly looked on expectantly, like a cat waiting for a little injured bird to fall off its perch so that it could go in for the kill.

There was only one thing to do.

I put my hand inside my bag, fished around, and pulled it out.

"This," I said timidly, holding the silk garment aloft, by way of apology. "This is what I was doing."

Alice's whole face lit up, her look softened and she embraced me.

"I lost sight of Molly and I just thought . . ."

"Oh you, beauty!" she cried, addressing the nightie—not

me—as if it were a long-lost friend. She snatched it away and tucked it into her carpet bag, which was stuffed with loot.

Then she turned to me. I was shaking like a leaf.

"Nell," she said, patting me on the knee, her diamond rings glinting, "I was trying to think of what to call you when we got in this car, for going off on your own, diso-beying orders, and generally behaving like a clot. And now I think I've found the word I was looking for . . ."

Alice gave a low chuckle as she pulled me into her embrace: "Hoister!"

In that moment I felt something totally new, a sense of belonging, like being part of the family I'd never really had; one that thought I was worth something. My heart swelled with pride.

It was the happiest day of my life.

I was one of the gang.

Chapter Six

ALICE

Elephant and Castle, June 1946

I love a good knees-up, especially when there's reason to celebrate, and after Nell's performance I was in the mood for a little party.

We all piled back to my place to unpack our shopping and freshen up. Poor little Nell, I did give her a bit of a fright when I thought she was putting our trip in jeopardy, but life's full of surprises, ain't it? The two quid I gave her for her efforts more than made up for it.

I love that about my line of work. It ain't just the thrill of getting away with it; it's the sense of playing with Lady Luck herself. Nell took a chance, and she proved her mettle. I'll be the first to raise a glass to that; reminds me of someone I know who I admire very much. Myself, in fact.

The Ship Inn over the road from Queen's Buildings is my local and the sound of raucous laughter was already ringing out by the time we made our entrance. The pub had survived the bombing in the Blitz, which was a cause for celebration at the time and every night since. There were a few boarded-up windows and it could have done with a lick of paint here and there, but everyone was usually too drunk to notice or care.

A gang of fellas were having all the best fun hammering

out "Roll Out the Barrel" on the ivories and hooting with laughter over their pints while their poor, dear wives sat in the corner, talking in hushed tones in headscarves, with little more than a thimbleful of sherry between them.

"Right, you shower!" I bellowed. "Let's have a decent round of drinks for the ladies, please!"

They stopped playing and sullenly put their hands in their pockets for a whip round. The money was passed to me in one of their caps and I tapped my cane on the filthy wooden boards while Molly inspected it. It was amazing how interesting the floor had become, judging by the way they were all staring at it.

"Ain't enough for that lot," she said, nodding toward the row of downtrodden wives in the corner.

"Dig deeper, boys," I said, clapping one of them right between the shoulder blades, almost knocking his teeth out on his pint glass. "Don't make me ask twice."

The barman rolled his eyes. It was the same procedure every bleeding week. I knew it, he knew it, but those greedy little punters would never learn, would they?

"You see, Nell," I said, turning to her, "that's the future of married life, sitting over there, miserable and kept on whatever crumbs he feels like giving you from his table."

The women were wearing patched-up skirts and darned stockings and looked little more than scarecrows. Meanwhile, their ruddy-faced hubbies were lording it in beer and sausages by the look of them.

"I know which side of the pub I'd rather be on," I laughed. "That's the trouble with men. They are all hearts and flowers when they want you, but when they've got you . . . well . . . just take a butcher's in that direction."

Nell glanced at the women in the corner and then opened her mouth to say something, but the music started up again, just as some of my other girls strutted in. Nell smiled at me instead, a beaming grin. It was a look that said it all. She was in my gang now. And I wanted her to feel right at home.

Molly had rallied a few of the other girls to come and celebrate Nell's first big success as a hoister, although from the look on her face, you'd have thought she'd lost a quid and found a ha'penny. That's the thing with Molly. She does have a tendency to get jealous. She's my deputy but she has a streak of the old green-eyed monster about her whenever I heap praise on one of the others. I like it that way; keeps her on her toes.

"Now, Nell," I said, settling myself beside her, so that I had a good view of the door of the pub—I don't like to be caught unawares if a cozzer pops his head through—"let's raise a glass to the finest little hoister in London town today!"

"Do you really think that?" She sipped at her drink, sheepishly.

"'Course I do! You had that old assistant dancing to your tune alright. And not just in some two-bit musty old department store, in Selfridges if you please! Talk about aiming high. You shot at the moon and scored a bull's-eye, my girl."

"I did, didn't I?" she said, sitting up straighter. "It was easy as pie. The silly old fool had no clue. I reckon I could have filched a few more if I'd had a bit longer."

She was puffed up with pride like a little pigeon strutting about Trafalgar Square.

"I couldn't be happier if you'd hoisted the crown jewels, love," I said, beaming at her, to give her a bit more of a gee. "Silk sells, and stealing a nightie like that on your first shopping trip takes courage, real courage." I gave her a reassuring little squeeze.

"It was foolish," said Molly, deadpan, into her sherry. "She took a huge risk." Nell's face fell.

"Oh, stop it, Moll," I chided. "Nell made the best of the situation, and we are all here to celebrate that."

I raised my glass and announced: "Let's have three cheers for Nell!"

The whole pub erupted into an impromptu chorus of "For She's a Jolly Good Fellow," and we were just getting to the last "*and so say all of us*" when the door swung open and Jimmy was standing there, all spruced up, as if he was going for a night on the tiles.

But the look on his face when he saw Nell in our midst and half of Queen's Buildings toasting her success was nothing like delight.

Jimmy strode across the floor like a man possessed and pulled Nell to her feet.

Everyone stopped singing and clapping and you could have heard a pin drop.

Then, he got down on one knee and pulled a something out of his jacket pocket. It was a little black box. He flicked it open. It was lined with velvet.

I peered at it, trying to get a closer look. Inside it was a gold ring, studded with sapphires. He'd be pulling the tallyman's cart for him if he'd got it on tick. I made a little cluck of approval. Not for the gesture, you see, it's just jewelry does have an effect on me, especially if it's a nice set of stones like those ones.

"Nell," he said. "I want you to come home with me now and we can see your parents and talk things through. I love you. Will you marry me?"

He offered her the ring.

She froze and then looked at me, her mouth falling open in shock.

"Well," I said, gesturing to the mother's meeting of misery, discussing their washing and their husband's tea in a huddle in the far corner. "It's your choice, ain't it?"

"Jimmy," she began as she took the ring and held it in

the palm of her hand. "This is beautiful, stunning, and God knows how you have afforded it but I'm not sure I'm ready for marriage and settling down and everything, and I don't know that you are either, if you are really honest. I don't know where you are half the time and you won't tell me, and I can't see that changing, only getting worse."

It wasn't quite the reaction he'd been expecting.

He lowered his voice to a whisper. "I'm not saying I'm a saint but I'm not that much of a sinner and you can't be having that on your own." He pointed to her stomach and stood back up, brushing the dust off his trouser legs. "Beggars can't be choosers, Nell, so don't be a silly girl. And don't believe everything she tells you." He nodded in my direction in a way I didn't particularly appreciate.

I don't know why, maybe it was the pregnancy that made her see red, but she lost it.

"Beggar?" she said, turning red with fury. "I'll tell you who's the beggar round here and it ain't me! I'm earning good money, better money than you from just one afternoon's work, actually. I've found something I'm really good at, that pays well, and you just want to take it away from me and chain me to the kitchen sink, just like all the rest. I won't have it!"

Oh, she was a right little firecracker when she got into her stride, this one. It was just a case of working out how to light the touch paper.

"Nell, you're working for someone who's got their claws right into you," he said coldly.

"Watch your mouth," I said, leaning over, so that I was right in his face. "Or you might meet with a nasty accident, if you know what I mean."

"This is between Nell and me," he spat. "So back off!"

"Oh, I ain't coming between two lovebirds." I laughed, rocking back in my chair. "No need to get overexcited."

At the same time, I swung my cane and gave him a sharp prod right in the middle of his chest, just to make a point.

Jimmy took a step back.

He stood there for a few seconds, his mouth opening and closing, like a fish out of water.

Nell stood up. "No," she said, thrusting the ring toward him. "No, Jimmy, I will not marry you, not now, not ever, so you might as well have it back."

Truly, it was better than a night at the varieties. The whole pub was watching with bated breath.

"You've got a screw loose, Nell," he said, tapping the side of his head. "I dunno what's wrong with you. A fella wants to marry you, to do the right thing, and you are throwing it back in his face! Well, you'll see what'll happen to you without my ring on your finger. You'll see what Tenison Street thinks of you, in fact, the whole bloody neighborhood!"

He had gone a really funny color, almost purple, and he snatched the ring and spun around on his heel, the turnups on his new trousers swishing as he went.

"Oh, naff off," she cried, as the rest of my girls jeered at him, for good measure. "Stay away from me. Just stay away, you bleeding spiv!"

Chapter Seven

NELL

Waterloo, London, June 1946

I numbed the shock of turning down Jimmy's offer of marriage with a good few sherries.

A week ago, I would have thought I'd lost my mind saying no to this proposal, but with Alice by my side and The Forty Thieves for company, things weren't looking so bad. Whatever he was offering me, I didn't want it, even in my predicament.

When the sad gaggle of married women in the corner got up and shuffled off home, I found myself thanking my lucky stars I had refused him.

It wasn't going to be easy doing it this way, but I'd keep the pregnancy secret for as long as I could, and get a pile of cash together so I could afford a place of my own. Then, I'd put the baby with one of the neighbors for the day, pay her good money, while I went off shopping with The Forty Thieves. It wouldn't be perfect, but at least I'd live life on my own terms. Maybe I'd give Jimmy the time of day, maybe not. But he wasn't the boss of me, that was for certain.

"Sounds like a good plan, love," said Alice, nodding approvingly. "Anyone who judges you round here will get a thick ear from me. You ain't the first woman to have a baby on the wrong side of the bedsheets and you won't be the last.

"And the thing is, being part of my gang offers you protection from the gossips."

Molly pulled out her hatpin and started brandishing it about the place. She was three sheets to the wind: "Oh, just show me someone who gets all hoity-toity about one of us and I'll have their eye out," she screeched. I knew she wasn't joking.

"But I ain't so sure how my dad will take it," I said, a horrible sick feeling rising in the pit of my stomach. "In fact, I reckon he'll have me out on my ear when he finds out."

Alice gave my knee a reassuring little pat.

"You can come and bunk up at my place anytime, until you find your feet," she said. "We're all like family, ain't we?"

Patsy and Em and some of the other girls raised a glass, and Molly gave me one of her grins.

"Now," said Alice, looking at her watch, "it's a working day tomorrow, so drink up, we'd better get home."

It was barely half past nine.

"I'm strict about that, Nell," she said, as we wandered out of the pub, and I made my way to the bus stop. "Working days mean early nights and woe betide anyone who's out on the tiles the night before a big shopping expedition."

She pointed her cane at my stomach. "And you need all the rest you can get, in your condition. See you at mine in the morning, nine o'clock sharp."

As the bus hove into view and I clambered aboard, I heard her shout.

"Don't be late!"

As we drew away from Queen's Buildings, I knew that I'd started out on a new path.

And there was no turning back.

Gamages department store sprawled right up the street and

around the corner on High Holborn, tempting customers with window displays offering everything from toys to fur coats. It was set over four floors, and was full of dark corners, corridors, and stairwells to get lost in, which was a hoister's delight.

The shop was full to bursting with hordes of unwashed, hot, sweaty women rifling through things they could never afford, never in a month of Sundays.

Even soap was a luxury item and the smell of so many fetid armpits in that packed store in the heat of a summer's afternoon was enough to make you gasp.

We were prepared to put up with it because we knew that crowds made it a lot easier for us to do what we'd come here to do.

"Stockings," said Alice. "Stockings galore. Stuff 'em in your drawers, hide 'em in your bags. I've got a big order from Queen's Buildings to fill, and I reckon we can make a pretty penny, so let's keep our wits about us and make the most of what's on offer."

Patsy and Em went off to find furs while me, Molly, and Alice headed for the stairs and the ladies' lingerie department on our stockings quest.

Alice turned to me. "Nell, after yesterday, I'm expecting big things of you! Don't panic if you get left alone for a while, just saunter around a bit, we'll come and find you."

The nerves of yesterday were long gone.

"Right," I said. "I won't let you down."

"Good girl," she said, smiling at me. "Let's make this a day to remember!"

Every inch of Gamages was filled with tempting goods, which made easy pickings: piles of leather gloves and tables filled with purses and rails of clothes rammed so tightly together that you had to stand on the toes of the person next to you just to get a look at them. In the confusion and the crush of bodies, it was easy to pilfer.

Molly knocked a few things off into her bag on the way past and I followed her lead, sweeping a couple of wallets and a spectacle case into the depths of my carpet bag, without breaking a sweat. It was just a case of being confident about it and people were so busy with their own business that they didn't have a clue what we were up to. The assistants were rushed off their feet and the queue for the till snaked halfway around the shop floor. But when we went upstairs to the ladies' underwear department, it was quiet as the grave.

I was learning a lot about the posh undergarments that rich ladies liked to wear, and I found them endlessly fascinating. As well as silk stockings, there were corselettes and those fine silk slips and brassieres that were nothing like the drab, coarse things my mum wore. Once I'd had the baby and I was earning well, I vowed I would spend my money learning to dress like a lady.

Alice got to work, immediately distracting the old shop assistant, who peered over her half-moon glasses and let out a weary sigh as she pulled out a drawer full of ladies' handkerchiefs. "Very nice," cooed Alice. "But which one do you think will go best with my hat?" She made a great show of looking in the mirror and holding them up to her face.

Molly and me were already around the other side of the counter, examining a neat display of silk stockings. The assistant had kept them right under her nose, but she was no match for Molly, who grabbed several packs while Alice slowly, very slowly, paid for a bright red silk hankie, counting out her coins on the countertop. Molly had already shoved the stockings in my bag, and we pretended to be sharing a joke as we walked briskly to the stairwell.

Once we got there, she fished around in my bag, pulling

out the stockings as well as the wallets and spectacle case I'd pinched from downstairs. Her face lit up: "Well done, Nell!" Then she hightailed it off down the stairs. I wasn't worried this time, not even when I went back onto the shop floor and there was no sign of Alice.

I just had to walk slowly to the exit on the other side of the shop, stopping to look at a few things along the way. One of the gang would be along soon; that's what Alice had said.

The minutes passed and I glanced around anxiously.

I took a deep breath, and was just heading for the stairs, when the assistant with the half-moon spectacles started walking toward me, with a look in her eye that said I was for it. There was someone else with her, a bigger woman, with thick-set shoulders and a chest like the prow of one of the big boats I'd seen going up and down the Thames near our house.

"That's her!" said Mrs. Half-Moon Glasses, pointing a finger at me. That big woman moved fast, because she had me in her grasp before I had time to think.

"Gotcha!" she said triumphantly.

"You're making a terrible mistake!" I squealed, but she wouldn't listen.

She marched me up to her office on the fourth floor, down a corridor with dark wood paneling on the walls. The whole place reeked of furniture polish, and I began to feel a bit queasy.

We stopped in front of a door with a brass nameplate that said "MISS G. HUNTER." Keeping a tight hold on my arm the whole time so I couldn't do a bunk, she pushed open the heavy wooden door.

A fella was in the office, gazing out of the window, smoking. He turned to face us, a broad grin spreading across his face.

"Well, well," he said, "your first kill of the day, Miss Hunter."

She gave him a look that could curdle milk, as if she wasn't the slightest bit interested in winning his praise: "Thank you, Detective Sergeant Hart."

"You're wrong about this, there's been a mistake," I cried. "I haven't done anything wrong." I was busy thanking my lucky stars that Molly had taken all the stuff I'd hoisted. In fact, it made me quite bold.

"You'll find you owe me a big apology," I said, crossing my arms and staring at her.

Miss Hunter snorted with laughter, took my carpet bag, and pulled out a pair of silk stockings. Just one. But that was enough to dob me right in it. Molly must have forgotten to take the packet when she cleared out my bag.

She raised an eyebrow as she sat down at her desk.

"What's this?" said Miss Hunter. "Why is our merchandise in your bag? Where is the till receipt for this item?"

"It must have fallen in by accident," I said. That took the wind out of my sails. Molly must have missed a pair, which were nestling right at the bottom.

My heart sank. Despite his suit, this bloke was a cozzer. I was done for, unless I could find a smart way out of it. Alice had told me that when a hoister's tumbled, she's got three choices: run, fight, or turn on the waterworks.

Well, I didn't fancy my chances against these two, who had more brawn between them than some of the blokes I'd watched bare-knuckle fighting at the top of our street on Sundays, and legging it was out of the question because the cozzer had walked around the office and was blocking the door. So, crying was my best chance.

The only thing was, when I tried to shed a tear, I just couldn't. Maybe it was fear? I dug my nails into the palm of my hand but still my eyes were dry as a bone.

"A likely story," scoffed Miss Hunter.

She picked up a pencil and began to slowly sharpen it to

a point. There was something very neat and tidy about her, from her immaculate black curls, which grazed her jaw, to her starched white blouse tucked firmly into the waistband of her navy wool skirt.

"Detective Sergeant Hart here is a plainclothes officer; I've been working with him to keep a look out because a lot of our most expensive stock has been going missing." She stopped sharpening her pencil and glared at me. "And that, young lady, is quite unacceptable. We have seen more and more of it since the end of the war, which is why managers such as me, who are prepared to do a little *detective* work of their own, are so vital."

She shot Detective Sgt. Hart a glance. He stifled a laugh when she called herself a detective, I could see that, and it pissed her right off, but she plowed on regardless: "It's as if the younger generation no longer has any respect. What do you think we were fighting the Germans for? So that you could come into Gamages and steal whatever takes your fancy?"

Well, yes, that was the general idea of The Forty Thieves, I suppose. I kept that thought to myself. The carpet was nice, thick pile, must have cost a few quid. I made quite a study of it, sitting there while she droned on.

"I can take her down the station and charge her," said the sergeant, placing a firm hand upon my shoulder.

Well, that got my attention. I stood bolt upright.

Suddenly, with this cozzer's hand on my shoulder, it was easy to start crying. I was scared witless.

"Please," I began, tears spilling down my face. "It was an accident. And the thing is, I'm pregnant."

You could have heard a pin drop.

Miss Hunter got up and smoothed her skirt down over her ample thighs.

"Oh, you silly, silly girl," she said.

"What will your husband say about this?"

"Ain't married, Miss," I said, sniffling and wiping my snotty nose on the sleeve of my dress.

She produced a handkerchief from her desk drawer and gave it to me, with a perfunctory: "I see, like that, is it? What's your name?"

"Well, yes," I wanted to scream, "it bloody well is like that, you stuck-up cow. You try living my life, scraping a living in a London slum." But I didn't.

"I'm Nell, Nell Kane," I said, wiping my eyes with her handkerchief. It had her initials embroidered on it in swirly golden thread and was rather lovely. I stuffed it into my pocket before she could ask for it back.

She looked over at the cozzer, who was looming over me like the grim reaper.

"Given that you are expecting, I think the best course of action is for Detective Sergeant Hart here to deliver you home to your parents . . . if he is willing to do so . . . to explain yourself to them."

I heaved a sigh of relief. She was a battle-axe, but at least she had a heart!

But then she picked up that bleeding pencil again and began to scratch away at the notepad in front of her.

"And for you to appear at Bow Street Magistrates' Court in the morning, because Gamages will be pressing charges for theft."

Oh, Christ!

Detective Sgt. Hart marched me down to his car, which was all chrome and leather fittings and smelled of tobacco. If the circumstances had been different, I might have enjoyed the novelty of it.

He was quite handsome—for a cozzer, that is. Most of them round our way had faces that resembled a King Edward spud. Our local bobby had sticky-out ears, which led the kids in my street to call him Wing Nut behind his back. This one, though, had a square jaw and regular features, apart from a scar on his cheek, which intrigued me. His back was broad and when he sat down in the driver's seat, the material of his jacket was stretched at the seams.

We made our way down Oxford Street at a snail's pace, behind a tram with a Bovril advert plastered on the back. I hated Bovril and now I despised it even more. The rest of the world hurried past, boys on delivery bikes, fellas with their coats slung across one arm, clutching a newspaper in the other.

Detective Sgt. Hart lit up and pulled the window down a bit and smoked, thoughtfully. I considered jumping out and legging it while he was looking the other way, but when we stopped at the traffic lights, he closed his hand around my wrist and said: "Don't get any ideas, I'd outrun you in any case. Just be sensible, for the baby's sake."

As we were crossing the river, he finished his cigarette and chucked the butt out of the window.

"What's a bonny lass like you doing mixed up with shoplifting?"

His voice was soft, persuasive, and he spoke with a Northern lilt. His eyes were deep set and they bored into me.

"Not from round here, are you?" I shot back.

"Tyneside," he said.

"Cold up there, innit? Did you leave because you tripped and cut your face on a lump of coal?"

A muscle twitched in his cheek. Perhaps I was getting to him.

"You're quite the minx, aren't you? And you haven't answered my question, Nell," he replied gently, placing a hand on my arm.

"You'd better keep your hands on the steering wheel," I said, shrugging him off and staring straight ahead.

"Is this what you want? To be a jailbird, as well as an unmarried mother? Sounds like a slippery slope to me."

"Dunno what you're talking about," I said. "The stockings must have fallen into my bag, that's all. I've never been in trouble before."

"Do your parents know you're pregnant?"

Well, that got me. I turned away, so he couldn't see the tears brimming in my eyes. This time, they were genuine.

A smile played on his lips. "I thought as much."

He paused for an instant, as a brewer's dray clip-clopped past at the junction.

"Nell, I saw another woman stealing and putting things in the bag you were carrying, because I was on the shop floor watching you. I know that you didn't put those stockings in the bag you were carrying; she did. But she got away before I could stop her. She was a professional by the look of it."

"So why the hell am I trouble for stealing, then?" I said, eyes wide with incredulity.

"If you tell me who you are working for, I'll let the matter drop. I can put you out of the car here, and you can walk home, and get on with your life, as if none of this ever happened. I can tell Miss Hunter that you did a bunk. If not, I will tell the court tomorrow that I also witnessed you stealing as well as receiving the stolen goods from the other woman . . ."

"But that ain't fair!"

He laughed. "Life isn't fair, Nell. And it's my word against yours. If I say that I saw you putting stockings into a bag, you put them in the bag. Maybe I saw you steal an entire rail of blouses and hand those over too. You'd already given a bag full of goodies to your accomplice and she'd got away with it. So, who do you think a court is going to believe? It's my word against yours, Nell."

God, he was right, but he was an evil sod, all the same. He chuckled. He was actually enjoying himself.

I watched his throat, clean-shaven, and imagined putting my hands around it, and squeezing hard: "It's often the way that gangs prey on the vulnerable. I expect they took advantage of your situation. If you tell me who they are, I can help you get away from them."

My mouth pressed itself firmly shut. I remembered the code. There was no way I was going to grass on Alice and the other girls.

The car was over Waterloo Bridge now, turning down the road at the end of our street.

"It's not too late, you can still tell me who you work for," he said, slowing down.

Kids heard the motorcar engine and started pursuing us, whooping and kicking their tatty football as they went.

"Nell! Nell!" they shouted. "Who's yer boyfriend, Nell?"

I scowled at him: "I'm saying nothing."

We turned into Tenison Street and another band of little tykes chased after us down the cobbles. Oh my God, I would never hear the end of this. It couldn't have created more of a stir if His Majesty the King had paid a visit to Waterloo.

He parked up and chucked a sixpence or two out of the window at them, to make them scatter, before clambering out, straightening his tie, and opening the car door on my side.

I stepped out, keeping my head down.

"Have it your way," he said, placing his hand firmly in the small of my back and ushering me toward our front door.

"You've gone and done what?"

Dad erupted like Vesuvius.

Detective Sgt. Eddie Hart stood in our front room watching me intently.

Mum was half in, half out of the door, not knowing whether she was coming or going. It was like looking at someone doing the Hokey Cokey in a panic.

"Your daughter has been caught shoplifting and she is expected at West London Police Court tomorrow morning at nine o'clock." Detective Sgt. Hart repeated it, in case Dad hadn't taken it in the first time.

"Is there any need to make it so formal and press charges?" said Dad protectively. "She's a good girl, our Nell, never been in trouble before. I will deal with her. Just leave it to me."

"The management at Gamages are insisting, to deter other pilferers because there has been a spate of it lately.

"I'm afraid there's more, isn't there, Nell?" said the sergeant, staring me down.

I couldn't believe it, he was dobbing me in it, good and proper.

"Well," said Dad, his face puce with anger, "spit it out, then."

The silence seemed to fill the room. Three china geese were flapping their way up the mustard-colored wall, going nowhere fast. I knew how they felt.

I wrung my hands, for what seemed like a lifetime.

"I'm pregnant," I whispered.

I didn't see Dad move in to wallop me one, but I felt it, right around the side of my face. It sent me reeling backwards onto my heels and I began to sob. I was a mass of snot and tears.

"You slut, Nell!" he yelled. "Never in all my born days. Your poor mother. She won't be able to show her face in church!"

Mum was a lapsed Catholic, she hated going to church, but it was pointless to protest. Anyway, she appeared in that moment to have found God again. She had fallen to her knees and was saying three Hail Marys and crossing herself.

Detective Sgt. Hart buttoned up his coat: "Well, I'll leave you to it, then. I'll be back in the morning to take her to court."

He'd walked in, lobbed a grenade into our lives, and walked back out again, just like that.

Once the front door was shut, Dad moved toward me and, grasping a thick clump of hair, pulled me toward the staircase.

I squealed with the shock of it, like a stuck pig.

"Please, Dad, no! Let me go!"

His jaw was set firmly, and his iron grip was tugging at the roots of my scalp as I scrabbled to get a foothold on the stairs.

A voice was crying out in pain. I realized that it was mine: "Please, you're hurting me!"

"I'll show you hurt, you whore!" Dad yelled, pulling me farther up the staircase, my arms flailing. I missed a step, and then another, my shins battering against the dark wood.

Mum stood as a silent witness to it all, tears coursing down her cheeks.

It was only two paces from the top of the stairs, across the landing, to my bedroom, and Dad threw me, bodily, inside and slammed the door shut.

I crawled across the floor, shaking and my scalp throbbing, strands of hair coming out in my hand, to peer out of the window. Down in the street, the detective and his car had caused quite a commotion.

Mrs. Avens, the parish foghorn, was holding court on the corner, glancing up toward my bedroom window, and kids were running pell-mell after him as he drove away. I sank to my knees in shame. Eventually the kids went in for their tea. I watched the sky turning orange and then fiery red as the sun went down over the city on the worst day of my life.

When darkness fell, my heart pounded at Dad's footfall on the stairs and I hopped into bed and cowered under the blankets, like I used to when I was little, and I was expecting a belting. He didn't come in, but I heard the sound of a key turning in the lock of the bedroom door. He was locking me in, like a bloody prisoner!

When he'd gone back down to the scullery, I tiptoed over to my dressing table and looked at myself in the mirror. A bruise was blackening on my face where he'd struck me, and my eyes were red-rimmed from crying.

"What the hell have you done, Nell?" I said to my reflection. I didn't have any answers, just the throbbing pain on the side of my face and a horrible sickly, twisted feeling in my gut that my life was going right off the rails.

The key turned in the lock and Mum came in and laid a sandwich and a glass of milk on the floor beside my bed.

I sat up and hugged her, burying my face on her shoulder. "I'm sorry, Mum, so sorry."

She stood up, all the color draining from her face.

"What have you gone and done, my Nell?"

She started to weep, and the sight of her crying broke me.

"Please, Mum, it was all a mistake," I blubbed.

"I can't save you from this," she said, burying her face in her hands as she pulled away. "God knows, I love you, Nell, no matter what you've done, but your father . . ."

She gave me a look and I knew then what she meant.

His word was the law in our house. He was disowning me.

"I'll come to court, to be there for you," she said. "But,

77

you know, it's going to be really difficult for us to see each other after this, what with the way your father is feeling about it all."

We clung to each other because we both knew this was goodbye, no matter what she wanted.

"You don't need to worry about me, Mum," I said, pulling myself together for her sake. She'd suffered enough and I'd made things worse. "I can face whatever they throw at me. This will all work out. I know it will."

I hadn't a clue what I was saying, really. They were just words, meaningless words, but I wanted to make it right, somehow, to take away all the pain I'd caused her. I should have stayed in the fur factory, where I belonged, I should have accepted Jimmy's offer of marriage, even if Dad had thrown me out, at least I'd have him by my side.

Now I had nobody and I was going to have to face the music alone.

Mum got up to leave and, as she turned away from me, the door closed on my old life in Tenison Street forever.

Chapter Eight

ALICE

Elephant and Castle, London, June 1946

There's an old saying that it's an ill wind that blows nobody any good.

And true to form, while little Nell was having her first brush with the law, I managed to stuff an entire rack of silk ties down my drawers, which was nice.

Molly, meanwhile, made easy pickings of some silverware, pilfering a dozen silver spoons. We draw the line at china, because that rattles like anything, although I did know an old hoister who swore that a maternity girdle was good enough for her to smuggle a whole tea set out of Gamages once.

Oh, don't think I'm being heartless. Every hoister ends up getting caught at some point and how you handle it can be the making of you, or your undoing. I've done more bird than most people have had hot dinners and it never did me any harm.

In fact, I'll let you into a little secret. It's a tradition in my gang for new members to be put through their paces a bit, to test their mettle. I like to know what they're really like under pressure and how likely they are to start squealing to the cozzers. Oh, I know, I can go over the Hoisters' Code with them until I'm blue in the face, and they can swear blind they will never breathe a word but the first time you get your collar felt it can come as a nasty shock and some girls take it upon themselves to sing like a bleeding canary—until I can find a way to shut them up.

As Queen of The Forty Thieves, I have a right to know what my girls are going to do under pressure. Some of them can get quite creative, punching people in the face, running like the clappers, putting on a show of fainting fits to get sympathy. They can discover they have an impressive array of hidden talents; acting skills that wouldn't look out of place onstage in the West End theatres and boxing abilities that would make a fella blush.

You name it, I've seen it all and thinking about it now does make me smile. Well, apart from the few silly cows who were daft enough to start blabbing, but let's not dwell on them.

So, a little bird went across the water and mentioned to the cozzers in the West End that The Forty Thieves were planning a little trip to Gamages with a sweet, innocent-looking girl, mousey brown hair, five feet five inches tall, brown eyes and a bit on a skinny side, wearing a rose-print cotton dress, at about half past three on Wednesday afternoon. She was planning, apparently, to hoist some silk stockings, the cheeky devil. Just fancy that!

And this ain't a case of me grassing her up. Perish the thought. No. Nell is not yet a fully fledged member of The Forty Thieves; she is still learning the ropes, so to speak. So, I was really giving her the chance to prove herself. She impressed me the other day with that silk chemise she half-inched from Selfridges but I needed to be sure of her loyalty to me and the gang. There's something unpredictable about Nell and I wanted to test her mettle. You can't blame me for that, can you?

The thing is, because she's in the family way, I was expecting she'd get off with a stern talking-to from the management. But one look at this new manager they've got in Gamages and I knew that things were going to be a bit more tricky for our Nell, and by then it was too late. The Hunter, they call her, and I'm determined not to have the pleasure of her acquaintance now I've had a good butcher's at her. She ain't doing this job just for the money, I can tell. She does it for the pleasure of catching us at it. Now, that is twisted in my book—it's not normal. It's just plain wrong. Who on earth gets pleasure out of stopping a few bits and pieces from going walkabout in Gamages, I ask you? It makes me wonder what the world is coming to. Is that what we had a war for? So women like her could get jobs like that?

Anyway, my spies in Tenison Street tell me there was quite a to-do when the cozzer brought her home to her parents. Nell's expected up before the beak in the morning. I do hope the magistrates will be lenient, as it's her first offense and with her being up the duff an' all. I was going to look in on Bow Street, just to remind her where her loyalties lie, but you'll understand if I don't because courtrooms aren't among my favorite places in the world, so I'll be sending a few of the girls along instead, just to give her moral support.

She's in a bit of tight spot, ain't she, with her bun in the oven and feckless Jimmy as the father? He's such a fly-by-night! What kind of a life would she be having if it wasn't for me helping her out?

Thinking about it, I haven't really got time for my girls to be looking after babies. They are adorable, the little mites, but they just get in the way of work and they're like buses, really. Once one comes along, there's always another following close behind. And another. And another.

Earning the kind of money that I've got on offer requires a level of dedication to duty that just don't go hand in hand with motherhood. Oh, I know she had some silly pipe dream about raising the baby on her own and I would be the last person to stand in her way, but we all know that real life has a horrible way of throwing a spanner in the works, don't it? She's down on Jimmy now but the wind'll change direction and he'll be flavor of the month again, sure as eggs is eggs, and then she won't be focusing on hoisting, will she? Let's leave the drudgery to the women who are born to it and whose husbands want them barefoot, pregnant, and chained to the kitchen sink, shall we? That's half of London from what I hear.

If she gets time, being in jail means Nell will have somewhere safe to deliver the baby, which will be taken care of once she's had it, in the way that's best for the baby. That's such a blessing for Nell.

And The Forty Thieves, of course.

So, really, even in these difficult circumstances, everybody wins.

Especially me.

Chapter Nine

NELL

Holloway, London, June 1946

Six months; six lousy months and all for one pair of stockings.

I swear my heart stopped beating for a moment as the magistrate banged his gavel and handed down the sentence. I gripped the edge of the dock, looking at that witch Miss Hunter practically clucking with pride and Detective Sgt. Eddie Hart flicking imaginary dust from his trousers as the beak heaped praise on the pair of them for catching me. You'd have thought they'd solved a bleeding murder.

"You are part of a pernicious evil in this society, a dangerous gang of criminals who are determined to purloin expensive goods for your own ill-gotten gains," said the magistrate. "I hope this sentence will persuade you of the seriousness of what you have done."

Now, I hadn't a clue what half of those long words meant but I caught his drift: I'd been nicking stuff and he wasn't swallowing my excuse that it was my first time on the rob because of the desperation of wanting to provide for my baby. He wanted to make an example, so he threw the book at me. It was such a stiff sentence for a first offense that I nearly fell over.

There were gasps from the public gallery and I could just make out the top of my mum's best hat as she hid her face and sniveled into her handkerchief. Iris was beside her, with a shiner to match the bruise on my cheek; there was no need to ask where she'd got that. Her Tommy had been hard at work throwing his weight around as usual.

Molly was there too, smiling at me, and Em beside her, dressed up in a beautiful plaid skirt suit. Most of what happened in court passed in a blur, except for the bit where the beak asked me if I had anything to say for myself.

I opened my mouth to say I was sorry but closed it, sharpish, as Molly very slowly drew a finger across her throat.

I got the message.

The last words I heard as I left the courtroom in handcuffs were that magistrate intoning: "Take her down, Officer."

I sat in the back of the Black Maria with my head in my hands, willing myself not to cry.

Through the bars on the window, the entrance to Holloway Prison loomed up ahead. It was like a bleeding fortress, a huge castle of a prison, with buttresses and thick, gray stone walls about twenty-five feet high.

There were three of us in the van; a tiny little sprite with hair the color of straw, who looked as if the cuffs would slide off her scrawny wrists. Beside her was an old flower seller, reeking of gin and piss. I kept my distance not only because she smelled like a dosshouse lavvy, but because the nits were just about jumping off her head and I didn't want them landing on mine. The little blonde girl intrigued me. She didn't look like she'd say boo to a goose, let alone commit a crime.

A fat prison guard sat by the back doors of the van, keeping a watchful eye.

It wasn't as if any of us was about to make a run for it. I was still in shock from my sentence, the flower seller was half cut from the night before, and the blonde-haired thing looked as if she just wanted her mum.

"What you in for?" I whispered.

"Thieving," she said, sniveling into her sleeve. "Stole a watch from the lady I clean for. Shouldn't have done it but my brothers and sisters were hungry."

The flower seller rolled her eyes. "A likely story! And I'm the Queen Mother . . ."

"No talking!" barked the prison guard, flinging open the doors and ordering us out.

We were marched across the cobbled courtyard to an enormous black wooden door, which creaked open. I glanced over my shoulder as we stepped inside, saying a silent goodbye to my liberty and the London I loved.

Holloway Prison was as big as a cathedral inside, but quiet as the grave. Five galleried prison wings radiated off the cavernous center, with row upon row of cells.

The chief prison officer squatted like an enormous toad at her desk in the middle of a highly polished floor.

She pursed her lips as we lined up in front of her.

"Welcome back, Rose," she said to the blonde girl, whose face hardened, making her less like a schoolgirl and more like a criminal.

"Fanks," she said, staring back, her slate-gray eyes unblinking and insolent.

"You will address me as Miss Fanshawe," she barked.

"Sorry, Miss Fanshawe."

I could tell by the sneer on Rose's face that she was hoping the chief prison officer would choke on her apology.

"I had hoped we'd seen the last of you, Rose," she said, a smile forming at the corners of her mouth.

"It weren't my fault, Miss, I shouldn't be here . . ."

Miss Fanshawe slammed her hand down so hard on the desk that I jumped. Her voice bounced off the stone floor, reverberating up the cast-iron staircase to the cell wings, where prisoners walked in silence, their eyes downcast. They were guarded by warders all dressed in black, with bunches of keys dangling from the belts at their waists.

This lot were at the back of the queue when they were dishing out the milk of human kindness and all that was left for them had gone properly sour.

"Part of your rehabilitation here is to face up to the fact that you are a thieving bunch of scum and pay the price for it," she spat.

She stood up, the gleaming buttons of her uniform straining across her massive bust, and frog-marched us across the circular center, with the other prisoners gazing down at us from the galleries. Her glossy black leather shoes squeaked beneath her bulk as she strode, intoning: "Rule number one, you never directly cross the center of this prison unless you are ordered to do so by a prison officer. Do so and you will be put on report to the Governor and lose your privileges."

Her voice ricocheted off the mustard-brown walls. A row of women were on their hands and knees scrubbing the floor and the whole place stank of disinfectant and despair.

We went down some metal stairs into the basement of the prison.

I reeled down the corridor after her, only half taking in the lists of dos and don'ts she was spouting.

"Punctuality, politeness," she chimed.

"Don't ask too many questions of the other girls; you are all criminals in here and they wish to focus on their tasks and not each other."

She was hurrying along at quite a lick and I was getting a little out of breath keeping up.

"You will never speak to the Governor unless you are first spoken to, do you understand? As far as you are concerned, she is God."

"Yes, Miss Fanshawe."

The door to one of the basement rooms swung open and a nurse in a starched uniform stood with a clipboard.

There was a row of showers on one side and a bench with three sets of clothes, neatly pressed and folded.

"So," said Miss Fanshawe, looking me up and down with bulging eyes, as if she were about to devour a particularly juicy fly, "you're new here, are you?"

"Yes, Miss Fanshawe."

"In that case, I'd like to wish you a pleasant stay," she smirked. She had a little ebony truncheon, which she pulled from her belt, waving it under my nose. "Do as you are told and you won't get into any trouble. Just ask Rose."

Rose's hands had balled into fists by her side.

"Now, strip off ladies, we've got some lovely things for you to try on once Matron has had a look at you." She paused in front of the flower seller, who was swaying gently, like a tall tree in the breeze. "And in your case, Lilian, a good delousing. We haven't got room for any unwanted guests in here."

She turned on her heel, chuckling to herself. "Welcome to the Holloway Hotel."

The matron peered down my ears and throat, searched through my hair and then looking at my bulging, pregnant tummy, said: "When is that due?"

"Sometime around Christmas, Miss," I said.

"A fit young girl like you will be fine to continue with your prison work right up until the point you deliver," she said. "You will move to the hospital wing to have the baby. I presume you are not married?"

"No, Miss."

Her face softened.

"You can call me Ma Doherty," she said, smiling briskly. It was the first and only glimmer of kindness I'd seen in the prison, and I found myself smiling back.

"I thought it was your first time in here," I whispered to Rose, as we pulled on our prison uniforms. There was a pair of scratchy-looking white bloomers and a worn, brown cotton dress. What a sight I looked in that, like a sack of spuds. There was a gray wool cardigan, so heavily patched that it could have come off the rag and bone man's cart, some hideous brown lisle stockings, and a navy cape and hood. The whole outfit was topped off with a gray cloth cap. If someone had told me this garb was a practical joke, I would have believed them but sadly, it was what I was going to be wearing for the next six months.

"Never assume. Makes an ass of you and me, don't it?" said Rose, with a laugh, setting her cap at a jaunty angle.

The flower seller brushed louse powder out of her bird's nest hair and said, "Young Rose here is one of the best burglars in the whole of London, ain't she?"

Rose puffed up her chest a bit, like a little blackbird rearranging its feathers: "If you say so."

Miss Fanshawe reappeared and we followed her through a warren of passageways to the back of the prison and down a narrow, winding set of flagstone stairs.

Before we entered, she gave us each a number and told us to answer to it or we'd be for it. I was 342, no longer a name, just a number. My luck couldn't sink any lower.

She pushed open the heavy metal door and we were hit almost immediately by great clouds of steam. Women with white aprons tied around their waists were toiling with their feet sloshing in the wet on the tiled floor and their heads bathed in vapor from giant coppers of boiling water. It was hot as holy hell in there. Miss Fanshawe had managed to put purgatory in the basement of Holloway Prison, I had to hand it to her.

The girls stirred the vats with wooden poles, before

heaving wet sheets out into baskets, which they lugged over to hand mangles. My mum had shown me how to use a mangle in the communal laundry down in Waterloo, so I knew what to do. I also knew that the weekly wash, just for our house, was a thankless and backbreaking task.

The heaps of sheets and clothes piled here looked like the prison was taking in dirty washing for half the district. It was a never-ending, miserable chore and one that I'd have to get used to.

"You can start over here, on the washtubs, with Rose," she said. "She knows what to do."

Rose gave me a toothsome grin as she picked up a metal washboard and a bar of soap and began to scrub at a dirty nightgown.

"Just take your time over each garment, there's no prizes for rushing it," said Rose, her lips barely moving.

She had a way of talking out of the corner of her mouth so that the warders couldn't spot we were gossiping. It reminded me of how the women at the Alaska Fur Factory spoke through gritted teeth to stop the rabbit fur getting into their lungs.

A tall woman, like a beanpole, was eyeing me from the ironing tables in the corner. She had a pigeon feather in her prison cap that set her apart from the others and a cat sitting beside her.

"That's Joan," said Rose quietly. "Don't cross her. Grasses everyone to the screws. She gets the extra milk and tinned salmon that the Governor thinks is going to her cat, the greedy cow. She runs a team of dippers on the outside, pickpockets, the lowest of the low."

After an afternoon scrubbing, my hands were so red raw that my knuckles had started to bleed. I took a heavy basket-load of sheets over to the mangle to run them through and Joan came over to me, with an iron in her hand.

A warder turned away.

"So, you're one of Alice's girls, are you?" she lisped.

I glared at her. "I'm saying nothing."

She held her iron up so that I could feel the heat of it near my face.

"Well, she ain't here to protect you now, so it pays not to be rude to me, dearie. She obviously don't think that much of you, or she'd have paid a copper off to let you go free, wouldn't she?"

I was doing my damnedest not to flinch or show weakness, but that took the wind out my sails. I don't know whether it was tiredness or hunger or shock, but I almost crumpled. Alice could have tried to pull some strings to get me off the hook, it was true. And she just hadn't bothered. I'd never thought of it until now, but the truth had been staring me in the face.

Joan adjusted the feather in her cap, put down her iron, and laughed until she almost split her sides. "Oh, we've got a right one here. Taken for a packet of stockings and got a six and it was only your first offense, ain't that right? You didn't even know old Alice had dobbed you in it with the cozzers, did you, love?"

Some of the other women were chuckling to themselves over at their washboards. I reeled backwards, as if I had been shot.

"I don't know what you mean . . ."

"Oh, love, face the facts. That's how Alice tests all her hoisters. She tips the boys in blue the wink and has them picked up for nicking to see if they'll cough or not. You don't just walk in off the street and become a member of The Forty Thieves, you have to pass the test. I'd never do that to my girls, seems a bit like being a grass."

Someone hooted with laughter at that. Rose was scowling and gave Joan a look that could curdle milk.

Joan leaned forward, so that I could smell her rancid breath. "Personally speaking I would never have turned you over to the cozzers. You're just too lovely, ain't you?" Her hand crept around my waist and gave me a little squeeze. "Up close, Nell, you're ever so pretty. It don't matter to me that you're soiled goods and a fella got there before me."

The Governor's cat came around and rubbed itself against her leg, purring.

"I'm here for you, sweetness, anytime you like; you come to Joanie and I'll look after you," she said.

"Pipe down and get back to work!" the warder shouted, trying to impose some order on the women, who were cackling with laughter. It was clear to me who ruled the roost in the laundry, and it wasn't the screws.

"Oh alright, keep your hair on," muttered Joan, "I was just being friendly, that's all."

She returned the iron to the pagoda stove in the corner, to get it hot enough to press the sheets again. "We've had our fun, haven't we girls?"

For me, the nightmare was just beginning.

My stomach was growling with hunger as we traipsed back up the stairs in twos, to go to the mess hall for supper.

A dollop of stew with a few lumps of gristle in it and some semolina that you could have plastered a wall with were slopped into metal bowls for us to eat in silence while the screws patrolled the long benches where we sat. I was so hungry, I scoffed the lot even though it looked and smelled like pig swill and I nearly broke my tooth on a lump of stale bread.

After that, it was up the spiral staircase to our cells on B block. I'd heard stories about women having to sleep on bare boards that had to be put up during the day, so I was grateful to find an iron-framed bed with a thin mattress and a pillow like a lump of rock. The sheets were stiff with starch and a scratchy nightgown had been laid out.

The cell was no more than six feet by ten, barely room to swing the Governor's cat, and there was a single shelf, and a washstand and a chamber pot under it. The thought of slopping out in the morning was gut-churning, so even though I wanted to go, I bottled it.

The sounds of the prison settling down for the night filled the air. Metal doors slamming, keys being turned in locks, and, in the cell below, someone weeping. A hatch on the door was thrust open and a tin mug of cocoa was passed through to me.

I sipped at it, feeling it warming me, as I shivered under the thin blanket.

As I lay there, looking up at the moon, which was just visible through the bars on the window, I had only one thought: getting even with Alice Diamond for putting me inside.

I pulled out my hairclip and began to scratch a little notch on the wall, imagining that I was cutting a deep gouge into Alice Diamond's broad, smiling face.

I'd be suffering for the next six months, but she'd be paying the price for a very long time if I had anything to do with it.

Chapter Ten

ALICE

Waterloo, London, June 1946

I don't know what the world is coming to since this blooming war, and the young folk are the worst of it, if you ask me. The girls have no respect for authority like they used to.

"No respect at all," said Molly, as I grabbed the factory girl by the hair and dragged her to the rickety wooden chair in the scullery. Molly had already told her friend to take a seat, in a manner of speaking. We'd met them at the factory gates down in Waterloo and walked them home for a nice little chat about what they'd been up to.

It was amazing how helpful the neighbors were, making themselves scarce as we turned the corner into their street. Children were pulled indoors, and men hastily beat a retreat to the pub. The cobbled street was quiet as the grave while we went about our business.

"I hear you've been quite busy at the cloth factory, Peggy," I said.

"There ain't a law against it," she said, bristling with anger at the way she'd been frog-marched down the road. She was putting a brave face on it, but her hands were shaking.

"We just wanted to try to help our families," her mate piped up.

I gave her a slap for her trouble.

"Nobody asked you," I said, smiling sweetly at her, as tears sprang to her eyes. "I want to hear it from Peggy here."

I put my face right next to Peggy's so that I could see the smoothness of her skin. "What made you think you'd wrap yourself up like Tutankhamun's sisters under your clothes in your lunch break and waddle out of that factory and fence your ill-gotten gains without me finding out?"

"It weren't done deliberately, to cut you out," said Peggy, in a small voice, staring at the table. "We just thought you'd be too busy in the shops to notice or care."

Well, that was like a red rag to a bull.

"You thought I wouldn't *care*!" I said. "Oh, that breaks my heart, that does."

I knew then, I'd have to up my game to keep control of things and there was only one person I could turn to in my hour of need: Mrs. Tibbs.

I'd put her into retirement after Britain declared war on Germany because it seemed a bit unpatriotic to use her against our own when we were fighting the Nazis, but now, well, I really had no choice.

The girls had brought it on themselves.

I pulled her out of my pocket and the pair of them started to weep like babies. "Shhh," I whispered. "Don't make it worse for yourself by getting her angry, she don't like a fuss."

Quick as a flash, Molly grabbed Peggy's face to hold her steady. Mrs. Tibbs is cold and hard but she's razor sharp, if you catch my drift. She just gave her a small stripe to be getting on with, but scars are so much more difficult to cover up when face powder is rationed, aren't they?

We let her friend go. She ran screaming from the house, which is good for business, really.

It was all over very quickly.

Peggy clutched her hand to her face, and I threw her

a teatowel to stem the flow of blood; I'm not altogether heartless, you see.

Crimson seeped through the white cloth, like the petals of the reddest rose in bloom. I always find it fascinating to watch how blood does that. It really is a beautiful sight. I gazed at it for a moment and when I'd seen enough, I turned to go.

"I'll be seeing you around," I said, tucking Mrs. Tibbs away in my pocket. "And if you get any bright money-making ideas, remember to come and find me.

"Or I'll find you. And so will Mrs. Tibbs."

Apparently, you don't feel the pain of it at first, just the shock. Mrs. Tibbs is fast, drawing down over the flesh. Fellas like to take their time, draw it out and maybe to do a couple of stripes when they do a shivving, 'cos it makes it harder for the doctors to sew two flaps of skin together when you're cut like that. Some jokers do it on the bum, so that a man can't sit down without splitting his stitches, but I never saw the funny side of that. It's just toilet humor, typical blokes. Mrs. Tibbs prefers it neat, quick, and to make her point. We women don't need to overstate matters with a six-inch cut when a nice, deep three-inch one will do.

I'm told that the pain comes later, when you're in the hospital, trying to eat or to talk. And then there's all the worry about what a mess your face will look; those kind of concerns really get to a woman more than a flesh wound, don't they? Not that I've ever been one to trade on my appearance. Oh, I know I can still turn heads, but you should have seen me when I was younger.

I was known for my good looks and my beautiful curls around the Seven Dials, where I grew up. People say that part of Covent Garden is a thieves' kitchen, a real slum.

Any Londoner worth their salt will tell you it's famous for the seven dark passageways leading to some of the poorest tenements in the city; places where most folk are afraid to tread. The houses we lived in had been thrown together on the cheap in Queen Victoria's day, so that the damp rose, and the bugs crept into the cracks between the peeling plaster and the dank wallpaper, adding to the misery of every poor sod who had to live there.

Don't let anyone tell you about the good old days in the Seven Dials because they are lying through their teeth. I'd bet you a tenner they'd never even set foot in the place if they can find a decent word to say about it. It was a pit of utter despair, never mind "Roll Out the Barrel," and raise a glass to London town.

There were three floors in those buildings and maybe one lavvy between all the families who crammed into two rooms apiece, with water from the standpipe in the yard.

The fellas round there said they were costermongers, bricklayer's assistants, and cabbies, but I mostly saw them leaning on lampposts or falling down drunk. Women went out charring if they could find someone to mind their babies, and there were bloody loads of them, crawling in the gutter, being bounced on a neighbour's hip, or careering down the lane in an old orange crate on wheels pushed by some little tyke who was supposed to be in school.

Women dragged themselves to and from the communal laundry or the market during the day with the weight of the world on their shoulders. The only time I truly saw them come alive was on a Friday night when they dished out a tongue-lashing to their husbands because they'd punched a hole in the week's housekeeping with one pint too many down the boozer.

That would see her pawning her clothes on Monday morning and putting on a sack until the next payday. The anger of how they were living, how they were forced to live, seemed to energize the women on my street and even now I can feel the crackle in the air that used to come before a really good domestic.

We were poor but at least I had shoes, unlike some of the kids. Perhaps because we had nothing to steal from each other there weren't any point in locking our doors. That's where I began my life as a thief but I'm getting ahead of myself because before I became a hoister, I had a different partner in crime. I'll let you into a little secret. This one was closer to home, my brother Lim.

It's short for William, but I named him that when I was a baby and he was looking after me. So, he was Lim and that was that. Lim, with his big, dark eyes and serious face, always trying to work an angle on something, even if it was just to find a way to break me out of my cot when my dad put a lid on it to keep me in there. Even as a toddler I was feisty, and I didn't want to be behind bars. God, I loved the very bones of my brother Lim and he thought I walked on water.

He was the eldest by two years and it was his job to look after me while my dad went out to work, burgling houses up Mayfair, and Mum was charring in Belgravia. I'd play with Lim for hours. He'd sit twirling his fingers around my curls, singing me the songs he'd picked up from the hawkers. Some of the language he taught me was a bit ripe for a little 'un but I had a fine pair of lungs on me, and people would toss us a ha'penny for my efforts if we hung around the theatres, which was the start of our partnership.

Sometimes our dad would come home drunk and knock seven bells out of Mum but she was always popping out babies, like shelling peas, and before we knew it, we had a houseful. Lim and me would save our coins and buy buns as a treat from the bakery round the corner. We'd sit down on the step and plot how we were going to make our fortune together, be rich like the toffs and stroll arm in arm down Pall Mall or ride about in a fancy carriage on Rotten Row on Sundays. Then the Great War came, and Dad got conscripted, and that was when the trouble really started.

Suddenly I had a load of uncles visiting that I never even knew existed, turning up at all hours of the day and night. Such a large extended family, don't you know? Mum was forever shooing us out in the street with the babies, even when it was dark and cold. Next thing we knew, the Poor Law was banging on the door and Mum had to put the little ones in the workhouse because she couldn't feed them, that's what they said, and so she had them adopted. There were raised voices in the scullery and more than one of the do-gooders from the Poor Law said something about her being an "unfit mother," which made her weep. Well, maybe she was unfit, but she was *our* mother.

Whatever they said, whatever she had done, she spent all her days crying for the children, especially the baby, and when she weren't crying she was spending whatever money she could lay her hands on drinking and still I had more uncles visiting than most people had hot dinners. Lim spat at one once and got a thick ear for his trouble.

We went out to work thieving from fruit and vegetable stalls up in Covent Garden just to make ends meet and I ain't ashamed to say I picked a pocket or two outside the theatres. Lim would do card tricks, he loved magic and was lightning fast with his fingers, and while the punters watched him, I'd sneak around and see what I could dip. I know it's the lowest of the low in terms of thieving, but I was just a girl, so I didn't know any better. Besides, Mum was pleased when we brought a few bob home, praising us and thanking God to have such lucky kids.

We could have carried on like that but then the bad news came and that changed everything.

We'd never had a telegram sent to the house before and I was excited when I answered the door to see the postman standing there. The only other letter we'd had was an eviction notice, if memory serves, but the look on Mum's face said it all. She sank to her knees before she'd even opened it. It said "War Office" on the back of the envelope.

I read the words: "*I regret to inform you . . .*" and then she snatched it away and threw it on the fire, wailing like a banshee. Dad spent his life as a thief, but he died a hero fighting the Hun, not that it did us any good. There were times she couldn't stand the sight of him but losing him like that, it broke her heart. I don't think she got out of bed for a week and when she came to, she went down the pub at opening time and downed the gin until she rolled home or ended up in the gutter. That went on for weeks, then weeks became months and still the rent man needed paying.

Lim wouldn't talk to anyone but me and he spent most of his time in the scullery, practicing his card tricks over and over, his brow furrowed in concentration. He scowled at every bloke who set foot over the threshold but that only made things worse because they'd ruffle his hair or tweak his nose to try to make him speak. He had a way of looking at them, with eyes as black as the ace of spades, which left them lost for words. If I hadn't seen it myself, I wouldn't have believed it but there was something in Lim's face that was pure evil when he was crossed and it brought a chill to the air and made men look away and leave him be.

We could have rubbed along like that: me and Lim hatching our plans to get rich and filching what we could, Mum drinking and opening her legs every time the pub landlord opened his doors, but one day she got caught up in a fight about a loaf of bread the grocer said she'd nicked. In the fray that followed, she knocked a policeman's hat off. Well, that caused quite a commotion. The next thing, she'd pulled out Dad's old flick knife and stabbed him with it, right in the arm.

By the time the news reached the Dials, we heard she'd cut his throat from ear to ear and the whole neighborhood charged round there to see what was happening. People loved a good fight, especially if it involved the law, and my mother did not disappoint. She was like a wild animal, howling, scratching, and biting, and there was blood all over the cobbles and the policeman was nursing a nasty cut on his forearm.

It took four cozzers to hold her down on a barrow and wheel her off to the police station. Men stood around cheering her on, admiring her strength, yelling, "Go on, Mary, give 'em hell!"

They locked her up in an asylum. She weren't mad, the shock of losing me dad is what done it, but I never saw her again.

After that, it was me and Lim against the world, nicking bits of fruit from the barrows up in the market, doing dances outside the theatres to earn our keep, but it was never going to be enough. I was fourteen when the war ended and we were on our uppers and things were looking bad, but Lim had a plan. We were running out of options; the cozzers knew my face too well and I had a few close shaves with posh ladies saying I'd stolen from their handbags.

"Don't worry," said Lim, as we sat by the grate warming our toes on the last of our chairs that we'd chopped up for firewood, "there's something else you've got that's worth more than pennies from people's purses, Alice."

That's what he said.

And like a fool, I trusted him.

Chapter Eleven

NELL

Holloway, London, November 1946

"Christ, it's freezing!"

I poked my nose out from under the blanket in the hospital wing and prayed that Ma Doherty hadn't heard me take the Lord's name in vain.

She was a Catholic and quite serious about all that religious stuff and though it weren't my cup of tea, I didn't want to upset her because she was nicer than the screws and gave me extra cocoa at bedtime.

She was busy shaking the other girls awake.

"Come on, you've no business to be lounging in bed. Get up! It's six thirty! You'll have the Governor after you!"

Any transgressions meant extra chores, and nobody wanted that, not in this weather. Our hands were already cracked and blistered from the carbolic soap and the cold.

I gingerly placed a toe down on the linoleum floor and steeled myself to go over to the washbasins. There was ice on the inside of the windows and the water for the morning wash was brought up in jugs the night before. That had iced over as well these last few days, but we were still expected to strip off and get clean before breakfast.

I shuffled my slippers on. I hadn't seen my feet since the weather turned the month before and now I was only a few days away from giving birth. The hour's exercise we had in the prison yard every day, walking round and round in single file, was more like a trek to the North Pole, but I did it anyway just to feel the wind on my face, and remind myself that there was life beyond the prison walls.

One by one, a row of bodies sat up, groaning and heaving their huge pregnant bellies before them. We were a mass of swollen ankles and heavy legs and the piles, oh my God, no one warned me about that! If someone had, I might have kept my knickers on. It would have been better contraception than a French letter.

I found out from one of the girls what one of those was, in one of our sewing classes. Even at nearly nine months gone, we were still on our hands and knees scrubbing floors all morning, but in the afternoons, we were allowed to settle down in the hospital wing with our sewing and knitting.

As well as patching up torn smocks and darning woollen stockings for the other prisoners, we were expected to make a full set of baby clothes for our little ones. After the drudgery of daily prison life, this felt like heaven to me. I'd always been a dab hand with a needle and thread, and now, with a few lengths of cotton material, some scissors and thread, I began to fashion a full layette for my baby. I poured all the love I could into little matinee jackets and sleepsuits.

Ma Doherty would keep a close eye on us and tell us what we had to do after having our babies, how to care for them. She'd seen so much childbirth it had put her off marrying or having one herself, that's what she said. If she hadn't come to the prison to work, she'd have been a nun. Having heard the screams from the girls giving birth, I knew what she meant but there was no way back for me now.

The Governor kept morphia in her room under lock and key, for pain relief, and that is where it stayed. Girls had torn themselves virtually in two during labor and she still refused to hand it over to them, no matter how much they begged and pleaded.

We'd heard that Ma Doherty had even asked the Governor if a girl who had ripped so badly that she had to be stitched right the way underneath, from front to back, could have some but still she would not budge.

"Pain is a natural part of childbirth," she told us chirpily on one of her visits to the hospital wing, to check we weren't slacking.

It was on one of those bitterly cold, wintery days that Ma Doherty brought me a letter and a small packet, which had been opened.

"Just keep it to yourself, Nell," she said softly. "I thought you should have this. You know you are one of my favorites."

I ripped it open and my fingers touched some pieces of rabbit fur, enough to make a little hood, and a beautiful offcut of sheepskin, to make bootees for the baby. They felt so welcoming and familiar to me, like a bridge to my lost life.

I hadn't heard a single word from my parents—I hadn't expected to—so this meant the world to me.

Dear Nell,

I hope you are keeping your chin up. I got you these offcuts from the basket at work, thought they might come in handy for the little one.

I miss you, Nell, and have lots of other news but we will see each other soon, I hope. I expect you know by now your parents don't want nothing to do with you anymore because of the baby. I'm sorry, Nell, it don't seem right because I know you are a good sort. Jimmy has been around asking about you. I saw him down the market 'cos he's giving your parents a wide berth for fear of the belting your dad will give him. He's really broken up that you're doing bird. He wants to make things right, to start over with you when you get out. He swears he only thinks of you and is so cut up that you turned him down. I know it ain't my business, Nell, and I'd like to box his ears for how things turned out, 'cos it's so unfair, but the way he talks about you, is like you are the only woman on earth. I told him it was his own stupid fault that he couldn't keep it in his trousers, and it weren't right that you had to take all the blame for it. He looked so ashamed, like he wanted the ground to swallow him up.

None of these fellas of ours are perfect, but Jimmy's heart is in the right place and he's working all the hours God sends over the water in Soho, which has got to be worth something, hasn't it? You can tell me to mind my own business and you'd be right but he made me promise I'd write and tell you he still feels the same way about you, if you can forgive him for everything.

The council are rehousing all of us in Tenison Street down at the Elephant and Castle because they say the streets have to be condemned because they are insanitary or something or other. Some of us wanted to put up a fight but it's useless because no one wants to live in these houses anymore, they all want a prefab down in Brixton if they can get it. We're all moving out in the New Year. Tommy says it will be a fresh start and he's hoping to get a job on the market down in the Borough. Come and find me there when you are back. You are always welcome in my house.

Love and best wishes,

Your pal,

Iris x

I put my hands on my swollen belly, feeling the baby inside me wriggle. Since being in the nick, I'd done my best to put

Jimmy out of my mind because, well, what was the point? I'd tried to see it as all a foolish mistake and that I was just so green, and he'd taken advantage and I was living with the consequences. But now Iris said he was serious about me. And this baby we had made was real. It gave me a huge kick that took my breath away, just to make a point of it.

I hadn't even considered us making a go of it as a family but if what Iris said was true, perhaps we could? Perhaps Jimmy would turn out to be a reliable husband and we could raise our baby together. Thinking back on it, Alice Diamond had done her level best to put me off married life and the way I saw it now, maybe she had a reason to because she didn't want me happily married. She wanted me to be one of her girls and to be the boss of me herself. The conniving old cow! But she hadn't switched off Jimmy's affections for me, no matter what, which was like a glimmer of hope for the future.

The thought of Jimmy and how I used to feel about him when we were courting made my heart flutter and I must have smiled because Ma Doherty said, "Whatever was in that letter has cheered you up, hasn't it?"

She was hovering over my shoulder, the nosy cow.

"Is it good news from the family?"

"Yes, they are all fine," I replied, folding the letter before she could read any more. Maybe I was just dreaming about how things could be with Jimmy and I didn't stand a chance anymore, but I wasn't going to give her the satisfaction of knowing about it.

I put it together with the offcuts at the bottom of my baby box, where I laid the baby's clothes, away from the prying eyes of the Governor. But Ma Doherty wasn't done yet. She had a funny look in her eye as she pulled up a chair and sat beside me. "Nell, you should really think about the baby's future. Will your parents be happy to have you at home, unmarried with a baby?"

I stared at the floor.

A clock ticked loudly on the wall. There was no point lying to her.

"No, Miss," I said.

"There are plenty of good families out there who would be willing to give a baby a home . . ."

I knew what she meant but I didn't want to face it. The thought of giving the baby away was like a knife in my heart.

"I'll manage somehow," I said flatly.

"On your own?" she replied swiftly. "That wouldn't be wise, would it?"

"Perhaps I won't be on my own," I shot back. "Perhaps the fella who got me into trouble is going to stand by me! My friend wrote me that he is sorry for everything that has happened to me, and he wants to make it right."

Ma Doherty put her arm around me, her face softening. "Oh Nell, dear, is that what made you so happy after reading that letter? Men who get girls pregnant out of wedlock will say anything to avoid facing the music in their community. They are just so selfish. If he was a decent man, he would never have got you into trouble, and if your parents thought he was a suitable type, they would welcome him into their home, but that isn't the case, is it?"

I felt tears prick my eyes.

All the hope in Iris's note was just a house of cards and it had come tumbling down.

"No, Miss, they don't want to see hide nor hair of him and not of me either," I mumbled.

There was something steely in her voice now: "You have to be sensible, stop living in a silly fantasy about how your life is going to be once you have this child. Your community will never accept it, even if you are married to the one who got you into this terrible, terrible situation; they will always gossip about you putting the cart before the horse. Everyone will know about it, love, everyone. Can you imagine the shame that little one will feel?"

It didn't take too much to think about Mrs. Avens, the parish foghorn, and her sly looks and snide comments. She'd relish the chance to make my child feel shame.

Ma Doherty brushed her skirt down and stood up. "You're one of the lucky ones to be chosen. This is giving you a second chance. All the clever girls come round to my way of thinking eventually, Nell. You'll see." Her voice was soothing and so reassuring.

"All I want to do is for you to be able to rebuild your life, free of the shame. You are in prison, and you are paying the price for your crime, but your child will live what you have done forever and it would be a lie for me to tell you otherwise. I have seen it so often. The most selfless thing a truly loving mother can do for her child is to give it a better life than her own."

I wanted to run away from her then, but deep down, I knew she was right, and I really only had one choice. But it was a choice I didn't want to think about.

She smiled and patted me on the shoulder. "Now, you look like you could use some extra cocoa. Would that be nice?"

The Governor absolutely relished Sundays, walking proudly like a mother hen at the head of a long line of us pregnant girls into the prison chapel. Even those who had just given birth were expected to come along and, what's worse, they had to kneel on the stone floor for the whole service, which lasted longer than the daily services after breakfast during the week, on account of the vicar's endless sermons about sin.

It was there that a miracle happened because I found that I could sing, really sing. I'd been raised on "My Old Man Said Follow the Van" and "Roll Out the Barrel" but now

I found my voice soaring through hymns and I even had a go at some of the Latin stuff.

Ma Doherty taught me the words, *Ave maria, grazia plena, dominus tecum benedicta tu in mulieribus,* and I hadn't a clue what they meant, but I mouthed them well enough and my voice soared up to the rafters because in that moment, I was free. It didn't matter that I was pregnant and unmarried or that I spent all day scrubbing the floors or toiling like a slave in the prison laundry, I didn't have to be silent and they couldn't tell me to be quiet because I was in church and I was singing. It wasn't just opening my mouth, it was opening my heart. I was singing for my unborn child, all the things I wanted to say to it, and the baby would kick and wriggle in response.

Chapel was the one place I could get a good chat with Rose, other than the exercise yard when Miss Fanshawe's back was turned, but she'd been missing for the last few days and I was beginning to get worried.

The last time I saw her, I'd put my hoisting skills to good use, swiping a bottle of surgical spirit from the hospital wing while Ma Doherty's back was turned. I hid it under my maternity smock and passed it to Rose one teatime, because she'd been planning to brew some booze in a chamber pot to trade for ciggies. She loved a ciggie, did Rose. I'd managed to get her a few dog ends from the fireplaces around the screws' rooms, which I was allowed to sweep out, on account of being a hospital inmate. But that wasn't enough to satisfy Rose's cravings so she decided to make a little distillery in her cell.

It was a crazy plan, and I'd almost wet myself laughing when she told me about it, but she'd managed to get some yeast from the kitchens, and she'd saved all the prunes from pudding for a week in the pocket of her cardigan. The whole lot were going into her jerry in the cell to make Holloway hooch.

But now as she shuffled in to sit at the end of our pew, I saw she was black and blue, with a bust lip and one eye half closed. A little slip of paper found its way down the line of prisoners to me. The chapel service was the usual place where deals were made and gossip was exchanged, or warnings were given, so everyone knew the drill. The racket of so many women singing was the perfect cover and notes could be passed with relative ease.

If the vicar had listened closely to what we were doing to his hymns, he wouldn't have been best pleased either, because sometimes messages were passed that way too. Who knew that the words to "Abide with Me" could be changed to *"Mary on B, has jam for tea"* or *"grass on me, I'll break your knee"*?

I hid the note in my hymn book and when the organist struck up, I unfolded it and began to read:

"Joan's got it in for me and you're next."

Rose loitered by the end of the pew as we filed back out of the chapel and fell into step with me. There wasn't much on her to start with but her cheeks were drawn, making her skin almost translucent, apart for the dark bruising around her eyes.

"Two days bread and water in the punishment cells," she said, out of the corner of her mouth. "Joan found out about my little gin still and when I wouldn't let her in on it, she tried to cop a feel in return for not grassing. I slapped the randy old bitch when she stuck her hand up my skirt, didn't I? And Fanshawe saw it and said I started a fight."

"What about the others in the laundry, didn't they vouch for you?" I whispered, as we made our way past the garden, where the most trusted and privileged prisoners were allowed to work in the summer months. It was either there or the library, but that was reserved for the Governor's top favorites, because they got to sit on their arses all day flicking through books or taking them from cell to cell for people to borrow.

"No chance, Joan has got the laundry dancing to her tune," said Rose. "They all said I started it."

"Once you've dropped your sprog, Joan will be after you too, you mark my words. I'm thinking of trying to escape. I don't think I can take much more. Fanshawe hates my guts to start with . . ." She was properly choked up, like the lifeblood was draining out of her.

The huge prison wall loomed in front of us. There was no way little Rose could get over it and we both knew that. She got a twelve-month stretch, so her suffering was going to go on a lot longer than mine.

"It's either escape or do something to myself," she said. "Then I might see you in the hospital wing."

"No, Rose," I said. "There's got to be a better way than that . . ."

I didn't get to finish what I was saying because we were just coming back into the cell blocks when I felt a trickle of something running down my leg, and in an instant, it had turned into a gush, which splashed onto the stone floor.

Miss Fanshawe must have thought I'd done it on purpose because, even though my waters had just broken, she made me get down on my hands and knees to scrub the floor with a bucketful of disinfectant, right the way through my labor pains.

Chapter Twelve

NELL

Holloway, London, February 1947

"I think the baby's coming!"

I was doubled up over the iron bedstead, groaning.

In the half-light of dawn, Ma Doherty appeared by my side.

She ran her hands over my belly, and her brows knitted into a frown.

I snatched at her fingers and clasped them hard as my belly went rigid. Then, I let out a terrible scream.

"Be quiet! You'll wake the whole prison. I'm trying to help you!" scolded Ma Doherty, getting down onto her knees and peering up my gown.

"This baby's breech," she muttered to herself. "Let's see what we can do . . ."

She began to prod and poke, making me wail, "Oh please, God, no! Can I see a doctor? Make it stop!"

"There's no time for that! Bear with it," said Ma Doherty as sweat ran down her face in rivulets from the effort of trying to manipulate the baby into the right position.

I was grunting like an animal and one of the other girls rolled over and said, "Shurrup, will ya?"

Ma Doherty told me to push and so I did, with all my might, and a tiny wriggling lump of humanity came into the world behind the walls of Holloway Prison.

★

My baby boy was the most beautiful thing I had ever seen.

His fingers curled around mine as he slept soundly in my arms.

The months of misery inside the jail melted away as I hugged this warm, wriggling bundle: my child.

Ma Doherty plumped the pillows behind my head to make me more comfortable.

I winced as she sat me up a little, as I'd torn badly during the birth, despite Ma Doherty doing her best to help me.

"Now, the sooner you are up and about the better. It will help you heal," she said.

"It is all worth it, for him," I murmured, ignoring the pain. Hearing my voice, the little mite opened his eyes.

"He's looking at me!" It was the most exciting thing ever.

"Oh, he can't focus on you just yet, you're just a blur to him, but he knows your voice right enough," she said with a smile. "A baby knows his mother. Have you thought of a name for him?"

"Joseph," I replied. It was my grandfather's name and it sounded strong and kind, which was everything I wanted him to be.

Ma Doherty beamed. "A good choice. I'll tell the Governor. Now, you need to get some rest." She eased the baby from my arms.

I opened my mouth to protest but Ma Doherty just kept on talking as she lifted my child and wrapped him in a blanket. "I'll take little Joseph to the nursery overnight so you can sleep, because you will need your strength for your chores back in the laundry during the day. You'll have time to feed him and change him in the morning and you'll have all evening with him too. It's a new routine, but you'll settle in quickly."

Tears pricked my eyes, but I fought the urge to cry. My baby's life was already planned out and I had so little say in it.

"We don't want him to get too attached," said Ma Doherty firmly, seeing the expression on my face. "He must learn to feed from the bottle while you are busy with your chores, and at night, it means you can get some rest, so this is the kindest way for both of you, do you understand?"

"Yes" was all that I could manage. My breasts were heavy with milk and every fiber of my being was crying out to cling to him. I longed to feed him again but all I saw of my son was his little pink face, peering out of a blanket as he was carried away in Ma Doherty's arms.

The chilblains on my feet stung like hell as I tried to warm my toes by the meager heap of coals smoking in the grate.

More than twelve inches of snow had settled on the ground outside over the past few weeks and the ice on the inside of the windows of the hospital wing was so thick that the Governor had finally relented, allowing fires to be lit.

But all that was left at the bottom of the coal scuttle by the time the screws had taken what they needed to heat their rooms were a few lumps of coke and slag, which barely burned when you held a match to them.

Days spent with water sloshing over my feet on the stone floors of the laundry combined with the freezing temperatures in the rest of the prison meant I was hobbling around in a permanent state of frostbite. And when things started to thaw, that made the chilblains started to burn and itch, which was an agony all of its own.

Only seeing little Joseph took my mind off it. The evenings after chores were what I lived for and the thought of holding him again saw me through the backbreaking days washing and mangling sheets. Sometimes I was glad to hide my face among the steam rising from the copper vats of boiling water in the basement, so I could forget the hell I was living in.

Baby Joseph was the one joy in my world. I clung to him, smelling his babyish head, reveling in his perfectness, for every moment I was allowed. When I came into the nursery and peered into his cot, he was smiling up at me.

"Don't be silly," said Ma Doherty. "It's probably just wind."

But it wasn't. The way he clasped my hand as he stared deep into my eyes meant Joseph recognized me as his mother. I was so careful with him, humming softly to him as I bathed and changed him, cradling him the right way, just as Ma Doherty had shown me.

That evening, after I'd bathed him and was settling down with him in my arms, Ma Doherty bustled up with a bottle full of baby milk.

"You must use this from now on," she said.

"But I need to feed him, I always do before bed," I said, unbuttoning my blouse.

"No," said Ma Doherty firmly. "The baby is two weeks old now and so we must start to wean him off you and onto the bottle only."

She produced a set of bandages from her pocket.

"These are to bind yourself with, to stop your milk from coming in anymore."

I took the glass bottle, fighting the urge to throw it on the floor and smash it into little pieces.

Joseph started to cry and turned his head away when it was offered it to him.

"He can smell you," said Ma Doherty crossly. "Here, let me do it and you go and sort yourself out."

She lifted the crying infant from my grasp and walked

away toward the window, where snowflakes were coming down so thickly that the exercise yard and the grounds of the prison were no longer visible.

I did as I was told. I took off my blouse and brassiere and began winding the bandages around my chest, wincing with pain as I did so. Milk seeped through the cloth as I tied it tightly.

"How long will I have to do this for?" I whispered. It just seemed so cruel to deny him my milk.

"A week perhaps," said Ma Doherty, turning to face me. Joseph was clasping the glass bottle now, rather than onto me, as he always did in the morning. There was a stab of longing inside me to feed him, to hold him once more.

"You mustn't dwell on this because it won't do you any good," said Ma Doherty, reading the look of sorrow in my eyes. We both knew what she meant. "You have played your part in feeding him, in giving him the best start, but now we must all begin to think of his future. Do you see?"

Out of the corner of my eye, I saw the chief screw, Miss Fanshawe, creep into the nursery.

"The Governor wants to see you now," she said smugly.

"Yes, Miss," I said, wondering what on earth I had done wrong.

The Governor sat at her desk, smiling sweetly. It was an unnatural look and one which made me feel sick to the pit of my stomach, especially when I when realized it was not for me, but as a show for the couple sitting opposite her, on a pair of high-backed chairs.

"Yes, come in, Nell," she said. "I'd like you to meet Mr. and Mrs. Carter."

The woman was immaculately made-up, with an expensive-looking coat, which she kept buttoned to the neck. Her handbag was perched precariously on her knee. Mr. Carter was balding and had a very well-fed look about him, with a paunch barely contained in his pin-striped suit.

"How do you do?" I said, remembering my manners, but wondering what the bloody hell a respectable couple like them were doing in a place like this.

The woman beamed at me, and the man adjusted his tie.

"They are interested in offering Joseph a permanent home. I have the adoption papers here," said the Governor.

She pushed a sheaf of paper toward me. A pot of ink and a fountain pen were ready and waiting beside it.

My legs almost buckled, and I clung to the edge of the desk to steady myself. It was all happening so fast.

I stared at the floor, as the blood started to rush in my head, making me dizzy. Joseph was my baby. How had these people even met him without me knowing?

"I'm a bank manager," said Mr. Carter, with such kindness in his eyes. "We can't have children, but we have the very best of everything ready for him at home and I can promise you, he will be loved and cared for. Joseph will have the best life we can afford to give him."

I bit my lip and stared at the floor. My boy would be raised by properly posh people. They'd give him so much more than I ever could; I knew it made sense, but it didn't make it any easier for me.

He was almost pleading with me as he went on: "We tried for so many years, but the good Lord never blessed us with children. Holding Joseph showed us that we can be parents but to a child who needs the security we can offer."

Mrs. Carter stood up, putting her handbag on the coffee table beside her, smiling with genuine warmth. "We can be sure to send you pictures of him on every birthday. I promise you I will love him as my own. We know that this is a difficult decision, but Ma Doherty knows us through our church, and she has explained that you won't be able to go home to your family with Joseph. We want to help you to get on with your life and to offer him all our love. I promise you he will be loved and cherished."

"Well?" said the Governor, with a note of irritation in her voice. "Come along, now."

To her, it all made perfect sense. What life could I give him, an unmarried mother from a London slum? This was just the way things worked. I picked up the fountain pen and dipped the nib into the ink pot, but then I hesitated. Something just would not let me do it. The Governor's face softened. "Nell, I realize this is a very difficult choice, possibly the most difficult a mother could ever make, but if you think things through, you will see that we here at Holloway are trying to help you and little Joseph. This way, you can return to your community without the shame of a child out of wedlock."

She lowered her voice: "As well as a criminal record."

It was true, I was just a low-life hoister with a baby out of wedlock, but what life would there be without the cuddles, the curling fingers?

Those snatched moments were all I lived for.

I thought of the look on my dad's face when he found out I was pregnant, how he'd turned his back on me and forced Mum to do the same for what I'd done. My boy would never know the cobbles of Waterloo. He'd play in a big back garden somewhere posh and go on to have a good job and a nice life.

It was the best gift I could give him as a mother, even if it broke my heart.

But if I was playing by their rules, they were going to give me something back. I'd had enough of being pushed around by everyone. Holloway Prison had shown me the only way to get to the top was by fighting for it, tooth and nail.

"If I do this, I want you to sign an order now for me to be moved out of the laundry, to the library, to get extra privileges, and Rose is coming with me," I said.

"I've never heard such a thing!" said the Governor, recoiling in horror. "Who on earth do you think you are to bargain with me?"

Rose had all but stopped eating in the last week and was completely broken by Joan and Fanshawe. I had to do something for her.

"It's not really helping me, it's for this lovely couple," I said coldly. "To help me give them what they want. And what they want is my baby. Ain't that right?"

These people hadn't the first clue what really went on behind closed doors at this prison. They just wanted to leave with a lovely plump baby—*my* baby—to make their perfect lives even more perfect.

Miss Fanshawe had been lurking in the corner, drinking it all in, and she moved toward me with menace, slapping her little ebony truncheon against the palm of her hand: "I can deal with this, Governor . . ."

Mrs. Carter shot up from her chair and blocked her path.

"Please," said Mrs. Carter, "surely there is a way to reward this girl for being so generous and thoughtful? It can't hurt to give her some kind of privileges for what she is doing, can it?"

I smirked at Fanshawe and then turned to smile sweetly at the Governor.

The Governor pursed her lips for a moment and then relented. She pulled a piece of paper from her desk drawer and began to write the order, which she handed to Miss Fanshawe, who looked a bit disappointed as she tucked her truncheon back into the belt straining around her fat middle.

My calloused hands were shaking as I scrawled my name

on the adoption papers. I was bargaining on my baby's life. I couldn't believe that I had sunk so low but that is what Holloway Prison had done to me. I wasn't about to forget it. It was just another notch on the wall, for the revenge I was going to take on Alice Diamond for putting me in here in the first place. This one would be a deeper cut than the others that I'd scratched over the past six months; much deeper.

I was marched back through the prison, with Fanshawe breathing down my neck, muttering under her breath: "You've got a bloody cheek talking to the Governor like that. You'd better watch your step, my girl."

But I let all her threats wash over me as she took me back to the hospital wing and locked the door behind her. There was only one place I wanted to be and that was by Joseph's side. He was sleeping soundly, like a little angel, in the clothes I had made for him. Now another woman would get to dress him and love him.

I picked him up, clutching him to me. Then I unbuttoned my blouse, yanking the bandages from my swollen breasts.

It only took a split second before he sleepily found his way to me. I began to feed him one last time, stroking his cheek, rocking him gently, trying to pour all the love I would ever feel for him, for his whole life, into that one precious moment together.

When I went to find Joseph in his cot the next morning, he was gone, along with the baby box full of clothes I had so lovingly made for him.

I pressed my hand to the sheet where he had lain, but it was cold. They must have taken him in the night.

I sank to my knees sobbing. "Oh, Joseph, what have I done?"

Ma Doherty appeared by my side and pulled me to my

feet: "Come on, love," she said, pulling me into a hug. "You have made the right choice, there's no point dwelling on it.

"Soon you will be free to get on with the rest of your life and put all this behind you."

But I knew then, gazing at the place where my baby had slept, that I never would.

Chapter Thirteen

ALICE

Elephant and Castle, February 1947

The weather's been properly filthy these last few weeks but every day I watch the girls from Queen's Buildings go off at the crack of dawn to the factory gates, like clockwork.

Some of them have taken to wrapping blankets over their thin coats, like shawls, to keep out the bitter cold. The courtyard is more like a skating rink and it's a right old game of ninepins if one of them slips, bumping into the other and sending them all flying. Makes me laugh at them for the fools that they are, going to work for somebody else. What a way to waste your life; skidding on your backside round the Elephant and Castle in the freezing cold just to earn a crust.

It's fair to say, I didn't always think that way.

When I was young and foolish, I believed in gainful employment; being paid by someone else.

I'll never forget it. I was high as a blooming kite with excitement because Lim had told me he'd found me a job, a really good one, which would me get out of the Seven Dials. It was a straight position and all, nothing crooked this time, he swore blind. It was a once-in-a-lifetime chance for a proper job that just didn't happen to girls like me, so I practically skipped my way through the warren of streets that led to Islington.

Now, this terraced street was a step up from ours because women were out on their hands and knees donkey stoning their front steps, and the sheets drying in neat rows between the houses weren't full of holes neither and the windows had glass in them, instead of boards where they'd had a brick or a bottle chucked through.

We rapped on a front door, which was smartly painted in shiny black, and a woman answered, with her hair up in a bun, and her skirt reaching to the floor and a white starched apron over it.

"Hello, Alice," she said, bustling me down the hallway to the scullery, which was filled with the smell of baking bread. "I'm Mrs. Tibbs, but you can call me Ma."

The whole place was sparkling clean, with the red tiled floor polished so much you could have eaten off it and neatly pressed sheets and towels piled on her kitchen table next to a Moses basket with a baby sleeping soundly inside.

Lim smiled at Mrs. Tibbs and they wandered back out to the hallway to exchange a few words while I had a bit of a nosey around. She had a nice carriage clock on the mantelpiece over the range—which must have cost a few quid—and some lovely lacework napkins.

Lim came back in and whispered in my ear: "For Gawd's sake, don't nick anything." And that made me giggle.

I whispered back: "I won't, I promise!"

He gave me a quick peck on the cheek. "I'll see you later, Alice."

With that he was gone, but I scarcely had time to draw breath before Mrs. Tibbs was talking nine to the dozen.

"Now, you will be meeting the captain, who is a very nice gentleman, but his life has been struck by the most terrible tragedy. He came back from the trenches only to lose his beautiful wife to the Spanish flu, leaving their poor darling daughter an orphan in this world."

Well, that would have drawn tears from a glass eye, wouldn't it? I found myself feeling pity for the poor fella losing his missus like that after surviving the horrors of the Great War. Life really wasn't fair.

"He needs a maid and someone kind as a companion to his daughter, who is just a little younger than yourself. What do you think of that?"

"It's like a dream come true!" I clapped my hands together. "But do you really think he will like me?"

"Well, from what your brother's told me, you are a good worker, kind and caring too. So, I can't see why not. But he'll be here soon so you'd better get ready.

"Tell me, dear, and don't be shy, when did you last have a bath?"

I blushed beetroot. My flannelette chemise stank to high heaven and although my face was no stranger to the dishcloth in our grubby sink, I hadn't bathed in weeks, maybe months actually. Laundry wasn't high on the list of my priorities in the Seven Dials either and there were so many stains on my dress I didn't know where to start getting it clean.

She was already helping me out of my filthy clothes.

"Why don't you have a nice wash, dear?"

Mrs. Tibbs poured a lovely copper full of hot water into the tin bath by the range and it looked so inviting. I was shy—my ma was the only person who'd seen me in my birthday suit—but Mrs. Tibbs didn't turn away for a minute as I stripped off. In fact, as I eased myself into the bath, she had a good look at me and gave an approving nod.

"That's right, don't be embarrassed. Get yourself nice and clean, there's soap on the side."

The baby in the Moses basket on the table began to cry

and the look of kindness melted away as she chided it: "Oh stop your bellyaching, for God's sake, you little bleeder!"

She took a glass vial down from the mantelpiece and poured a few drops onto her fingers before sticking them into the baby's mouth. The little one sucked and then his eyes fell closed and he was quiet again.

"Ma's magic drops, just to help the teething pain," she said, screwing the lid back on the vial. "Works wonders."

She bustled off and returned with some new clothes for me. This was like heaven and I had to pinch myself to be sure I wasn't dreaming. I put on the crisp, white bloomers and a new chemise of broderie anglaise cotton. It was so beautiful, I couldn't believe it, nor the smart new pinafore she gave me. I'd never had clothes like this. Mine were bought secondhand at Berwick Street market. Sometimes they were fashioned from my ma's castoffs and were more like patchwork than a skirt.

"You need to make the right impression for this job," said Mrs. Tibbs. "Smart girls make good money, don't they? The captain is a very fine man and he wants a girl of quality, so dirty old clothes just won't do."

She put my cracked leather boots in the corner and presented me with a pair of soft velvet ballet shoes to wear.

"So why are you helping us?" I said, as I pulled them on and admired my feet in them. "I mean, Lim's never mentioned you until now."

"I act as a sort of go-between to help girls find places in good families, and I take my commission but that will be all sorted between me and your brother and the captain, don't worry your pretty head about that."

She helped me button up my pinafore and then shooed me toward the staircase in the hall.

"Go on, you'd better get up there, he'll be here soon."

"But isn't it better to wait in the parlor?" I said.

She waved her hands in the air. "I can't be receiving guests in my scullery, Alice! There's a baby here and it's just not presentable. I have made my best room upstairs and the front is ready for you to have a little chat. Just go on up."

The bedroom door creaked open and I stepped lightly across the floorboards and sat on a chair by the window, peering out of the heavy drapes into the street below. The whole room smelled of furniture polish because behind me stood the most enormous mahogany bed, which was covered with feather pillows. I walked over and touched the bedspread, which was red silk with little Chinese ladies on it. It was the kind of bed a princess might sleep in. I sat on the edge of it and had a little bounce, just for fun. There were no squeaking bedsprings and no bedbugs either, I was pretty certain of that.

I began to wonder what kind of a bedroom the captain would provide for his staff. Even a poky little attic room would do for me. I was getting so excited to meet him when I heard a heavy footfall on the stairs and a handsome blond-haired man in a light tweed suit pushed the door open.

Mrs. Tibbs peered over his shoulder from the landing.

"You must be Alice," he said. "You're just perfect."

"Well, I'll leave you two to get better acquainted," she said with a tight smile.

I heard the key turning in the lock and glanced up into this stranger's face, as he moved toward me with a look in his eyes that I'd seen round our way, when a fella had some business with one of the girls from the back alleys.

"Why has Mrs. Tibbs locked the door?" I said. "Can you get her to open it, please?"

I didn't like being locked in there with a strange fella.

He was already pulling off a fine pair of leather gloves

and he took off his gold-rimmed glasses and put them on the table by the bed.

"Don't be silly," he said.

The penny dropped. I leapt to my feet and made for the door, but he blocked my path.

"Now, then . . . I thought we were going to be friends," he said, but I didn't feel like being friendly to him, I just wanted to get out of there, so I kicked him in the shins, quite hard.

"Oh, you little devil!" he spat, baring his beautiful white teeth. Then he slapped me with the back of his fist, so that I fell back onto the bed, my face smarting like hell.

Before I could get up, he had me pinioned and his free hand was tearing at my knickers. I thrashed around and spat in his face, so he slapped me again and I started to cry.

"Please, mister, there's been a mistake . . ."

His moustache bristled against my face and his breath smelled of tobacco. "No mistake. I know what you are here for as well as you do."

I screamed, drumming my heels on the floor, and he tussled with me so that he had me facedown on the bed, to stifle my cries. I've always been strong and I'm no stranger to fighting these days but back then, I was just an innocent girl and against a big fella like him, I didn't stand a chance.

The next thing I knew, he flipped me over to face him, and my nostrils were filled with his expensive cologne as he lay on top of me. I felt something hard jabbing at me between my thighs.

I clamped my legs together, but he used all his might to force them apart. The harder I fought, the more pleasure he got out of it.

"Come on, you little bitch," he leered as he pushed his way into me.

A searing pain tore through me and still he didn't stop.

He was grunting and sweating and then suddenly it was over, and he rolled off and got up.

I lay on my side, all the fight beaten out of me, pain coursing through my broken body, blood seeping crimson onto the crisp, white sheets.

He gazed at me for a moment and then leaned over and stroked my hair. "You have such a pretty face. You're much nicer when you are not snarling at me, Alice. That really was your first time, wasn't it?"

I was sobbing so hard I didn't reply.

Then he chucked me a pound note on the bed, buttoned up his fly, turned on his heel, and left.

I didn't have the energy to run away, so I just lay there, numbly staring at the ceiling. He'd only been gone a moment when Mrs. Tibbs appeared.

Her hands flew up to her face at the sight of me. "Oh my dear, what has happened?! I thought he was going to offer you a job but look at the state of you! You're like the Wreck of the Hesperus!"

I sat up, shaking and barely able to string a sentence together: "Please help me, I'm bleeding."

Mrs. Tibbs rushed around the room, peeking out of the curtains.

Then she came to me and hugged me tight. "He's gone. There's no sign of him out there. You poor, poor little mouse. You sweet, innocent little dear. You have a good cry. What a beastly man! He's tricked us all."

"I want Lim. I want my brother!" I sobbed. "He'll kill him."

"Oh, he's busy at work tonight, my love," she said. "He left me strict instructions that you are to stay here until the morning and I daren't cross him, that wouldn't be right, would it? And you can't leave, not now, not in this state."

She swept my fringe back from my face and lowered

her voice to a whisper. "The thing is, the captain is such a respectable gent. I don't know what you said to make him behave in the way he did, but you are just a girl from the slums whose mother's in the asylum, aren't you?

"They'll say you're mad like her and making up stories if you tell anyone. I think you need to keep this a secret. That's the best way. People like him get away with all sorts. They'll say girls like you just do this for the money then feel bad about it afterwards, so you cry wolf."

Her fingers crept over the bedspread. "And, why, there's a pound he's left you! That's lucky, ain't it?"

She handed it to me. "Here, you'd better take it and I will bring you some warm milk with my special drops in it to help you sleep. And you can let me have a look at you and see what I can do to make it better? How's that for an idea?"

I sank back onto the pillow and closed my eyes, wishing the nightmare would go away, but I was too weak to fight anymore.

I woke at first light feeling groggy and light-headed, but I found the bedroom door unlocked.

Mrs. Tibbs was asleep in the rocking chair downstairs so I grabbed my boots from beside the range, not even stopping to fasten my laces, before I lifted the latch into the street. The knocker-up was still banging on windows to turf people out of bed to get to their factory jobs as I limped home through the city, past the costermongers wheeling their barrowloads of fruit and vegetables and last night's drunks lolling in the gutter.

My new pinafore was torn where the captain had grappled with me and every step I took led to searing pain inside, but still I walked on to get to the Seven Dials, where I knew I'd be safe.

When I got in, Lim was nowhere to be seen. I squatted in the corner of the kitchen, waiting and waiting for him to return.

The gas lamps had been lit by the time he barreled through the front door, drunk as a lord. "I had a great win at the spielers, Alice." He was waving paper money around. A fistful of cash, the like of which I'd never seen.

"Fella wants me to buy into his business 'cos I'm so good at the cards. I'm thinking about it. Could be the start of something big."

He waved two ten-pound notes under my nose.

I sat in silence.

"What's up, Alice?" he said, grabbing a crust of bread and chewing it thoughtfully. "How did your job interview go?"

"Something bad happened," I began and started to sob.

Lim put his arms around me and the whole story came tumbling out.

"So, will you find him and kill him, Lim, for what he done to me?" I said, looking up into his face, searching for the rage that I knew he must be feeling for what happened; that someone hurt his little sister in that way.

But his eyes were inky, like deep, dark pools, and so cold.

"Sounds like a good way for you to make money, Alice," he said. "You're pretty, Mrs. Tibbs can keep an eye out so you don't get beaten or hurt. What do you say?"

"You want me to sell myself to men. To go on the game?"

"I want you to earn your keep," he said, brushing me off him. "I've got business interests of my own now. I can't look after you, I have to think of my own gang."

His gang. Lim's gang.

"But what about us?" I blubbed. "You said it was you and me always."

"I ain't a charity," he said. "Brothers and sisters ain't in this game together when they grow up. It's not like that in the real world, that was just kids' stuff, us nicking bits of fruit. We can't make a living off a few silly dances and half a pound of stolen apples, Alice! There's plenty of work for girls, you just have to know how to roll the fellas and get the most out of them with what God gave you."

I couldn't believe my ears and I sat there with my jaw practically on the floor.

There was no letup from him: "I've seen the way men look at you. You'd be a fool to waste your good looks any other way."

But I wasn't listening to the rest of what he said because I was running through the door, up the lane, away from our home and everything in it, away from the Seven Dials and the life Lim had planned out for me.

And no matter how far I ran, or how much I stole over the years that followed, the truth of it sat with me like a lead weight on my chest.

I had been sold by my own brother, like a lamb to the slaughter.

Chapter Fourteen

NELL

Holloway, London, February 1947

When they set me free from Holloway Prison, two weeks after Joseph was adopted, my whole body still ached with the grief of being parted from my baby.

It was a sentence I would carry with me for the rest of my life.

As I walked away from the prison at first light, my eyes were blinded by tears and my head was full of thoughts about Joseph's little pink fingers clasping mine, the curve of his cheeks, his babyish smell and soft, downy blond hair. As Joseph grew up, his laugh, his walk, his voice, would all bear traces of me.

But he would be loved and enjoyed and cherished by another woman, one who the world said was better than me, because she was married.

Snowflakes were falling as I made my way down the Holloway Road, in a thick, pea-souper of a freezing fog, with feet like blocks of ice. The wind whipped through me, chilling me to the bone as I shuffled along through a foot of snow which made the houses look like they were dusted in icing sugar. My teeth were chattering as I pulled my coat close around me against the cold, but the dress I had on was just a thin summer frock with roses printed on it, the one given to me by Alice Diamond. I hated it now, as much as I despised her, with every fiber of my being.

Every step I made was a step closer to home and my goal of getting even with the monster who had lied to me and ruined my life.

The muffled thud of horses' hooves approaching made me spin around. I came face-to-face with a milkman, with a half-lit ciggie dangling from his lips.

"You're up early! Need a lift, love?"

I nodded gratefully, handed him the suitcase, and clambered up onto the cart.

"You won't find a bus for love nor money," he said, helping me up. "Drivers are on strike. Coalmen are on strike. Half the flaming world's on strike, except me," he grumbled. "Makes me wonder whether the war was worth winning if this is the peace we get."

"Oh," I said. "I had no idea."

He eyed me suspiciously: "You ain't been in the clink, have you?"

"No," I lied. "It's just I don't read the papers much and we haven't got a radiogram in the house."

He drew on his cigarette and then coughed deeply and spat in the gutter. "Running away, are you?"

I set my face to the wind. "I'm going back where I belong."

With suitcase in hand, I made my way down through the city as people wrapped like mummies battled against the elements. There was an eerie silence as I crossed Waterloo Bridge and the gray waters of the River Thames swirled beneath me. When I got to the other side and the stone steps which led down to my street, I had to catch my breath.

Tenison Street and Howley Terrace had survived everything the Germans could chuck at them during the Blitz but now the wrecking ball had done its worst. The wastepaper factory had gone, and the Feathers pub had a "closed" sign on it and the windows were boarded up, so that was surely next in line for demolition.

Piles of bricks and plaster, homes crushed to matchsticks, and a row of cobbles were the only proof that people had made this their community. Kids had played, families had struggled, hopes were raised and dashed in the sculleries and the backyards of Waterloo.

Now all that was left of my childhood was a pile of rubble and bitter memories, a love for a baby I couldn't keep, and a pipe dream of bettering myself with The Forty Thieves, only to be played for a fool.

I decided then, staring at the ruins of my life, that I would take back what I was owed: my happiness.

When a brewer's dray came past, I hitched a lift down to the Elephant and Castle. By the time I got there, I could barely feel my fingers, which were turning blue.

The tenements of Queen's Buildings loomed up ahead. Graying flannelette bedsheets stiff with frost were strung high up between the flats. Crossing the frozen courtyard, I ignored the stares from snot-nosed kids using a lump of ice as a football, which skittered across the filthy ground.

I hesitated for a moment before climbing the stairs to the third floor and tapping softly on the door of number 32.

A blast of heat escaped when the door swung open, as if a furnace was blazing inside, and the smell of toast wafted down the hall, making my stomach rumble.

Alice Diamond stood there beaming.

"Nell! As I live and breathe! It's good to see you," she said, pulling me into a warm, motherly embrace. "Welcome home, love."

There was only one way to get to her. If friends were

close, enemies had to be closer. I had learned that the hard way.

"Thanks, Alice," I said, allowing myself to be enveloped in her arms, "I missed you so much. It's good to be back in the gang."

She didn't know it, but I was plotting to be the best hoister in the whole of London because this time, I would steal from the person who was least expecting it—from the Queen of Thieves herself.

And what's more, I had my eye on one thing in particular.

Her crown.

Chapter Fifteen

ALICE

Elephant and Castle, London, February 1947

Nell was like a waif and stray when she turned up on my doorstep that winter's morning. I don't know what they're feeding them in the clink these days but it ain't a patch on the good old-fashioned prison diet from my day, with plenty of suet.

I pinched her hollow cheeks and steered her to the kitchen table. Bacon was sizzling in a pan on the stove, and Molly slid a couple of slices onto a plate and brought them over.

It was the most delicious thing she'd tasted in ages judging by the way she wolfed it all down.

I was pleased to see there wasn't a pram in sight.

"Gave the baby away, did you?" I said, pouring some tea and watching her intently.

"Had him adopted, posh couple," she replied eventually, fighting back tears.

"It's for the best," I said gently. I knew it couldn't have been an easy choice for her to make, but it was the right one as far as I was concerned. "You'll forget in time. You're young."

She nodded but there was a look on her face, as if talking about him was like a knife twisting inside her.

Luckily, I had more pressing matters to discuss with young Nell, to take her mind off it. "We've got lots of work for you to do, to keep you busy, ain't we, Molly? And besides, you still owe me for all the things I taught you already, not to mention the nice underwear you took from me."

Her mouth fell open, like a stupid fish caught on a line. "But I thought it was a present . . ."

"It was on tick," I said with a laugh. "You don't think any of this comes for free, do you, Nell? I ain't a bleeding charity!"

"No, of course not," said Nell, shutting her trap sharpish. Snowflakes were still coming down outside the window and she didn't want to be chucked out in the street. She knew which side her bread was buttered. "I want to work. Just tell me what you need me to do."

"Well, that's the right attitude," I replied, settling myself down on my favorite chair. "I was worried you'd lost your love of hoisting. Things have been getting more difficult up West. Cozzers are clamping down on law-breaking and the likes of us."

"Yeah, times have been hard since you were having a nice time putting your feet up in the Holloway Hotel," said Molly, puffing on a smoke and flicking ash into her teacup.

"It weren't a bleeding holiday," said Nell, her jaw tightening.

"That's not what I heard," Molly replied with a smirk, flicking her red hair over her shoulders. "Apparently you were the star singer in church and got yourself some extra privileges sucking up to that baby-snatcher of a matron, didn't you?"

Now, most of my girls would have kicked off at that, even against Molly, but Nell didn't flinch. She just eyed her coolly. I found that a bit troubling because it was out of character, but I put it down to her being tired from the emotion of handing over her baby and the fact that she'd just had her first decent meal since leaving the nick.

"I hope you ain't got too religious to be hoisting," I said smoothly, "because while you were saying three Hail Marys, the miners went on strike and the rations got cut.

"People need a bit extra these days, just to get by. In fact, I've been helping your mum out since she moved down this way."

That got her attention. She sat up straight.

"What do you mean?" she gasped. "Mum would never take anything crooked . . ."

Oh, I'm full of surprises. I just couldn't wait to share them with Nell. My day was getting better and better.

"That was before your dad's gambling debts got out of hand," I said matter-of-factly. "He had a bit more of a flutter after you left to have the baby, think he was quite upset. Likes the dog racing, does old Paddy. Turns out he ran up quite a lot on tick."

"How much?" A look of panic swept across her face.

"About a tenner, plus interest," I said. "I stepped in, seeing as you are one of my girls, and I paid it off before the racing gangs could get to him, but he's paying me back with interest, so I've been helping your ma out, when I can, with a few extra coupons here and there. She lives over in the next building, with the rest of the people from round your way who got rehoused. I told her not to worry because you will make it up to me, won't you, love? We're just like one big, happy family, ain't we?"

She swallowed hard. "Of course we are."

I was so glad that me and Nell were on the same page again. It can be tricky when one of my girls comes out of the nick. You never know if they're going to have had the spark beaten out of them by the screws or whether fending for themselves has given them a bit too much of a gee, and then they're like a wild horse who just needs the bit and bridle to calm them down again.

Having Nell's family in debt to me was a nice touch, I must admit, and I hadn't seen it coming. But then fate does sometimes put chances like that in your lap. I pick them up gratefully and wring every last drop I can get out of them. It's the connections that matter in a place like the Elephant and Castle; how people all fit together, and as Queen of The Forty Thieves, I make the most of that.

It was a bit of a gamble helping them out because I guessed that Nell didn't have much time for her dad, after he'd called her a little whore for getting up the duff, but every girl loves their mum, no matter what. So, of course Nell was going to do what she could to help her old ma out, wasn't she?

While Nell was still reeling from the shock of learning that her dad owed me money, Molly pulled open a cupboard, which was stacked with tins of sardines, evaporated milk, and sugar.

"We're onto a nice little earner, black-market food and goods and fake coupons," she said, pointing to the sideboard which was piled high with ration books and packets of silk stockings.

"But things have been getting harder for us in the West End shops. They've been catching us at it when we're hoisting. Seems that the management know we are coming even before we get there, which means someone is tipping them the wink."

I chipped in: "I reckon that our little sideline of fake coupons and things falling off the back of lorries in Waterloo might have upset a few faces over in Soho."

"What do you mean?" said Nell. "Surely no one would be daft enough to cross Alice Diamond and The Forty Thieves? Word would get around and they'd get a belting, for starters."

"That's nice of you to say but I have a feeling someone has been grassing me up," I said, stirring my tea.

"But who?" she leaned forward, with a look of real interest. "Who's grassing you up?"

"I have my suspicions, but I need to know more, which is where you come in, Nell. You're a fresh face, no one over the water will know you're one of my girls, so I need you to go and be my eyes and ears in Soho."

"What does that involve?" she said. She weren't really in a position to say no in any case.

"I want you to go and get a job in one of the clubs down there, it's run by a fella called Billy Sullivan."

"Billy who?"

"Calls himself the King of Soho," I said. "Quite a title but he's cut a lot of people up West to get it and he runs protection rackets in the clubs, amongst other things."

"I've heard he likes blondes," said Molly, brandishing a bottle of peroxide she'd pulled from the sideboard. "So, first, we need to sort your hair out."

Molly sat by the kitchen sink and coated Nell's head with a foul-smelling concoction and then covered the lot with an old shower cap.

After about twenty minutes, Nell started fidgeting and scratching her head.

"Sit still," said Molly, "you'll get it everywhere."

"But it's starting to burn!" she yelped.

"Alright," said Molly, pulling off the cap, "let's get it rinsed then we can put it in curlers for a bit of lift."

Nell sat in front of the fire with her hair in curlers for a good hour to help it dry. When Molly handed her a mirror, she gasped at her reflection.

Gone was the mousey-brown-haired schoolgirl who had been caught thieving stockings in Gamages. In her place was a platinum-haired starlet, someone who wouldn't look out of place in the *Picture Post*, stepping out on the arm of a famous actor.

"Blimey, you're a dead ringer for Jean Harlow," said Molly. I moved closer to get a proper butcher's.

"My, my," I said, pinching her cheek. "You've turned into a proper stunner."

She shook her head, as if she didn't believe me.

"Here," said Molly, pulling some makeup out of her handbag. "You'll need to learn how to put this on."

Nell took the red lipstick, powder in an enamel compact case with a puff, and a block of black mascara with a little brush. Molly spat in it and it turned inky before she swirled the brush in it and carefully applied it to Nell's eyes.

Next, she showed her how to outline her mouth with the lipstick before blotting it on a handkerchief and reapplying.

"That helps it stay put no matter how much you drink," she said. The fumes on Molly's breath at close quarters were testament to that.

All the months of misery scrubbing sheets in the prison laundry had melted away. The blonde hair set off her big, chestnut-brown eyes, making her cheekbones stand out. Those lips, coated with red, were almost indecently kissable. When she smiled, the young woman in front of us lit up, as if she were breathing for the first time in her life. There was something beautiful about her, like a pearl when you hold it in the palm of your hand and it's all sheeny. I felt a tingle that I usually get when I'm about to nick a particularly lovely fur. This girl was special.

And what's more, she was mine.

"Right," I said, holding her by the shoulders and taking another good look at her, "let's sort your wardrobe out."

She traipsed after me down the hallway like a little lapdog, to the front room, where the clothes rail was still chock-full of hoisted goods.

There were day dresses in the finest wool cloth, which looked so warm and stylish. I knew she couldn't wait to try them on.

I slapped her hand away: "No! You've got to dress the part. You're supposed to just be a factory girl from the East End, who happens to be good-looking. Fancy clothes will make you stick out like a sore thumb. Here, this'll do."

I pulled out a shapeless utility frock in a rough brown wool, which was every bit as drab as the wallpaper in the hallway.

"Did someone nick that for a laugh?" she said.

Well, I wasn't having that. She was getting above herself already.

"You've no idea how hard it's been! They're even putting the furs in glass cabinets these days, so no, it ain't a joke. This is all some of the girls could get away with and they risked longer than you had in prison to do it. You'll find people still willing to pay a decent price for stuff like this, with clothing on the ration."

"I'm sorry," she stuttered.

"Count yourself lucky you ain't on the streets," I muttered to myself, as I flicked through the rail. "Here!"

I thrust a Fairisle cardigan at her and she took it without saying a word. Next, I gave her a pair of leather ankle boots and a set of Fairisle mittens to match the cardigan.

I topped it off with a belted coat in navy blue gaberdine and a navy wool beret to match.

"Get that lot on then," I ordered.

As Nell was hoicking her way into the dress, which was scratchy as hell, I filled her in on Billy Sullivan.

"He owns quite a few pubs and clubs but his favorite is The Windsor on Wardour Street. I will give you a few outfits for the club in the evening. You can say you got them on tick if anyone asks."

I pulled a black skirt and blouse from the rail, along with a polka-dot viscose dress and a jacket with a nipped-in waist. Her eyes lit up at the sight of those. I wanted her to have something to catch Billy's roving eye.

"What kind of work do you want me to do in the club?" said Nell.

"Oh, use your imagination," said Molly, lighting a cigarette. "Pretty girl like you will think of something, I'm sure."

"I see," she croaked.

She'd just had a bun in the oven so the last thing I wanted was for her to get herself in the family way again.

"Just be a bit creative," I said. "But keep one foot on the floor at all times. Take whatever job he offers you, be nice, and keep your ears open for any gossip but keep your knickers on.

"He likes to have a meet with his fellas on Friday nights at the club. I'll meet you in a week's time for lunch at the Lyon's Tea House on the corner of Shaftesbury Avenue and you can tell me what you've found out and where I can find you when I need to."

Molly gave her a handbag and slipped something into it—it was a billiard ball in a sock. "Just in case you need to defend yourself, Nell. A smack with that will fend off anything. Works a treat."

"But what if I don't find anything out?" she said. Nell was starting to panic now, even with a secret weapon in her handbag.

I thought I'd better make myself clear.

"You'd better find something worth saying. I've had enough of snitches and I want to know who's been grassing me up."

"I probably ought to look in on my parents before I go," she said, picking up her suitcase.

"There's no time for family visits now and your dad ain't too keen on you showing your face round here anyway from what I've heard. Word is, he thinks you're a little slut."

She stepped back, as if I'd punched her right in the kisser. I do like to keep my girls on their toes.

I put my face right next to hers, so she could see into the depths of my eyes, which were narrowing like a cat's. "You ain't on holiday, you're working for The Forty Thieves. Now, get going!"

Chapter Sixteen

NELL

Soho, London, February 1947

The lights of Soho glowed like an ember in the heart of the frozen city.

People huddled together in doorways, sharing a ciggie and a laugh, while pubs overflowed with punters drinking to take their minds off rationing, food shortages, and the relentless cold.

As I made my way to The Windsor in Wardour Street, I must have looked like just another new girl in town who was down on her luck. Don't get me wrong, I hadn't been expecting an easy ride from Alice and The Forty Thieves, but the way she sent me packing had left me feeling a bit punch-drunk.

She had me and my whole family over a barrel but that only made me more determined to get my own back. I knew my plan was going to take some time, but I'd gone from the frying pan into the fire where Alice was concerned.

It wasn't even as if I cared about my dad, but I didn't want Mum to suffer. She was putting up with enough from him without having The Forty Thieves making her life a misery down at Queen's Buildings.

Some folks would have thrown in the towel at this point, abandoning any hopes of getting even with someone as powerful as Alice Diamond. But as I picked my way through the filthy backstreets, I realized that this seedy place, full of people splashing their cash, might turn out to be the making of me. Here, I wasn't the foolish teenager who'd got up the duff. On this side of the river, I was a blonde bombshell looking for an opportunity to shine—and the chance to outwit Alice into the bargain.

Nothing ever gets handed to girls like me on a plate, I knew that well enough.

So, as I went down the grimy staircase into the underground club, I took a deep breath and stepped toward my new life.

A coat-check girl rolled her eyes when I asked if there was any work going. That didn't put me off. I pushed through the double doors and into a room which was blue with smoke.

It was like another world in there; it was packed with fellas, tables full of drink, raucous laughter, tunes being bashed out on the piano, and on the stage, a row of scantily clad girls were high-kicking their way through a dance routine which left little to the imagination.

"You here for the auditions?" said the barman, who was bald as a coot and looked like he'd been polishing the crown of his head all afternoon.

"I'm looking for work." I tried to muster some enthusiasm. I could hardly believe I was here, dancing to Alice Diamond's tune.

The barman looked me up and down.

"You and half of London want a job at the moment," he scoffed. "You can have a tryout after the next act, if you like?"

I glanced over to the stage.

"But I can't really dance . . ." That was an understatement. I'd always had two left feet.

"In that case you can clear off home, blondie," he said, turning his back and running a dishcloth over some glasses.

The image of Alice Diamond loomed large in my mind for a split second. I got in quick, before he turfed me out: "But I can sing."

"Alright," said the barman, turning to face me, revealing a gold tooth as he flashed a smile, "you're on after the next act."

The dancers trooped off to a smattering of applause and a thick-set girl with raven hair tumbling to her shoulders teetered onto the stage. She was swathed in strips of white silk that looked like they'd been cut up from a wartime parachute and she was sporting a pair of long evening gloves that reached to her elbows. The silk was draped from her neck almost to the floor, which was quite a sight, and just her toes were visible, in a set of high heels.

As she started to move to the music being hammered out by the pianist, she became fluid, like water. One by one, the punters stopped talking and turned to stare at her. She was mesmerizing as she shimmied across the little stage, framed by moth-eaten velvet drapes, performing as if it was her moment on the silver screen. When she started to unravel the silk scarves to reveal her creamy white flesh, jaws hit the floor. Her hips took on a life of their own, gyrating and grinding, and as she unwound the silk from her ample bust, she revealed a couple of tassels covering her nipples. She twirled them to wolf whistles of appreciation.

After five minutes of stripping, this woman was standing starkers, except for that pair of long, black velvet evening gloves. She made a great show of peeling them down her arms and pulling them off before flinging them to her admirers. She finished her act with her back to the audience, giving them the full benefit of her peachy behind, before turning and blowing a kiss, to rapturous applause.

"How the bleeding hell am I going to follow that?" I said under my breath. I had no intention of taking my coat off in front of this bunch of perverts, let alone my underwear.

I was just making my way to the stage when the whole club was plunged into darkness and there were a few muffled screams from backstage as the stripper tripped over the dancing girls.

"Power out!" yelled a fella.

Candles appeared from under the bar and matches were pulled from jacket pockets to light them.

I stumbled up the steps at the front of the podium in the gloom, to shouts of "Get on with it or get off!"

"Just get 'em off!" boomed another voice.

"Show us your knockers, love!"

In the flickering candlelight I could just about make out a roomful of faces turning to look at me. I blushed crimson and began to sing.

My voice was clear as a bell: *"We'll meet again, don't know where don't know when . . ."*

And the piano player picked up the tune.

I sang from the heart: *"But I know we'll meet again some sunny day . . ."*

A few blokes started humming along and when I finished, someone at the back yelled, "Give us another one, then!"

The lights came on again just as a stocky man walked in, wearing the smartest pin-striped suit I'd ever laid eyes on, with a silk handkerchief protruding from his top pocket. He had slicked-back hair and a toothsome grin and was soon glad-handing blokes at the bar. He accepted a large whisky, lit up a smoke, and turned to watch me.

Well, I stood there, feeling like a complete idiot because when I opened my mouth, no sound came out.

He sipped at his drink, a smile playing on his lips, his eyes boring into mine with such intensity it made me feel hot.

"Come on, love. Give them something else, keep 'em happy," said the pianist, his fingers poised, ready to pick up the tune.

The candlelight cast shadows up the walls and in that moment, I wasn't in a Soho dive but back in chapel, singing to give myself hope.

"Come on!" hissed the pianist. "You haven't got all day, or they'll turn nasty."

I shuffled my feet for a moment, to find my footing on the stage, and then began to sing: *"Ave Maria, grazia plena, dominus tecum in mulieribus . . ."*

People stopped talking.

It was just me, and my voice, filling the room.

About halfway through the song, I realized the bloke at the bar was still watching me intently. This time, I met his gaze and sang the rest. He glanced away.

By the time I reached the last *"Ave Maria,"* my voice soared to the rafters and in the silence that followed, you could have heard a pin drop.

The big fella in the nice suit started to clap first, and others followed, whistling and cheering.

He whispered something to the barman, who came scampering over as I was leaving the stage, to rapturous applause. It was like being a star at the varieties.

"Mr. Sullivan says you have the voice of an angel, but you'd be better sticking to popular songs in his clubs."

"I'm sorry," I stammered. "It just came into my head. I don't know why I sang that." I'd only gone and messed up the audition in front of Billy Sullivan. What on earth was I going to tell Alice Diamond now?

The barman grinned. "But he told me to tell you, you're hired. You can start tomorrow."

My mouth fell open. I looked over to the gangster, who raised his glass.

"Well," said the barman, "what are you waiting for, blondie? Get yourself backstage to meet the others. If you ask nicely, one of them might sort you out with somewhere to stay."

The side door led down a narrow corridor to a dressing room the size of a postage stamp, where six dancing girls were crowded around a single mirror lit by a flickering light bulb.

One of them already had a thick layer of cold cream plastered on her face and the others were taking turns dipping their fingers in it, to remove their makeup. Up close they were pasty and a few of them had rows of bedbug bites up their scrawny arms. None of them said a single word to me.

The stripper was on her own in the corner, half-dressed, fixing her stockings to her suspender belt.

She glanced up. "Well, if it ain't the singing nun! Aren't you late for evening prayers?"

"Quite the comedian for someone who makes her living flashing her bits, ain't you?"

My hands clenched into fists. I'd just about had enough of today and the way I was feeling, I was ready to knock this mouthy bird into tomorrow.

"Oh, give over, I'm only joking," said the stripper, pulling a packet of cigarettes from the pocket of her blouse. "Smoke?"

I shook my head and bit my lip. Now I felt foolish for being so moody.

"It was just nerves made me forget what to sing, so 'Ave Maria' was all I could come up with," I said. "First time I've done an audition in my life."

"You'd never know from the way you were belting them out," said the stripper, smoothing her skirt down over her hips. "I thought you were a natural." She offered her hand to me. "I'm Violet, but everyone here calls me Gypsy."

The tallest of the dancers turned, her eyes narrowing to slits. "That's because you're a bleeding didicoy, ain't it? Should have stayed in your caravan in Wanstead."

Quick as a flash, Gypsy pulled off her shoe and lobbed it right at the dancer, hitting her in the mouth, making her cry, "Ow! You bitch!"

"Call me that again and I'll scratch your eyes out, you daft cow," said Gypsy.

The dancer made to launch herself at Gypsy, but I blocked her path.

"Don't talk to her like that, she's my pal," I said, squaring up to her, trying to imagine what Alice Diamond would do at a time like this. "I wouldn't want you to hurt yourself 'cos then you wouldn't be able to do that stupid dance of yours, would you?"

The dancer stared at me for a moment, but I stood my ground and glared back.

Gypsy threw her head back and laughed as the dancer scowled and slunk back to the dressing table mirror. Gypsy went back to tucking her skirt into her blouse and as she was pulling on her coat, she said, "You put her in her place good and proper. Fancy going for a cuppa and a bite to eat?"

I nodded.

"Good," said Gypsy, "'Cos it smells bad in here, don't it? I think it's those dancers with their rotten fannies."

That was the funniest thing I'd heard in ages and it set me off giggling. Gypsy and me linked arms and we strolled out of the dressing room, like old friends.

★

British Restaurants were still doing their bit all over London, serving up meat and two veg to the nation, just as they had during the war. Gypsy took me to her local just off Shaftesbury Avenue. You could get a two-course meal for little more than a shilling but as Gypsy piled rabbit stew onto her plate, I'd pretty much lost my appetite. Yes, I'd got myself a job in Billy Sullivan's club, but I was still miles away from finding out anything useful to Alice and The Forty Thieves and that was enough to put me off my dinner.

"So," said Gypsy, as she shoveledd in a mouthful of stew, "why are you up in town, Nell?"

"Don't get on with my dad, so I left after a fight," I said, giving my story a tryout. "I walked out and left my job in the sugar factory in the East End." It wasn't too much of a lie, so I was convincing enough. I didn't get on with Dad and had no intention of ever speaking to him again. "Thing is, I can't go back home because things got so bad indoors . . ."

"You can bunk up at my place, it's above a cobbler's off Drury Lane," said Gypsy. "It's only got one bed, but we can sleep top-to-toe, if you don't mind?"

I smiled. I would have slept in a pigsty at this point, I was just grateful to have a roof over my head in this weather. "I don't mind at all and can help with the rent. But what about your landlady, won't she have something to say about it?"

"Oh, she's deaf as a post and blind as a bat and going doolally, so she probably won't tell the difference between us," said Gypsy with a snort of laughter that made the couple at the next table look askance. The idea that I, with my newly platinum blonde hair, could be mistaken for the buxom brunette Gypsy was frankly ridiculous. That made me laugh out loud.

"You going to eat that?" said Gypsy, eyeing my plate of stew.

"Help yourself," I said, watching as Gypsy consumed it with gusto.

"So, what brought you to The Windsor?" I asked, as I sipped my tea. I was trying not to be a nosy cow, but Gypsy was something special.

"You mean why do I take my clothes off for a living?" said Gypsy, twirling a thick lock of hair around her fingers. "Anyone who performs is selling themselves, even those stuck-up dancers who think they are better than me. Well, they ain't. You might as well be hung for a sheep as a lamb, that's my motto, and I've got something worth looking at. I'm a solo act, I don't need a line of dozy cows high-kicking behind me to turn heads. You're the same with your singing. We're the stars. They're the support act."

"What about your family, don't they mind?"

"Me mum ran off with a Canadian airman at the end of the war, so she don't care. She was supposed to send for me, but she never did. And me dad, well, I don't care if he lives or dies. He's probably drunk in a ditch in Essex somewhere."

"Did you run away from home, then?"

Gypsy stopped smiling and a dark look crossed her face. "Things got difficult when Mum left. Dad was drinking and he kept finding his way into my bedroom after the pub . . ."

She stopped herself and stared into the depths of her tea. I understood, without Gypsy needing to say any more about what had happened.

"I didn't mean to pry."

"You ain't prying, it's fine," said Gypsy. "It's nice to have someone who's interested in what makes me tick without judging me. So, there was a fair in Wanstead Flats every year, with travelers and gypsies, and I ran away with them one summer and never went back home."

"Did you stay with them long?"

"Long enough to learn their language, didicoy, to pick up a few tricks of the trade like reading the tea leaves or telling fortunes," she said. "I tried to make a living doing that when I came to London after I left them. The winter after the war ended, they were moving up north and I wanted to stay down south so we parted company.

"Well, I can tell you, Nell, it's blooming hard making a living telling fortunes in pubs. People thought I was on the bleeding game half the time. I used to sneak into the cinema to keep warm and while I was watching the talkies for hours on end, I got the ideas for my act from the film stars."

"Don't you feel shy about getting your kit off?" I'd rather be burned alive than stand in front of strangers in my birthday suit.

Gypsy thought about it for a moment: "Nah," she said. "They can look at the goods, but they can't touch and anyway, I'm saving myself for the man of my dreams."

"Who's that then?" I said.

"Someone rich and good-looking, who's going to walk into the club one day and fall in love with me and treat me like a princess."

"You really think you're going to find that kind of a fella round here?" If I looked incredulous it's because I was.

"'Course I do!" said Gypsy, chucking a lump of sugar into her tea. "That's who I'm thinking about when I strip off."

Gypsy's eyes twinkled, and I could see why her parents had called her Violet because they were a stunning shade of mauve-blue when you looked at them up close. "Everyone should have a dream. What's yours, Nell?"

My dreams were mostly of how to get rid of Alice

Diamond but I wasn't about to spill the beans on that. Besides, dreaming about pushing her off a tall building or chucking her in the river with a knife in her back made me sound mad and I was trying to make friends. Gypsy wanted a roommate, not a deranged killer.

But in that moment, sitting in the British Restaurant, surrounded by glum couples silently struggling to force down a jam roly-poly, I said: "I'm going to have so much money that I don't need any man to take care of me."

Gypsy threw back her head and laughed loudly, so loudly that the couple at the next table got up and moved away in disgust.

"You are properly bonkers, Nell," she guffawed, slapping the table so that her tea spilled out of its china cup. "That'll never happen, never in a month of Sundays!"

I smiled at Gypsy but as we were rising to leave, something inside me snapped.

I muttered under my breath, "We'll see about that."

Chapter Seventeen

ALICE

Elephant and Castle, London, February 1947

I watched Nell trudge across the frozen courtyard with her little suitcase in her hand when she left Queen's Buildings to go to Soho on a little job for me. I've learned the hard way that it pays to make sure my girls are doing what they're told.

And as I was gazing out over my manor, I spied something else that piqued my interest, so I went downstairs for a closer look.

The tallyman's cart was pulling up and who should happen to be perched up there by his side, but another one of those Tenison Street girls. This one's called Iris and she's always got bruises. Most folks say her bloke is a nutcase.

The tallyman handed her a basket and then gave a cheery wave and flicked his whip over his old nag's haunches to get her moving through the snow.

I caught up with Iris as she was making her way to her tenement. The kids who were mucking around with lumps of ice as a football moved out of my way when they saw me coming. It's always like that. Sometimes I feel like Moses and the parting of the Red Sea whenever I leave Queen's Buildings.

"That looks heavy," I said, pointing to her basket full

of coney pelts. Fur-pulling—that's a bloody thankless task. Girls bring the piecework home to skin the rabbits in their flats. A basket full of bunny fluff gets everywhere and there's hardly any cash in it.

She took one look at me and flinched.

I know I have a reputation, but I wanted to show her I'm kind and caring at heart.

"Careful you don't slip, dearie," I said, linking my arm through hers.

I smiled at her. "You'll set tongues wagging riding with the tallyman like that. All the other housewives in Queen's Buildings will think you're getting a bit extra, if you know what I mean."

She bridled at that comment.

"He was just helping me get home safe 'cos I've taken on piecework to make a few bob and this filthy weather makes it hard to get home, that's all," she mumbled.

Snowflakes as big as florins were laying thickly on the ground in front of us.

"How's things indoors?" I said, spotting a fading bruise on her cheek.

"That's none of your business!" she shot back at me, pulling her coat closer around her middle.

"I'm just being friendly, as your neighbor," I soothed. "There's no need to be so chippy, love."

She looked as if she would crumple then.

"I'm sorry. I didn't mean to be rude. It's just I don't like people prying into my business."

"Then you shouldn't go around sporting a big black eye, should you? Looks like your hubby's been knocking the hell out of you. Am I right?"

"Tommy's a good man."

"Never said he wasn't," I replied. "Just think he's a bit handy with his fists, ain't he?"

"There's no work for my Tommy," said Iris, stopping for a moment, her eyes brimming with tears. "No one wants him on account of his moods, but he can't help it.

"Even minding the barrows over in Covent Garden's too much for Tommy's nerves. He nearly broke some kid's neck the other day for giving him lip and that was the end of that. People don't care that he's a war hero. He's just a nuisance to them now."

She sank to her knees on the cold, stone step and started to weep.

I sat down beside her.

"Us women look out for each other round here," I said. "You just have to let me know and maybe you can help us out and we can help you."

"I don't need your help," she said, standing up and drying her eyes. "My Tommy wouldn't hear of it either. Thanks for your concern all the same."

Now, I could have been offended by her giving me the bum's rush, but it was early days with Iris. She picked up her basket of fur pelts and disappeared inside the dark stairwell up to her flat and another evening walking on eggshells with Tommy.

Desperate women do desperate things, so I always like to know who might have their door open to me, so to speak. Even a tiny crack is enough for me to get my foot in.

And once I'm over the threshold and involved in your life, you won't find it easy to get rid of me.

Chapter Eighteen
NELL

Soho, London, March 1947

The gas was a blue ghost, flickering lamely on the stove as I heated the water to make a cup of tea.

Old Ma Harris hadn't noticed that Gypsy had a visitor lodging upstairs because we waited until she had battled her way out of the front door and through the snow to the grocer's shop before getting up. Gypsy and me would roll out of bed late in the morning, taking turns to brave the freezing scullery to make a cuppa, before getting dressed and scurrying off to the club for breakfast.

It was so perishing cold, all the girls were finding excuses to turn up well before their shifts. Even the mice were in early.

Dancers were endlessly sewing on sequins or mending their costumes and we pretended to work on our routines. The "come on" girls, whose job it was to persuade the punters to spend, spend, spend on watered-down drink, were hanging around so long in the club they'd practically taken root. Lou, the barman, didn't mind too much as long as we all did our best to foist something on the early customers: an overpriced greasy fry-up, a nasty little chop that passed for lunch, or some watered-down beer. He gave us commission on whatever extras we could flog and never missed an opportunity to make an extra bob or two.

Tomorrow was Saturday and I'd have to face Alice and persuade her to give me a bit more time to uncover the snitch. All the while, I kept my ears pricked for the slightest bit of gossip that could be useful but so far, apart from fellas coming in and handing over wads of cash to Billy as he sat at the bar every afternoon, I'd failed to even get a titbit of information.

As I sighed, my breath formed a little cloud in front of me. Mold bloomed up the ancient wallpaper, which was peeling where it met the cracked ceiling plaster. It was hard to say which was worse: Holloway Prison or this. I tiptoed across the freezing tiled floor to reach the kettle, which was whistling its head off. Back in Queen's Buildings, Alice Diamond was sitting pretty in that cozy kitchen of hers, with enough food to feed five families. It wasn't fair that the likes of her ponced off girls like me. My eyes hardened into little pebbles of hatred as I thought about how I'd trusted her like a fool, and she'd betrayed me and my baby.

The desire for revenge was a like a small fire inside me and I found myself stoking it to remind myself why I was here, in this shithole, and how I was going to claw my way out and bring Alice Diamond down a peg or two.

The water sploshed into Old Ma Harris's teapot. I swilled the used leaves around and around before refilling the kettle to get enough warm water for a quick wash in the basin upstairs.

Everyone smelled unwashed because everybody was these days; the reek of cheap perfume was the best most of the girls could do to cover it.

I carried two cups of weak tea upstairs to Gypsy, who

had the bedspread pulled over her head, so that just a mass of raven curls was visible, spilling out over the pillow.

I set the teacups down on the floor, beside a jam jar full of cigarette butts, and reached across the bed to pull open the gingham curtains that I'd made from a tablecloth hoisted from the British Restaurant. I was quite proud of those.

Gypsy was in awe of my daring, especially when I shoved a whole load of cutlery into my handbag for good measure, but right now, rubbing sleep out of her eyes, she was in a foul mood.

"Oh, give over!" cried Gypsy. "Can't a girl sleep?"

"Suit yourself," I said, "I'm not hanging about. It's like the Arctic in here."

I swigged the tea down in one gulp, pulled on my dress, and grabbed my shoes, stepping over a pile of Gypsy's discarded belongings. The floor was a mass of tangled stockings, lipsticks with no lids, half-empty jars of face cream, and empty aspirin bottles. A graying corselette and some knickers hung forlornly over the fireguard by the empty grate and Gypsy's dress from last night had been flung across the dressing table. The place looked as if it had been burgled and Gypsy snoozed on in the middle of the chaos, like Sleeping Beauty in a dosshouse.

As I was heading down the stairs, the front door pushed itself open and Old Ma Harris stood there, squinting up at me. I froze.

"Changed your hair?" the old woman said, her mouth pressing itself into a thin line of disapproval.

I nodded mutely and hurried down the stairs as Ma Harris shuffled off down the hall, before she realized that I wasn't her lodger.

As I was heading through the front door, Ma Harris shouted after me, "Makes you look like a cheap tart. And don't forget you still owe me for last week's rent!"

Gypsy was a terrible spendthrift. Most of her wages went on tat from Berwick Street market or on ludicrous high heels that were either too big or too small, so it was no wonder she was keeping Ma Harris short.

"I had to 'ave 'em!" she'd cry, cramming her feet into a teeny pair of court shoes, like some desperate Cinderella, or stuffing tissue paper down the ends of a pair of size nines, to stop them slipping off altogether. It was a wonder that Gypsy ever made it to the stage without falling flat on her face.

Outside on the street corner, a paper boy was flapping his arms about to keep warm and yelling the headlines about the Royal Family arriving in South Africa. It was all well and good for them escaping the big freeze. Meanwhile, the rest of the country had to put up with power cuts three days a week and the worst winter in living memory, which was dragging on with no sign of a thaw.

Soho was sugar-dredged in snow but even that couldn't disguise the grime as I made my way to Wardour Street, past firemen blasting the frozen tram points with a flame-thrower to shift the ice, as if they were battling the enemy.

Every doorway was dotted with piles of cigarette butts and old newspapers and shop windows were either black with filth, or bomb-damaged and boarded up.

Pushing open the door, the grimy staircase lay ahead of me. Down in The Windsor, the pianist was already tickling the ivories. The lights in the club were dimmed to lure the customers into forgetting the time and staying longer and the whole place was cocooned in semi-darkness, which left me half blind for a moment.

But I recognized the tune and started to sing along: *"I'll be seeing you, in all the old familiar places, that this heart of mine embraces . . ."*

I'd always loved the Billie Holiday song; Mum had sung it

to me during the blackout as we huddled in the tube station, when I was scared witless as bombs dropped overhead.

"All day through, in that small café, the park across the way . . ."

But as I got to the next line, about the children's carousel, the words stuck in my throat and my head started to spin. My life flashed before me. There we were, me and Jimmy, strolling arm in arm around the market in Waterloo, making plans for the future, and then me, full of rage, throwing his engagement ring back at him. I saw Joseph wrapped up in his pram, wearing the clothes I'd made him to keep warm, being pushed around the park by his adopted mother. A pang of longing shot through me. My knees went and my legs almost buckled.

A figure stepped out of the shadows and steadied me.

It was Billy Sullivan.

"Don't just stand there gawping, Lou," he barked at the barman, as he held me in his steady grip. "Get her a brandy."

Billy steered me gently by the elbow to a seat at his table, the one nearest the chrome-topped bar, which he used as his office during the day. His accounts ledgers were neatly stacked and Billy was always noting down the money that a steady stream of his Chaps brought to him.

I accepted the drink gratefully, craning my neck to have a peek at the names in that book of his, but Billy swiftly shut the ledger, away from my prying eyes.

"I'm sorry, Mr. Sullivan," I blurted, "I didn't mean to make a fuss . . ." The brandy was warming me from the inside and the room had stopped spinning.

Billy pulled up a chair, which screeched on the stone floor, and sat down opposite.

"You upset about something, Nell?" he said, his coal-black eyes searching my face. "Because I like to look after my staff and I'm here to help if you have any troubles . . ."

"No," I lied, banishing the image of baby Joseph from my mind. "Not at all, I just forgot to have breakfast, that's all."

"Well, in that case, Lou will get you some eggs, won't you, Lou?" he said. "Can't have my songbird starving, not in this weather."

The barman nodded and shot me a look that was nothing like pleasure at the prospect of having to fix me something to eat, because the cook hadn't managed to make his way in yet.

Billy pulled a silver cigarette case from the breast pocket of his immaculately pressed suit and flipped it open.

"Smoke?"

"No thanks," I said. Perhaps it was nerves, but my throat had started to feel dry and the last thing I needed was ciggie smoke when I had to sing for my supper.

Billy settled back in his chair and eyed me, thoughtfully. His hair was graying at the temples and slicked back. Everything about him was perfectly polished: shoes, nails, belt buckle, and even his white teeth, which he flashed when he smiled. He was thick-set, but his face was handsome, a bit like Humphrey Bogart, and there was something intense in his eyes that made me feel like he was undressing me. To my surprise, I quite enjoyed that thought.

"So, tell me a bit about yourself then, Nell. What brings you up to town to work at The Windsor?"

I flinched for a second at the question and a sip of brandy slipped down the back of my throat, setting off a coughing fit.

He leaned forward to pat me on the back and I caught a whiff of his aftershave. It smelled delicious, like lemons.

When I had recovered, I forced a smile and said, as casually as I could: "My family are from the East End, but we all got bombed out during the war. I had a job in the

Tate and Lyle factory for a while, but I left when I fell out with my dad, which is why I came to Soho. Things got bad indoors, I couldn't go home."

It wasn't too much of a lie. I began to relax.

"Know the Tate and Lyle factory well," said Billy, lighting up his smoke. "In fact, I remember old Banksy the foreman. Used to knock me off a few bags of sugar when we were running short. I like a sugar in my tea. You must know him?"

I swallowed hard and had to remind myself to keep breathing.

"Yes," I squeaked, taking another teensy sip of brandy to give me the Dutch courage needed to continue with my barefaced lies, "old Banksy was a real character. He loved a joke. Got me into trouble for laughing too much on the shop floor more than once." Now my heart was thumping ten to the dozen but there was something else, a lightness in my stomach, which was fluttering every time he looked at me. I clasped my hands together in my lap, willing it to stop.

Billy seemed satisfied with my answers and he chuckled to himself and stood up.

"Well, you take care, Nell. I've got a bit of business to attend to, but I look forward to seeing you perform the song later. Sounded nice."

He picked up his ledger, tucked it under his arm, and sauntered out of the club.

Lou slammed a plate of scrambled eggs down in front of me.

"Breakfast is served. Don't get used to it, Lady Muck," he grumbled. "And you can do your own bleeding washing up."

Flirting with the punters wasn't something I was very good at because my heart wasn't in it. Not like Gypsy and Alma, the lead dancer.

Those two would square up to each other like a pair of alley cats the moment someone wearing a half-decent suit set foot in the building because it meant he had money to spend. The fella had probably pawned his gran to buy his threads but no matter, in The Windsor, blokes liked to have cash to splash. Wedding rings were slipped off at the door and her indoors, with her headaches and housecoat, was out of sight and out of mind.

I had no illusions about what the blokes were after. I knew where it led, and I wasn't going to go there under any circumstances.

"Oh, be nice, blondie, come and sit on my knee, I'm lonely," said a horrible greasy-looking type with a beer gut spilling over his trousers. He reached out to paw at me as I tried to get past to go backstage.

The last thing I wanted was to make a fuss, because it would upset Lou the barman if I wasn't nice to the punters, and he was watching with a gimlet eye. But the thought of cozying up to this lump of lard was gut-wrenching.

"I ain't feeling too clever," I said apologetically. "Think I'm coming down with something—I wouldn't get too close if I were you."

But the man made a grab and pulled me to sit, planting a wet kiss on my cheek and pinching my bum. He smelled vile, like piss and boiled cabbage. I fought the urge to retch.

So's not to offend him, I started to laugh, nervously, and I was trying to wriggle myself free as his hands found their way up my skirt.

"Now, now! Don't touch the goods . . ."

But his fingers were dangerously near the tops of my stockings now, so I clamped my legs together in desperation.

"Let's order you a drink? What would you like?" I said, trying to fight him off. It was like wrestling a flaming octopus.

Glancing over to the bar, Lou was standing watching

with a look of amusement on his face. He wasn't going to stop this punter feeling me up, the bastard, and all because he'd been forced to cook breakfast.

Just then, a voice came from over my shoulder: "I think the lady has had enough, don't you?"

A tall man, smartly dressed and smooth-shaven, with a broad jaw and thick, wavy hair, strode across the club toward us. The big fella seemed to shrink visibly at the sight of him, relaxing his grip. I managed to stand up, smoothing down my skirt, which had found its way somewhere up close to my armpits. But not before the fat guy had muttered, "Prick tease," under his breath.

"What did you say?" said the man, putting his hands on the fat bloke's lapels and pulling him to his feet. A muscle twitched in his cheek.

"Nothing . . . didn't say anything," said the fat lump.

"I think you should apologize to the lady because this is a respectable establishment and not a knocking shop," said this knight in shining armor. I glanced around to see where he'd parked his horse.

"That's not what I've heard," replied the bloke, spittle forming at the corners of his rubbery bottom lip. "Everyone knows Billy doesn't mind if we get a bit friendly with the girls from time to time."

The other man pulled something out of his pocket and flicked it open. The flash of a steel blade glinted in the light as it was held to the big lump's cheek.

"I'll pretend I didn't hear that, and it's Mr. Sullivan to you, you lousy piece of shit," said the man, whose suit was as sharp as his razor.

"No offense, honest," said the fat bloke, putting his hands up, "I was only fooling around. Sorry, love." He pulled on his grubby overcoat, quick as lightning, and headed for the door.

My rescuer turned to face me, greeting me with the most startling pair of deep-set blue eyes I'd ever seen. "Are you alright?"

For a moment, I was speechless.

Out of nowhere, Lou loomed large, barging into the conversation.

"She's alright but the silly moo just lost us money for drinks by being so prim and bloody proper, that's what! I keep telling the girls, Albert, but they won't listen. Maybe you should have a word with Mr. Sullivan about it?"

"Oh, belt up, Lou!" said the fella. "You can't have oiks like that feeling up the girls. It ain't right. Cheapens the place. Now why don't you sod off and polish some glasses?"

Lou scowled and turned on his heel back to the bar.

The man smiled and out of nowhere, Gypsy appeared by my side, dressed in a silk dressing gown, gazing coyly from under her curls.

"I'm Albert, Albert Rossi," he said, leaning over to shake me by the hand. He was, quite simply, the best-looking bloke I had ever seen. Gypsy offered her hand as well, just for good measure, and he took his time giving it back to her.

"I'm a friend and business partner of Billy Sullivan's, and you two must be his top acts. He's told me so much about you both. Perhaps we could all get together for a drink one evening after work?"

Gypsy almost swooned at that.

"We'd love to!" she gushed before I could get a word in edgewise.

For some reason, I couldn't get Billy Sullivan off my mind all afternoon even though I had to put up with Gypsy yacking on about the delectable Albert Rossi.

Gypsy had filled me in on everything she knew about him, at least ten times.

"Ooh, the Italian dreamboat," she swooned, as we got ready backstage. "He's got a whole fleet of cars that he runs for Billy, from Tottenham Court Road. There's a petrol coupon racket going up there, mark my words, but Albert could drive me home any time of the day . . . or night."

She shrieked with laughter and Alma and the other dancers shot her a dirty look.

"He's a proper charmer but he's never tried it on with anyone here," said Gypsy, doing up her suspender belt. "And more's the pity. Some girls practically *throw* themselves at Albert, but that just makes them look like tarts 'cos he ain't interested.

"But, of course, it's different when he's the one inviting *us* out for a drink," she said, with a note of triumph in her voice.

Gypsy looked pointedly at Alma, who flicked the V sign back at her.

"Albert is only interested in the quality," drawled Alma, "so don't get your hopes up, Gypsy. He's way out of your league. Someone told me he had his heart broken by a proper toff.

"And what about you?" Alma sneered in my direction. "We saw you sucking up to the boss. Don't think for a minute that Mr. Sullivan would give you a second glance!"

"I wasn't thinking about him in that way at all," I shot back, turning away and applying some lipstick so she wouldn't see the blush that was forming on my cheeks. "He just wanted to know a bit more about me."

Alma laughed like a drain and gathered into a little huddle with the other dancers, who started whispering loudly about "tarts."

Gypsy lowered her voice. "Do you think Billy Sullivan fancies you, Nell? I reckon you might have hit the jack-pot!"

"Don't be daft," I replied, blotting the lippy carefully

with a handkerchief, to give it staying power. "He was just concerned because I didn't feel too well, that's all."

But the very mention of his name made me feel a little flutter of excitement again, as if a candle had been lit and was glowing in the darkness. I tried to snuff it out because it was wrong. Billy was a dangerous man and someone I was supposed to be spying on. But it glowed on, regardless.

The club was packed to the rafters that evening and I scoured the audience for any sign of Billy, while Gypsy ran around picking up the feathered boas that she'd flung off at the end of her act.

But he was nowhere to be seen and, as I stepped up to the microphone and began to sing, I felt a little stab of disappointment at that. The punters were in high spirits, calling for an encore, and so I decided to try my new song.

I'd only sung a few notes when a crowd of fellas tumbled through the doors, with Billy Sullivan at their center, and Albert Rossi by his side. They were in high spirits, laughing and joking, and a few of them were nursing cuts and bruises and reliving whatever fight it was they'd just been involved in.

My voice faltered over the din. It was like having to sing in assembly in front of the whole school with kids chattering away. Then Billy's eyes locked onto mine and I found I wasn't scared anymore.

He signaled for hush and the fellas around him fell silent and turned to look at me.

There were whoops and cheers at my rendition of "I'll Be Seeing You" and Billy Sullivan pushed his way through the crowded club to the edge of the stage. He held out his hand to help me down, clapping along with everyone. I felt proud that he was making a point of coming to greet me, as if I was the star of his club.

I smelled the whisky on his breath as he whispered, "I'd like a word in private."

Before I knew what was happening, his hand was on the small of my back, guiding me through the side door and up the corridor, past the changing room, to a back room that was out of bounds to the girls. Lou had made that much clear.

He pulled a key from his trouser pocket and unlocked it, holding the door open and ushering me inside. The room stank of stale smoke and was rather bare. There was a faded carpet and some leather easy chairs along one wall. The blind at the window was pulled firmly shut. I realized this must be where Billy had his business meetings, the most secret ones, with his gang.

There was a leather-topped desk with a lamp, a letter opener, ink and a fountain pen on the blotting pad, and a stack of accounts ledgers in a neat pile. A faded photograph of a couple of kids in old-fashioned clothes stood in a silver frame and beside that was an expensive-looking cigar box and a cut-class decanter filled with amber liquid on a tray with crystal glasses. Squatting in the corner was a large safe and beside that, a metal filing cabinet.

He pointed to a rickety wooden chair in front of the desk and I sat down.

"Feeling better?" he said, flipping open the cigar box and selecting one for himself. He rolled it back and forth between his fingers and then struck a match from a packet in his pocket. It flared for a moment and he lit the cigar.

"Yes, I'm back to my old self," I said, shifting nervously in the chair. What on earth was I even doing here?

"Quite a performance you put on tonight," he said drily.

"Thanks," I replied, biting my lip. "Very kind of you to say so."

I looked more closely at the old photograph, desperate

to find something to say to break the awkward silence. The boy was Billy Sullivan in his younger years, dressed in a flat cap, white collarless shirt, and breeches; glaring insolently at the camera with those unmistakably devilish dark eyes. The girl was gazing up at him adoringly, her long, dark hair tumbling over her shoulders.

It was strange to think of Billy belonging to a family. He was the kind of bloke who looked as if he'd been born a gangster but here was a girl, looking up at him as if he were her handsome prince.

"Is that your sister?" I said, my mouth running away with me.

"Yes," he said, moving around to my side of the desk and picking up the frame for a moment. "She left me when she was young, too young," he said, with a note of regret in his voice. "I think of her often."

"I'm sorry for your loss," I whispered, afraid that I'd put my foot in it. "It must be hard to lose your sister."

Suddenly, he clasped hold of my wrist, puffing on his cigar until the end glowed red. Then he took it out of his mouth and placed it close to my arm, so close I could feel the heat of it starting to burn my skin.

"Please," I said, tears welling in my eyes as I tried and failed to pull away. "You're hurting me!"

He smiled and it was more like a snarl, as he placed the cigar back between his teeth, still keeping a firm hold of me.

"Yes, quite a performance you gave us, Nell. Old Banksy ain't the foreman at Tate and Lyle because he don't exist. But you know that, don't you?"

I stared at the carpet, which was flecked with dark stains, as if someone had spilled ink all over it.

"But I like you, so start explaining yourself before I change my mind and show you what happens to women who cross me."

★

My mouth was drier than the desert as Billy's coal-black eyes bored into mine. He relaxed his grip and I sank back into the wooden chair.

"You'll only get one chance," he said, perching himself on the edge of the desk and pouring himself a whisky from the cut-glass decanter. "So, I'd make it good before I find a way of loosening your tongue. I think you get the picture, don't you?"

He rolled the cigar smoke around his mouth and blew it out, slowly.

My mind was racing but everything was moving in slow motion. I stared at the floor. No words came.

"Who sent you?" he said, lunging forward and clasping a clump of hair at the nape of my neck so that I had to look up at him, bringing tears to my eyes.

"I'm one of Alice Diamond's girls," I said hoarsely. "I had no choice but to come over here and spy on you." He raised an eyebrow and relaxed his fingers, letting them trail through my hair, stroking my neck, very gently. My scalp throbbed but his caress almost made me purr.

"Well, well. Now you've got my attention," he said, moving away from me to the chair on the other side of the desk and settling himself down in it. "Tell me more."

"I was learning to be one of The Forty Thieves, before I got my collar felt by the law a few months back," I began. "I only went shopping with them once, but I'd learned the tricks of the trade with Alice." I was fumbling with my fingers, which seemed to have developed a life of their own.

"I see," said Billy icily. "Go on . . ."

"Thing was I was already in trouble because I was pregnant, so the cozzer took pity and he didn't arrest me. He took me home and told my parents. I got a right belting off my dad and then I was sent away to have the baby." The words came rushing out. I didn't want to confess to being a jailbird, so I was a bit economical with the truth, not that it was going to get me out of this tight spot any easier.

"Quite a story. I don't know what it is about you girls these days," said Billy, tutting and smiling to himself.

That made me blush crimson. Telling Billy about getting myself into trouble with the baby was humiliating but there was no other way.

"By the time I came home, my dad had run up gambling debts and the whole family was in hock to Alice. I couldn't go home because my dad didn't want to see me, and in any case, Alice had other plans . . ."

"What kind of plans? She ain't exactly a criminal mastermind, is she? Good at hoisting but that's about the sum of it!" He guffawed. "Alice Diamond, indeed! She should stay in Woolworths, on her side of the water, where she belongs."

"Alice was worried that someone was grassing up her girls because they kept getting nicked when they were going shopping. It was like someone was tipping the cozzers the wink. That's what she thought," I said.

"Did she now?" said Billy, thoughtfully blowing a smoke ring up to the ceiling. "Thought I might have had something to do with it, I suppose?"

I nodded. You could have heard a pin drop.

"I hear lots of things, as you can imagine, in my line of business," Billy said softly. "But, as it happens, someone round the Elephant and Castle was singing like a canary about the comings and goings of The Forty Thieves. So, on this occasion, she was right."

My heart was pounding. This wasn't how I'd expected to find out about the snitch, not directly from Billy Sullivan himself. I had a horrible feeling about that, right in the pit of my stomach.

"Times are getting harder for businessmen like me and the cozzers don't like all the high-profile thefts from the stores when everyone is tightening their belts. The Forty Thieves like their luxury goods, don't they? It makes people, decent people, feel . . . uncomfortable, cheated and at times like that, the police start trying to make my life a bit difficult. So, of course, I was happy to pass on what I could about the hoisters from The Forty Thieves, just in the interests of doing my civic duty."

I bristled at the thought of what Alice would say about that. The King of Soho was dobbing us in it to save his own skin, just as she had suspected.

Billy was warming to his theme and seemed to be enjoying every minute of my discomfort. "Oh, don't be offended, Nell. This is just how business is done among us fellas. Up here in Soho, we have good relations with the police. We hear things, they hear things. It works both ways. People don't want gangs of shoplifters steaming through their stores, not after there's been a war on and we're all still living on the ration. These silly girl gangs grab headlines. It ain't good for business, real business. And that's what us men are all about."

Well, I almost laughed at the thought of Billy, struggling to get by on rations with his petrol coupon fiddles and his nightclubs and his expensive tailored suits. But I didn't dare.

He leaned forward, so I caught another whiff of the whisky on his breath, as he whispered conspiratorially, "I'll let you into a secret. The information I got about Alice and The Forty Thieves was payback of sorts, because the fella that told me owed me for a consignment of silk stockings that got nicked off the back of his cart outside Queen's Buildings, right on Alice Diamond's doorstep. We all know who the likely culprit was, but of course, nobody there would breathe a word about it. All his customers said they were busy having a cup of tea at the time and nobody had seen a thing. Funny that.

"So, the tallyman had to find a way to make it good before I showed him how upset I was about losing so much good stock."

"The tallyman!" I said, before I could stop myself. "That slimy bastard. I never liked him. I knew he was a rat."

Billy laughed.

"It weren't actually him who grassed, though. It's some bird he's shagging who's his eyes and ears who really did the dirty work."

"Someone with a debt to pay him?" My heart sank as I thought back to Iris and how much she was struggling when we were back in Tenison Street. God only knows how she was coping now, but would she have sunk so low?

"Do you know who it was?" I asked.

"Can't say I know or care," said Billy airily. "People always have their reasons to talk, don't they? But I have to say, your tallyman has got a big mouth and he can't keep his dick in his trousers. If he'd been doing his job properly instead of getting his leg over, those stockings would have earned me a pretty penny. So, you're welcome to that bit of information, as long as Alice Diamond don't find out it came directly from me."

He blew another perfect smoke ring and it seemed to please him. He watched it for a moment before it disappeared.

"But now we are better acquainted, in future, Nell, I expect you to keep me filled in about what The Forty Thieves are up to. You could be quite a good source of information."

I gasped. "She'll bloody kill me if she finds out!"

"I'd hate to think what will happen to you if you decide not to help me," he murmured.

"But how I am supposed to convince her that I found out so much about the grass in the first place?" I said desperately.

"Oh, you'll think of something," said Billy, standing up and brushing the creases out of his trousers. "You're quite good at making up lies, aren't you? Just ask Old Banksy."

He moved back around the desk toward me, like a tiger stalking his prey.

"You're taking money from me, Nell, which means you are loyal to me," he said, with such menace that my heart skipped a beat.

"I don't mind you going out hoisting with Alice and her girls, that's fine, nick yourself a few nice outfits for the club while you are on about it because I like my girls to look their best." He waved his hands in the air, like he was conducting an orchestra. "Play along, keep her sweet. But the minute I find out you're ratting on me, I will make whatever Alice Diamond can threaten you or your family with look like a stay in the Ritz Hotel, do you get me?"

"Yes, Mr. Sullivan," I stammered.

"It's alright, sweetheart," he said. "Now we're friends, you can call me Billy."

He smiled warmly, leaning over to tuck a stray strand of hair behind my ear, but his eyes were cold and dark and I felt if I stared too long, I might drown in their depths.

"You've such a lovely face, nice features," he whispered, his hands working their way across my shoulders. I could feel my body responding to his touch.

"It would be such a shame to have to spoil it, because people like to look at the club singer, especially when she's pretty, like you."

He let that thought sink in. I began to tremble from my head to my feet, which were practically tap dancing. The more I tried to keep still, the worse it got. More alarmingly, my insides felt all squishy every time I looked at him and I was powerless to stop it.

I turned away, studying the ink stains on the carpet in front of me.

It was only when I looked more closely that I realized, with horror, that they were not ink, but spots of dried blood.

Billy Sullivan was expecting me to be his eyes and ears, to spy on The Forty Thieves, and Alice wanted me to spy on him.

I was in gangland now and I was playing with fire.

The question was, whose gang was I in?

Chapter Nineteen
ALICE

Soho, London, March 1947

I always get butterflies in my stomach when I go shopping up West. It's the excitement of knowing there's going to be some good stuff to nick. Lately, I know there's more of a risk of getting caught and that's been making me rather nervous in a way I'm not very fond of.

The newspapers are full of headlines about rascals on the take, stealing rather than doing an honest day's work. Well, let the cozzers round up the spivvy fellas selling paper flowers and tat on street corners for a few shillings. I'm all for a clear-out of the chaps who are so feckless they are poncing off decent folk.

I've had enough of all the patter that their wares are "speshul, love" because, frankly, it makes it harder for me to sell decent stuff at a good price to my punters who are counting the pennies more than ever. I'm sick and tired of being undercut by their rubbish. Most of these spivs are draft dodgers or deserters who never did their bit in the first place and their shoddy knockoff goods are giving us hoisters a bad name. I'd love it if the cozzers would go one better than that and call on the Mr. Bigs, all the gangland bosses over in Soho who sit there sipping whisky in their spielers until all hours, while they pull the strings on the spivs plaguing our street corners.

Round 'em up, I say, and get them down the Labour Exchange to do an honest day's work. But leave me and my girls to do a fair day's thieving because the price of clothing these days is just daylight robbery for us ladies and we have dug for Britain and kept the home fires burning during the long war.

Now it's time for us to at least have a few nice threads to put on, ain't it? We ain't harming anyone by hoisting a few dresses, because it's all covered by the shop's insurance, so who are we stealing from exactly?

As we glided through the backstreets of the West End in my Chrysler, I couldn't help noticing that the streets were full of people queuing patiently. Truly, I have never known a nation like it. If there was a prize for queuing, the British would win it. Queues for tobacco, for the cinema, for spuds even in this perishing weather under such leaden skies. Why anyone would want to stand around freezing on the pavement is beyond me. My toes were nice and toasty in a lovely fur-lined pair of boots I hoisted from Derry and Toms up on Kensington High Street last winter and that is how they would stay if I had any say in the matter, snowdrifts or no snowdrifts.

Molly leaned over to give me one bit of good news, in between slugs of gin from her hipflask.

"The blackout's back from tonight," she slurred. "Newspaper seller told me this morning the gas lamps and electric will go off overnight for the foreseeable because of the power and coal shortages."

That took the chill off the air because the blackout meant it would be easier for us to shift our wares to our fences. I don't really go in for religion, but I said a prayer of thanks. Shop assistants were already bumbling around by candlelight in the late afternoons because of the power cuts, but this was like hitting the jackpot. A genuine cloak of darkness would make thieving so much simpler. For a moment, I almost got a bit teary-eyed remembering the good old days of the Blitz.

But then we drew up outside the Lyons Corner Tea House on Shaftesbury Avenue and I remembered I had to have a meet with my underworld spy: little Nell.

Nell was waiting for me, dunking a biscuit in a cuppa, with a face like a wet weekend.

"How's clubland treating you?" I purred, sliding into a seat next to her.

"It's about as welcome as cancer," she replied.

"That bad, is it?"

"Punters are feeling me up, the digs I'm in are colder than Siberia, and the pay is lousy, but other than that, life onstage is just fantastic, thanks," she spat.

Honestly, she was such an ungrateful little wretch, after all I'd done for her.

"Beggars can't be choosers, can they, Nell?" I said smoothly. "Everyone has to start somewhere. At least you aren't fur-pulling and doing piecework to make ends meet like your old chum Iris . . ."

"Have you seen her?" said Nell, leaning forward with eyes like a little eager bunny. "How's she doing?"

"She looked like a woman who's got a lot of trouble with him indoors last time I caught sight of her," I quipped, watching Nell's face fall. "But enough of her. Did you find out who has been snitching on my gang, in between enjoying the limelight?" I said, pinching one of her biscuits and taking a bite.

"I did hear a bit of a whisper," she said, averting her gaze. She spoke slowly, as if she was choosing her words carefully. "The barman told me that someone's been grassing up The Forty Thieves, from inside Queen's Buildings."

"Interesting," I said, chewing thoughtfully. "Any ideas who that could be, Nell?"

She glanced around the room, as if the answer was sitting at one of the little gingham-topped tables and might dash over to help her out. Then she spluttered into her tea, "No, no idea, sorry."

"Try harder, love," I said, putting my hand on her knee and giving it a squeeze, so that my nails were just starting to dig in. "Think."

She winced under my grip.

"I think I heard someone mention the tallyman was involved but I couldn't be sure. Billy told the barman it was probably some gossipy housewife who was helping him because she was just jealous of all the finery the Forties go about wearing," she stammered.

Well, you didn't need to be Sherlock Holmes to work out who the most likely snitch was, did you? The vision of Iris sitting alongside the tallyman on his cart, like the Queen of Sheba, was etched in my memory. But it was more fun to keep Nell guessing whether I'd worked out her friend Iris was a blabbermouth because that way I could test her loyalty to me a bit more.

I relaxed my grip and smiled at her. "Billy? Not Mr. Sullivan? Sounds like you have got to know him quite personally, Nell."

"God, no!" she said, recoiling in horror. "Nothing like that! He lets all the staff call him Billy, that's all. I don't know him from Adam. He just pays my wages."

There was a flicker of something in her eyes. Just a flicker, but it concerned me. What was she up to? I began to wonder how cozy she'd got with Billy Sullivan.

"Is that right?" I said. "I thought *I* paid your wages . . ."

"I didn't mean it like that!" she muttered, turning red in the face. "You pay my wages, Alice, I ain't saying otherwise. I'm in The Forty Thieves—that's why I'm working my arse off in that stupid club. It just came out wrong."

She hissed at me through gritted teeth, "I know where my loyalties lie."

"There, there," I said, giving her arm a little pat, "don't upset yourself, we ain't falling out and certainly not over a blooming fella like this Billy Sullivan."

That seemed to make her relax. She forced a smile. But my interest was piqued.

"But tell me, what's he like? Is he scary?"

"Terrifying," said Nell, the color draining from her cheeks. "He's got eyes like a bottomless pit. Fellas come in at all hours to pay their dues and give him a cut of whatever they've earned. He keeps a big ledger in his office with all the figures in it. He's got the whole of Soho dancing to his tune."

"Has he?" I drummed my fingers on the table in front of me. "Well, we'll have to see about that."

"Do you need me to try to find out more? To see if there's some other way to get one over on him?" she said, brightening. She almost looked quite keen.

"Are you volunteering?"

"I just overheard something at the bar, it's probably nothing . . ." she said, glancing away.

"What did you hear? You'd better spit it out," I said. If Sullivan was up to something, I wanted to be the first to know.

"Just that the grassing you up was the start of it," she said. "I didn't want to worry you, but I think they're going to try to drive you out of the West End. Billy Sullivan and his mob are trying to take the heat off their bit of business by making the cozzers focus on yours. I might be able to find out more, but I'm going to need to stay undercover in Soho to do it."

I mulled it over for a moment. I quite liked the idea of a permanent spy in Billy Sullivan's camp. But it troubled me a little that she was so keen, especially given how much she said she hated clubland.

"You can stay in Soho, for now," I said. "But I'll keep a close eye on you and it won't be forever. Don't get too comfy in your sequins."

I pointed to her tea, which was stone cold.

"Drink up, we're going shopping. Did you remember your hoister's drawers?"

She downed it in one gulp and traipsed after me to the car. "Yes, Alice."

Now, I don't know which bright spark it was who decided to put a garden on top of a shop in Kensington, but if you've never seen the view from the famous roof gardens of Derry and Tom's, you ain't lived. Whoever it was had more money than sense because they even brought in a load of pink flamingos to strut about and startle the posh ladies while they eat their cucumber sandwiches.

I love it up there, mainly because hiding behind the bushes is a perfect place for a bag swap, but also for the view. I can see right over the roofs to Kensington Palace, where the other Queen of London likes to take her tea. Granted, it's always a bit chilly in winter, but the pleasure gardens of Derry and Tom's truly are a hoister's paradise.

As we drew up to the store, I told my driver to keep the engine running outside, in case we needed to make a quick getaway.

We turned heads, stepping out of my car, looking like three well-to-do ladies on a nice afternoon jaunt.

"Tell me we don't have to go and freeze our knockers

off on the top of the shop again," groaned Molly, pulling her mink stole tighter around her shoulders as we shuffled through the snow.

Molly hated heights, especially when she'd been on the sauce. She claimed it brought on her vertigo up on the roof but I think it was just the ride up in the lift made her feel sick as a dog because she was half-cut and unsteady on her feet.

"Oh, show some enthusiasm, Molly," I chided. "It's Nell's first time in Derry and Tom's and she needs to know the lie of the land."

A blast of heat escaped as we pushed open the heavy glass doors to the shop and stepped inside.

The color returned to Nell's cheeks as we wandered the length of the elegant downstairs shop floor, stopping at glass cabinets filled with bracelets, watches, rings, and every kind of jewelry. I let her linger and take it all in while Molly scoured the shop for walkers.

I could see by the look on Nell's face that she was dying to nick something; she was like a kid in a sweet shop. I liked that, it meant she hadn't lost her bottle.

"We'll do those last," I said. "Let's start with some nice furs. There's a good market for them in this freezing weather."

Nell nodded in agreement.

"Nervous?" I said, tucking a lovely woollen scarf into my handbag as we walked past a display stand near the door, which was piled high with knitted goods.

"A bit," she said. "I just don't want to get caught like last time."

"Oh, you won't, that was just bad luck," I chided.

She gave me a funny look and then glanced away. "Really bad luck."

"Once you get back into it, you'll remember everything,"

I said. "It's like riding a bike. I promise I will look after you, Nell, you are one of my girls."

She seemed mollified by that.

We climbed the staircase to the first floor and I had to stop halfway and lean on my silver-topped cane. My legs weren't as fast as they used to be and although I didn't admit it, that was troubling me. That stick weren't just for show these days or for thwacking people round the head with. I needed it because sometimes, out of the blue, my legs were going all sort of numb and tingly; a bit like when you've slept badly and you get that dead-leg feeling.

Nell clocked me resting.

"Everything alright, Alice?"

"Yes, just out of puff," I lied, gritting my teeth and climbing the last flight of stairs.

The fur floor at Derry and Tom's was packed to the rafters with women trying things on, parading up and down in fur mufflers and hats, while shop assistants darted to and fro, laden with pelts.

The sight of such rich pickings made my heart beat a little faster. There were beautiful musquash, long sable wraps, blue fox stoles, and rails full of marmot and mink. It was like half the Canadian wilderness was in there, ready to be nicked. The only question was how many trips could we make before we were spotted?

Molly sidled up, having scouted the place, and pulled off her beige wool overcoat, to reveal a thigh-skimming sable fur. With Nell by my side, I went to the rails and found another fur exactly like it and all three of us stood by the mirror as I slipped it on.

"Looks very lovely on Madam," said an elderly female shop assistant. "Would Madam like to try the hat to go with it?"

"Yes, Madam would," I said, as Nell suppressed a giggle.

While her back was turned, Molly and me swapped coats.

Quick as a flash, I told Nell to pull another sable from the rails and try that on, to create a bit of a distraction. Nell was fumbling around over the other side of the rails as I saw the shop assistant returning, brandishing the most enormous fur hat.

"Hurry up, Nell!" I hissed.

Quick as a flash, Molly put her woollen coat on over the top of the fur I had given her and strolled off, and soon just her red hair was visible, at the other end of the shop floor.

Nell stood there, twirling around in her fur coat, while I tried the hat on.

"No, I don't think it suits me after all," I said, struggling to keep a straight face as I handed it back to the assistant. I looked like one of the guards on parade outside Buckingham Palace, in one of those massive bearskin hats.

"Nell, you do look a sight in that coat, put it back on the hanger, darling, because Mummy is not going to pay for that," I added sweetly.

Molly was already nowhere to be seen, so the pair of us went to walk off toward the staircase when the shop assistant grabbed at my arm.

"You need to return that fur!" she said, rather too loudly for my liking.

"You are mistaken," I said, brushing her off and opening my coat to show her the label. "How dare you accuse me! This is a Gamages fur!" And that was no lie, for indeed it was; one I'd hoisted from Gamages in my drawers last week.

"I'm so sorry, my mistake, Madam," she said, returning to the rails and flicking through, as if she was counting her stock.

"I should think so too!" I huffed.

I had already stuffed the spare hanger in my handbag, safe in the knowledge that Molly would be depositing a fine sable coat from Derry and Tom's in the trunk of my car outside.

"That was the shuffle," I explained to Nell, as we went down in the lift to have a closer look at the jewelry on the ground floor. "It's all about distraction. It's a bit like a music hall act or one of those chase-the-lady card games, where the punters are the mugs because they always lose. Well, the shop always loses on this one. When we go back up you can have a go at clouting a mink stole, to see how much you can remember."

"I already have," she said with a laugh, waddling along like a duck. "I did it when you were trying on the hat. It's tucked down the leg of my knickers."

"You are a crafty little devil," I murmured in approval.

"Oh, you have no clue," she said, smiling at me, her eyes dancing with delight. "That was fun!"

I knew I was right about her from the get-go, but that proved it. I pushed the niggling doubt I had about her and Billy Sullivan getting too cozy to the back of my mind.

Nell was born to be one of The Forty Thieves, just like me.

Chapter Twenty

NELL

Kensington, London, March 1947

They say diamonds are a girl's best friend and that day in Derry and Tom's, I became mates with them for the first time in my life.

As we swept back into the shop, the sight of so many wealthy women swarming around displays of opulent gold jewelry almost overpowered me. They had long, elegant necks, like swans, and they wore beautifully fitted leather gloves that showed off their delicate fingers as they picked their way through tray after tray of gems that would cost more than a year's salary for any man.

I ain't ashamed to say I wanted to be like them. I wanted to have so much money that I could afford to flit like a butterfly between precious stones. Being with The Forty Thieves offered me some hope of owning a few stones of my own. Don't get me wrong, I hadn't forgotten about getting even with Alice but as I was here anyway, I wasn't going to look a gift horse in the mouth, was I? Besides, I had to keep her sweet, to get her to trust me, so that she'd never see the fatal blow coming until it was too late.

"See anything you fancy?" murmured Alice.

"All of it," I said, my eyes gleaming with desire.

"My daughter would like to look at some engagement rings," Alice chimed in her plummiest voice.

As a creaky old shop assistant pulled a velvet-backed tray full of sparklers out from under the counter, I began to understand the thrill of hoisting, the pleasure of touching luxury and the temptation to tuck it away in a pocket, rather than paying for it at the till. It was like a drug and I was hooked. He laid the tray in front of me and I held a dazzling square-cut emerald ring up to the light, mesmerized by it.

"Let's see what we can filch," Molly breathed in my ear. "Can I have a closer look at that one, please, my good man," she said, grandly pointing a fat finger at another tray in the glass case.

While the bald-headed assistant bobbed down to oblige, she deftly swiped a diamond solitaire from my tray and Alice quickly replaced it with a paste one she had concealed in her gloved palm. They were like a double act; well rehearsed, with perfect timing. I felt like an onlooker but I didn't care. I was in heaven surrounded by so much luxury and I was learning fast. These were all skills I was planning to steal and use for myself, once I had put paid to Alice's hoisting career.

Through the window, dusk was falling on the snow-covered streets and dim lights flickered softly, making everything feel so cozy. Assistants spoke in whispers to each other, their voices little more than quiet echoes in the showroom. There were marble columns and mirrors everywhere, so that the women could see how gorgeous they looked in their winter coats, with swagged shoulders and huge turned-back cuffs, diamonds glinting at their ears and throats.

I put the emerald ring on my finger and it shone. I imagined being the kind of Kensington lady who would get up and choose what jewels to wear, perhaps to have a different one for every day of the week, instead of freezing half to death in a shared bedroom above a cobbler's in Soho.

"May we see some watches?" said Alice, pulling the ring off my finger and handing it back to the assistant. There was another emerald ring next to it, smaller, round, but just as lovely. My fingers traced across the stone, longingly, for an instant before Alice dug me in the ribs, quite hard, to get me to focus. I wanted to slap her for that but instead I smiled placidly.

He nodded his approval and we moved to the next counter, where he produced another tray of ladies' wrist-watches; dainty little things in yellow gold. One had diamonds around the clockface and I knew from the moment I laid eyes on it that Alice was going to nick it. She just glowed when she looked at it.

"Coughing fit," she whispered, and I dutifully pretended to choke, clasping my throat.

"Oh, my dear!" cried the assistant. "Are you alright?"

"I think it might be the flu," I gasped. I flung myself forward over the counter, knocking the tray of watches flying, as Alice shoved something in my pocket with one hand and slammed a couple of fake watches down on the glass top with her other.

Other shoppers turned around, startled, and I pulled myself up straight, clearing my throat, as Molly slapped me on the back, harder than was necessary. She nearly knocked me flat again.

"I think my daughter might need a little air," said Alice smoothly. "Thank you for your time."

With that, we strolled toward the lift.

"I am not going up to that sodding roof garden," scowled Molly. "I'll take the stairs back to furs, nick a few bits and pieces, and then meet you in the car."

"Oh, suit yourself," said Alice. She was grinning from ear to ear as she turned to face me.

"Well done, Nell," she said. "Quite a performance. You are a natural at this."

I was honing my acting skills by pretending to be in her thrall the whole time. Shakespeare himself would have been proud of me.

I put my hand in my pocket and felt the roundness of a clockface and the leather strap.

"You can give it to me but don't take it out, not yet, it's not safe," Alice whispered as we got into the lift.

And then I saw him, striding toward us, just as the lift doors were closing. Alice stepped forward to press the button to make the lift go up, but he pushed through and practically bumped into her, forcing his way inside.

I'd like to think it was my desire for revenge that made me do it, but in the moment, it was more like fear. I dropped the watch into Alice's pocket while she had her back to me.

Then the doors closed and all three of us were heading skywards, to the top floor.

"Hello, Nell," said Detective Sgt. Eddie Hart, as I shrank back in terror. "Who's your friend?"

"I'm Annie Black, a close chum of Nell's family," said Alice. They stood almost eye to eye. If she was scared, she didn't show it: "And who might you be? Someone without any manners?"

She was as tall as any fella and twice as bold.

I was plastered to the back of the lift, knowing full well I had a stolen mink wrap hidden in the left leg of my drawers and I had just planted a stolen watch on the Queen of Thieves. The mink appeared to be taking on a life of its own and was getting hot and uncomfortable. I swear I felt it wriggle.

I didn't want to go back to jail but there was no way out. And in any case, when Alice found out what I'd done, planting that nicked watch on her, she'd probably make sure my life was no longer worth living. Either way I was in deep.

"Turn out your pockets," said Detective Sgt. Hart, grabbing hold of me roughly, plunging his hands into my coat.

"Get off me!" I cried.

Alice tussled with him to try to stop him searching me. They were like two blokes in a bar brawl and she kneed him in the groin just as the lift stopped at the roof gardens and the doors opened, to a crowd of startled shoppers. She was defending me, as if her life depended on it.

"Get your hands off her!" shouted Alice, in a voice loud enough to wake the dead. "Help! We are being attacked by a madman!"

A couple of chivalrous have-a-go heroes yanked the cozzer out of the lift and away from us. "I'm a police officer and these two are thieves!" he spluttered, windmilling his arms, trying in vain to shake them off. "I have reason to believe they have stolen a very expensive watch."

"Nonsense!" scoffed Alice. "You made a pass at my beautiful daughter in the lift and she rebuffed you and now you are making up these silly stories." She straightened her hat and smoothed down the front her coat.

Several ladies gasped in horror and one shouted, "Shame on him!"

I started to cry, right on cue. I was scared witless so finding a few tears was easy. The thought of Holloway Prison again was enough to make me blub.

"Will no one save us from this beastly man!" said Alice, flinging her arms wide. "As God is my witness, there is nothing in my pockets, look!" She pulled the pockets of her fur coat out, so that the lining was visible.

Then she pointed a finger at Detective Sgt. Hart, who was spluttering with rage and indignation. "I wonder if the same can be said for you! I fancy *you* are one of those spivvy types."

There were clucks of indignation from the women and one of the men put his hand firmly inside Detective Sgt. Hart's pocket and pulled out the gold-and-diamond watch.

"So!" said Alice, triumphantly. "*He* is a thief! Come along, my dear, I think you have been through enough." She turned to me and pushed me back into the lift, as a mob surrounded Detective Sgt. Hart.

She pushed the button and sped back down to the ground floor.

My heart was doing somersaults as her eyes bored into mine.

"Seems you are more light-fingered than I realized, aren't you? I know I said you could palm the watch off on me but that was quite a stunt you pulled. Were you trying to drop me in hot water, little Nelly?"

She loomed over me.

"I knew you'd get rid of it," I gasped. "If I'd kept the watch, we'd have been done for! I wasn't thinking straight, I'm sorry!"

She put her hands on my shoulders and her face softened. "It's alright, I understand. It was your first time in a tight spot and sometimes the rules go out of the window and we all have to rely on our wits. I admire your spirit, Nell, if the truth be told.

"But now it's time for you to do a little favor for me in return."

We sat in silence as the car crawled through the backstreets toward the river in near total darkness. The blackout was back, enveloping the whole city, so that only the lights of the tugboats and barges could be seen dappling the swirling waters of the Thames.

"Are you angry with me?" I stammered, eventually. My

hands started to shake, and Alice offered me a swig from her hp flask.

"Oh, love, I've seen it all before," she said. "My girls have to do all sorts to get themselves out of a scrape and if we are in it together, we work as a team. Ain't that right, Molly?"

Molly smirked at me, a horrible grin that showed off her rotten teeth. "That's right. Things go wrong on jobs and as long as everyone gets out alright, there's no hard feelings. Besides, I got a lot of nice stuff while you were having a tussle with that cozzer."

"I don't understand how he even knew we were there," I said. "Of all the shops in London . . ."

"Probably just chance," said Alice. "But he had a good look at my face, which means I will have to be careful in the future. We might find ourselves going up to Whiteley's or farther afield down to Bentall's in Kingston for a few weeks, just until things have calmed down," she said.

Molly nodded in approval.

We crossed the bridge and the car crawled at a snail's pace past a brewer's dray and a rag and bone cart plodding aimlessly through the darkened streets. Waterloo was silent in the snow.

"I've got to get to work later," I said, my nerves getting the better of me. "Can't you drop me my side of the river and I will help you out with this favor another time?"

"No, it can't wait," said Alice, with a glint in her eye. My heartbeat quickened as I struggled to stay calm.

"What is it you need me to do?" I asked.

"You'll see, all in good time," said Alice, settling herself back on the leather seats and gazing out of the window.

Queen's Buildings loomed like a ghost ship, with sheets billowing between the tenements, like tattered sails.

We got out of the car, with Molly tottering behind across

the ice-covered courtyard, and Alice linked her arm through mine, steering me away from her building and to the other side of the tenements.

The stairwell was just as grim as Alice's block, and as we climbed, our breath formed freezing clouds in front of our faces.

"Where are we going?" I said.

"Shh," whispered Alice, as we stopped outside a door. "It's a surprise."

She took out her silver-topped cane and rapped loudly. Behind me I saw that Molly had taken something out of her carpet bag. It looked like one of those metal handles that the fellas used to start their cars.

A split second later, the door swung open and Iris was standing there, with a look of surprise on her face and a half-skinned rabbit pelt in her hand.

"Ain't you going to invite us in?" said Alice, putting her foot across the threshold. "It's bleeding cold out here."

"Who's there?"

Tommy came staggering down the hallway, with a half a bottle of beer in his hand, swaying from side to side.

"Just some friends, paying a little house call," said Alice, barreling past him as Iris stood like a statue, all the color draining from her face.

"Get of my house!" he shouted, but Molly thwacked him in the knees with the starting handle and he crumpled.

Alice cracked him on the back of the head with her cane, for good measure, and he fell to the floor and started to sob and shake. He put his hands over his head: "Please don't!"

Iris ran to him. "Can't you see he's not right in the head? He's a war hero! He's been through hell in Burma. Stop hitting him!"

"Oh, save it," said Alice, grabbing Iris by her housecoat and propelling her into the tiny kitchen. "He's the man who knocks seven bells out of you; don't stick up for him, you dozy cow. Have some self-respect."

Alice turned and kicked him like a dog.

"I'd go out for an hour, if you know what's good for you, mate," she said. Molly brandished the starting handle again in a way which made it clear she meant business and Tommy grabbed his coat from the peg on the wall and stumbled off out of the front door.

"That's right!" yelled Molly to his departing back. "Naff off down the boozer."

"Now," said Alice, turning to Iris. "I've got a bone to pick with you."

Iris was white with terror as she rushed to my side.

"Please, Nell, tell them I'm your friend. Don't let them hurt me!"

"Nell works for me," said Alice, her mouth twisting into a snarl. "She does what I say. Tell her to sit down, Nell."

I turned to face her.

"Just sit down, Iris, it will all be fine," I said gently. "Whatever this is all about can easily be sorted." I had a horrible, sinking feeling that I knew exactly what it was all about. Billy's words about the tallyman getting his leg over with a housewife who owed him money were ringing in my ears. But if I said too much, I'd give myself away and find myself having to take on Molly and Alice. I wouldn't stand a snowball's chance in hell against both of them.

I prized her fingers off my sleeve, and she plonked herself at her tiny wooden table, which was filled with coney pelts. A basket full of white and brown fluff sat at her feet. The kitchen was spotless, but she barely had a pot to piss in. Tommy must have pawned everything they owned to pay for drink. It was such a pathetic sight.

Iris put her head in her hands and began to cry.

"Oh, don't turn on the waterworks now, you little snitch," said Molly, slapping her around the back of her head, making her yelp.

"I don't know what you mean . . ." she sniveled.

"Oh, but you do, Iris. Don't be so silly, there's a good girl. Just tell the truth," said Alice, smiling at her. "Now, it ain't every day you get the Queen of Thieves round your house for tea, is it? I like to make it an occasion to remember."

Alice put the kettle on while Iris sat there, dumbfounded. I swear it took forever for that water to boil and in that time, you could have heard a pin drop.

Then, Alice used up all the tea leaves in the caddy to make the strongest brew imaginable and poured the three of us a cup each, filling each chipped mug to the brim. She pointedly didn't make one for Iris.

I sipped at my tea. It was so strong it could have stripped paint. Iris looked up at me, but I looked away.

Iris was pleading now: "I don't know what you are talking about, honest to God, Alice, I don't."

Alice put down her tea and took something out of her pocket.

It was a lace handkerchief and there was something inside it that she unwrapped carefully. To my horror, I saw it was a cutthroat razor with a beautifully carved whalebone handle.

"My old friend here can usually find a way of making people like you remember the truth, Iris," she said, handing it to me.

"Now, Iris, why don't you tell us all about the tallyman?"

Iris put her head in her hands and addressed her comments to the floor.

"I had to sleep with him because I couldn't pay my bills," she said, her shoulders shaking.

Somehow, she found the courage to look directly at Alice and she raised her voice.

"Is that what this is all about? I've been cheating on my husband and he knocks me about. But you show me a woman around here who hasn't done something like that when their fellas were away in the war! And we all know men can all get a bit handy with their fists, so what business is it of yours?"

Her eyes blazed with barely suppressed anger. "You can judge me if you like but I don't care!"

"I don't give a toss who you get your leg over with, love," said Alice. "But you still ain't telling the truth." She prowled around the back of Iris's chair and then grabbed a lock of Iris's beautiful chestnut curls, which had grown all the way to her shoulders since I last saw her.

"Nell, cut that off," she ordered.

My hands were shaking but I knew then, I didn't have a choice, not if I wanted to get out of here unscathed. Still, I hesitated for a moment.

"Whose side are you on? Hers or ours?" said Alice menacingly.

In that moment, the gulf between Iris's life and mine seemed wider than the River Thames.

"I'm sorry, Iris," I whispered, slicing through her hair, which fell to the floor at her feet.

But Alice was just getting started. She grabbed another fistful of hair from the other side of Iris's head. Tears were coursing down my friend's face.

"Tell us the truth about what you really did, Iris," said Alice. "No more silly stories. Just the truth or I swear I will leave you bald as a coot."

"I kept watch for the tallyman," she blubbed. "I told him when you were going out shopping; what days and what times, so he could follow you up West. I didn't mean any harm by it . . ."

"Now we are getting somewhere," said Alice, pulling Iris's hair so hard that she cried out in pain, as Molly cackled to herself.

"And why did he need to know, that nosy little tallyman? Tell me that!"

"It was for one of the bosses up in Soho," said Iris, her voice barely a whisper.

Alice turned to me, still clasping a clump of Iris's hair, and said matter-of-factly: "Cut this bit nice and short, down to the scalp."

"You are letting her off too easy!" cried Molly, swigging from her bottle of gin that she liked to carry in her coat pocket. "You should cut her face and be done with it."

Alice ignored her and looked at me. "Well? Get on with it!"

"Nell," moaned Iris, her face a mass of snot and tears. "Please, don't."

Something in me snapped.

"You shouldn't have done it, Iris," I said, grabbing hold of her hair myself, and cropping it as close to the scalp as I could. "You've brought this on yourself."

Then I grabbed another hunk of it and sliced through that too. Rage came bubbling up from deep inside me; rage at being forced to do what Alice wanted, at what had become of my life, and at Iris for not keeping her big mouth shut.

I felt the softness of her hair in my hands and I wanted to destroy it, all of it. I saw Iris running down Tenison Street toward me, late for the factory, her curls escaping her hair band. Iris and me gossiping on the bus, as she tucked a stray lock of hair behind her ear; her curls shaking as we laughed at our old boss Miss Pritchard and joked about spam fritters in the canteen at the Alaska Fur Factory. The more I cut, the more I wanted to keep going, to slice away every memory of life the way it used to be.

Iris begged and pleaded but I kept cutting and chopping

until her hair lay in heaps all over the kitchen floor and all that was left on her head looked more like one of those skinned rabbit pelts, with a few tufty bits sticking up behind her ears.

"Grass!" I spat, as I stepped back to admire my handiwork.

Chapter Twenty-One
ALICE

Elephant and Castle, London, March 1947

Watching Nell at work with my razor brought back a few memories. In fact, it made me rather nostalgic for the time when I started out with The Forty Thieves.

Things were a bit harder in those days, shortly after the Great War, because they only let you work as a lookout for the first year or so. South London was chock-full of really skilled hoisters back then. Every woman worth her salt knew how to clout a fur or steal a frock for the gang and I had my work cut out earning my stripes.

This last war changed all that. Girls got ideas above their station, working in offices and the like, so The Forty Thieves had to adapt. Now I let my girls hoist from a much earlier stage in their training than they did back in the old days. And, yes, if an occasion arises when I can test their loyalty to me and the gang, then of course I will take it. Life is full of surprises, and you've got to keep them on their toes.

Iris had it coming, the dozy mare. She needed to be cut down to size and now everyone in Queen's Buildings knows that she has done wrong and been punished. Oh, her hair'll grow back in time, so I wasn't that hard on her, was I?

Meanwhile, it'll make her more pliable for what I have in mind: storing a few nice things of mine in her flat if the need arises, in the knowledge that she will not dare breathe a word of it to anyone. And in return, I will knock that lousy husband of hers to kingdom come if he so much as lays a finger on her again. That is the deal.

So, you see, I'm quite fair really, given she has been a very silly girl indeed. She needs my protection. I can save her from herself and stop her having to shag that little prick, the tallyman, because working for me, I will take care of the money side of things.

In fact, I heard his old nag got a bit poorly because someone put glass in a nosebag full of oats and she cut her mouth to ribbons. Shame, that. I don't suppose we will be seeing him round our way for a while.

I caught a spark of something in Nell when I introduced her to my shiv that gave me high hopes for her and I gave her a little treat as a reward; it's only a small sparkler, little more than a chip in a band of gold, but she's pleased as Punch with it. Molly looked askance when I handed it over. I've never given her a reward like that, but then again, she's never been too far out of my sight, so she ain't needed one.

The only place I ever had to look for Molly was at the bottom of an empty bottle of gin down the boozer. Young Nell is different. She's across the water in Soho, doing good work for me, and she's still getting over the loss of her little one. I think it does a girl good to have a treat now and again.

Besides, old Molly's been getting a bit too reliant on the sauce of late and I had in mind that young Nell might be deputy material for me, given her liking for violence, so I wanted to make my gratitude clear.

I thought she might be a bit squeamish, or refuse me, given that she and Iris go all the way back to Waterloo but, blooming heck, she went hell for leather on Iris. It was like watching Sweeney Todd at work! It did make me laugh.

There is the small matter of her chucking that wristwatch in my pocket in the lift at Derry and Tom's but after her performance with Iris, I'm prepared to let that slide. No hard feelings. Of course, the moment she put it in there, I felt it, but I had my hands rather full of that cozzer's bollocks at the time, so I couldn't plant it back on her, which I might otherwise have done, just to teach her a lesson. When it comes to being light-fingered, I'm the best in the business.

So, putting a razor in a woman's hand is always a risk because some girls just aren't used to it. They see it as something male, something that belongs to their brothers and fathers, and they daren't touch it. I never felt that way. In fact, I like to think that my shiv found me, the day after I was let down so badly by my brother, Lim.

The day after my brother Lim abandoned me to start his own gang, the pound note I earned from my night with the captain was burning a hole in my pocket.

I bought myself a pint of prawns and picked at them with a wooden toothpick as I wandered through the Seven Dials. A plan was forming in my head and I found it gave me quite an appetite.

The lights of Theatreland burned brightly and crowds of people bustled in and out of the foyers, dressed up to the nines. It was 1919, little more than three months after Armistice Day, and everyone wanted to forget the war and their losses, and they were out for a good time.

Women called from the shadows in the alley and blokes would appear, adjusting their hats or doing up their trousers, whistling to themselves. It was all just part of the fun for them; women were at the bottom of the pecking order in this city. I looked at one old drab, doing whatever she could on her knees, for a few pennies, and decided I'd rather be dead than selling my body on the streets.

I was worried I wouldn't remember the way to Mrs. Tibbs's house, but it all came back to me as I meandered through the streets and alleyways of Little Italy and into Snow Hill.

The street was shrouded in a thick pea-souper of a fog as I made my way to her door and knocked softly.

She pulled it open and stood there with her arms folded, eyeing me coldly. "Oh, so, you're back, are you? You still owe me for those clothes you nicked; I've a good mind to report you to the law for stealing."

"No need to be like that, Mrs. Tibbs." I smiled. "I had a long chat with Lim, and he explained how things would work between you and me. I think it's a good idea. Can I come in?"

"I knew you'd see sense eventually!" she cried. "Come over here and give old Ma Tibbs a hug." She pulled me across the threshold and I felt the softness of her body as she pressed my bones so hard, I thought they'd crack.

She cupped my face in her hands. "You look tired."

"I've been walking around all day," I said. "How about a nice cuppa to seal the deal on our new working relationship?"

"Oh, you are a card!" she laughed. "You don't have to worry your pretty head, just leave all that stuff to me and I will tell you how to keep my clients happy. I have a lot of very good-quality men through my door. A vicar, a teacher, and even one or two with titles, who sit in the House of Lords, if you please! I can guarantee girls who are clean, like you, because they're so fresh and young."

I nodded in agreement.

"How much do you think I can earn? I mean, how much did Lim get for me?"

She gave me a suspicious glance. "If he didn't tell you, I'm not going to. That deal is between me and him and it's all water under the bridge now."

"Oh, it don't matter, in any case," I said, with a wave of

my hand. "But what I really want to know is, how much do you think I could earn in a week, after paying you, that is?"

She bustled over to the sink and filled the kettle. "Three, maybe four quid," she said. "But I ain't joking about those clothes. They will have to come out of your first week's wages."

"Sounds grand," I said.

She clattered the copper kettle on the stove and struck a match to light the gas. Soon enough it was whistling and she unlocked a tea caddy and spooned a generous heap of leaves into her teapot, with great ceremony.

"Got anything to eat? I'm starving," I said, suppressing a fishy burp from all the prawns I'd scoffed on the way round.

While she was rootling in the pantry for a lump of cheese, I crept over to the mantelpiece and took her glass vial of magic drops, the ones she'd used to calm that baby, and tipped the whole contents into her teacup and put the empty bottle back on the shelf.

Then I poured the tea and offered her a cup.

She took a sip and screwed up her face. "Milk must be off."

"Mine tastes fine," I said, hurriedly taking a slurp, so that I almost burned the back of my throat.

I forced a smile as she continued to drink hers.

"Let's have a toast!" I said, taking another sip of the scalding liquid.

I slugged it down and she laughed and did the same.

"To happy days, rolling the fellas at your house, Mrs. Tibbs!"

I chattered on for England. Her eyes were getting heavy and soon enough she was snoring like a train. I took the muslin from the kitchen table, tore it into strips, and tied her tightly to the rocking chair.

Then I had a good look in her sewing basket.

What a treasure trove that turned out to be! Amongst the

knitting needles, crochet hooks, and pins was a cutthroat razor. I thought I was going to have to make do with her best carving knife but this was something else. I tested it on my finger first and it was sharp alright, a drop of blood was proof of that.

There were a few other things that caught my eye. Her hatpin—I swiped that—and a little pocketbook with lots of names and addresses in it, and how much they'd paid and for what. Some of the things those fellas paid for would make a whore blush. I thought it all looked very interesting and could come in handy, so I tucked the book in my pinafore pocket.

Next, I put on the spare apron that was neatly pressed and folded on the kitchen table and then I went over to her. She was still snoring away like a bear in the woods as I drew the razor, slowly and deliberately, along her arm. She didn't open her eyes at first, in fact I was halfway through my handiwork when she opened her eyes. I don't know if you have ever seen that look on someone's face when they are shocked awake, but it really is something to witness their terror at the sight of their own blood. I was ready with her best teatowel and I stuffed that over her mouth as I finished it.

"Shhh," I told her. "It's alright, Mrs. Tibbs, it will all be over soon." She struggled quite a lot, splatting blood all over herself as I carved the letter deep into her forearm.

A is for Alice, ain't it? And it was a name I never wanted her to forget.

"Oh, now look what you've done!" I said, as I stepped back to admire my work. She'd need stitches to sew the flaps of skin back together, but even then, the scars would be permanent. At least, that is what I hoped.

"It was ten pound he paid me for you, ten pounds! I can

pay you back, just let me go and stop cutting me. Stop!" she shrieked, "I'm begging you. I thought we were working together!"

"You were wrong about that," I laughed. "If you were on fire, I wouldn't piss on you, you rotten old bag."

She was rocking to and fro, like a mad thing, and gurgling like crazy.

"Let me go, I will pay you money. Please!"

"I ain't going to take your filthy, tainted money," I said. "Now, stop screaming, or I will cut your throat."

That shut her up.

I boiled some water on the range and washed away the blood from my hands in the sink, using that nice bar of soap she had, humming to myself.

"I'll have the law on you," she said.

I waved her pocketbook under her nose.

"I don't think so because this will make very interesting reading, won't it? So, if you so much as think about going near a cozzer, I will sing like a fucking canary. And the alleyways round here are so dark, I'd be careful if I were you. You never know who might be lurking. London town can be so dangerous after dark."

With that, I walked out of that house, to get on with the rest of my life.

And it was a life that was going to be lived my way.

I took the shiv with me in my pocket, wrapped in her lace handkerchief. I'd taken quite a shine to it. Over the years, it's almost taken on a life of its own.

You see, when someone gets cut, it's her voice I hear. It ain't me doing the shivving, it's Mrs. Tibbs. She's made me do so many bad things I've almost lost count, but she's a greedy mare because no matter how many cuts she makes, it's never quite enough, and sometimes I feel her itching to get out of my pocket.

I think Nell felt the same as I did. That razor wants blood.

Now there is only one other person who still owes me that I'd like to reacquaint with Mrs. Tibbs.

And that's my brother, Lim.

Chapter Twenty-Two

NELL

Soho, London, March 1947

After weeks of snow falling silently in the night, the pattering of raindrops on the window woke me from a drunken stupor.

Gypsy groaned as I leaned over her to peek out of the thin curtains into the street below, where the pavement had turned to a mass of gray slush. The thaw was finally here; spring was on its way.

Alice had rewarded me with my own diamond ring, after what I did to Iris. It sparkled on my finger as I rubbed sleep out of my eyes. A dull ache throbbed in my temples. I wasn't a big drinker, I could barely take a couple of sherries at the best of times, but when I got back to The Windsor, I wanted to blot out what I'd become with that razor in my hand. After my act, I hit the bottle, hard.

I felt queasy after cutting her hair, as if I'd gorged myself on the violence of it. It reminded me of the time I'd stuffed myself with cake on VE Day and almost threw up. What I'd done bubbled up my gullet, and drink felt like the only way to force it back down again.

The last thing I remember was Lou the barman chuckling to himself as he poured me another large whisky after closing time, and Gypsy and me staggering home, singing at the top of our voices.

Now, as I watched the newspaper boy struggle up the street with his soggy bundle of papers, I wondered if I'd done the right thing punishing Iris. She belonged to the world of mugs: people who did straight jobs for a living and grassed on the likes of us. Alice said she had it coming, and I suppose she did.

"To forge new ties, you have to cut old ones, Nell," she said. "You have to make painful decisions at times in this game and you've proved you are willing to do that. We don't live by their rules, we live by ours, remember that."

Oh, I'd have liked to have snatched her shiv and slashed her to ribbons with it, to teach her all about the pain I was still feeling because of what she'd done to me.

But instead, I smiled and accepted the ring while Molly was turning green with envy.

So, this diamond ring proved that I was getting somewhere in The Forty Thieves, even after that stunt I'd pulled with the watch in the lift backfired so badly. Now, I was enjoying a winning streak and I intended to keep playing my cards close to my chest.

Gypsy sat up in the bed and grabbed hold of my hand to admire my diamond again. She'd been trying to get the truth out of me about it, but I wasn't telling.

"Come on, spill the beans, where did you get that?" she cooed. "Got a fancy man?"

"If I have told you once, I have told you a thousand times: it was a family heirloom from a friend over the water," I said, holding it up, so she could get a better view.

"It really is lovely," she said. "You are a lucky so-and-so. And you were celebrating something last night, I know you were. I bet your fancy fella bought it for you!"

I didn't need a man to buy me jewels.

I had earned it. And I was sure of one thing: this would be the first of many.

She lay back down, so that her hair spread out around her on the pillow, like a great cloud: "I wish I could get a fella to buy me a sparkler or two! I never get anything nice, can't afford it, bloody ration coupons and economy drives," she said, pouting. The room was littered with shoeboxes from her last spree up Berwick Street market. Nothing she bought had fitted her and the dressing table was strewn with bunches of paper flowers from Woolworths because she'd taken a fancy to those and wasted all her money on tat, as usual.

Maybe it was guilt about my old pal Iris, but I felt Gypsy needed someone to take care of her, in the way that only a member of The Forty Thieves could.

I gave her a wicked grin. "Tell you what, why don't we go and have a look around the shops before work? That'll cheer you up!"

People were still muffled up to their chins, with the rain falling like stair rods, as we sauntered through the West End to Gamages. The tramlines up on High Holborn were glossy in the wet for the first time in months, instead of white with snow.

"Oh, I'm like a drowned rat," laughed Gypsy, shaking water from her head as we stepped into the shop. Everything stank of soggy woollens and people still had their wartime faces on: tired, lined, and now thoroughly cheesed off with the great British weather, which had gone from subzero to downpour overnight.

We pushed our way through the crowds, who were sheltering from the elements rather than buying, and Gypsy stopped at a heap of buttery-soft leather gloves. She picked up a black pair and examined the price tag.

"Nineteen shillings and sixpence!" she scoffed. "Who can afford that these days?"

"I know," I said. "It's daylight robbery."

She plonked them back on the pile and was rifling through for a cheaper pair, while I moved my handbag to the edge of the table and idly swept the ones that she wanted inside it. A shop assistant glanced over from the till, and I smiled at her sweetly. I wasn't nervous in the least. I looked down at my diamond ring and it glinted under the electric lights. I could be like Alice Diamond; all it took was the guts to carry it off.

"Fancy a look upstairs?" I said and we wandered on through the shop together.

"I could do with some new underpinnings," said Gypsy, twanging the strap of her brassiere. "They might have something on sale." It was true, most of her undergarments had seen better days, which was another reason she performed starkers.

She stopped at a rail of rayon slips and camiknickers and picked a few up to try. I pulled some silk ones from their padded hangers, which brought the shop assistant running like the clappers.

"Would you like to try those?" she said, snatching them from me, as if they were the crown jewels.

"They're for my friend," I said, gesturing to Gypsy, who was waiting patiently by the changing room, with a handful of underclothes in the cheapest, scratchiest material imaginable from the bargain counter. The shop assistant looked her up and down, with something approaching pity, which really got me riled.

Gypsy was oblivious to how she was being sneered at. She was so excited just to be in the shop trying on some nice things, rather than bartering with some market stall trader in Berwick Street.

"Try this," I said, handing her the white silk slip and some drawers to go with it. "It looks gorgeous."

"Price tag to match, I'll bet," she said. "But no harm window-shopping!"

I pretended to look through some stockings for a moment and then stuck my head around the changing room curtain, where Gypsy was shimmering in the slip. It clung to her curves.

"Imagine if Albert Rossi could see me in this." She giggled. "He'd fall at my feet, wouldn't he?"

She did look stunning. It didn't seem fair that she couldn't afford such a lovely piece of lingerie.

She pulled it off and hung it up, before putting on the rayon one, which looked every bit as cheap as the material it was made from.

"This one's only three shillings and sixpence, plus one of my clothing coupons, so I'm going to take it," she said chirpily, twirling around to admire her reflection.

We took everything she'd tried on over to the till in a big heap and as the assistant was ringing through her purchase, I put my coat on top of the silk slip and camiknickers, just as Alice Diamond had taught me.

"Might I trouble you to show me those handkerchiefs?" I said, pointing to the neatly folded tray in the cabinet below.

She pursed her thin lips, giving me a look that let me know I was being a nuisance, but she had no choice but to oblige. As she bent down to get them, I picked up my coat and one of the silk slips with it, shoving it up the sleeve.

Gypsy was so busy counting her pennies she didn't see what I was up to.

I felt a warm glow inside, that I was doing something nice for my friend and getting one over on that snooty cow of a shop assistant. And it was easy too. I couldn't wait to show her what I had nicked.

Gypsy carried her purchases proudly in a brown paper

bag, while I had my hoister's haul concealed up my coat sleeve and in my handbag. It wasn't bad for a first trip out on my own. My heart was beating a little faster, but I took my time, smiling at the shop assistant as we left, just like Alice did.

At the other end of the womenswear department, there was a crowd gathering around a mannequin in a glass cabinet, which was dressed in the most extravagant, long, swishy skirt I'd ever seen. There was enough material in it for two economy suits and one pair of curtains, at least. The gold-colored jacket had a nipped-in waist but it flared out across the hips and the whole lot was topped off by a fine felt hat, with a sweeping brim. It was so different from the clothes we were used to; ours were cut on the knee, with teensy collars or tiny little pleats. This outfit was so generously cut that it was almost shocking.

"Just look at the yardage on that!" said one woman, nudging her friend in the ribs. "War Office won't like it!"

"Far too showy, all that wasted cloth," said another matronly woman, peering over her spectacles to get a closer look.

But we were all drawn to it, like bees to honey.

"Well, I *love* it!" said Gypsy, loudly, pressing her nose to the glass for a closer look.

A big sign at the bottom of the glass case read: "DIOR— NEW LOOK for Spring 1947" and there was a display poster about a fashion show on a stand beside it which read: "SPRING FASHIONS 1947. Ladies! GAMAGES proudly presents the NEW LOOK by the House of Dior at our spring fashion show, featuring furs from the Alaska Fur Factory, at 4pm on Wednesday March 23rd. Tickets 6d. On sale now."

Beneath that, on a little card, was written "*Models wanted, apply to manager.*"

"We could go to that," I said.

"Might be nice," said Gypsy.

"As models, I mean," I said. "That way at least we'd get to try on some of the clothes. It might be fun."

Gypsy nodded.

The only hitch was whether that witch of a manageress, Miss Hunter, would tumble who I was.

But I was a pathetic, scared, mousey brunette when our paths had last crossed and now, as a platinum blonde and a fully fledged member of The Forty Thieves, I was brimming with confidence. The old Nell was history.

By the time we reached Wardour Street, Gypsy was still high as a kite with excitement about the little gifts I'd hoisted for her.

"But I didn't even see you do it!" she squeaked. "You are so clever. Where on earth did you learn to do that?"

"Oh, here and there," I said. "It's just like nicking the tablecloth from the Lyons Corner Tea House, only you have to be a bit more game. With prices the way they are, it's only fair that girls like us get a few lucky breaks, don't you think?"

She nodded in agreement and chucked her cheap rayon slip in the bin. "Never liked it anyway. Don't know why I even bought it! Thanks, Nell, you are such a pal!"

The stale stench of last night's booze and cigarettes wafted up the staircase as we descended into The Windsor. Lou, the barman, was like a blue-arsed fly, buzzing about, with money on his mind.

"Wet weather means more punters," he boomed. "Cocktails are our special for today."

He was studiously ignored by a gaggle of dancers who pretended to mend their costumes.

"Are you lot even listening to me?" he barked.

I walked over and perched on a stool. Alma, the lead dancer, strutted up and sat beside me, picking at her bed bug bites. Gypsy stifled a yawn and joined us. Lou seemed mollified by our presence.

"That's lemon cordial with some white wine, but you will sip at it as if it's nectar because we're charging the mugs three shillings a glass and I will pay you sixpence, clear?"

We nodded.

"And Mr. Sullivan has just got a consignment of chocolates in that are very special," he breathed, wiping the sweat from his brow, as he heaved a cardboard box onto the bar for us all to admire. They were probably filled with sawdust because God only knows where you could find chocolates with rationing as it was, but at least they looked like chocolates on the box outside. Pity the poor sods who had to eat them.

"I'm thinking a pound a box and you can get five shillings back from me for every one you shift. Got it?"

We made a great show of hanging on his every word. Nobody wanted to get booted out on the streets in this weather.

Something heavy thudded down the stairs and a man crashed through the doors, with one end of a rolled-up carpet tucked under his arm.

Bringing up the rear, sweating like a pig, his sandy blond hair flopping over his forehead and his trilby hat pushed back on his head, was Jimmy.

Our eyes met.

"Nell!" he cried, putting his end of the carpet down and rushing toward me.

My heart was pounding, and he hesitated for a moment, almost drinking me in, before he took a step toward me, his hands encircling my waist.

"You look stunning, Nell," he said, his voice hoarse with longing.

Before I knew what was happening, he'd pulled me into

a fond embrace, kissing me on the cheek. My stomach somersaulted the way it always did with Jimmy. Even after everything I'd been through, he only had to look at me with those cornflower-blue eyes and my heart started to melt. I fought that feeling as hard as I could but it was useless. My mouth could tell a lie, but my heart couldn't. I still fancied him something rotten and the anger about everything I had been through got tangled up in it all. The words got stuck in my throat.

"How've you been, Jim?" I croaked.

Alma whistled. "Lovebirds!"

Gypsy started preening herself, the way she did whenever a half-decent bloke stepped into her orbit, but Jimmy only had eyes for me.

Then he seemed to remember he was meant to be working, so he adjusted his tie and glanced back over his shoulder. His mate still had tight hold of his end of the rug. Something in the rug emitted a muffled groan.

"Pick it up, you clown!" said Jimmy's companion. "For Gawd's sake, Mr. Sullivan told us to take it straight into his office; no hanging about!"

The rug started wriggling around. Lou turned away and started polishing some glasses as Gypsy, Alma, and me stood there, open-mouthed.

"What you got in there?" said Gypsy. "A crocodile?"

Jimmy picked up his end of the rug, which was kicking like fury, and tucked it under his arm. "No, just a particularly troublesome snake."

He gave me a wink. "I'll catch you later, Nell. Fancy a drink when you knock off work?"

"Perhaps," I said casually.

He grinned at me again and the pair of them lugged the body in the rug across the club, as if it was the most natural thing in the world to carry someone bundled up like that.

My stomach lurched as I thought back to the bloodstains on Billy Sullivan's office floor.

Lou must have caught the look on my face because he pulled a bottle of champagne out from under the bar and uncorked it. He poured three glasses, with bubbles fizzing over, and handed them to me, Gypsy, and Alma.

"Now, did any of you ladies see anything unusual just now?"

Alma took a large gulp and said, "Not me."

Gypsy sipped at it and thought for a moment. "I saw a perfectly normal carpet being delivered, didn't you, Nell?"

I drank deeply.

"Same here," I said. I knew which side my bread was buttered in gangland.

"Good," said Lou. "What happens in The Windsor, stays in The Windsor, and that is the way Mr. Sullivan likes it."

"Taking my name in vain again, Lou?"

His voice echoed across the room, making me jump out of my skin. How long had he been there watching us?

Billy Sullivan strolled over, flicking raindrops off his fedora, and bellied up to the bar. "Mothers' meeting, is it? Haven't you got work to do?" The temperature dropped several degrees at that, and the cheap champagne went flat. He was in no mood for chitchat. We knew he had business to attend to in the back room, for one thing.

We emptied our glasses as quickly as we could and made our way over to the stage to begin rehearsals.

But not before Alma's mouth ran away with her. "So, Nell, who's your secret boyfriend? And how come you know one of Billy's Chaps so well?"

I looked over my shoulder to see if Billy Sullivan had overheard me. By the look on his face, he was digesting that piece of information, as if it were tastier than one of his knockoff chocolates.

★

The muffled cries coming from Billy's office could be heard in the club, no matter how hard the pianist hammered on the ivories to try to disguise it. Dancers exchanged glances as they practiced their steps, and I belted the songs out but I couldn't help wondering what on earth was going on in there.

After a couple of hours, when it was time to let the punters in, Lou traipsed down the corridor and the rolled-up carpet was once again carted out and up the stairs by Jimmy and his chum, who gave me a cheery wave. This time the carpet was not moving.

That evening, I sang my way lamely through my set, to a packed audience of whey-faced punters, with condensation rising from their damp clothes. Gypsy and Alma set about the tables with boxes of chocolates, perching on laps, stroking thighs, and draping themselves over anything with a pulse and a fat wallet, much to Lou's delight.

Billy held court at his favorite table by the bar, and when Albert came in, Gypsy made a point of hovering near him until he bought her a drink. She'd put her new silk slip on, and he watched her backside, mesmerized by it, as she strode to the stage for her act.

At eleven o'clock, Billy and Albert and the rest of the gang got up and left, with much glad-handing and straightening of ties. It was close to midnight when Jimmy strode back into the club to find me, nursing cuts and bruises on his knuckles.

"Fancy that drink? We've got a lot to catch up on, haven't we?" He ruffled his hair, showing off his handsome features.

My stomach went all floaty, but I fought that feeling.

"I don't know, Jim, you look like you're trouble, and I've got to see that Gypsy gets home too."

"Don't you two lovers worry about me," shouted Gypsy,

glancing up from a table, where she'd spent hours hanging on to every word from a pair of twits with shiny shoes to match their slicked-back hair and old-school ties. The table was piled with empty glasses and she'd managed to foist not one, but two boxes of chocolates on the unsuspecting pair. "I don't want to be a gooseberry, you go on without me, Nell."

"Alright," I said, "one drink."

He pulled me to him, but I brushed him off. "And no funny business."

Ivy's Café was a proper dive, on the corner of Frith Street, but it was always open late. Nobody minded the chipped china or greasy cutlery because everyone got a warm welcome and she buttered her toast so thickly. The grocery store next door was under the protection of Billy Sullivan, so there was no shortage of black-market food on her plates, unless the boys in blue darkened her doors, in which case cuts of bacon, trays of eggs, and pats of butter would be hurriedly shoved under the sink or rushed out of the back door and into the alley.

Ivy toiled over her gas stove by the light of a paraffin lamp in the blackout and wax oozed over saucers in the middle of each table in the café, where stumpy candles had burned down almost to the wick. The smell of cooking made my stomach rumble, as I realized I hadn't eaten all day.

I devoured my piece of toast with such gusto, licking my fingers, that Jimmy took pity and gave me his as well.

A muscle twitched in his cheek, as he leaned across the table toward me.

"So, how have you been keeping?"

"Fine," I said tightly.

He lowered his voice so that the fella reading a newspaper at the next table couldn't hear. The headlines read:

"Spivs and Drones Order—*Police to clamp down on the scum of London.*"

"I thought about you a lot, about the baby. I heard you'd gone inside . . ." said Jimmy.

"Well, a fat lot of good that did, all your thinking," I spat.

"I tried to get a message to you, through Iris. She promised me she'd write to you, to tell you how I felt about everything . . ." He looked hurt.

"Yes, I know," I said.

"So, you got the letter? Why didn't you get in touch?"

"Because, Jimmy, I thought about it and decided it was just a load of old flannel. And I had to do what was right for the baby . . ."

"Did you have it?"

"Of course I had it. And it was a boy, a beautiful baby boy," I said. God, he was so flipping clueless. I felt rage boiling up inside, but I managed to keep a lid on it.

Jimmy was lost for words, for once.

I looked up at the flies stuck on the gummy paper hanging above the counter and started to count them.

"Had him adopted, didn't I? He was gorgeous. Looked a lot like you." Well, that was just too much. Tears welled in my eyes and I blinked them away at the thought of my baby, my Joseph.

Jimmy swallowed hard: "A baby boy, our son . . ."

"My son, Jimmy," I said sharply. "I carried him for nine months, and I pushed him out and then I had to make the right choice for him, which was to give him away and now I'm living with the guilt of it."

Tears were running down my face and I wiped them away with the back of my hand.

"Oh, God," Jimmy said, reaching out to me. "It's all my fault, Nell, but I can make it up to you."

He made it sound so easy, but he was pissing in the wind, as usual.

"It don't matter now," I said, looking away. He had no idea what I had been through in Holloway and what I was going through now in Soho. He never would. "What's done is done."

"It don't have to be this way," he said. "We can make a go of it. You and me. I'm onto something big now, good money; we could move out to one of the suburbs, out West, Ealing way, to start over. What do you think?"

He clocked the ring on my finger and a dark look swept over his features.

"Who gave you that? You got a fella, Nell?"

"No, Jimmy, I haven't got a fella, not that it is any business of yours! I earned it myself."

He rocked back on his chair and ran his hands through his hair. "You ain't on the game, are you, Nell? Because God knows I would never forgive myself for it . . ."

"Who do you think you are, questioning me?" I scoffed. "I won't let the greasy punters in that dive lay so much as a finger on me. I earned it myself through other little jobs I do outside the club, if you must know, not that it is any of your business!"

"You ain't still in with The Forty Thieves, are you? Because Billy's got it in for them from what I've heard . . ." he murmured.

I shook my head. "I take in piecework for the theatres, sewing and mending. I've always been good with a needle and thread, ever since the fur factory. So, a posh actress gave it to me, as a thank-you when I saved her modesty one night."

He seemed satisfied with that.

He stirred his tea. "I know you're angry with me, Nell, and you've every right to be, but there's no other girl like you as far as I'm concerned. I tried to make it right, to walk you up the aisle, but you wouldn't have it . . ."

"Oh, the spielers are full to the brim with floozies, I'll bet," I said, buttoning up my coat. I'd heard enough of his patter. He was worse than the spivs up Old Compton Street, with loudly painted ties, selling dolls wrapped in cellophane, which dropped to bits the minute you bought them.

"Please, Nell," he begged, "give me a chance. Things just took a bad turn for us because I was stupid that night when you told me about the baby. It was the shock of it, I was drunk as a lord, and I didn't take care of you. I should have shown you I was serious about us, I could've faced your dad down, man to man at the start, and persuaded him to let us marry because . . . because I love you, Nell."

"You can't go saying that you love me, Jimmy, not now, not like this . . ."

But there was something desperate in his eyes, something I hadn't seen before in the old Jimmy, which stopped me in my tracks.

"The way I feel about you is precious, and I know that now because I've seen things, done things . . ." he murmured. We both knew what he was talking about. The body in the carpet at The Windsor was only the tip of the iceberg, I suspected.

"I want us to have a life, like other people do. I want a wife and a baby and a home, away from this. I can keep us safe. I want to take care of you, if you will let me try. All I'm asking for is a second chance."

The bloke at the next table rustled his newspaper and peered at us both. I didn't like the look of him, and he was clearly earwigging. What with the law clamping down on spivs and gangsters, for all I knew there could be spies everywhere in Soho.

"Jimmy, we can't talk here," I said. "It's getting late . . ."

"Well, tomorrow?" he said, hope lighting up his face. "You get a night off, don't you? I can take you to the pictures and you can see that I'm serious about us. I can explain everything then. It will be fun, like it used to be. I promise."

I let him kiss me on the cheek and he made a great show of unrolling a wad of banknotes to pay the bill.

"Alright," I sighed. "I'll meet you tomorrow. But I ain't promising anything." I wasn't going to let him back into my life that easily, even if my heart was aching for him.

We strolled out of the café through the darkened Soho streets, which were still glossy and wet, laughing as we avoided the puddles, looking like any other couple heading home after a night on the town.

By the time we got to my front door, we were arm in arm, and I felt the familiar warmth of his body next to mine.

Jimmy bent his head to kiss me, and I tilted my chin up so that our lips met.

At my feet, a discarded cigarette packet bobbed along the gutter in a torrent of rainfall.

I clung to him for a moment, watching as it was swept away, down into the drains below London.

Chapter Twenty-Three

NELL

Soho, London, March 1947

The queue for *An Ideal Husband* snaked halfway round Leicester Square, but as the minutes ticked by and I found myself nearing the doors of the cinema, my heart sank.

Jimmy was nowhere to be seen. He'd obviously got a better offer. So much for an ideal husband; he was a crap boyfriend, for starters. I should have known better than to trust him.

Inside, the foyer was plush, in gold and red, with velvet drapes. A grand clock on the wall chimed loudly, echoing off the ornate plasterwork.

"Do you want a ticket or not?" clucked the woman at the box office, shooting me a pitying glance over the top of her glasses. "The film starts in two minutes, love."

I caught the eye of another no-hoper who'd been stood up. She was pretending to do her lipstick as she loitered by the entrance. A few moments later, she gave up the ghost and headed out of the door, back into the remains of her evening.

I handed over my two shillings, pretending that I'd planned to come alone anyway, and the usherette guided me to the stalls, her face illuminated by the glowing end of a ciggie, which perched on her bottom lip, as if by magic.

I can't remember when I started to cry but by the interval, my mascara was running down my cheeks and an old fella in the row in front turned around and gave me his handkerchief.

"Ain't any of my business, sweet, but whoever he is, he ain't worth it," he said.

Those words were like a knife in my heart.

I gathered what was left of my pride and left the cinema, picking my way through the backstreets, ignoring the shouts from drunken blokes falling out of pubs, until I found my way to somewhere familiar.

It wasn't exactly home, but it was the only place I knew I'd get a warm welcome; alongside the dregs of Soho and those desperate to make a bob or two, just to keep their heads above water.

The sound of the piano being bashed for dear life drifted up the dank stairwell and as I pushed through the doors and into The Windsor, Alma and Gypsy were strutting at the head of a conga line, flashing everything that God gave them, while the fellas queuing up behind sang "The Lambeth Walk" at the top of their voices.

Presiding over the whole scene, leaning on the bar in a double-breasted navy wool suit, his eyes drinking it all in, was Billy Sullivan.

"Evening, Nell," he said, with a grin slowly spreading over his face. "You look like you could use a bit of cheering up. Fancy a drink?"

I forced a smile as the cheap champagne bubbles exploded on my tongue. "Thanks, Billy."

"I wonder if you might like to do me a little favor," he said, leaning in close, so that I caught a whiff of his lemony cologne. I should have known that nothing in his clubs came without strings attached, not even a free drink.

"I've got a game of cards tonight, important clients, and

I need someone to help serve the drinks and look decorative, who knows how to behave in decent company," he said, watching me closely.

I must have recoiled slightly because he very gently laid his hand over my forearm. "There's no pressure, Nell, if you have other plans, but I like to have people I can trust by my side when I play, so that I can focus on the game. And I will pay you handsomely for your time."

Gypsy waved at me from the conga line as she twirled her feather boa. "Come on, Nell, don't be a wet weekend! Come and join in!"

"Can Gypsy come too? I'd feel better about going if she came with me . . ."

He thought about it for a moment, as he lit a cigar.

"Don't see why not. Albert would probably like that. But she'll have to keep her trap shut unless she's spoken to and mind her p's and q's. I'm talking about a high-stakes game in Mayfair, Nell, not some backroom spieler where you'll get a thug's boot in your face the minute you try to leave the card table. There will be lords and ladies there, most likely. Do you understand?"

"Yes," I said, fumbling with my cardigan, feeling self-conscious. I was just a girl from the slums. What would I know about talking to posh people who were born with silver spoons in their mouths?

"I've got a feeling you can hold your own in good company but to help you, there are a few nice things in my office that I've just got in from one of my suppliers. I reckon you'll find something in your size that might take your fancy. I'll be waiting in the car outside when you are ready. Meet me in half an hour."

He handed me the key to his office.

"And, Nell," he said, brushing a thumb across my cheek, "go and fix your face, there's a good girl."

★

I pushed my way through the crowded club to go backstage and into Billy Sullivan's lair, wondering how I could think up an excuse to get out of having to go to his stupid card game. I just wanted to go home, pull the bedclothes over my head, and forget about Jimmy standing me up.

But when I turned the key in the lock, the sight that greeted me was not the gangland den that I had expected. Roses and freesias in cut-glass vases on the desk filled the air with the most delicious scent and the blood-spattered carpet had been replaced with an oriental rug.

A clothes rail of the fanciest-looking gowns I'd ever laid eyes on stood next to the leather sofa. I knew from the first glance they were dead ringers for that Dior New Look dress I'd seen in a glass case in Gamages. I peeked down inside one of the linings to check the label and my heart skipped a beat. They *were* Dior gowns, the real thing, not some knockoffs from an East End tailor. God only knows how Billy Sullivan had managed it, but he had a whole rail full of them; they must have been worth hundreds of pounds each.

I felt like a kid in a sweet shop, as I touched sumptuous satin ribbons and pleated, heavy silks. These were the dresses that the women in Derry and Tom's jewelry department wore to go to their fine dinners when they wanted to look their most elegant. And now I was getting a chance to step into their world and into their shoes. It was a notch up from anything I'd seen at Alice's place, in Queen's Buildings. It made what The Forty Thieves hoisted look like they'd fallen off the back of the rag and bone man's cart.

I unbuttoned my cardi and took off my skirt and blouse, folding them neatly on his leather-topped desk. As I stood there in my underwear, I couldn't help noticing his accounts ledger was open, so I took a peek, leafing through row upon row of neat, copperplate writing; names of pubs and clubs and amounts of money received for "protection" services rendered by Billy Sullivan, Esq.

But something stood out like a sore thumb. Among the list of names and meticulous notes were payments to cozzers—Sgt. this, and Constable that, and at the head of it all was a Ch. Insp., which I knew stood for the top brass. Billy Sullivan had half of the police force in London straightened and on his books by the looks of it. He was so powerful, there would be no stopping him.

I felt a creeping sense of dread that I'd seen something I shouldn't have done.

Out of nowhere, there was a rap at the door that made me jump out of my skin and then, to my relief, Gypsy appeared.

Her mouth fell open at the sight of all the beautiful flowers and clothes.

"Oh my Gawd, Nell! Look at this lot! I think I've died and gone to heaven!"

She was talking ten to the dozen as she rifled through the rail: "Mr. Sullivan explained that we're going somewhere really classy and I have to keep my trap shut unless he says otherwise. I don't care because I get to have a night out with Albert Rossi wearing one of these beauties. You are the best friend in the whole wide world, Nell!"

I picked out a baby pink gown with a silk bodice and a frothy silk crepe and skirt that reached almost to the floor. There was more yardage in it than most people could afford in a month of Sundays, even with coupons. And it was nothing like the underskirts made of parachute silk that you sometimes found on the markets. This was pure class and I wouldn't have been surprised to see it on the likes of

Princess Margaret. My hands were shaking with excitement and I struggled with the zip.

"Here, let me help," squealed Gypsy. "Don't bust it, for God's sake."

She dashed to my side and fastened it up and I stood smoothing the folds of material down over my hips.

"How do I look?" I said self-consciously. It was such a showstopper of a dress, there would be no shrinking into the background in it, even in a room full of lords and ladies.

"Ravishing, darling," she said in her poshest accent. "Now it's my turn!"

She pulled out a plunge-neck black velvet gown, which looked tiny, a bit too tiny for her ample frame. But there was no stopping her. She hoicked it on over her head and wriggled herself down into it before turning around and asking me to zip her up.

I was almost knocked out by the cleavage on display.

"Albert'll have a couple of things on his mind all night other than the cards if you don't cover those up," I laughed, flinging her a mink stole that was hanging over the rail.

"Spoilsport," she pouted. But she put it around her shoulders, making her neckline a bit more modest.

Shoeboxes were lined up beside the sofa and I opened one, relishing the crinkle of the tissue paper as I unwrapped a beautiful pair of pointy-toed stiletto-heeled silk shoes in pink to match my dress. I tried them on. They fitted me like a glove.

Gypsy, meanwhile, was forcing her feet into a pair of peep-toe velvet platform sandals, which were at least a size too small.

"Perfect," she breathed.

I rooted through my handbag and flipped open the tiny mirror of my powder compact to apply lippy, rouge, and lashings of mascara, which Gypsy then retouched, as if she were painting the Sistine Chapel.

"There!" she said eventually, when she was satisfied with how I looked.

She held my arm as we tottered out of the office and through the club, to wolf whistles from the fellas and glacial stares from Alma and her mob of dancers.

"Oh, lah-di-dah," she crowed. "S'pose you think you're better than us now, do you?"

Lou the barman waved at me and produced a bunch of daffodils from under the counter.

"These are from Jimmy," he said, thrusting them toward me with a guilty look. "He left them here earlier, to say sorry that he couldn't meet you because some urgent work came up. You were so busy talking to Mr. Sullivan that I forgot to tell you . . ."

I looked at the wilted blooms, wrapped in an old newspaper, and thought back to me sitting in that cinema on my own like a maiden aunt. It was such a pathetic gesture of apology, compared with the roomful of flowers that Billy Sullivan had just laid on. I scoffed. "It don't matter now, Lou, I got a better offer, didn't I?"

I turned to Gypsy as we stepped out into the street, where Billy had the engine to his gleaming black Bentley running, and Albert was sitting beside him in the passenger seat.

"I don't think we're better than those other girls," I whispered to Gypsy. "I know we are."

She gave my arm a little squeeze.

"Act like you were born to it," I said.

Chapter Twenty-Four

NELL

Mayfair, London, March 1947

The engine of Billy's Bentley thrummed softly in the night air as we drew up outside a three-story mansion in Berkeley Square.

A doorman in a top hat and tails with shiny buttons on his coat opened the car door for me. I hesitated for an instant before stepping uncertainly onto the pavement. Billy offered me his arm and we walked up the front and into another world.

"You look beautiful, Nell," he murmured, his eyes lighting up as he appraised my form. "Any prince would be proud to have you on his arm."

"Welcome to The Lucky Seven, ladies," said the doorman.

We strode through the grand entrance hall, lit by gilt chandeliers with dozens of flickering candles casting shadows up the wall. In front of us lay a thickly carpeted staircase with ebony balustrades.

A hush fell over the drawing room. Murmured conversations between bored ladies perched on overstuffed sofas faded into silence. I felt all eyes on me, or rather, my dress, as they wondered how on earth I was wearing Dior when their seamstresses, their private accounts at Derry and Tom's and Marshall and Snellgrove, had been unable to procure it for them.

The silk rustled as I teetered along beside Billy, who started glad-handing men dressed in dinner jackets and bow ties as if they were old friends. But their accents gave them away as toffs, who knew little of the underbelly of London that Billy inhabited.

Albert was striding across the room after him, with Gypsy struggling to keep up in her too-small shoes.

One of the toffs had a little moustache that reminded me of Hitler. He just about devoured me and Gypsy with his eyes, while his wife looked daggers and twiddled with the string of pearls at her throat.

Posh Hitler took Gypsy's hand, clasping it longer than was necessary. Then he bit into the olive in his martini in a way that was almost indecent as he leered with a rubbery bottom lip. Gypsy, who was rather flustered, let her mink stole slip, exposing the mounds of white flesh of her bosom, barely contained by the velvet dress. Albert's lip curled at the edges as he noticed that; it was more like a sneer than a smile.

"Can we make ourselves useful? Perhaps we could fix some drinks?" I ventured, desperate to break the ice and stop the posh fool from falling headlong into Gypsy's knockers in front of his wife.

Billy nodded, and carried on backslapping his way around the room, as chairs were moved back and the men sat down at an oval table, topped with a green baize cloth.

"Thanks for your patience, gentlemen," said Billy, speaking softly. I went over to the drinks trolley and started to mix a whisky and soda for him. I'd seen Lou do it often enough, but now my hands were shaking.

"And my thanks to Lord Dockworth for hosting us here at this special meeting of The Lucky Seven Club."

Posh Hitler, Lord Dockworth, cleared his throat in approval.

Spielers, illegal private gaming dens, were operating all over London in back rooms and basements, but The Lucky Seven was clearly a top-class joint that evaded the cozzers by moving from mansion to mansion in Mayfair.

I carefully placed the crystal tumbler by Billy's elbow. Gypsy was busy fussing over a martini for Albert, as Lord Dockworth licked his lips in my direction. Lady Dockworth rolled her eyes as if she'd seen it all before and marched over to the other side of the room, where she gathered in a huddle with her chums, who were a mass of pointy elbows and nipped-in waists. They had a way of draping themselves over the expensive furniture that came with years of practice, to ensure they still looked charming. But when she turned her back on me and Gypsy, she made it abundantly clear that we were not going to be having any cozy chats with her or her friends this evening.

Thick, swagged curtains kept out the evening chill and a fire blazed in the grate beneath an enormous marble mantel-piece. In a painting on the wall above it, a cheery-looking cavalier was waving his hat in the air on a horse that was rearing up but going nowhere fast.

I had no idea how to cope with the amount of material in my dress if I sat down, so I stood, pretending to admire the painting, with Gypsy hovering at my side.

"Right, gents, chemin de fer is the game of the night," said Billy. "Can we agree a minimum stake of fifty pounds per chip on the black this evening, one hundred on the white and five hundred on the red?"

There were piles of ivory discs of different colors on the table in front of each chair. I could hardly believe my ears. These people must have pots of money sitting at home.

A servant brought in six new packs of cards on a silver

tray and took each one in turn from a cellophane wrapper. Players took a pack each and shuffled them and then they were all put together and a player to Billy's left cut them.

The cards went into a box on the table and Billy used a long wooden paddle to deal them. It was quite a palaver for a game of cards.

It took me a while to get the hang of the game, but I watched closely while Gypsy yawned and fidgeted as if she was bored in a lesson at school.

I could understand why men gambled at the dog track. There, at least you could have a tip-off about a dog or know its running form; but with cards, there was so much at stake and so much more was down to chance. It seemed like madness to me and for such huge sums of dosh.

The cards were dealt in pairs, facedown, and the aim was for each player to try to beat the bank, betting on whose cards added up to nine. The winner of each round took over as the bank. It was fast-paced and Billy seemed to be on a losing streak at first, with the chips stacking up in front of all the other players, but when he was down to his last two fifty-quid pieces, he started to win and win big. The more rounds that were played, the better he got. It was mesmerizing.

Lord Dockworth wasn't smiling anymore and had started to write checks like they were going out of fashion to get more and more chips. Hours whizzed by. In the end, his missus and her stuck-up friends called it a night and their haughty goodbyes echoed in the hallway. I kept refilling Billy's glass every time he signaled me, by clicking his fingers. He'd drunk so much whisky, I began to wonder if he had hollow legs, but he seemed more focused than ever. My feet were killing me, but I stood watch, trying to work out Billy's secret for winning, hardly daring to move in case he wanted another drink.

Then I spotted it. It was just a tiny bend in the angle of the high-value cards, so that when you held them in your hand, they inclined slightly outwards on the right corner. I rubbed my eyes to make sure I wasn't imagining it, but it was there alright. My time at the Alaska Fur Factory meant I had a great eye for detail and once I saw it on one card, it was plain as day on the others. Somehow, Billy Sullivan had fixed the decks. It was all a con. His winning streak wasn't down to skill or luck. He was cheating, plain and simple.

I coolly poured myself a long drink of soda, with plenty of ice, and I kept my discovery to myself.

Gypsy, meanwhile, had availed herself of the free drinks and was lounging, half asleep on an armchair.

When the grandfather clock in the corner struck three, Lord Dockworth threw in his cards and pushed his chips toward Billy, who called in the rest of his winnings. The peer took out his checkbook but Billy waved his hand, dismissively.

"That won't be necessary, Ernest. I'm sure we can find another way for you to repay the favor, some other time . . ."

Lord Dockworth looked visibly relieved. I fancied he'd have to have sold that cavalier over the mantelpiece to clear his debt. They shook hands.

Albert pulled Gypsy to her feet and she rubbed sleep out of her eyes.

"Come and have a nightcap with Lord Dockworth and me in the library," he whispered in her ear, holding her up, with an arm around her waist. She laid her head on his shoulder.

I started moving toward her, to make sure she was alright, but out of nowhere, Billy held me in an iron grip: "You're coming with me."

"But what about Gypsy?"

"She's a big girl, she can look after herself," he said.

Gypsy glanced up at me with those big violet-blue eyes of hers. "I'm fine, Nell," she slurred. "I'm making an evening of it with Albert."

The moon disappeared behind some thick clouds as we left The Lucky Seven. Billy got behind the wheel of his Bentley and we set off at a snail's pace through Mayfair, with only the headlamps to light the way.

At Bond Street, he turned a sharp right and then pulled in, right beside a jeweler's store. He flipped open the trunk and pulled out an iron bar, which he wrapped in his coat. Before I knew what was happening, he'd smashed through the plate glass and seized a necklace from the display case.

The sound of a policeman's whistle echoed in the dark but Billy was already back in the car, laughing like a maniac, as he tossed the necklace into my lap.

He put his foot on the accelerator and we screeched away down the street.

I don't know whether it was fear, or the sheer thrill of it, but I found myself laughing out loud too.

"So, do you like your present?" he grinned.

It was a massive ruby, about the size of a walnut. I held it in the palm of my hand, and it thrilled me to the core.

"It's beautiful. Can I really keep it?"

"I said I would pay you handsomely," said Billy. "And I am a man of my word. Just ask anyone in my gang."

We drove up Piccadilly and through the warren of back-streets, with Billy humming softly to himself.

As he parked the car, he turned to me. "Let me see you in the necklace, Nell. Try it on for me."

I held it to my throat, feeling the weight of the gem against my skin, and then his hands were at the nape of my neck, fastening the heavy gold clasp. As his fingers stroked downwards over my bare shoulders, a tingle shot through me, like a jolt of electricity. His touch was like the pull of a silken thread somewhere deep inside me.

"It looks beautiful, just like you," he murmured. "A woman like you deserves the best in life."

Billy pulled me into his arms. "I know where you belong, Nell, even if you can't see it yet."

Then he kissed me, full on the lips.

And before I knew what I was doing, I kissed him back, hungrily.

I loosened his tie and unbuttoned his shirt to get to him. He was so strong, but he treated me like I was his most precious jewel, covering me with tender kisses.

The streetlamp glowed dimly, lighting up his face, with those eyes as black as coal staring into the depths of my soul. Billy held me in his gaze, his lips brushing against mine. "Is this what you want, Nell?" he said softly, unfastening my dress.

"Yes," I said, my body aching with longing.

I knew it was wrong, but it felt so right being in the arms of the evil gangland boss, Billy Sullivan, the King of Soho.

Chapter Twenty-Five
ALICE

Soho, London, March 1947

Now, I don't know about you, but when someone goes a bit quiet on me, I start to worry.

It had been a few days since I'd heard from Nell, and so I thought I'd pay her a little visit to see what she'd been up to.

Her landlady didn't half grumble when I knocked her up out of bed to answer the door and she kept calling Nell "Gypsy" for reasons I couldn't fathom. Lord only knows what porkie pies Nell had been telling, but I played along with it.

"That's right, she's always been a gypsy, roaming the city, footloose and fancy-free, but I promised her late mother, poor soul, that I would take care of her, and that is what I must do," I said, huffing and puffing my way up the narrow staircase, ignoring her demands for rent.

So, imagine my surprise when I found Nell lounging in bed, dressed like a princess, wearing a necklace fit for a queen.

I yanked the bedclothes off her and she tumbled out of the bed, landing in a heap at my feet, where I happened to give her a little kick, just to make sure she was fully awake.

"What the bleeding hell do you think you are playing at?" I spat. "Did you hoist that yourself?"

She looked up at me, startled, like a rabbit in the head-lights. "No, it was a present."

I grabbed a fistful of the finest silk of her dress, as I hauled her up on her feet: "Present? Who from?"

There was enough quality cloth there to pay a king's ransom.

She was stunned into silence and looked at the floor.

I clasped the ruby at her neck with one hand and held my cane right against her cheek with the other: "And where in the name of God did you nick that from? You will have the law on us with a stone that size going missing, you little fool. Was it from someone's drum or a shop window?"

She didn't answer.

I slapped her around the face, hard. She clutched at it, tears welling with shock, but there was defiance in her eyes. "The dress was a gift from Billy Sullivan. I was spying on him for you. I got into his inner circle, for a card game, and he gave me the dress to look posh for his hoity-toity friends, that's all."

I was far from convinced.

"And what about the necklace? Fell off the back of a lorry, did it?"

"He gave me that as payment. He smashed a shop window down Bond Street last night." She addressed her comments to the bare floorboards.

"Oh, I bet he did, the reckless idiot. And pay you for what, exactly? I thought I gave strict instructions for you to keep your knickers on."

"It was just for looking decorative when he was playing cards, that's all, serving him drinks, I swear it."

I seized her, shaking her like a rag doll. "Looking decora-tive! Is that what you want to do with your life? Look like a trinket for Billy Sullivan to display, to show the world he's controlling you? And taking his jewels, which will probably lead the cozzers to my door. You stupid little fool."

"Please, Alice . . ."

But I was just getting started.

"And at what point were you going to tell me about this lovely present of yours?"

"I never got a bleeding chance . . ." she whined. "You came bursting in here and turfed me out onto the floor. You can't just march in here like you own the place . . ."

I was having none of it.

"Let's get this straight. I am the Queen of this gang, you know the Hoisters' Code: anything you earn comes to the Queen. You should have been at my door with this last night. So, hand it over."

She undid the clasp and parted with the stone, miserably. I pulled Mrs. Tibbs from my pocket.

"Give me a good reason not to use this on you, to teach you a lesson you'll never forget." My fingers twitched but Nell didn't flinch. She sat there, with that defiant look in her eye again, as if she was willing me to do it.

Then, just as suddenly, the look was gone.

"I had no choice but to go with him to Mayfair," she said calmly. "If I hadn't, he'd have been suspicious of me. I was doing it for us, for The Forty Thieves."

I put the shiv back in my pocket and sized up the jewel; it wouldn't have looked out of place on a maharajah. "I suppose this will have to make up for my disappointment in you. We'll lay low with this one for a while. I'll have a word with my contacts in Hatton Garden, maybe sell it on abroad."

"But what if Billy asks to see me wearing it?" She looked panicked at the thought.

"How likely is that, Nell? For you to be parading that

in his club in front of all the low-life punters who would squeal to the cozzers for the price of a pint? Unless you are planning on having a private showing of some kind for him?"

"God, no!" she spat. "What do you take me for? He's a monster. Makes my flesh creep . . ."

"Well, you'll have to make up a story to cover yourself, won't you?" I said icily. "You seem pretty good at that. Who the bloody hell is Gypsy? Been reading the tea leaves for the landlady, have you?"

The door swung open and a girl stood there, squaring up to me, with her hair all over the place, her tits falling out of her dress and a cut on her lip.

"I'm Gypsy," she said. "Who the effing hell are you?"

"I'm Nell's fairy godmother," I said, brandishing my cane in her direction. "So, watch your mouth. Although, by the look of things, it seems someone has beaten me to it . . ." Nell jumped up as if she'd been scalded and went toward her friend.

"It's alright, Gyp, she's my aunty from across the water. The one who gave me the sparkler."

"I heard raised voices," said Gypsy, with an apologetic shrug. "Thought there was trouble. No offense."

"None taken." I smiled, appraising her form. She was a very good-looking girl, the sort that shop assistants would fawn over if she spoke differently and dressed right. She was game enough to front up to me as well. I started to wonder about smoothing off her rough edges a bit.

"Nell's been telling me all about her adventures in Mayfair last night. I don't suppose you went along on that little jaunt, did you?" I said.

"It didn't turn out the way I hoped," she replied, sitting down at her dressing table like a deflating balloon.

"Oh dear," I soothed. "Why don't we all have a nice little cup of tea and then you can tell your Aunty Alice all about it?"

Nell shot me a worried glance.

"You don't mind me getting to know your pal Gypsy better, do you, Nell?" I said archly. "After all, we're family, ain't we?"

"Albert hit me," said Gypsy, blowing her tea to cool it down before she took a sip.

"What did he do that for?" said Nell, with a gasp of disbelief.

"It was all my fault," said Gypsy with a shrug. "I was too mouthy and a bit rude to that toff, when all he wanted was a little kiss and a cuddle, which wouldn't have hurt, just to be nice. And instead, I pushed him off me. Albert got mad, said I'd caused embarrassment to Mr. Sullivan by doing that, and I gave him some backchat.

"So, he did this."

She touched her swollen lip, as if she were trying to make sense of it.

"He doèsn't have the right to lay a finger on you!" said Nell. "I've a good mind to . . ."

"No!" said Gypsy, shaking her head and looking at the floor. "It was a misunderstanding. The drunken old fool Lord Dockworth probably won't remember it anyway. Mr. Sullivan had won so much at the cards that he was drowning his sorrows. I was Mr. Sullivan's guest and I was supposed to be nice to people, that was the deal, wasn't it? Albert apologized to me after. It's fine."

"But, Gyp," said Nell, "you can't let a fella get away with it."

"He ain't just a fella," said Gypsy. "He's Albert Rossi and he wants to take me out to dinner tonight to make up for it." She brightened at the very thought.

"Blokes aren't saints, are they? Just ask your Aunty Alice. I bet she understands where I'm coming from . . ."

Gypsy turned to me and I noticed she had the most stunning eyes, violet, like a flower.

"Love makes women foolish, Gypsy," I said. "Sometimes you have to listen to your head, not your heart. I wouldn't stand for a man beating any of my girls."

"Have you got daughters?" said Gypsy. "I bet you'd go around and give any bloke what for with that cane of yours," she said with a laugh.

"Oh yes, lots of girls look up to me as their mum, don't they, Nell?"

"I wish I had someone like you to watch over me," said Gypsy. "My mum ran off with a Canadian airman and couldn't get shot of me fast enough."

"Well," I said, giving her a little pat on the shoulder, "now we're friends, you can talk to me anytime you like. I'm always there to lend a sympathetic ear."

"You've certainly raised Nell the right way. She's the best friend in the whole wide world. She even nicked me some silk knickers and a slip the other day when I couldn't afford it . . ."

Nell had gone very pale.

"Did she? Stealing is wrong, Nell, don't you remember what you learned in Sunday School?!" I scolded. "Lord knows what your mother would say if she knew what you'd been up to. I've a good mind to take you home with me right now!"

"Oh, me and my big mouth," said Gypsy. "She didn't mean no harm by it, Aunty Alice, it was just helping me out because I was desperate. Please don't tell her ma. She won't do it again, will you, Nell?"

Nell shook her head.

"Well, here was I thinking you were making a decent living and it turns out that you are nothing but a bleeding tea leaf, Nelly. I am shocked," I said, folding my arms in consternation. "I've never heard anything like it in all my born days."

"She earns her money singing in a nightclub and is a respectable girl," said Gypsy. "Did she tell you we are going to be models in a fashion show? Maybe you could come and watch? It's going to be fun. You should be proud of her, please don't be cross."

"No," I said, glancing at Nell, who had now gone white as a sheet. "She hasn't mentioned that yet, but we've got such a lot to catch up on, haven't we, dear?"

I took a sip of my tea. "Oh, it's gone cold. Be a love, Gypsy, and go and top it up with some nice hot water from the stove, will you?"

Gypsy took my teacup and traipsed off down the stairs.

I turned to Nell and pulled out the shiv. "You'd better start talking."

"There ain't a law against me going into shops," she said, sulkily.

"There ain't. But there is a law against you nicking stuff and not handing it on to me," I said, holding Mrs. Tibbs to the light and admiring the sharpness of the blade.

"I just helped a friend out. She needed something nice. Gypsy's a sweet girl but she's a bit hopeless with money," she said. "I shouldn't have done it . . ."

I kicked over a heap of paper flowers and empty shoe-boxes.

"No, you should not. You've been giving away my secrets, like an ungrateful wretch. It's disloyal. Very disloyal. And do you know what I do to girls who are disloyal to me?" I moved closer to her.

"I know it looks bad, but I was in Gamages checking out the lie of the land for a fashion show, something big," she said. "I will make it up to you."

She grabbed the hem of her dress and showed me the label, which said DIOR.

"There's going to be dresses like this one, which is called the New Look, and is the latest thing from France. All the posh women want it. You should have seen them in Mayfair looking daggers at me!

"There'll be going more furs than you know what to do with and we can clean up because The Forty Thieves can be the models."

I stopped and thought about it for a moment.

"Models?"

"Yes," said Nell. "Me, Em, and some of the girls can do it and I can rope Gypsy in on it too. If we can get half a dozen of us in there, we can nick whatever we can lay our hands on, right under their noses, and no one will be any the wiser. We will just walk off the catwalk and disappear. What do you think?"

"I think you are on your last chance," I said. "There's a lot of groundwork to do if we are going to pull it off. But you might just have played a blinder, Nell."

She heaved a sigh of relief but I turned to her as I tucked Mrs. Tibbs back into my pocket: "Only time will tell if it's enough to save your skin."

Chapter Twenty-Six

NELL

Soho, London, March 1947

GANG WARS! *West End or Wild West?*

The newspaper boy was shouting the headlines at the top of his lungs as we left the house to go up to Gamages, to try out as models for the fashion show.

I stopped by the newsstand and my heart leapt into my mouth as I read the front page.

Gangster slashed by rival in open warfare on our streets!

Businessman Alfred White, known in the underworld as Big Alf, was this morning recovering in hospital from a deep gash to his face, which required fifty stitches, after a fracas outside his mansion block in Bayswater. He was slashed by a thug wielding a razor, after returning from a night at the pub.

A man was seen running from the scene of the crime by Mr. White's wife, Winifred, who is now under police protection. Officers are expected to interview Mr. White later today, but sources told the Morning News: *"He's saying nothing. The gang bosses prefer to sort their differences out without police interference. Whoever did this is a marked man. Big Alf's men will have their revenge. Police fear a breakdown of law and order on the streets of London."*

Lord Dockworth, the former Home Secretary, is an outspoken critic of the gangland culture infesting the West End, which has worsened since the end of the war. MPs are calling for a Spivs and Drones order to give police greater powers to clean up our streets.

"Our shops are overrun by thieves and our streets are ruled by violence. And I shall be raising these matters in the House of Lords," said Lord Dockworth, speaking at his Mayfair home.

"Whoever did this should face a very stiff prison sentence indeed. People need to be protected from these razor gangs. One may ask whether we are living in the West End or the Wild West."

I could hardly believe it! That hypocrite Lord Dockworth had spent the evening rubbing shoulders with the biggest criminal in Soho and here he was publicly denouncing a razor gang attack. He had some brass neck to do that.

"Something catch your eye?" said Alice, peering over my shoulder. "Typical men spilling blood all over the place," she tutted, reading the headline. "They'll only make matters worse for themselves, the stupid fools. But while the law is after them, that means they have less time to spend watching us, don't it?"

She had the bit between her teeth on my fashion show ruse and I was happy about that, because after she caught me out wearing the dress and the necklace from Billy, I thought my number was well and truly up.

But she was positively bubbling with enthusiasm at the prospect of nicking designer dresses and the best stock that the Alaska Fur Factory could muster.

She'd made us make ourselves presentable and I'd done my best to disguise the cut on Gypsy's mouth with powder and lippy.

"Just let me do the talking," said Alice, as we pushed open the doors to the shop. After making inquiries in ladieswear, one of the snooty shop assistants took us up to the fifth floor to see the manageress, Miss Hunter.

The scent of furniture polish filled my nostrils as we

walked out of the lift and I couldn't help thinking back to the last time I was here, frightened, pregnant, and alone, with a stolen pack of stockings in my bag.

"Bringing back a few memories?" whispered Alice, reading the expression of fear that was written all over my face.

I dug my nails into my palms as I smiled sweetly. "Not at all," I lied.

I hadn't worked out exactly how yet, but I was determined that I would be the only one walking free from that fashion show and she would be up here, with Miss Hunter and half the cozzers in London, facing the music.

"Come in," boomed Miss Hunter. She was sitting at her desk, still sharpening her favorite pencil. She must have had a drawer full of them because God only knows what else she did all day, other than make people's lives a misery. The leaves of the potted plant in the corner were polished almost as highly as the floor. It's fair to say she may have spent a bit of time doing that.

"I've brought some young ladies who want to try out for the fashion show, Miss," said the assistant, practically bowing and scraping before her boss.

"Very good," she said, shooing her away with a flick of her bobbed hair, "you may get back to work."

All three of us stood there, clasping our handbags.

"The girls are such huge fans of Mr. Dior's work," gushed Alice. "We saw the dress on the shop floor. They couldn't resist the chance to model for you."

Miss Hunter put down her pencil and strode across the office and looked me and Gypsy up and down. She actually got hold of my waist and gave it a little pinch, before turning to Alice. "Are these your daughters?"

"This beautiful girl is my daughter, *Ruby*," she said,

pointing to me, with an evil glint in her eye, "and that is her friend, from the office. They are both secretaries. Lovely girls, aren't they?"

Miss Hunter looked at me closely, as a flicker of something approaching recognition crossed her face.

"Have we met?"

"No, Miss," I said, standing on tippy-toes to make myself appear taller.

"I'm sure I would remember making your acquaintance," I simpered, like one of those Mayfair women I'd met the other night. She seemed to like that.

She appraised Gypsy's buxom figure. "I'm not sure she has exactly the look that we require . . ."

"Oh, but you must take her," said Alice, "because she is French, like the lovely dresses you are going to show. Who better to model them than a lovely young French woman?"

"I see," said Miss Hunter. "Comment vous appelez-vous?"

"She's called Edith . . . Edith Piaf de Paris," said Alice proudly, as I stifled a giggle.

"Like the singer?" said Miss Hunter, raising an eyebrow.

"The very same," said Alice. "Her parents were huge fans."

"Vous aimez habiter a Londres?" said Miss Hunter in a perfect French accent, smiling warmly. "Votre famille vient de Paris?"

Gypsy hesistated, twiddling with her hair, and then said: "Oui. Mon dieu, oui, oh, la, la, oui."

"She finds it too emotional to speak her own language," said Alice, in a whisper. "Lost most of her family in the fighting, best not to ask her about it. She can understand English perfectly well. But just look at her eyes and think of how she'd light up a room in one of your lovely Dior creations."

Miss Hunter peered into Gypsy's eyes and made a little "hmm" of satisfaction.

The next thing I knew we were parading up and down her office with books perched on our heads, praying that they wouldn't tumble off.

"Very well," said Miss Hunter. "There will be a rehearsal next week. Report to my office at 2 pm on Wednesday."

"Oh, wonderful," said Alice. "There are a few more girls from the typing pool who might be useful to you, but meanwhile these two won't let you down, will you, girls?"

"Erm, *non*," said Gypsy.

Gypsy and me collapsed in a fit of giggles as we rounded the corner from Gamages onto High Holborn.

"Edith Piaf de Paris!" I hooted. "I nearly wet myself laughing."

Alice seized hold of me. "You'd better not blow her cover or screw this up, or you will be laughing on the other side of your face."

I was only saved by a van with a huge placard on the top, and a fella yelling through a megaphone: "*Women!* Your country needs you. Sign up here for vital work. We need you to work to get Britain back on its feet!

"Don't stay at home when you are needed in our factories and offices."

The van drew up right beside us and he clambered out of the passenger seat.

"You, ladies, can I interest you in signing up today, to help your country?" he said, brandishing a clipboard.

I'd heard about women being accosted by government officials who were so desperate to find staff after the war that they were recruiting girls on the street to get them to go to work.

"Oh, that's all we need," said Alice, through gritted teeth. She turned to face him.

"I'm so sorry," said Alice, almost sweeping him into the gutter with a flick of her arm. "We are all in gainful employment, my good man. We work all the hours that God sends, in Gamages."

"You can say that again," I muttered under my breath, as I escaped Alice's clutches.

That afternoon, Gypsy did her hair and had a bath in the tin tub in front of the range before leaving early to go to the club. She was still high as a kite about the prospect of dinner with Albert Rossi, even though he'd belted her one.

I tried warning her that a leopard doesn't change its spots but she wouldn't hear a word of it. The scummy gray water was cold in the old tin bath and Gypsy was long gone, in a waft of her cheap Coty perfume, when there was the most almighty hammering on the front door.

I pulled it open to find Jimmy standing there, his collar pulled high up around his chin, his hat low over his eyes, and bloodstains on his hands.

"Nell," he said, "thank God you're here! Please let me in."

"What in the name of Christ Almighty have you gone and done?" I said, my mouth falling open at the sight of so much blood. It was on his overcoat too, a great splodge of it.

"I'm on my toes, Nell," he said, white with fear, stepping over the threshold. "Half of London's after me. If the law gets me looking like this, I'm going to have some explaining to do and if Big Alf's men get me, I'll be in the foundations of one of them new buildings they're putting up all over the East End. I've just got to lie low until Billy sorts it all out."

Suddenly the newspaper headlines made sense.

"Tell me you weren't involved in that shivving," I whispered, taking hold of him by the shoulders, knowing full well what the answer was. The damp, fetid air of the little hallway stuck in the back of my throat as I gasped, "Tell me you didn't go and stripe that fella's face!"

"This is a war, Nell," he said. "The war with Germany is over but this is our war, right here on the streets of London, and I'm a bloody good soldier."

"You did everything you could to get out of doing your duty in the army, Jimmy!" I cried. "You made up dodgy eyesight, flat feet, and every other ailment you could bleeding well think of to keep your barrow and now you are fighting for the King of Soho as if your life depends on it. What the hell has got into you?"

He pulled a wad of banknotes from his pocket and handed them to me. "This."

I stared at it. There was at least two hundred quid there, in used notes. It was a bleeding fortune. It was enough for us both to get out of Soho, just as he had promised.

Old Ma Harris started to stir from her afternoon nap in her bedroom right beside us. "Gypsy? Is that a fella I can hear?"

"No, Mrs. Harris," I said, "just some kid playing Knock Down Ginger. I've sent him off with a flea in his ear. You go back to sleep."

Jimmy lowered his voice as we made our way down the hall to the scullery. "It's enough for us to make a fresh start, to rent a house together, start over. I did it for us, Nell."

I shut the door and turned to him.

"Oh, Jimmy," I said, "You bloody fool. They're going to throw the book at you. You'll be looking at a seven for this, hard labor and everything. How can we be together if you're in the nick?"

He was crushed by that.

"I had no choice, don't you see," he said, with a wild

look in his eyes. "I'm in the gang, one of Billy's Chaps, and he was testing me out with the biggest job he's had for a very long time. I'm made in the gang because of this. The Chaps are already calling me Jimmy the Razor."

"And where are they now?" I said despairingly. "Where are they, your gangland mates? They've run back into the sewers where they belong, and they have hung you out to dry. I don't see you banging on their doors. You're right here, banging on mine."

He stared at the floor. "They told me to lay low, until the heat is off, because their drums are the first place the cozzers will come looking. And I can't go to Billy. It just ain't done. That's not the way it works. I've got to keep him out of it. It's a loyalty thing. It's the gangland code. He's the boss."

Jimmy took off his blood-spattered coat, rolled up his sleeves, and started to scrub himself clean in Gypsy's dirty bathwater.

Suddenly, the penny dropped for me.

"It was in the paper, Jimmy, earlier on this morning. Billy Sullivan has set it up so you will take the fall for him. He's got an alibi and he's got one of his posh politician chums to cover his back."

"What do you mean?" said Jimmy, looking more like a frightened child than a gangster on the run.

"Billy Sullivan can distance himself from the attack on Big Alf and say it was nothing to do with him because he will say he was having dinner with other people that night," I said flatly. "He's taken out his rival by using you, but his hands are clean as far as the establishment are concerned. He has witnesses."

"How do you know that?" he said. "Billy wouldn't do that to me."

"Wouldn't he?" I said. "He's running a fancy spieler in

Mayfair; The Lucky Seven they call it. And the posh git who was in the paper calling for whoever done the shivving to be banged up in jail for a very long time was sitting next to Billy Sullivan all night playing cards. He was being taken for every penny while you were slashing Big Alf. He owes Billy big-time and so he is going to dance to Billy's tune, you mark my words."

"That's bollocks," said Jimmy. "You're just making this up. That is just dancers' gossip from the dressing room, ain't it?"

"No, Jimmy," I said. "It's the truth."

"What do you mean?"

"I was there, I saw it with my own eyes."

"What the hell were you doing there?" he said, anger flashing across his face.

"You are not the boss of me, Jim," I said. "You stood me up at the cinema, remember? So, I went for a drink at The Windsor to drown my sorrows, if you must know, and I got roped into it."

"I'm sorry," he said, looking crestfallen. "I was given the job, I had to see it through. I left flowers at the club, to apologize. I tried to do the right thing, honest I did. Didn't you like them?"

"Of course, I liked them," I lied. "I loved them but that is not the point. Billy Sullivan used me too, as part of his alibi. He made me and Gypsy go to Mayfair to serve them all drinks. He gave me a new dress . . ."

His face fell, like I'd just smacked him in the jaw.

When he glanced up again, he was consumed by anger. "Did he touch you?"

"You don't own me, Jim!" I spat. "It's none of your business what he did or didn't do and if that's the way you are going to talk to me, you can get out now."

I waggled my finger at him, the one with the diamond on it.

"This ain't your ring, and it never will be, let's get that straight. It's my ring, I earned it myself. No man will ever be the boss of me."

"I don't want to be the boss of you, Nell. You are your own woman. I just didn't want to think of him laying his hands on you, making you do things. I just want to take care of you . . ."

I looked away and walked over to the kettle. Water sploshed from the tap, breaking the silence.

"We've both been played by Billy Sullivan," I said eventually.

"I don't want to lose you, Nell. I'm sorry, for everything. I was trying to show you I'm a man you can be proud of, a man worth marrying." Jimmy sank his head into his hands and began to shake. "I can't go to prison, Nell. I don't want to be locked up. I want to be with you. I want us to have the life we should have had with our baby, our firstborn, Joseph. I think about him all the time. I dream about him, Nell. I swear I can see his face every time I close my eyes."

He was crying now, tears coursing down his face. "I want to have children with you, come home to you and feel you next to me in the bed, every night.

"I want to see your face every morning and watch our kids run off to school and kiss them good night and keep them on the straight and narrow."

I went to him and put my arms around his shoulders.

He pulled me close and the moment we kissed, all the desires and hope we had for our lost life together collided in that grimy little scullery.

Jimmy wasn't perfect by a long shot, but we came from the same streets, we understood one another, and we weren't out to fleece each other like everyone else in Soho, so perhaps he was perfect for me.

He carried me upstairs in his arms and laid me gently

on the single bed. It wasn't like the first time, in the back alley, when I was fumbling and excited and scared at the same time and he was leading me astray.

I unzipped my skirt and undid my blouse while he peeled my stockings down my thighs. Then I felt for him, urgently, wanting him inside me. I felt the hardness of him and the firmness of his body as he nudged his way into me. He brushed his fingers across my breasts, and I tingled at his touch.

"Oh, Jimmy," I whispered.

We lay there, in the fading light of the afternoon, making love to each other, for the first time in our lives.

Outside in the street, the shouts of kids playing kick the can died away and the sun set over Soho.

Chapter Twenty-Seven
NELL

Soho, London, March 1947

Jimmy lay in a tangle of bedsheets, staring at the ceiling, as he lit another cigarette.

The muscles in his chest tightened as he stretched like a cat, before he turned to put an arm around my waist. His eyes sparkled, like they used to when we were courting, but he treated me differently now, gazing at me as if I was something so precious, he didn't want to let me go.

"You are a very beautiful woman, Nell," he murmured, nibbling my ear.

"And you are a very wanted man," I said, pinching his cheek and wriggling myself free. "I've got to get to work, Jim, they'll be wondering where I've got to."

I pulled on my stockings and fastened my suspender belt, as he watched me, mesmerized.

"I can't believe Billy would rat me out," he said eventually. "I just can't believe it."

"It isn't a case of ratting you out," I said, leaning in closer to kiss him again. "It's about distancing himself from you, while getting the benefit of the dirty work you've done because the rival gang will be broken.

"He doesn't care if you do time in jail; he's paid you off

and you get the reputation in gangland, but he keeps his position as the King of Soho."

It was as if a light bulb had gone on, right over Jimmy's head.

"The Whites are his biggest threat, since the Italians were all but cleared out of London in the war," he said. "They were trying to muscle in, and Billy didn't like it because Big Alf wouldn't do a deal, 'cos it would have left him short-changed. The fella you saw in the carpet was just one of his foot soldiers. We beat out of him where Big Alf would most likely be."

"So, Big Alf had to be publicly humiliated by being cut by one of Billy's men," I said. "He's lost his power now, no one will line up behind him. He's a spent force."

"But Billy keeps his hands clean and what's more, he can even get toffs like Lord Dockworth to take the heat off him."

"How am I going to get out of this, Nell?" said Jimmy, running his hands through his hair.

"I'll think of something, Jim," I said. "I've got a few tricks of my own up my sleeve to outfox Billy Sullivan."

I was thinking about breaking into Billy's office somehow, but I didn't want to worry Jimmy with that because it was a dangerous plan. When I was in Holloway, I'd heard Rose talking about making a copy of a key using bath soap.

I glanced around the room. Gypsy had a nice bar of scented soap on her dressing table and so I stuck that in my pocket.

I turned to Jimmy. "Jim, you can't stay here. You'll get me and Gypsy thrown out if the old bat downstairs hears you."

"I know," he said, propping himself up on his elbow. "I might be better across the water down around the Elephant. There are more places I can hide out there."

"So true," I said with a giggle. "You did a bloody good

job of hiding from me often enough. You were like the
Scarlet Pimpernel of the fruit and veg stall!"

He pulled me to him, and I tumbled over on the bed.

"I ain't letting you go ever again, Nell," he said, his voice
hoarse with longing.

"We will meet again, Jim, just like the song says," I said,
prizing him off me. "But I really do need to get my skates
on or I'll miss my singing slot."

"I'll wait for a few hours then I'll lift the latch and go,"
he said. "But I'm going to leave most of this here, for you,
for safekeeping."

He handed me the wodge of notes. "This is the start of
our new life together, Nell. I mean it," he said. "Whatever
happens, keep it safe. For us."

That evening, I strolled into the club and slap bang into
Billy Sullivan, who was propping up the bar, dressed in an
immaculate suit, as always.

"You're late," he said. "I was about to send out a search
party. Everything alright?"

I felt his eyes traveling over my body and it revolted me
and thrilled me at the same time. I tried not to think about
that because it seemed so disloyal to Jimmy. Billy was like
a virus, coursing through my veins, and I just wanted it to
burn itself out.

"Fancy a drink before you go on?" he said, pouring me
a glass of champagne.

I accepted it and sat beside him, sipping at it.

"I read some interesting headlines this morning," I said
sweetly. "I saw your friend Lord Dockworth in the paper
talking about the dangers on our streets after that razor
attack."

He flinched, just slightly, as a few punters started
earwigging.

"Dreadful business," said Billy, loudly enough for them to overhear. "I was just having some drinks with friends that night. It was a very convivial evening as I recall. But then you know that, because you were there, weren't you, sweetheart?"

He put his hand around my waist, firmly.

I leaned my head toward his shoulder and whispered in his ear, "I heard Jimmy's in the frame for the attack on Big Alf. But you know that anyway, don't you?"

His eyes were like molten lead as he murmured, "You watch your mouth."

"You don't scare me, Billy, because I know you cheat at cards," I said under my breath.

The next thing I knew, he'd pulled me to my feet and was steering me across the club, in the direction of his office.

"Keep playing," he barked at the pianist, who was looking confused because I was due to start singing. "This won't take long." Alma and the dancers sighed and started another high-kicking routine.

Billy frog-marched me up the dank corridor and into his office, slamming the door shut. He turned to me, with a face like thunder.

"What in the name of God do you think you're playing at?"

"I could ask you the same thing," I shot back. "You used me and you used Jimmy! You don't care about him, even though he is loyal to you. You've got to help him get out of the frame for this razor attack," I said.

He seized my wrists and held me tight. "You don't tell me what to do, Nell. No woman ever tells me what to do. And you have no idea about my feelings for you, so don't presume that you do."

Just as suddenly, he let go of me, turned his back, and walked around to the desk, running his hands through his hair. As he did so, I slipped his office key off the desk and into my pocket. I had Gypsy's bath soap in there and I pushed the key into it, as hard as I could, praying that it would leave an imprint.

Billy was pouring himself a whisky as I quietly sneaked the key back onto the edge of his leather-topped desk, my pulse quickening with the fear of being discovered.

"But what about Jimmy?" I said, trying to calm my nerves.

"What about him? He's paid well, he knows the risks, he's one of the gang," he said, watching me closely.

"But if he goes to prison . . ."

"That seems very likely, wouldn't you say?" He smiled at me, that toothy grin of his, as he sat down. "He will do his bird and I will make sure he gets paid a salary when he comes out. Jimmy's one of the little people, a foot soldier if you will. He knows his role."

"But he thought he was onto something big . . ."

"Turns out he was, he's all over the papers. And that's before we get to the court case." Billy laughed.

I turned away in disgust.

"Nell, with things the way they are after the war, people want to see the streets of Soho being cleaned up. They need to know that people who wield razors go to prison, and that is what they will get.

"Alf White and his mob aren't going to be a trouble to anyone anymore. People can feel safe under my protection and I can keep a handle on things. That's what the cozzers want, that's what I want. It's how things work."

"But Jimmy believed in you . . ."

"I know you're fond of Jimmy," he began.

"You know nothing," I shouted.

"Let me finish!" He slammed his hand on the table, hard.

"You may be fond of him, but he is beneath you, Nell. You don't need a barrow boy. You need a man like me, and you know it. Deep down inside, you know that's the truth. You knew it the other night. Why fight it?"

"You disgust me! The way you set this all up . . ." I felt hot tears of shame prick my eyes at how far I'd let him go with me after The Lucky Seven and how much I'd wanted it too.

"Oh, Nell, don't be a silly girl," he said, coming to my side and pulling me into his arms. "You need a man like me, not a boy like Jimmy. Has he got what it takes to satisfy you? Can he give you designer dresses from Paris, flowers and jewels to call your own? I think we both know the answer to that."

"It's not about that!"

I tried to pull away but that only made him laugh. "Well, I didn't hear you complaining about anything else. In fact, you looked like you were thoroughly enjoying it the other night. And you get as much of a thrill from stealing as I do; we're quite a combination, aren't we?"

I scowled at him. "Stop it!"

"Oh, you are so beautiful when you're angry," he said. He gazed down at me and I was drowning in his eyes again. "Jimmy belongs in the past. Your life is here, by my side, and you'll realize that soon enough."

I stared at my feet, wishing they could take me away from all of this. I pulled away and sat down to catch my breath.

I studied the photograph in the picture frame again. Billy's little sister was staring up at him as if he walked on water, the poor, deluded cow. I pitied her, growing up with him for a brother.

But Billy hadn't finished with me yet. "Talking of which, what are The Forty Thieves up to these days? Any plans you've heard of that I need to know about?"

"There is something they are planning that I caught a

whisper of," I murmured. "But I'm not sure I should tell you. Alice will kill me . . ."

He loomed over me.

"Oh, come on, Nell, don't be coy. Spit it out, for your sake . . ."

It was quite easy to sound as if I was only reluctantly parting with the information, which I wanted him to know. If he felt Alice Diamond was muscling in on his patch, there was a chance he'd finish her off himself. She was outsmarting me at every turn, so it didn't hurt to stir up trouble between them a little more.

"There's a fashion show at Gamages in a week or so, with lots of furs from the Alaska factory and those posh Dior dresses, like the one you gave me," I said.

"I'm listening," said Billy, picking up a cigar and rolling it between his fingers.

"The Forty Thieves are going to try to hoist some of the stock before it gets onto the catwalk, or that's what I've heard. But it's only a rumor, and I don't see how they think they're going to get away with it."

Billy's eyes lit up. "Fashion show? There might be enough goods there to interest me and my boys, if we could get away with enough stock in a lorry. I can always find a buyer for furs. That's very interesting, Nell, thank you for the tip-off, which I will treat with the utmost discretion. And as for The Forty Thieves, well, we'll see how much they get away with when they are up against my gang, shall we?

"Now, you'd better get yourself on that stage to sing for your supper, hadn't you?"

He came back around to my side of the desk and slapped me playfully on the bottom as I was leaving.

"Oh, and you'd better forget about what you saw at the card tables of The Lucky Seven, if you know what's good for you."

"I know you fixed those packs. I know how you did it," I said flatly.

"You've got quite an eye for detail, haven't you?" he said. "Which is another reason why I'm fond of you."

He wagged his finger at me. "But you've got to learn, Nell, to stop meddling in things you don't understand and leave it to the men. Don't let me hear you talking about that ever again, not if you value that pretty little throat of yours.

"It will be hard for you to sing if I have to cut it to shut you up, won't it?"

I was shaking like a leaf by the time I made it onto the stage. A row of expectant faces greeted me, and a hush fell over the room. Word had got round Soho that I had a voice worth listening to, and the club was packed to the rafters.

I started to sing, miserably:
"They asked me how I knew,
My true love was true
I of course replied
Something here inside
Cannot be denied . . ."

I was halfway through the song when I saw a familiar face in the audience. I don't know who was more surprised—me or Detective Sgt. Eddie Hart, quietly sipping a pint, trying to blend in with the lowlifes. I fancied he might have been one of Billy's straightened coppers, but I hadn't spotted his name in the ledger of payments the other night and that made me curious. I was taking a huge gamble being in Billy's world but the thrill of winning everything or losing everything made me bolder. The stakes were high, and I had to take a chance.

I slowly made my way down into the audience, sashaying past the little tables full of grubby oiks in dirty macs, to the detective's spot. It's fair to say, he looked as if he'd seen a ghost.

"They said someday you'll find,
All who love are blind
When your heart's on fire
You must realize
Smoke gets in your eyes."

"Ain't you pleased to see me?" I whispered, putting my arms around his neck and sitting on his lap. "Are you one of those naughty policemen who's been taking Billy Sullivan's crooked shilling?"

"For God's sake, Nell, no, I'm not," he hissed. "Can we go somewhere and talk about this? If you don't blow my cover, I promise I'll make it worth your while."

"One word to the fellas at the bar, and you'll be cinders. Ash don't tell no tales, from what I hear, and Billy Sullivan don't like cozzers in his club." I smirked. The boot was on the other foot now and I was thoroughly enjoying myself.

"You'd better look like you're paying me for all this attention, or the barman will be over here emptying your pockets for you."

I stood up and carried on singing:

"Now laughing friends deride
Tears I cannot hide
So I smile and say
When a lovely flame dies
Smoke gets in your eyes."

He produced a ten-bob note from his wallet and stuffed it down my cleavage. "That's just for starters. I'm undercover, Nell, even my own boss doesn't know I'm here." Sweat was forming on his brow. He was very handsome, and I quite liked him when he was looking scared.

"I think you will have to do me a very large favor," I

said. "But if you scratch my back, I'll scratch yours. Meet me in the back alley after my set."

"Oh, ain't he saucy?" I giggled to the audience. "Now, who else wants to hear another song?"

The rats were scampering around the overflowing bins like it was Derby Day around the back of The Windsor.

The lighted end of the cozzer's ciggie glowed red in the darkness as I picked my way over the cobbles toward him.

"Well, that was a turn-up for the books, wasn't it?" I said chirpily. "Who'd have thought you'd be darkening my door like that? Whatever is the world coming to, Detective Sergeant Hart?"

"Who's there?" A voice came from the other end of the alley and someone started walking toward us.

Before I could protest, Detective Sgt. Hart had pulled me into an embrace and was kissing me passionately. I cannot tell a lie; it felt quite nice.

He pulled a flashlight from his pocket and shone it toward the intruder. "Piss off, mate, we're just trying to have a bit of peace and quiet here."

The shape in the alley moved away.

"Sorry about that," he said, releasing me and adjusting his tie.

"Do they teach you that in police school?" I said, grinning like the Cheshire cat.

I could have sworn, even in the middle of the blackout, that I saw him blush.

"Now, why don't you level with me about what you were doing in Billy Sullivan's club?"

"I was hoping you might do the same," he said. "The last time I saw you, you were running with The Forty Thieves. Had a sudden change of career?"

"I'm doing what I need to do, to make ends meet, like

most folk," I said. "But you'd better start talking because if Billy or one of his men comes looking for me and they find you, you are done for."

"Alright," he said. "The top brass believe that Sullivan's got right into the force, paying people off, because he's always one step ahead of us. The Home Secretary has set up the Ghost Squad, to root out corruption."

"And they put you in charge?" I said incredulously.

"No, they didn't put me in charge, but I'm one of a very small number of trusted officers who are undercover, to try to find out who the rotten apples are. I'm an outsider, from Tyneside, and the London bobbies don't trust me because I'm not one of them."

"Hmmm," I said, twiddling with my hair. "I might be able to help with some information. But you've got to help me first and I will need guarantees. I'm not putting myself at risk to get stitched up by the likes of you."

"Is it money you need? I can pay you well for whatever information you can get me," he said. "And I swear you will be protected. I will never reveal my sources, Nell."

"Well, we can start with you promising to turn a blind eye if you see me out shopping," I said.

"Fair enough." He shrugged. "But if anyone else catches you, you're on your own."

I thought about it for a minute. "But it's not just that. I need a favor for a friend who's in trouble with the law. I might need you to bend the rules to get him a lower sentence."

"Depends what he's done and I can't wave a magic wand, but I give you my word, if you help me nail Sullivan, I will do everything in my power to help your friend. I'll take it all the way to the Home Secretary if I have to. These are extraordinary times and the powers that be want to clean up Soho for good from bosses like Sullivan.

"So, we can set up a meeting place, somewhere safe, where we won't be spotted and you can tell me everything."

I hesitated. Billy had eyes and ears everywhere.

"I've always liked a walk by the River Thames," I said. "I'll be by the river, just the other side of Big Ben, around three o'clock tomorrow."

"Deal," he said, handing over a ten-pound note. "This is to show you I'm serious."

"Fine," I replied, pulling the lump of soap from my pocket. "You might find this comes in handy."

He took it from me and shone his flashlight on it.

"What's this?"

"It's an impression of the key to Billy Sullivan's office," I said, as his jaw hit the floor. "I'm hoping you might know a good locksmith."

Chapter Twenty-Eight
ALICE

Elephant and Castle, London, March 1947

I always said that Jimmy was a good-for-nothing but, blooming heck, it seems I underestimated the barrow boy, didn't I?

There he was, in handcuffs, with his mug all over the front page of *The Daily News,* being paraded as London's answer to Al Capone.

GANG WARS! RAZOR ATTACK ARREST

Police yesterday caught the man they believe is behind the gangland attack which left a Soho businessman needing fifty stitches. The appalling assault on Alf White is believed to be part of an ongoing gangland feud which has stepped up since the end of the war.

Jimmy Feeney, 22, of Waterloo, South London, was captured after a dramatic chase through the backstreets of the Elephant and Castle. The fugitive ran riot through several shops before he was apprehended.

Feeney, a petty criminal, is known to police for selling black-market goods from his fruit and veg stall. He was charged with assault in relation to the attack on Mr. White and is due to appear before West London Magistrates Court tomorrow. He was also picked out of an identity parade by Mr. White's wife, Winifred, who is being treated for shock.

Chief Inspector Hardy, of Scotland Yard, said last night: "This is an important step toward cleaning up Soho. We will not tolerate gang violence on our streets. Law-abiding people have had enough of it. Violent thugs will be caught. Gang bosses should take this as a warning. Your time is running out."

I can't say it made me feel any safer knowing Jimmy was behind bars. He was best known for slipping a rotten orange into your paper bag or perhaps an overripe plum. The real culprit—and we all know who that was—was still sitting pretty in his clubs in Soho. Poor Jimmy was just his messenger boy and as the saying goes, they always shoot the messenger.

"I never liked him," said Molly, sloshing gin into one of my best teacups. "He just weren't trustworthy. And now we find he's been doing the King of Soho's dirty work. Well, it serves him right that he got caught." She took a sip, and smiled to herself, just as Nell walked in with Em, and the Partridge twins from Queen's Buildings, who were going to do some training to be models for the fashion show.

"I see your boyfriend's made the papers," Molly gloated, thrusting the front page right under Nell's nose.

Nell sat down, with all the stuffing knocked out of her, like a boxer dangling on the ropes when they are on their last legs.

"Oh God, Jimmy," she mouthed. "No!"

"He kicked one right over the bar with that shivving, the silly fool," I said, watching her closely. "That's what you get for getting cozy with the likes of Billy Sullivan," I added pointedly.

"Yeah," Molly crowed. "It's a good job you gave that baby away, Nell, because imagine it growing up and finding out that both his parents are jailbirds!" She was so pleased with her wisecrack, she started laughing like a hyena.

Nell saw red and before any of us knew what was

happening, she'd knocked Molly off her stool and had her hands around her throat and was throttling her.

"Stop that!" I yelled, cracking her on the back of her head with my cane before Molly went a funny color. Molly got her free hand up to her hair and yanked out her trusty hatpin: "I'll put your eye out! Come here, you little witch!"

She waved her arms around wildly, trying to get a stab at Nell's face, but she was fairly pissed, so the risk of that was vanishingly small.

I smacked Molly one with the back of my fist, for good measure, sending the hatpin skittering over the kitchen tiles.

"No, you will not, Molly," I said crossly. "The pair of you will pack in this nonsense now." Honestly, they were like squabbling children.

Molly got up and dusted herself down on one side of the room, while Nell scowled at her from the other.

"I told you, Alice! That girl has got ideas above her station and she's got no respect for the gang," said Molly.

"You let your mouth run away with you, Moll," I chided. "And you!" I said, turning to Nell. "Who the bleeding hell do you think you are slinging your weight around in my house? If anyone is dishing out the beatings within these four walls, it's going to be me!"

"I'm sorry, Alice," she said. "I just won't have her talking about my Joseph like that. It's taking a liberty."

Molly brushed her hat off and plonked it back on her bird's nest of hair.

"I'm going down the boozer," she said. "And you are very much mistaken if you think this is over, Nell."

She turned on her heel and stalked out of the door, leaving Em and the Partridge twins gawping like idiots.

"Welcome to our happy little gang," I beamed. "Take these!" I handed them some books I'd swiped from the local library—and that was a rare visit, because I don't go in for book learning. "Stop standing there catching flies and copy Nell as she shows you how to walk with Charles Dickens on her head."

Nell adjusted the book and started to walk slowly across the kitchen, swaying her hips a little, but I could tell her mind was on Jimmy.

"Can I have a go?" said Em, who was itching to be a model, so she had something to tell the girls at the jam factory.

I picked up a few books by Jane Austen and parked those on her blonde curls. She'd only tottered a few steps when they fell off.

"No," I said. "We need you to get this job, so concentrate. Maybe work in a twirl at the end, where you stand so she can see your profile because you've got a lovely button nose. Then spin around and smile at the old battle-axe of a manager. Oh, she's a right sourpuss, so anything you can do to charm her will help."

Em grinned like a corpse when rigor mortis has set in.

"Oh, for God's sake," I cried, pulling my hairpins out and letting my hair loose over my shoulders. I picked up *Oliver Twist* and stuck that on my bonce, shimmying across the room toward the window, sticking my nose in the air to show my profile, before turning slowly and smiling sweetly.

"Do it like this!"

Nell had been watching me the whole time, but when I turned around, she was looking at me differently, as if she was seeing me for the first time.

"Well, Nell, what do you think?" I said.

"I think you look really different with your hair down," she said, staring at me. "It makes you look younger. Much younger."

★

It took a few hours to get everyone looking like they belonged on the catwalk, but me and Nell managed to make a silk purse out of a sow's ear where Em and the Partridge twins were concerned.

"Alright, you lot, sling your hook," I said, when they went to help themselves to yet another brew from my teapot. "This ain't a soup kitchen. Go and get yourself up to Gamages to see the manageress and earn me some money."

Nell hung back, as if she wanted to ask me something.

"What's the matter?" I said. "Cat got your tongue?"

She waited until she heard the front door slam shut.

I felt for Mrs. Tibbs in my pocket, just in case, because she did have a funny look in her eye.

"I know who you really are," she said, matter-of-factly.

"I'm your boss, the Queen of Thieves," I said. "And you'd better watch that tongue of yours after your performance in here today."

Her next words stopped me in my tracks.

"You're Billy Sullivan's sister, aren't you?"

"You don't know what you're talking about," I scoffed. "You're making up fairy stories, Nell. I think you might have had a funny turn after I clumped you one in that scrap with Molly." I forced a laugh.

"I've seen the picture on his desk, of you both when you were kids. I hadn't realized it until you let your hair down, but it's you in that photograph, isn't it?"

"I dunno what you're talking about," I said. "He's no brother of mine."

But she wouldn't let up.

"Is that why you sent me to spy on him? You want to settle an old score? I can't say I blame you . . ."

"If I do have scores to settle with Billy Sullivan, it's no business of yours . . ."

"I don't appreciate being a pawn in your game with

Billy Sullivan," she said, her eyes burning with anger. "You should have told me at least."

I rushed at her and grabbed her by the lapels of her coat.

"Who do you think you are, talking to me like that? You were a clueless, snot-nosed little nobody from the backstreets of Waterloo who couldn't keep her knickers on when I found you.

"Now look at you! I've made something of you. I've given you a life and I get to say what you do with it. That's the way things are. There are dozens of girls like your old mate Iris out there, girls who have come off on the wrong side of me, who rue the day they crossed me, so don't start now."

My legs started tingling again, that dead-leg feeling. I swear this girl was raising my blood pressure and it weren't good for my heart. I didn't want to show it, but I had to sit down for a moment and catch my breath.

I could see Lim's callous face, sneering at me all those years ago, telling me to put myself on the game. Nell had brought it all back to me and suddenly I was fourteen again, with my whole world turned upside down. I pushed it away and pulled myself together.

"The Forty Thieves has only lasted this long because of the Hoisters' Code and loyalty to the Queen is the first one," I spat. "Testing that loyalty as I see fit is part of that because we offer such a lifestyle and a wage. I had to know you were game enough. That is why you went to Soho.

"You found out who was snitching on me, and you've got your foot in the door in Billy's world. You've proved yourself and you've got more to do, for the good of The Forty Thieves. That is all you need to know. Now, get out of my sight."

Nell buttoned up her coat and got up to leave.

But as she was standing in the doorway, she turned and

said, "He keeps the picture of you because you are the one that got away from him, Alice.

"If there's one thing I've learned about Billy Sullivan, it's that he hates to lose. After all this time, he's never forgotten you, has he? And you've never forgotten him either because you are two sides of the same coin. Blood is thicker than water."

I jumped to my feet, with all the energy of a spring lamb. Mrs. Tibbs was screaming to get out of my pocket, to taste blood, but I knew she'd have to be patient. My fingers worked at the lace handkerchief that was wrapped around the blade.

"You know nothing of who I am or where I've come from," I said. "Don't ever mention Billy Sullivan's name and mine in the same sentence again; not if you value your life. The past is just that, the past. And that's where it's got to stay, Nell. Stay out of it, if you know what's good for you."

All these years of carrying my secret and this girl, this nobody, this thing I had shaped out of the dirt in Tenison Street, had seen right through me.

She stood there, her blonde curls brushing against her jaw, her shoulders pulled back and her chin tilted up, to face me. She was the most beautiful hoister I had ever seen in that moment; daring and determined, as if furs would fling themselves off clothes rails in her presence and follow her anywhere. The power coursing through her veins almost crackled at her fingertips.

It winded me.

"I want to get even with Billy Sullivan too, for what he done to Jimmy," said Nell, turning on her heel.

"Jimmy?" I scoffed. "You ain't still harping on about that good-for-nothing, are you? I can give you a better life in my gang than he can provide in a month of Sundays and anyway, he's up to his neck in it with the cozzers now . . ."

She glared at me, a look that could have stopped traffic.

"He may be good-for-nothing but at least he's honest about it. How's a man like Jimmy supposed to make it in this life, with the likes of Billy Sullivan pulling all the strings? He didn't even stand a chance. I said I'm going to get even with Billy Sullivan for landing Jimmy in it.

"And one day, I'm going to."

Chapter Twenty-Nine
NELL

Westminster, London, March 1947

As the chimes of Big Ben rang out across the River Thames, I felt time was running out for me and Jimmy.

He'd been collared by the law and was now sitting in a police cell, waiting to come up before the beak in the morning. He'd been hung out to dry, just as I feared he would, and a little knot of anger tightened in my stomach at the sneering way Billy Sullivan had cast him aside. The newspapers were having a field day and he was being blamed for all the violence that ever happened in Soho. Jimmy and I were just pawns in the game for the Queen of Thieves and the King of Soho, but I'd had enough of it.

I was still reeling from the realization that Billy Sullivan was Alice's brother, even though she wouldn't admit it. Talk about crime running in the family! But there was no love lost between either of them; that was something I was determined to turn to my advantage. Alice's threats rang in my ears, but for once, I was unafraid. Something about me knowing her secret weakened her. It may only have been a chink in her armor, but perhaps that was all I needed to pierce it and run her through.

The wind whipped through my coat and swept my hair around my face as I ran down the gray stone steps to the riverside. Detective Sgt. Hart was already there, walking along, his hands thrust deep into his pockets.

He smiled as he saw me approaching, lighting up his handsome features.

"I was worried you wouldn't show up," he said, as I fell into step beside him.

He tried to pull me into an embrace, and I knew it would feel good, but I resisted, out of loyalty to Jimmy.

"That was last night," I said. "For show. It's different now."

"I wasn't taking a liberty with you, Nell," he said, looking hurt. "I was trying to make it look like we're a couple."

"Well," I said, with a shrug. "We ain't. So, why don't we talk business? I've seen ledgers, in Billy Sullivan's office, which might be useful to you in your investigation into bent cozzers."

"What exactly?"

"Lists of officers' names and payments, dates and times, that sort of thing," I said.

He looked gobsmacked. "Are you sure?"

"Of course I'm sure," I said. "He's always noting down payments he receives and what he pays out for business, his protection rackets, that sort of thing. Billy Sullivan is ruthless but he's also meticulous."

"I know," said the detective, his finger tracing down the long scar on his face.

"Did he give you that?"

"I can't prove it was him, no, but I suspect he did, a long time ago when I was a bobby on the beat and I broke up a fight between some Italians and some thugs in a Soho shop."

"It must have hurt," I said.

"Like hell," said Detective Sgt. Hart.

"So, did you get that key cut?" I asked, watching as a tugboat struggled its way upstream towing a barge full of rubbish.

He fished deep into his coat pocket and pulled out a shiny brass key.

"I'm not sure if it will work, but it's the best we could do with what you gave me."

"It's the only way I'm going to slip into Billy Sullivan's office unnoticed," I said. "So you'd better pray it works."

"I need to see that ledger, to get the proof of his protection rackets and the bent officers on his payroll. But how will you get it out?"

Then I said those three little words that every hoister in The Forty Thieves knows, but men never really understand: "In my knickers."

"You heard me right," I said, catching the look of disbelief on his face. "I am going to hoist it down my drawers, like the best shoplifters."

The detective didn't know whether to laugh or throw the key in the river, for all the good he thought I'd be able to do with it.

"We can meet here at same time tomorrow, and I will hand it over, but there are other conditions, or I will just chuck it in the river myself and you will never nail Billy."

"Tell me your terms," he said.

"I am modeling in a fashion show at Gamages tomorrow afternoon. The Forty Thieves are going to hoist a few bits and pieces. I want you to let us get away—all except Alice Diamond and you know what she looks like, because you've seen her at close quarters, haven't you?"

He shifted uncomfortably at the memory of her clumping him one in the lift.

"My, my," he said. "She really has upset you, hasn't she?"

"Yes, she bleeding well has," I said. "She landed me in it that time I went hoisting by telling the Old Bill where

I'd be and what I'd be up to. It's some stupid test that she's got for new girls in the gang, to see what they will do. I think she thought me being a first offense and pregnant that I'd get off with a warning, but the world has changed. You walked into my life and the rest is history."

I stared at the water, swirling and churning in the wake of the little boat, as it struggled against the tide. Joseph was three months old now and someone else was loving him, while my arms were empty. And Jimmy was sitting in a cold, hard police cell for his trouble.

"I intend to repay the compliment, see how she likes it," I said. "I think the time has come for a new Queen of Thieves, don't you?"

He laughed out loud.

"Oh God, Nell, your naked ambition is showing."

"And so is yours, Detective Sergeant Hart," I replied. "Don't be a silly boy and pretend you don't need me. Times are changing in gangland. Alice Diamond belongs in a world from before the war, a time that is past. And you will find me a lot easier to deal with than the likes of her or Billy Sullivan."

He couldn't disguise a look of admiration for my sheer brass neck.

I went on: "And you might want to tell a few of your Ghost Squad cozzers that after the show, Billy Sullivan and his mob plan to use a lorry to block the street off and nick all the furs and designer dresses they can get their grubby little mitts on. Might be nice to pay them a surprise visit?"

"Sounds like a plan," he said, smiling at me.

"But I'm going to need guarantees about what is going to happen to my friend," I said.

"Who is that, then?"

I could tell he was still trying to imagine me shoving that

book down my underwear and walking out of The Windsor, with the secrets to Billy Sullivan's empire in my drawers.

"Jimmy Feeney. He's up on a charge of assault."

He threw his hands up.

"He's one of Billy's henchmen, Nell," he said. "He's in the frame for that razor attack on Alf White."

"I know exactly who he is, and I know what he's done," I said. "He's just a foolish barrow boy from Waterloo who was trying to make money so we could start a life together, the life we would have had if you hadn't collared me for those stockings I nicked from Gamages."

"Oh, you can't go dragging up the past and blaming it all on me, Nell," he said. "You were the one breaking the law that day, as I recall. And Jimmy Feeney's already been identified as the culprit by Alf White's wife. There are other witnesses who will swear it was him. The case is very important. The public want to see justice done, in the current climate."

"You and I both know that the real culprit, the man who stood to gain and who is getting an easy life of it, is Billy Sullivan," I shot back.

"Well, perhaps your friend Jimmy should talk to the police about that . . ."

I grabbed hold of him. "Perhaps I should walk away now and the next time I see you in Billy's club I will tell them exactly who you are and what you are up to? Jimmy was my fella . . ."

"And is he your fella now?" There was a look in his eye, and if I didn't know better, I'd say it was disappointment.

"He ain't perfect but then you show me a man who is." I sighed. "His heart's in the right place. He was trying to make things go right for us both and he's landed himself right in it instead. Jimmy ain't the brightest button in the box.

"He hasn't got what it takes to survive in prison. He

will crack up. I know, I've been there, and I can tell," I added quietly.

"He should have thought of that before he—"

All the anger of the past year came bubbling up inside me, like a great tide: "Do you have any idea what it's like for people like me and Jimmy? We don't stand a chance; we are just used by the Alice Diamonds and Billy Sullivans of this world and tossed aside when they've finished with us. Jimmy was foolish enough to think he was one of the gang, but I know different.

"I'm giving you the chance to break Billy Sullivan's grip on Soho, but you have to help me save Jimmy or there's no deal."

Detective Sgt. Hart furrowed his brow.

"The best chance he's got is to cop a guilty plea and I will try to get his brief to come up with some mitigation, self-defense, maybe," he said, mulling it over.

"He can't grass on Billy Sullivan or he'll be a dead man," I said. "But if he admits it, will he at least get less time in prison?"

"I'm sure I can have a word with the powers that be, see what I can do," said Detective Sgt. Hart. "He's very likely to get a shorter sentence, especially if you can provide the information you are promising."

Then I remembered something: that posh idiot Lord Dockworth, the former Home Secretary.

"You need to be careful because Billy Sullivan's even got spies in the House of Lords," I said. "Lord Dockworth owes him thousands in gambling debts but if he looks at the cards they played with, he will see that they are marked. Billy Sullivan's running a game with a fixed deck, which meant Lord Dockworth could never win. He's been played by Billy Sullivan too."

"This is getting more intriguing, Nell," said Detective

Sgt. Hart. "There was I thinking you were nothing more than just a little shoplifter—"

"You have no clue who I am or what I've done or what I'm prepared to do," I spat. "I'm a woman from a slum that's been knocked down because people say it was no good but I'm still standing."

"I think I'm just beginning to understand that, Nell."

"It pays to be a woman on the sidelines in gang-land, watching the men while they are swinging their dicks around being powerful, because sooner or later, they will screw it up, won't they?" I said. "And it's always the little details that catch them out. We women have a good eye for detail. I learned that down the fur factory."

I was turning to go when he caught hold of my sleeve.

"As you've been so honest with me, there's a piece of information I need to share with you," he said. "That day in Derry and Tom's when I caught you in the lift, I'd been tipped off."

"Yes, I know," I said. "It was my old mate Iris. I still can't work out how she did it, but she paid the price for her big mouth."

He looked puzzled. "No," he said. "It was someone much closer to Alice Diamond, someone in the gang with an axe to grind, and she was the one who shopped Jimmy Feeney when he showed up down the Elephant after the razor attack too.

"It was Alice's second-in-command, Molly."

They say revenge is a dish best served cold but as I crossed Westminster Bridge to catch the tram back down to the Elephant, I was burning with anger and raring to serve it up to Molly, piping hot.

Iris was a snitch, nothing could change that, but Molly had betrayed not only the gang, but my Jimmy. I always thought she'd been jealous of what I'd had with him and now I knew it. The spiteful cow had it coming, and I was going to give it to her, good and proper.

I felt in the bottom of my handbag for the billiard ball in a sock she'd given me when I first crossed the water into Soho. That would come in handy.

The problem was, Molly was a wildcat, even in drink. I knew I needed someone else to help and there was only one person I could rely on.

Darkness was falling as I made my way into Iris's tenement and climbed the stairs to her front door. I knocked softly and her frightened little face appeared, her shorn head covered by a scarf.

"Go away," she said, pushing it shut, but I'd already got my foot in the doorway.

"Let me in, Iris," I said. "We need to talk."

When Tommy caught sight of me in the hallway, he avoided my gaze, grabbed his coat and cap, and left.

"Are you happy now?" said Iris, pulling off her scarf to show the tufts of hair left on her head. "Have you got more to do to me?"

"No," I said. "I'm here to explain things and to ask for your help with something."

"I don't know you anymore, Nell," she said, tears welling in her eyes. She was shaking as she spoke: "You ain't my friend; you ain't the girl I used to know from Tenison Street. You're a monster, that's what you are."

"You don't know what I've become or why," I shot back. "You are in no position to judge me, Iris. You done wrong by grassing to the tallyman and you know it. It was a risk you took for reasons I understand, but you were playing with fire and you got burned."

"But the way you hurt me," she said. "It was like you were enjoying it."

"No," I said. "I wasn't." Something else had taken over when I was cutting her hair, it was true, but I wasn't even sure what that was or where it had come from. It was a side of myself I was only just beginning to understand but if I was going to be the Queen of Thieves, I was going to need it.

"I had to do it, or Alice Diamond would have done worse to me," I said. "I want to change things around here, but it's going to take some time. I had to stay in the gang. Don't ask me to apologize for the life I'm living, Iris, because you are on a hiding to nothing with that."

Iris swallowed hard and dried her eyes on her apron. "God knows I've paid the price for what I've done, and Tommy won't even touch me now, not even to kiss me or nothing.

"He's shit-scared of me, his own wife, because if I say a word, Alice Diamond will come down on him like a ton of bricks. That's what she told him."

"Tommy is a bully who was beating you, Iris, there was no respect for you," I said. "I want to make life better for you, but you've got to show willing and help me."

"What more do The Forty Thieves want of me?" she cried. "Molly's been round here gloating that when my lovely hair's grown back, she's got some wealthy fellas who will pay me for my time."

"What?" I said, sitting down, with all the wind knocked out of my sails.

"She reckons she's going to put me on the game because I've got to do what the gang says, that's what she said."

"That's nothing to do with The Forty Thieves," I said.

"That's Molly, the evil bitch. And let me tell you, she has got it coming because she grassed on my Jimmy to the law the other day and that is why he's behind bars. That's why I need your help tonight.

"I know you'd rather not be part of it, Iris, but this is the world we are living in. Look around you. There are times when you have to stand up and be counted. You are worth more than this. You can play by their rules and be a victim all your life or we can make up a few of our own. What do you say?"

Iris glanced around her. The threadbare tablecloth was covered in fluff from her fur-pulling work, the china stacked neatly on the mantelpiece was chipped, and a pair of Tommy's trousers, which were more patches than cloth, lay ready for mending.

She undid the straps of her apron and grabbed her rolling pin. "Count me in."

The evening mist rolled off the River Thames and through the backstreets of the Elephant, shrouding the rubble and ruins left by the Blitz.

The pub had survived the bombing, which was a cause for celebration at the time and every night since. Smoke and laughter escaped in little blasts whenever someone pushed open the doors to take a piss up the green tiled walls or puke one pint too many into the gutter.

Iris and I loitered up the back alley by the side of the pub, tucked away behind the bins, waiting for our moment. A cat prowled past, followed by a mangy dog, which squatted and did its business, right by my feet.

"I'll tell you one thing, Iris," I said, as we watched it perform and strut off, with a satisfied wag of its stumpy tail, "I take you to all the best places. Stick with me, I'll show you all the shites of London town."

She giggled, just like the old friend I used to know in Tenison Street.

The door of the pub swung open and people started to spill out into the street, staggering back to their lives on the never-never in Queen's Buildings, buoyed by drink.

Iris started walking down the alleyway, but I held on to her arm. "Wait!

"When we do this, you follow my lead and we keep silent, understood?"

Iris nodded.

I tied my headscarf so that it covered my face, and all you could see was my eyes. Iris did the same.

A full ten minutes passed before Molly barreled out, three sheets to the wind. The landlord slid the bolt on the door, locking it firmly, in a way that said good riddance to bad rubbish.

We gave her a moment's head start before we set off in pursuit. I could hear her singing "Molly Malone" at the top of her voice, which was handy because the fog was getting thick. Queen's Buildings loomed a few hundred yards ahead of us, and I knew we had to reach her before she got to the safety of the courtyard, where a fight could easily be heard.

She still had that arrogant swagger about her walk, even in drink, and as we tiptoed closer, I could see the red fox's brush of her hair swishing out from under her hat. She'd just got to the chorus, "*Alive, alive-oh,*" when I ran at her, swinging the billiard ball in a sock with all my might, and landing it squarely between her shoulder blades to fell her.

Molly landed like a sack of spuds, facedown in the gutter, and before I could do anything, Iris was whacking at her with the rolling pin in a frenzied attack.

Molly screamed, putting her hands up to protect herself, and I pulled Iris back. Then, I raised the billiard ball and cracked Molly one on the side of her head, making her moan. Iris kicked her in the ribs, over and over, until I felt she'd done enough. And judging that was a tough call, it has to be said, because as much as I hated Molly's guts, I didn't want to end up at the end of the hangman's noose for killing the cow.

We'd just about had our fill, when a costermonger appeared at the top of the street, with his empty barrow.

"What's going on?" he shouted into the gloom. "Who's there?"

Molly was on her side, knees drawn up and whimpering, blood coming from her busted nose. I'd be lying if I said I didn't get satisfaction from seeing her like that. She belonged in the gutter.

I signaled to Iris to get going and we scarpered back to her tenement before the costermonger could reach us, tucking our weapons into our coat pockets as we went.

We were breathless and giddy from the thrill of it.

Iris turned to me, shaking but smiling, as we climbed the stairs. "She had it coming, didn't she?"

I knew then I had found a partner in crime who I could rely on.

"Welcome to my gang," I said.

Chapter Thirty

NELL

Soho, London, March 1947

I awoke at first light, to the sound of stones being chucked at my bedroom window.

Down in the street, Alice was hopping mad. "Nell, for Gawd's sake, wake up, you lazy moo!"

I pulled up the sash and stuck my head out. If Molly had worked out who'd beaten her up, I was done for, but I had to make a show of being innocent.

"You'll wake the landlady," I hissed. "What on earth's the matter?"

"I need to talk to you," she said, glowering at me. "Come down and let me in!"

My heart was pumping as I put on Gypsy's dressing gown and ran downstairs. I darted into the scullery and pulled a knife from the drawer, tucking it up my sleeve. Suddenly the game was all too real.

"What took you so long?" said Alice, as I opened the front door.

"I had to make myself decent," I said, holding the shaft of the knife in place inside my sleeve with my curled fingers. "Come on through, before you wake the whole street."

I held the front door open and let her go down the corridor first, in case she tried to jump me.

But as Alice paced up and down the scullery, with anxiety etched on her features, she was like a woman possessed, ranting and raving about what had happened to her deputy.

"Molly's been put in the hospital by Billy Sullivan's men," she said. "Oh, I should have done him earlier. I should have listened to Mrs. Tibbs. But no, I thought I knew better than old Tibbsy, didn't I? And now they've gone and done in my Molly."

"Poor Moll, I can't believe it!" I said, edging over to the sink, to drop the knife without being spotted. "I know we had our differences, but to be laid low like that is just taking a liberty, ain't it? And who is Mrs. Tibbs? Is she someone in the gang I ain't met before?"

But Alice was already looming over me.

"This," she said, pulling out her shiv and bringing it dangerously close to my face, "is Mrs. Tibbs. You've already made her acquaintance and you two get on quite well from what I recall." She cackled with laughter.

Truly, she had flipped her lid. She'd given that shiv of hers a name. I began to regret letting her into the house.

"I think we could both use a nice brew," I soothed. I breathed a sigh of relief as she walked over to the kitchen table, tucked her shiv back in her lace handkerchief, and sat down.

Turning away, I sneaked the knife down my sleeve and onto the draining board and filled the kettle, trembling with nerves in case she'd spotted what I was up to.

"Molly got jumped as she was leaving the pub in the blackout last night," said Alice, as I set the kettle on the range to boil. "She's had a nasty clump round the lughole which has left her so dizzy she can barely walk, and they've broken her face in bits and smashed three or four ribs. She said it was Billy's men that jumped her. Doctors say it'll be weeks before she's up and about."

"God almighty," I said. Who would have thought Iris could be so handy with a rolling pin? She'd done more than I gave her credit for. "The bastards!"

"I know it's a shock but don't upset yourself too much, Nell," said Alice, eyeing me closely. "Molly is tough as old boots. She'll live."

Well, that was a relief because I didn't intend to get topped for it.

"I think you and I could use some sugar," I said, wandering into the pantry, in case I gave myself away. "Calms the nerves."

Alice shouted after me, "Molly says there was at least three of them, maybe four. Big fellas with hands like giant hams. She tried to sock one or two of them in the kisser, but they just overpowered her, the four of them."

"And that was just the four bottles of gin she'd drunk," I murmured to myself, suppressing a smile.

I walked quickly back into the scullery and chucked a lump of sugar in her tea. "It's a gang attack, four on one. It's dirty tactics, Alice."

"This is a declaration of war, Nell. I'm going to have him for it," she seethed. "The bastard Billy Sullivan won't know what's hit him."

I saw an opportunity to wind her up, and so I was off, like a rat up a drainpipe.

"The thing is," I said, stirring my tea, "I heard something in the club the other day and I thought it was just men being all mouth and trousers but now I'm starting to wonder . . ."

"What!" she cried. "What did you hear? Spit it out, for God's sake."

Oh, she was like a fish on the line, and I was yanking it in.

"I heard Lou the barman say that Billy Sullivan was going

to knock the crown off your head over this tallyman business and you weren't going to be Queen no more. He wants to take over the gang and run it himself. He wants to put a fella in charge. King of Thieves, that's what he said. No more Queen of Thieves. I didn't want to believe it; you know how men are always talking themselves up."

This was stretching it a bit, but in her current state, she swallowed the whole tale, hook, line, and sinker.

"Does he now? The cheeky swine," said Alice, puce with rage. "I'll have his guts for garters! It's a bloody liberty! King of Thieves, my arse!"

"That's what he's been plotting all along," I said, warming to my theme. "He's been after your title the whole time."

"Nell," she said, taking hold of my hands, her green eyes glistening, "you've done well telling me this. I know you're young, but the others look up to you because of you being here in Soho, helping the gang out. I was going to find a way to do this without upsetting Molly in a year or so, but now she's out of the picture and with Sullivan on our case, it needs to happen sooner not later."

I listened with bated breath.

"You are loyal to me, and that loyalty may be tested further but, will you be my deputy?"

I couldn't have been happier if Prince Charming had got down on one knee and asked me to marry him.

"Oh, yes!" I cried. "Yes, I will."

We hugged each other for a moment. It would have looked to anyone as if we were a mother and a daughter, holding each other in a fond embrace. But I wasn't burying the hatchet. The only place I wanted to stick that was in her back.

She finished her tea, set her hair and her hat straight, and pulled herself together. The Queen of The Forty Thieves, Alice Diamond, was more like her old self again.

But I wasn't finished with her yet.

"I saw the way you were looking at Billy Sullivan in that old photograph in his office. He was your world, wasn't he?"

She flicked open Mrs. Tibbs.

"You may be my deputy, but I told you never to speak about that, Nell," she said, moving toward me. "I wasn't joking."

I put my hands up.

"Whatever happened between you is your business, I didn't mean anything by it. We both know blood is thicker than water. But if it's revenge you want, why don't you take it? He's just a bloke, you're the Queen of Thieves and he's coming for your crown," I said. "It's you or him, time's running out, can't you see?"

Truly, all I needed for Christmas was a wooden spoon because I was so good at stirring things. I was thoroughly enjoying myself, but it was a dangerous game.

She thought about it for a moment, her eyes narrowing, like a cat's. I held her gaze.

"Mrs. Tibbs feels the same way as you do, Nell," she said, folding the blade away and wrapping it in her lace handkerchief. "She does, but I have to tell her to be patient, because only I will know when the time is right. You can't rush these things. That kind of understanding about gangland comes with years of experience. You'll learn."

"Why did you give your razor a name?" I ventured. I knew there must have been a good reason and I was wondering if I might turn that to my advantage at some point.

"Oh, Mrs. Tibbs and me go way back," said Alice, patting her pocket fondly. "She used to belong to an old gal called Mrs. Tibbs, who I met through . . ." She stopped herself and cleared her throat. "Through close family. It was thanks to her that I found the guts to do my first shivving. After that, everything else came easy for me.

"She made quite an impression on me as a girl, so let's just say, I made one on her."

She leaned in closer. "But sometimes I do wonder if there is a little bit of something in that blade, something special, magical almost. You felt it the other day with Iris, when you cut her hair, didn't you? It's as if Mrs. Tibbs likes doing her work, doesn't she? That's how I knew you were right to be my deputy. Mrs. Tibbs chose me and perhaps she's chosen you as well?"

A shiver ran down my spine at that and I looked away. Maybe I was more like Alice Diamond than I had given myself credit for. I hoped whatever madness she had wasn't catching.

"What's the matter, Nell?" said Alice, reading the look of concern in my eyes. "You are up for the job, ain't you? You do like Mrs. Tibbs, don't you? Because she gets easily offended . . ."

"Yes," I said. "The Forty Thieves need me, and I won't let the gang down."

I added hastily, "Or Mrs. Tibbs, for that matter."

"Right," she said, getting up. "I will see you at Gamages this afternoon with the others. Once the models are showing their final outfits, send the girls to sneak out down the staircase to the car, and then I will make sure that you and me get away safely."

"Sounds brilliant," I said. Me and Alice would be alone on the stairwell together, just as Detective Sgt. Hart came to catch her, red-handed. My whole plan was coming together very nicely indeed.

A dark look crossed her face, and in that moment, you could see the family resemblance between Alice and Billy, plain as day. "Then, when I've had a think about it, you and I will work out how to get this bastard Sullivan once and for all."

"You can count on me," I said, knowing full well that both of them would be behind bars before the day was done. Excitement fluttered in my chest. I was so close to toppling her now, I could practically see her going over the cliff edge.

I've never gone in for superstitious nonsense, but I was beginning to think there might be something in it. Not just about that shiv, and how it made me feel when I held it in my hands, but there was something else. They say good things come in threes, don't they?

Well, I was deputy of The Forty Thieves, I was going to get Billy Sullivan arrested and Alice Diamond too, so there was the proof.

It didn't matter that it was pouring with rain, the sun had come out in my world. I whistled to myself as I pulled on my hoister's drawers and made my way to The Windsor.

After six long years of war, London was battered and broken but Soho was its beating heart. From the shouts of the barrow boys at first light to the drunken yelling of boozed-up blokes falling down in the gutter in the early hours, I was caught up in its relentless rhythm, and stepping lightly down the pavement, I felt that Soho belonged to me.

Lou was already in his favorite position behind the bar at The Windsor, polishing his glassware.

"You're in early," he said.

"I was hoping to get a message to Mr. Sullivan," I said, batting my eyelashes at him. "Is he in?"

It didn't exactly come naturally to be charming to Lou, the grumpy old git, and that only made him more suspicious.

"You can tell me, I will pass it on," he said, watching me with a gimlet eye.

"It's personal," I replied. "It would be better if I could tell him myself. I'll just pop down and see him in his office . . ."

"He's out," said Lou. "Got a bit of work on with the Chaps, I don't suppose he'll be back until later."

"Fine," I said, making my way across the club, "I've just got to pick up some of my clothes to take to the dry cleaner's . . ."

My hands were clammy as I pushed through the door into the back corridor, glancing over my shoulder in case Lou was following me. I swept into the filthy little dressing room and grabbed the clothes I'd left behind the night I went to The Lucky Seven.

Then, I darted back into the corridor. Billy's office door lay up ahead. Running toward it, I felt in my pocket for the key and stuck it firmly into the lock. I twisted it and turned the door handle, but it didn't open. I tried again, rattling the key around in the lock a bit. Finally, after what seemed like a lifetime, I heard a click, turned the handle and gave it an almighty shove, tumbling through the door.

The flowers and dresses were gone; that had all been part of Billy's plan to seduce me, I realized that now. The room stank of blokes, cigar smoke, and fear.

I ran to the desk, but the ledger was nowhere to be seen. Frantically, I began to pull open the desk drawers one by one and although I found a handgun, a cosh, a wad of cash, and some very nice diamonds in there, the ledger was missing. If he kept it in the safe, I was done for. The hands of the clock on the wall moved at lightning speed, as one minute and then another sped by.

With beads of sweat forming on my brow, I pulled out the whole of the middle drawer. It caught against something, as if it was jammed. Billy Sullivan was a trickster and a conman, wasn't he? I ran my hands along the underside of the desk and there, hidden in a secret compartment, was the ledger. I flipped it open, and the list of policemen he was paying off lay before me. I had struck gold.

Then, to my horror, I heard Lou whistling out in the corridor and the unmistakable sound of footsteps approaching. My heart raced as I stuffed the ledger down my drawers, pulling my blouse out over the waistband of my skirt to cover the bulge.

Quick as a flash, I sat down, picked up the fountain pen, and started to scrawl a note. This was no time for half measures, I had to make it convincing.

Lou poked his head around the door.

"What the hell are you doing in here?" he said, his eyes wide with incredulity. "How did you get in?"

"The door was unlocked," I said, as calmly as I could while my knees were knocking together under the desk. "And I'm writing a note to Mr. Sullivan, it's personal."

"I told you I would tell him . . ." Lou began, moving toward me, his shoulders brushing through the doorframe.

"No," I said, hiding what I had written. "Look, Lou, there are some things that are between a man and a woman and you may think you know everything your boss gets up to, but trust me, you don't.

"Mr. Sullivan asked me a question and gave me time to think about it and I am just leaving him a reply."

"Let me see that," he said, angrily snatching the paper from my hand.

The ledger was digging into my ribs, and I swear in that moment I could barely breathe.

The note read: "Billy, you are right, we belong together."

He took a step back.

"Oh," he said, swallowing hard, "I see, it's like that is it? Well, you'd better sling your hook because Mr. Sullivan don't like people in here without his say-so. You should have asked his permission."

"Don't you see, Lou, that Billy and me, we are beyond

that stage? We know each other . . . personally," I replied, with a twinkle in my eye.

Poor Lou, he looked rather crestfallen.

"I'm sure he'd hate to think you'd shouted at me just for saying 'yes' to him. In fact, I think he'd be quite cross because this was the answer he was waiting for. Billy always gets what he wants, doesn't he? Billy always wins," I said.

I got up, with my dry cleaning in front of my stomach and my heart in my mouth as I walked toward the office door.

"And I won't mention the door was unlocked if you don't," I said, over my shoulder. "It's your job to check it, isn't it? I expect Billy will blow a gasket if he finds out about your lapse of security. Shall we keep it as our little secret?"

"But I could've sworn I locked it," Lou murmured to himself, scratching his bald head, as I waltzed off down the corridor.

Men in bowler hats were scurrying to and fro outside the House of Parliament, like a bunch of worker ants. What on earth did they do all day, those toffs at Westminster, with their briefcases full of important stuff? We were worlds apart but beneath their collars, suits, and hats they were just men, with desires and weaknesses and needs that I was beginning to understand. Soho had taught me that, and it was a life lesson I would always be grateful for because now I knew how to take advantage of them. No man would get the upper hand with me again.

Detective Sgt. Hart was waiting for me on Westminster Bridge, looking like all his Christmases had come at once.

I pulled the ledger out of my drawers and held it firmly in both hands.

"You have actually gone and bloody well done it, Nell!" he cried, picking me up and spinning me around.

"And now you had actually better bloody well keep your side of the bargain," I said, handing it over to him as he gently put me down. He flicked through it, raising an eyebrow at some of the names on Billy's list of straightened cozzers.

"I've already got the Ghost Squad on standby in Holborn," he said. "It's all hush-hush, so the regulars haven't a clue, which will keep Sullivan in the dark. I cannot wait to get him in the back of my Black Maria. And will you be able to deliver Alice Diamond to me as well, like you said?"

I started running him through my secret plan: "The rest of the girls from The Forty Thieves will take the back exit out of the shop after the show, just as the last models are starting off up the catwalk. Alice has told me she will create a distraction, to allow me time to get to the exit, and she will follow me down the staircase.

"I'm going to delay her by tripping on the stairs, which is where you come in. You'll have to move fast because once she's on her toes, she's a force to be reckoned with. I will have to fight you off to make it look convincing, but you will let me get away and collar her instead."

He nodded. "Sounds good."

I could hardly believe I was going to double-cross her with this cozzer, but it was really happening. The waiting game had been worth it.

"Billy's men will be parked up in a lorry down one of the side streets, because they want to steal the Alaska fur van, so once we have got out of the way, you can move in and catch them at it."

"Oh, don't worry your pretty head about Billy Sullivan," he said. "Leave him and his mob to me." There was a glint in his eye. "It's been a long time coming and I'm not going to let him slip through the net. Besides, now I have the proof of his protection rackets, he's banged to rights."

"And Jimmy?" I said. "How is he doing?"

"I've made sure he's being made as comfortable as he can be in the cells, without drawing attention to it," said the detective. "But it's fair to say he isn't someone who is used to losing his liberty. You were right about that."

"Poor Jimmy," I murmured. "God knows how he's going to cope inside."

"He's lucky to have a strong woman like you in his life," he said, gazing at me intently.

I poked him in the ribs. "Oh, flattery will get you . . . nowhere."

He smiled. "The Home Secretary is waiting to see the strength of the case against Sullivan, but he will make sure the sentencing for Jimmy is lenient. I gave you my word and I will stick to it."

"Well," I said. "It's been nice doing business with you . . ."

"Might you fancy a drink with me sometime?" he said, as I was turning to leave, with the raindrops pattering on my face. "I can leave my police badge at the door. I mean just you and me, getting to know each other a bit better . . ."

"Oh, Detective Sergeant Hart." I sighed. "It's like a cat going out with a mouse, isn't it? You and me would never work because I will always want to steal and you are as honest as the day is long."

"I'm sorry you think that way, Nell," he said, shuffling his feet about. "I was hoping I might reform you a little, persuade you to mend your wicked ways."

There was something boyish about him. He really was quite charming when he wasn't arresting people.

"I'm flattered," I said. "But no man will ever be in charge of me, as long as I live. I'm happy the way I am and, as it happens, I love going shopping up West. If the hoister's drawers fit, then wear them, as the saying goes.

"Still, we will always have our afternoons by the River Thames to remember each other by, won't we? And the day you collared me in Gamages. That was very memorable, for all the wrong reasons."

His shoulders drooped a bit.

Life was full of surprises.

Sgt. Eddie Hart may have won the war in Soho, but he'd lost the battle for my affections, and he looked quite defeated by that.

Chapter Thirty-One

NELL

Holborn, London, March 1947

I hadn't seen crowds like it since Stan Laurel and Oliver Hardy brought Piccadilly to a standstill when they visited London.

High Holborn was buzzing with people coming to the Gamages fashion show and spivs were milling about offering fake tickets, in the hope of making some easy money. It was a taste of luxury when we were all still being told to tighten our belts on our utility wear and that proved irresistible.

It was handbags at dawn to secure a seat, a real stampede by ladies who should have known how to mind their manners. But in that moment as the minutes ticked closer to four o'clock, they forgot everything they'd learned at finishing school and prepared to fight each other to catch a glimpse of Dior New Look dresses and the most beautiful furs.

I met Gypsy by the shop entrance, and we forced our way through the crowd. She was brilliantly pushy, like a steamroller: "Corblimey, get out of my way, why don'tcha?"

When women turned to protest that she was elbowing them out of the way, she preened: "We are models for Monsieur Dior. Make way! Coming through . . ."

Upstairs in ladieswear, a section of the store had been closed off with screens, with rows of chairs at either side to form a catwalk down the middle. Some bright spark at Gamages had borrowed scenery from the theatre in Drury Lane. Roman columns with fake ivy hanging off them stood at either side of the changing room doors. A pair of heavy velvet curtains hung on a brass rail between the columns and to the side of that, some poor workmen were heaving a baby grand piano into position. The manageress, Miss Hunter, was strutting about with a clipboard giving orders to fellas in overalls who looked like they wanted to smack her one in the chops rather than adjust the ivy or shift another sodding chair into the right position.

"No, Stanley, left a bit, please," she chirruped, while shop assistants darted about with a dustpan and brush to make the place presentable. "We must give as many of our customers as possible the chance to get close to the haute couture."

She spied Gypsy and me approaching: "N'est-ce-pas, Mademoiselle Piaf?"

"Oui," said Gypsy, who was beginning to enjoy being French. "Definitely, oui."

"You girls go on through to the changing rooms to start getting ready," she clucked. "Allez, *vite!*"

There were a few professional fashion models getting ready in the changing rooms and they looked askance as we came in. They were tall and thin as string beans and as graceful as racehorses. The Forty Thieves were just a bunch of pit ponies next to them, but what we lacked in experience, we made up for in enthusiasm—particularly because we were on the take and that was enough to give us a gee.

The Partridge twins were sensational, with their jet-black hair parted down the middle and pulled back into neat chignons, dressed in identical gold jackets with full black knife-pleated skirts. Em was a dead ringer for Judy Garland, but with blonder hair and freckles. She glanced up at me excitedly as a shop assistant helped her into a raspberry-pink silk taffeta dress, which was fit for a princess. The Forty Thieves were always known for being almost like film stars around South London and now we were living up to our reputation on this side of the water.

"Oh my Gawd, Nell," squeaked Em, "ain't it beautiful?"

"We'll have that one, for sure," I whispered.

My outfits were hanging on a rail next to Gypsy's and beyond that were rows of the finest furs from the Alaska. I could hardly believe that I was going to wear the pelts I had spent my days perfecting in the life I lived before.

I reached out and touched a beautiful full-length mink coat, and the snowiest white Arctic fox fur cape, feeling a glow of happiness as I meticulously planned how I was going to nick them.

"Five minutes, girls!" boomed Miss Hunter, peering at us over the top of her clipboard, like an officious little sergeant major.

Gypsy was busy pouring herself into a silk polka-dot creation, topped off with a massive hat. The material clung to every curve and she was a total knockout in it. After I'd done up her dress, she helped me into a day suit, made of the finest black gaberdine, with a skirt that swished out from the waist like the petals of a flower every time I moved. The jacket was trimmed with fur and I pulled on gloves and a hat. I peered at myself in the mirror and a very posh lady stared back at me. I wouldn't have looked out of place at Buckingham Palace. Miss Hunter must have agreed because she bustled by and hung a little handbag over my arm to complete my outfit.

I poked my head around the velvet drapes to see if I could spy Alice. The room was filling up fast and she'd promised to turn up. I couldn't spot her anywhere, but it was too late to back out now.

But someone else was there, right in the middle of the front row, adjusting his silk handkerchief in the top pocket of his immaculately pressed suit. Billy Sullivan glanced over in my direction and I felt my stomach lurch, before I quickly pulled the curtains closed.

"What's the matter?" said Gypsy. "You've gone a funny color. Is your dress too tight?"

I was beginning to regret telling him about the fashion show, not to mention writing that note to him. It was like inviting a bear to a dinner party and wondering if you were going to end up on the menu. I had no way of knowing whether he'd read my letter, but even if he had, once he realized his ledger was missing, I would be skating on very thin ice indeed.

"I'm fine," I said, taking a deep breath. "Just remember to do what we discussed with Alice and everything will work out."

The pianist started up. It wasn't the sort of stuff you'd hear in the club or down the boozer, but it set the mood for the fancy clothes we were wearing. The professional models opened the show, gliding effortlessly down the catwalk, and we trooped off after them.

We followed in their footsteps, tottering along as if we wore clothes like this every day of the week, to gasps from the audience: "Oh, how divine!

"Look, there's so much material, the skirt's almost to the floor!"

We twirled slowly at the far end of the catwalk and on the way back, I felt Billy undressing me with his eyes. Luckily, I wasn't wearing the pink dress like Em was, or my face would have matched it by the time I got back to the changing room. He had such a way of making me blush.

I could have tried to pretend otherwise, but Billy Sullivan had an effect on me that I was powerless to control. It was like the funny flip I used to get in my stomach when I was a girl, standing on Waterloo Bridge looking down at the River Thames. Being around him was knowing that if you fell, you'd drown, but despite everything, I couldn't help imagining the thrill of jumping in anyway. I realized then that putting him behind bars for what he did to Jimmy wasn't going to switch my feelings off. But to give me and Jimmy a fighting chance, I had to get rid of him. A long prison sentence meant he'd be out of sight, out of mind, at least. While he was still running Soho, I'd be forever under his thumb.

I was gambling on a win against Billy Sullivan, but this time, I had fixed the deck in my favor.

In the changing rooms, gowns were hastily unzipped and in the confusion, as we changed into our next outfits and priceless dresses were chucked over chairs, the Partridges stuffed their Dior skirts and jackets into a shopping bag and one of them—I couldn't say which, they were identical and only their ma could tell them apart—slipped out to the back stairs for her meet with the rest of Em's girls. The girls took the bag and scarpered down the stairs to Alice Diamond's Chrysler and the Partridge twin came back to the changing rooms, as if butter wouldn't melt in her mouth.

I waited until Miss Hunter was helping to dress the models in houndstooth outfits, with hats to match, before rolling that lovely Arctic fox fur into a tight little bundle and shoving it down one leg of my hoister's drawers. I pulled a mink stole from the rail and pushed that down the other leg, because you might as well be hung for a sheep as a lamb. Then I put on a silk evening gown, with a full skirt and plunging neckline, and stepped out onto the catwalk. As I strode along, to murmurs of appreciation from the assembled ladies, I decided that the New Look was perfect for hoisting because you could have got a house underneath those dresses and no one would have been any the wiser.

The Partridges continued their ruse; one went onto the catwalk, the other flapped off to the staircase. I'd have loved a whole brace of Partridges in the gang; they were worth their weight in gold for the confusion they caused and the amount they got away with.

Gypsy was loving every minute of the show, even if she was almost falling out of some of the dresses, and she hammed it up every time Miss Hunter told the audience: "And now, we have our very own *French* model . . ." which gave me more time to hoist stuff. I was having the time of my life doing that.

I threw on a beautiful sable coat and then, having told Miss Hunter I needed to answer a call of nature, dashed to the staircase, where I quickly took off my evening dress, pulled the furs from my knickers and handed the lot to one of the Forties to take down to the car.

Miss Hunter was fuming by the time I returned because I almost missed my slot on the catwalk. I darted on, pulling my fur coat tight around me as I gave my twirl at the end, because I had nothing but my underwear on and I didn't want the hoity-toity ladies to have to pass the smelling salts.

We only had the final party dresses and evening furs to go now, and I had started to get really anxious about where on earth Alice had got to. I'd promised Detective Sgt. Hart she'd be here and collaring her was part of the deal.

Worse than that, what if she'd seen through my plan and known the truth about Molly all along? What if she was waiting for me in the stairwell with Mrs. Tibbs at the ready? I tripped over myself getting into a beautiful silk evening dress as I worried about that and Miss Hunter shot me a dirty look: "Do please be careful with the gowns, girls!"

"Sorry," I mumbled, fiddling with the huge velvet bow

at the bust, as I pulled a fox fur around my shoulders. "It won't happen again."

Gypsy was resplendent in an olive-green silk dress, buttoned all the way up the front, and white calfskin gloves. The Partridges and Em managed to hoick themselves into the most stunning beaded gold tulle evening gowns, leaving the professional models' noses out of joint, because they were supposed to be wearing them.

"Right, this is it," I whispered to them. "Just sneak straight out after you've done your turn."

"But where's Alice?" said Em. "And what about you?"

"Don't worry, I'll think of something," I said.

The pianist struck up a chord and we were just stepping out for our final walk, to applause, when a drunk old flower seller staggered into the crowd, knocking over a few chairs, singing at the top of her voice, *"My old man, said follow the van . . ."*

As people scrambled out of her way, shouting with indignation, she tipped up the brim of her hat and gave me a wink.

My heart was thumping ten to the dozen as I recognized the glint in her emerald-green eyes.

It was Alice Diamond.

Chapter Thirty-Two
ALICE

Holborn, London, March 1947

Half a crown!

I had to pay Old Lizzie Lumps, the flower seller, half a bleeding crown to part with her piss-stinking skirt and moth-eaten old shawl. She charged me sixpence extra for the battered straw hat, and some bunches of lucky lavender that were little more than dried twigs. It was robbery, plain and simple. She could have made it as a thief—if only she hadn't been so fond of the bottle.

As I looked around at the horror-stricken faces of the well-to-do ladies assembled in the womenswear department of Gamages, I decided to put on a bit of a show of my own, not only to give my girls a chance to get away, but just for the hell of it.

It was easy for me to make a proper nuisance of myself, bothering the posh folk: "Oh, buy my lovely flowers! Go on! Spare some coins. Have a care for an old lady!"

The smell of my clothing alone had them running for cover. You'd have thought a German bomb was about to explode in their midst, so it tickled me pink to go after them as they scrambled to get out of my path.

And that's when I saw him.

Billy Sullivan was sitting in the front row, looking like he owned the place. I recognized the cut of his forty-guinea suit, the crisp whiteness of his starched collar, his silk tie from Bond Street, and the entitled shine of his handmade leather shoes.

Out of the corner of my eye, as I walloped that manager Miss Hunter away with my cane, I spotted a cozzer walking toward Billy. It was that plainclothes fella I'd had a tussle with in the lift at Derry and Tom's.

Now, it might have just been a coincidence, but I was beginning to think it was a bit strange that he turned up like a bad smell wherever I went. And, in fact, wherever Nell went too. What were the chances of that?

Billy turned to look over his shoulder, to see what all the fuss was about, but he didn't budge. He was a man who could handle himself and he wasn't going to let a bit of a fracas with a drunken old tramp like me spoil his afternoon, was he?

The cozzer quickened his pace and pulled out a pair of handcuffs. The look of grim determination on his face and the way he was making a beeline for Billy made me realize he wasn't the least bit bothered by me, an old gal who was three sheets to the wind and being rowdy in a posh shop.

Sometimes in this game, you have to make a split-second decision. It's hard to explain that to mugs who have never stolen anything in their lives, but you get to read a situation and you know when to take a chance. My brother taught me that when we were kids growing up in the Seven Dials and I watched him swizz the punters out of pennies in his card tricks.

Whatever he had on Billy Sullivan, the cozzer was cocksure of it because he marched toward him like he was judge, jury, and executioner, all rolled into one.

The thought that this cozzer was going to put Billy Sullivan behind bars might have been enough for some people who've been cheated by him. But I got no satisfaction from that.

Nell had brought it home to me that what I had against Billy was personal in a way few could understand. The kind of justice I was interested in was meted out on the streets, by people who weren't born with a silver spoon in their mouth; who'd had to claw their way up from the gutter, simply to survive.

Blood is thicker than water, like she said. And Mrs. Tibbs was screaming at me to get to know him better. So, who was I to deny her?

With the brim of my hat low over my eyes, I pulled her out of my pocket and flicked her open. Mrs. Tibbs glinted under the electric lights. It was as if she was drawing breath for the first time in her life.

And for the first time in mine, since I was a girl, I forgot all about The Forty Thieves and the Hoisters' Code and what I had come here for.

I was just inches away from his broad shoulders; I could smell his expensive aftershave and see the neat line where the barber had clipped his jet-black hair at the nape of his lovely neck.

"Wotcha, Lim," I murmured.

He spun round to face me and before he knew what was happening, Mrs. Tibbs was scoring her way down his cheek, opening him up from just below his eye to his chin, blood spurting everywhere. She was lightning quick. She did a proper number on him; oh, she was unstoppable, just as I knew she would be. She went in hard and fast and cut deep.

Somewhere over the other side of the room, a woman screamed and another fainted at the sight of so much blood.

Billy clutched his hand to his lacerated face, his mouth

rounding in horror and disbelief, as the cozzer wrestled me to the floor, knocking Mrs. Tibbs out of my hand. She skittered away from my grasp.

I heard a madcap laugh.

"You bitch," yelled Billy, throwing himself at me, blood spurting all over the place. Out of nowhere, a mob of plainclothes policemen piled in, and he was cuffed.

"That looks nasty," said Detective Sgt. Hart, his eyes shining with glee, as he pulled Billy to his feet, with drops of crimson spattering all over the floor. "I think you might need a few stitches. It could leave a nasty scar."

"Get your hands off me," said Billy, shaking with rage. "I am a respectable businessman. I will have your job for this. I'll have you know I'm a friend of the Chief Constable."

Detective Sgt. Hart smiled. "William Sullivan, I am arresting you for demanding money with menaces, bribery, and corruption."

I tussled a bit with a young cozzer, just to make him feel brave, but I was giggling so much I couldn't put up much of a fight.

As I was led away to the police station, Billy was shouting one word and one word only at the top of his voice.

I'd waited decades but it was worth it to hear my brother yelling so loudly that the whole of London town could hear it.

"Alice!"

Epilogue

NELL

Elephant and Castle, London, July 1948

She's so beautiful, sleeping soundly in her cot.

My little girl's fingers curl around mine as she dozes in the late afternoon.

You could have knocked me down with a feather when I found out I was in the family way, but this time I was ready for motherhood because I already had a nice flat. Alice Diamond didn't have much use for it anymore after she got herself arrested. The Forty Thieves look on me as their Queen now, so it was only fitting that I moved into her old drum.

When I wrote to Jimmy in Wandsworth Prison to tell him my news, he was really made up about the baby. We decided to call her Ruby, just like my favorite necklace, and she came into the world just in time for Christmas 1947. It was the best present ever.

Jimmy's just about bursting with pride for his daughter. He wants to know every little detail about her life, and he writes to me at least once a week. Neither of us can forget about our firstborn, Joseph. Truthfully, it don't get any easier, but when we speak of him, we like to think he's happy with that well-to-do family, getting the best of everything. I send him a mother's love every night before my head hits the pillow and hope that somehow, through the skies over London, it reaches him.

I have high hopes for my Ruby. I felt her first kicks when I was shoving a few blouses down my drawers in Marshall and Snellgrove, in Oxford Street. I plan to teach her everything I've learned, to make sure she stays out of trouble. I was hoisting right up to the birth because having a bump makes it so much easier to clout things and people are less suspicious of you.

Jimmy got a three-year stretch for the shivving of Alf White, which all the Chaps in Soho said could have been a lot worse. I made sure he had his best suit, all neatly pressed, when he stood in the dock and he looked so handsome as he blew me a kiss when they took him down after sentencing. My Jimmy only has to look at me to make my heart skip a beat, even if it's across a prison table at visiting time. They say absence makes the heart grow fonder and it has in my case, but I don't tell him that too often in case he starts taking it for granted.

A little bird told me he'll get out early for good behavior and I'm pleased about that because we've got a lot of lost time to make up for. Meanwhile, he's got himself a nice job as a prison barber, because it turns out he's quite good with a razor after all.

Jimmy wants to make an honest woman of me when he gets out but I told him there's not a snowball's chance in hell of that happening because I am as bent as a nine-bob note and proud of it. And anyway, I've already got more diamond rings than I know what to do with. As luck would have it, Alice left her jewelry behind when she disguised herself as a flower seller that day in Gamages and her rings fit me just perfectly. So now I've got a nice row of diamonds, which I can use as a knuckle-duster whenever the need arises.

The girl I was before will always fancy the pants off Jimmy

but the woman I am now has got her head screwed on right and she don't care one jot about respectability and wedlock. Those things are for mugs. Being Queen of Thieves means I'm married to the job in some ways, and I quite like that.

Funny, but I find everyone round Queen's Buildings is always very polite to me and I've never heard even a whisper of malice about the fact that I haven't made it up the aisle.

I never feel lonely because Iris pops around to babysit when I need to go out to do some shopping up West. And my girls, The Forty Thieves, keep me company, coming and going all day long. Some days it's like Piccadilly Circus in here and I wish I had one of those revolving doors like they do in Selfridges.

Nobody talks about Alice Diamond anymore, not after she was so disloyal to the gang that day in Gamages. She forgot all about us and selfishly went off and got herself arrested. The way she striped Billy Sullivan's face like that! Anyone would have thought she was trying to start a gangland war. It was very unwise. Luckily, I was able to smooth things over with Albert Rossi and the rest of the Chaps. Turns out it was a family feud and had nothing to do with The Forty Thieves. Just fancy that!

I went to see her in court after she was charged with assault. She was still dressed as a flower seller, glaring at me from the dock, as the judge handed her a hefty sentence for causing such a public outrage.

None of the girls could understand why she did it, but I told them sometimes people bear grudges, and it eats them up and drives them mad. Blood is thicker than water as the old saying goes and being Billy Sullivan's sister must have made her forget her loyalty to the gang and lose her marbles. Luckily, I was on hand to get us all out of that shop and to safety, with our loot.

The Forty Thieves were made up about the amount we

hoisted and we still chuckle about it down the pub. When Miss Hunter came to do the stock check, she found about half a dozen of Mr. Dior's finest gowns had gone walkabout.

I'd like to have been a fly on the wall for the conversation when she rang Paris. I expect they taught her a few words of French she wasn't too familiar with.

So, I've made a few other changes to the gang. It ain't easy being Queen and sometimes you have to be cruel to be kind. Molly was never the same after her unfortunate accident, you see.

She can't really remember what happened, other than she was hit on the back of the head, but what with that and the booze, I had to let her go. It was a bit like putting down a horse when it's only fit for the knacker's yard. We were all glad to see the back of her; she'd become a bit of an embarrassment. Last I heard, she was working as a prostitute's madam up in one of those rat-infested hotels up in Waterloo. Shame, really.

Meanwhile, I've caused a bit of a stir in Soho by opening my own club. They say gangland's a man's world, but times are changing, aren't they?

The Windsor got shut down when Billy Sullivan was arrested and all the girls would have been out of work, so I put forward a plan to reopen it as a new place, really classy, for dinner and dancing. I had the cash that Jimmy left me, and I put it into the business, which has made a fabulous return. Soho has never been busier.

Lord Dockworth volunteered to be my guarantor, after I had a lovely little chat with him and his wife about The Lucky Seven gambling club. I did so enjoy taking afternoon tea with them in Mayfair. They were utterly charming, which was quite unexpected, although from the look on Lady Dockworth's face, I think she surprised herself with how polite she could be to me when she made a bit of an effort.

Thanks to Lord Dockworth, the magistrates were prepared to overlook my one conviction for shoplifting, as the folly of a misspent youth. So, I got my license and had the club fitted out nicely and we're one of the top nightspots in Soho these days.

Gypsy is my manageress. Turns out she's got a good head for figures, but I do have to watch how much she spends on shoes. I kept Lou the barman on, as well as Alma and the other dancers, because familiar faces are good for business, aren't they? Lou has just about got over the shock of having me as his boss, but if he weren't grumpy I'd think he was sickening for something.

There's never any trouble at the Silver Slipper because the Chaps all look out for me, as Jimmy the Razor's girl. Albert Rossi stuck a ring on Gypsy's finger, but he keeps coming up with excuses as to why they will have to delay the wedding. He's yet to tell her the truth: that he's already got a missus and three kids up in Clerkenwell, but knowing Gypsy, she'll forgive him for that.

The fallout from Billy Sullivan's corruption trial was monumental. Half the London police force got booted out, with Billy's accounts ledger for evidence. The cozzer who nailed him is Detective Chief Inspector these days but if he ever pops by my club, I tell him he still has to pay his drinks bill, just like any other punter. I don't want him getting ideas above his station, even if he is very good-looking for a policeman.

And Billy Sullivan?

Well, he jumped bail from hospital after he had thirty stitches in his face and never stood trial. Some say he got out of the country on a private airplane. Others say Billy was last seen in South Africa, where he's running a diamond mine.

I expect in time, people will forget all about Billy Sullivan and he'll be just another one of those gangland legends, who fellas talk about over their pints in the darkest corners of the pub, reliving his wicked deeds in hushed tones.

Those of us who knew him personally might struggle to find a kind word to say about him.

Although, I must say, sometimes when I hold my Ruby and she gazes up at me with a familiar look, I remember him fondly.

ALICE

Now, let's be honest.

It's been a while since I last set foot in the Holloway Hotel, and I am quite pleased with what they've done with the place.

The walls are painted cream and brown and those of us staying at His Majesty's Pleasure are allowed to put pictures up in our cells and add a few homely touches. The bed is a bed, with a mattress, and not just a board that you have to put up during the day, like it was when I was last here. It's altogether a nicer experience for us guests, especially those of us facing a long stretch.

The prison clock bashes out the hour just the same as it always did, echoing up the stairwells, but I find that reassuring as I count down the days until I get my liberty.

And the cocoa! Well, that is just as delicious as back in the old days before the war. I got myself a nice little job in the library, on account of the fact that I caught that no-good dipper Joan from the laundry selling ciggies and trying to force herself on the younger ones, the dirty cow.

The warder Miss Fanshawe and me go back a long way, you see, so she was all ears. I knew her when she was little more than a girl, starting out on her first job here, and I helped her get a foot on the ladder for promotion, by maintaining a sense of order in the prison. Those little favors last a lifetime.

I had a lovely welcome from all the prisoners who found it in the goodness of their hearts to share their rations with me and make sure I didn't have to do much heavy work, because of my legs, which are a constant trouble these days. Funny that I can still skip up the stairs when the warders ain't watching but I feel a bit of a limp coming on whenever I see the Governor.

I was given extra blankets and the softest pillows, and I barely had to say a word to get them. It's nice when you don't have to ask twice.

I've been offered a nice comfy stay in the hospital wing if I feel the need for extra rest and I may take old Fanshawe up on that but for now, right here, in the heart of the prison, is where I truly belong.

Oh, it ain't the same as life on the outside, I know. But I can't help it if the women look up to me, can I? They need a Queen to guide them and if being a Queen of Holloway is the role that fate has handed me, then who am I to refuse it?

I hear someone else is a pretender to my crown with The Forty Thieves while I'm languishing in jail. I've been doing a lot of thinking and certain things have fallen into place as far as she is concerned.

When old Queen Bess banged her sister up in the Tower, did she stop being Mary, Queen of Scots, queen of people's hearts? No, she bleeding well did not.

As Nell will discover in the fullness of time, some of us are born to it and some of us had better watch their backs when I get out.

Acknowledgments

I am delighted to be part of the Orion Dash family, and in Rhea Kurien I have found a dynamic editor who shares my fascination for The Forty Thieves, the era, and the characters I have created. That makes working on a book a real pleasure.

I would like to thank my agent, Giles Milburn of Madeleine Milburn Literary Agency, for believing in this book from the outset and sharing my enthusiasm for the world of Alice Diamond, Nell, and the Queen of Thieves.

My family and friends have supported me in more ways than I can mention while I was writing this book and I am so grateful for their love. Thank you to Reuben and our boys Idris and Bryn, you rock my world; and also to my friends Sally and Marcus, Clare, Tania, Al and Fiona, Hannah and Carli, Lisa, Jules, and the coven.

Finally, a huge thanks to my readers.

About the author

About the book

Insights,
Interviews
& More . . .

Meet Beezy Marsh

Gail Fogarty

BEEZY MARSH is a #1 internationally and *Sunday Times* top ten bestselling author who believes that ordinary lives are extraordinary. She is also an award-winning journalist who has spent more than twenty years making the headlines in newspapers including the *Daily Mail* and the *Sunday Times*. Beezy is married with two young sons and lives in Oxfordshire with a never-ending pile of laundry. ❧

Author's Note

Writing this book during the long months of lockdown allowed me to escape to an exciting world in a bygone age in London, and I am thrilled to share that with you. Gangland has always held a fascination for me, but this extraordinary set of women gripped my imagination because their story is so unusual.

Working-class communities in London in the early twentieth century—where part of my immediate family has its roots—are so often portrayed as women having little to do but cook the dinner, raise the kids, and be "her indoors."

The Forty Thieves gang, which had its heyday from the 1920s to the 1960s, took that notion and threw it out onto the cobbles, challenging any bloke who dared to try to stop them.

To those who knew them, they were like film stars who dressed glamorously, fought harder than the men, and refused to bow down to the law. Yet they could be caring, standing up for wives whose husbands frittered the housekeeping on drink or were handy with their fists behind closed doors.

The moment I got to know some of the leading lights of the original gang and their daughters and granddaughters—including one of ▶

Author's Note *(continued)*

the later "Queens"—I knew that there was more to their story than met the eye.

The Forty Thieves and their Queen were bound up with London's underworld in a way few people realize, and these women held extraordinary power in their communities. Some had reputations that would make the toughest gangsters think twice before crossing them, and their influence was enough for their names to be whispered by hardened criminals in a way that is still almost reverential.

They lived outside the law at a time when women, especially poor women of their class, had few opportunities other than going to work at the local factory. Married women were usually expected to give up work. I know from my own family that rationing and the long years of the Second World War had left the most decent working-class people tempted to take "a bit of crooked" to get desirable items such as a nice cut of meat, stockings, or a new dress.

In this environment, the Queen of Thieves and her shoplifters, or "hoisters," flourished.

Sometimes, the lives of the hoisters intertwined with underworld bosses, so that they became lovers, or they had family ties through siblings or marriage, but even then, they fiercely guarded their right to earn their own money and to run their own gang, free from male interference.

Creating a fictional world for these women in *Queen of Thieves* was an absolute joy because their voices demanded to be heard.

And there is still so much more for them to say . . . ∾

Behind the Book
The True Stories That Inspired *Queen of Thieves*

Contrary to popular belief, London's gangland was not just a man's world in the turbulent years of the first half of the twentieth century. When I sat down to talk with the descendants of some of the Forty Thieves' leading lights, I heard stories that made the Peaky Blinders look like a bunch of choirboys.

But just to backtrack: my own family's roots in London go back to the 1800s. They were working-class people, laundresses, barmaids, servants, and laborers. When I was growing up in the 1970s, I heard stories from my grandmother about a fearsome gang of female thieves who ran amok in the posh stores in London's West End. Many years later, as an author and journalist fascinated by London's history, I began my research.

Almost immediately, I was hooked.

Alice Diamond's gang is believed to have had its roots in Victorian London around the slums of the Seven Dials in Covent Garden. The neighborhood was infamous in Charles Dickens's day, but by the 1930s the breeding ground for the gang's recruits was South London. The grim terraces of Waterloo and the tenements of the Elephant and Castle provided a plentiful supply of girls desperate enough to join the Forty Thieves. Many started as little more than children, acting as lookouts.

The secrets of the Forty Thieves were passed on from mother to daughter and from aunt to niece, so that whole generations of families saw thieving as a way of life. The only time they regretted their crimes was if they were caught, because that usually meant a spell in the grim confines of Holloway Prison.

So, the women quickly learned to hone their skills to evade capture.

Their specialty was "hoisting"— stealing items from shops—and "clouting" by shoving them down their voluminous underwear, which had elastic at the knee to hold their stolen loot in place. The full skirts of the time would hide the contraband nicely.

From the 1920s, Alice Diamond ruled the gang. Born in the workhouse in Lambeth, she stood a towering five feet, ten inches tall and had a punch as strong as a man's, using her diamond rings as a knuckleduster. Newspaper reports denounced her as the "Queen of the Terrors" and warned that it once took six policemen to hold her down when captured. ▸

Behind the Book *(continued)*

Her hoisters dressed like film stars: in the latest fashions, with beautifully coiffed hair. They carried razors wrapped in lace handkerchiefs in their handbags and thought nothing of whipping out their hatpins to blind and maim anyone who crossed them, from the police to other gangsters who wanted to muscle in on their lucrative business. Yet they could also be caring, standing up for wives whose husbands frittered the housekeeping on drink or who were handy with their fists behind closed doors.

The years immediately after the Second World War were a boom time for the gang, as clothing was restricted by rationing until 1949. Even decent folk were only too happy to "take a bit of crooked" from the Forty Thieves to have something new. Some received stolen goods, so that dank tenements became Aladdin's caves stuffed full of furs and beautiful dresses.

Mothers in the gang would take their babies with them to the shops, hiding hoisted clothes in their prams, then to move them on to pubs to be handed off. Tallymen would be drafted in to shift stolen clothes from one side of London to the other on their carts for a fee. Alice Diamond would organize the resale of the stolen goods. It was a strict rule and a matter of pride that hoisters never wore what they had pinched. Instead, they were paid in cash and went back to the posh shops to legitimately buy beautiful silks, furs, and jewels with their generous pay, which could be up to ten times what a man would earn in a factory.

There was a Hoisters' Code of loyalty, which included rules such as going to bed early before "going shopping," handing over everything they'd pinched to Alice in return for weekly wages, and never stealing each other's boyfriends (the last because it was bad for group morale). In 1925, a man and his teenage son who had the misfortune to offend the gang were savagely attacked with iron bars and knives on the orders of Alice Diamond, who led the ambush.

At her kitchen table, Alice Diamond taught her girls how to roll furs on the hanger and shove them down their hoister's drawers and how to fool shop assistants. Alice herself was famous for clouting three furs in one go—one down each leg and one under her gusset—and then walking out of Selfridges as if she hadn't a care in the world. She'd send her girls out in teams of three or four at least three days a week, to different stores all over London, or even as far afield as Birmingham and Brighton. Men were employed as drivers but were never allowed to join the gang.

Mink stoles and furs were the ultimate prize, but some of the gang stole silverware, and one even put on a ▶

maternity girdle to pinch an entire china tea set, although she later complained it did rattle a lot on the way out of the shop. Jewelery was a favorite, as it was easy to hide up a sleeve, and rings could be switched for worthless fakes.

Members of the Forty Thieves were expected to be resourceful and daring and if they couldn't talk or cry their way out of a situation, they knew how to stand and fight. One unfortunate policeman was blinded by Alice Diamond's deputy when he tried to apprehend her. She later expressed no remorse for her appalling assault and even flirted with the judge when he sentenced her to jail. Loyalty to Alice meant never spilling their secrets or "grassing" to the police.

The gang's heyday was from the 1920s to the late 1950s, but I discovered that although the Forty Thieves had effectively disbanded by the early 1960s, their thieving ways continued on a small scale. Some granddaughters and great-granddaughters of those who worked with Alice Diamond had themselves been shown the tricks of the trade by the gang's former members. Some even confessed that they occasionally used them today.

The women I spoke with revealed some trade secrets to me, laughing at the memory of how their forebears had flashed their hoister's bloomers and joked about what they had pinched as they all joined in a knees-up down at the local pub. One descendant of the gang— who had learned to steal as a young girl in the 1970s under the watchful eye of her relative, who in turn had been taught by Alice Diamond herself in the 1930s— told me: "They didn't see anything wrong in it because these things were too expensive for most people to afford, and shops had insurance. I felt the same way.

"My gran liked to go for tea at the Ritz, especially if she could pinch someone's fur coat from the cloakroom on the way out. She was still hoisting well into her seventies."

With her blonde hair and immaculately cut jacket and trousers, this woman in her early fifties looked like butter wouldn't melt in her mouth. But I realized that she too shared the twisted criminal mindset of Alice Diamond and her gang as she laughingly told me: "The only thing that isn't hoisted is my knickers. And I still have my gran's hoister's drawers—more for a laugh than anything else, but I have used them." ‿

Questions for Discussion

1. When Alice Diamond recruits Nell, she tells her: "We are skilled workers. The posh folk are pinching from us every day of our lives. They treat us like mugs. We work our fingers to the bone. . . . We ain't really robbing from anyone if you look at it that way. We're helping ourselves because no one will help us." Is there some truth to what she says, or is this attempt to justify their crimes just part of how Alice manipulates people?

2. Nell accepts Alice's offer to join the gang, thinking, "Alice was offering me a different life: money, big money, more than I'd ever earned, standing on my own two feet with no man being the boss of me." Is Nell joining Alice simply because pregnancy has made her desperate, or does Alice tap into an aspirational streak in Nell? Is this promise of independence and security merely an illusion?

3. Was Nell right to refuse Jimmy's offer of marriage? Why do you think she turned him down? What would you have done?

4. Alice makes sure Nell is caught shoplifting to test her loyalty, but also because, "If she gets time, being in jail means Nell will have somewhere safe to deliver the baby, which will be taken care of once she's had it, in the way that's best for the baby. That's such a blessing for Nell." Is Alice truly looking out for Nell and her baby? How does this scheme ultimately work out for Nell and Alice?

5. Does Alice's backstory—about her hardscrabble childhood in Seven Dials—teach us anything new about her? How did her early life turn her into the Queen of Thieves?

6. When she rejoins Alice after her time in jail, Nell reflects: "Nothing ever gets handed to girls like me on a plate, I knew that well enough," and "This seedy place, full of people splashing their cash, might turn out to be the making of me." Is she motivated by ambition? By her desire to take her revenge on Alice? By both?

7. What did you make of Nell's relationships with the other women who cross her path: Iris, ▶

Rose, Gypsy, and Molly? Is Nell a good friend? How do women's interdependence and relationships with one another drive the action of this story?

8. Were you surprised to learn Billy's relationship to Alice? Did it change the way you felt about her vendetta against him? What do you make of Nell's observation that Alice and Billy are "two sides of the same coin"?

9. When Nell turns down Detective Hart, she says, "It's like a cat going out with a mouse, isn't it? You and I would never work because I will always want to steal and you are as honest as the day is long." Is she right? Or should she have made her escape from a life of crime with him?

10. What do you think the future holds for Nell and Alice and the other characters in this book? If there were a sequel to *Queen of Thieves*, what do you think might happen? ⁓

Discover great authors, exclusive offers, and more at hc.com.